ER F...
UN...
MISTLETOE

BY
SCARLET WILSON

S NOWBOUND WITH
OR DELECTABLE

BY
SUSAN CARLISLE

MILLS
BOON

I2512146

Scarlet Wilson wrote her first story aged eight and has never stopped. Her family have fond memories of *Shirley and the Magic Purse*, with its army of mice, all with names beginning with the letter 'M'. An avid reader, Scarlet started with every Enid Blyton book, moved on to the *Chalet School* series and many years later found Mills & Boon®.

She trained and worked as a nurse and health visitor, and currently works in public health. For her, finding medical romances was a match made in heaven. She is delighted to find herself among the authors she has read for many years.

Scarlet lives on the West Coast of Scotland with her fiancé and their two sons.

Susan Carlisle's love affair with books began when she made a bad grade in math in the sixth grade. Not allowed to watch TV until she'd brought the grade up, she filled her time with books and became a voracious romance reader. She has 'keepers' on the shelf to prove it. Because she loved the genre so much she decided to try her hand at creating her own romantic worlds. She still loves a good happily-ever-after story.

When not writing Susan doubles as a high school substitute teacher, which she has been doing for sixteen years. Susan lives in Georgia with her husband of twenty-eight years and has four grown children. She loves castles, travelling, cross-stitching, hats, James Bond and hearing from her readers.

HER FIREFIGHTER UNDER THE MISTLETOE

BY
SCARLET WILSON

First published in Great Britain 2013
by Mills & Boon, an imprint of Harlequin (UK) Limited.
Harlequin (UK) Limited, Eton House, 18-24 Paradise Road,
Richmond, Surrey TW9 1SR

© Scarlet Wilson 2013

ISBN: 978 0 263 89922 1

Harlequin (UK) policy is to use papers that are natural, renewable and recyclable products and made from wood grown in sustainable forests. The logging and manufacturing process conform to the legal environmental regulations of the country of origin.

Printed and bound in Spain
by Blackprint CPI, Barcelona

Dear Reader

This year has been a cause for celebration.

I celebrated a big birthday *(shh!)* in New York with my family, and two of my books were nominated for the Romantic Novelists' Association's RoNA Rose Award. I was delighted and honoured to have two Mills & Boon® Medical Romances™ on the shortlist, and to see the line that I love recognised.

This has also been the year I wrote my first non-medical hero. I'd like you all to meet Callum Kennedy, a firefighter in the rope rescue unit, who appeared fully formed in my mind—and funnily enough in uniform! I also got to set my story in my nearest city—Glasgow.

Glasgow is gorgeous at Christmas time, with beautiful lights along Buchanan Street and on into George Square, with its ice rink and Christmas tree. Perfect for a Christmas story!

In this story Callum meets Jess—his childhood sweetheart—and he's shocked by the changes in her. Life has dealt Jess a cruel blow, and she's having a hard time recovering—but maybe Callum and his gorgeous son Drew can bring her all the Christmas cheer that she needs!

Please feel free to contact me at my website www.scarlet-wilson.com. I love to hear from readers!

Merry Christmas!

Scarlet

Recent titles by Scarlet Wilson:

ABOUT THAT NIGHT…**
THE MAVERICK DOCTOR AND MISS PRIM**
AN INESCAPABLE TEMPTATION
HER CHRISTMAS EVE DIAMOND
A BOND BETWEEN STRANGERS*
WEST WING TO MATERNITY WING!
THE BOY WHO MADE THEM LOVE AGAIN
IT STARTED WITH A PREGNANCY

*The Most Precious Bundle of All
**Rebels with a Cause

**These books are also available in eBook format
from www.millsandboon.co.uk**

DEDICATION

This book is dedicated to my good friends Jane Bell,
Kirsten Gallacher and Lorna McCririe,
who all enjoy getting into the spirit of Christmas!

CHAPTER ONE

Bzzz…bzzz…

The noise jerked Jess out of the delicious tranquil state that had been enveloping her.

Her eyes blinked at the bright light outside, the fuzziness of her brain trying to adjust and make sense of it all.

Her pager usually woke her in the dark of the night—just like it had three times last night. Having it wake her in the middle of the day was an entirely new experience.

A baby with RSV had kept her awake most of the night in Paediatric ITU, and when the ward had finally quietened down around an hour ago, she'd brought her coffee in here to do some paperwork.

Fat chance. She touched the coffee cup on her desk. Stone cold. Had she even managed a sip before she'd wiped out?

How long had she been asleep? She wriggled in her chair, rolling her shoulders back and trying to ease the knots out of her back.

Bzzz… Bzzz…

She glanced at the number. A and E. Another admission. Probably another respiratory problem.

It was Glasgow, at the start of November, but it felt like the middle of winter. The temperature had dropped dramatically in the last few days and paediatric emergency admissions had soared. Trips and falls on the slippery pavements had resulted in a whole host of strains, fractures and head injuries. Asthma and respiratory complaints were through the roof. Infections and nondescript viruses were causing mayhem with new babies and toddlers.

Just as well she didn't have anyone to go home to. She hadn't seen the inside of her house for days.

She picked up the phone and dialled A and E. 'It's Dr Rae. You were paging me.'

The voice was brusque, skipping over any pleasantries and getting straight to business. 'Assemble a flying squad. Nursery minibus in the Clyde on the city outskirts. Unknown number of casualties. We're waiting for more information from emergency services. You need to be ready to leave in five minutes.'

She was on her feet in seconds and throwing open the door, her tiredness, sore muscles and fatigue instantly forgotten. 'I need a flying squad,' she yelled, glancing down the corridor as the sister of the ward hurried towards her, 'Where's Jackie? I want her with me.'

Jackie appeared at her side in an instant. 'What is it?'

'Nursery minibus in the Clyde.'

The experienced nurse's face paled. 'In this weather? In these temperatures?'

'Go!' The ward sister waved her hand at them. 'Leave everything else to me.'

Jess started jogging down the corridor, heading for the stairs. It took less than a minute to reach A and E and one of the staff thrust a green suit into her hands. She climbed into it immediately, noting the fluorescent 'Doctor' sign on the back. It was essential that all staff could be picked out easily in an emergency. One of the paramedics thrust a pair of gloves towards her. 'Take these, you'll need them out there.'

She glanced at her watch. It was only two-thirty in the afternoon. At least a few hours of daylight left. She prayed they wouldn't need more than that.

'Let's go!'

The shout came from the front doors. Jackie appeared at her side again, similarly clad in a green jumpsuit with 'Nurse' emblazoned across the back. They picked up the pre-packed paediatric emergency kits and headed outside.

Jess climbed into one of the emergency vehicles and fastened her seat belt as the sirens sounded and they headed out onto the motorway. She turned to the man sitting next to her, 'I'm Jess, paediatric consultant. Have you heard any more?'

He nodded. 'Stan, emergency service co-ordinator. Lots of problems. Someone sideswiped the minibus and sent it down a thirty-foot slippery bank and straight into the Clyde.'

Jess tried to stop the sharp intake of breath. Her brain was into immediate overtime, imagining the types of injuries the children could have sustained.

'How many?'

He shook his head. 'Still waiting for confirmation. Three adults, at least ten kids.'

'Age range?'

'From two to five. We're getting more information all the time. The other nursery minibus missed everything. They didn't even know there had been an accident. The police are there now, collecting details of all the kids.'

Jess swallowed, trying to ignore the huge lump in her throat. The flying squad wasn't called out too often. She was the consultant on call—it was her job to be here.

But that didn't mean her stomach wasn't churning at the thought of the scene she was about to face.

Yes, she could appear calm. Yes, she could use her skills and clinical expertise. Yes, she would do everything that was expected of her and beyond.

But would she sleep tonight?

Probably not.

There was a crackle of the radio and some voices she couldn't distinguish. The driver turned his head. 'Five minutes. They've called out the rapid response and specialist rope rescue team. They should arrive just before us. Let's hope Callum got out of bed on the right side today.'

'Who is Callum?'

The words were out of her mouth automatically, before she even had a chance to think. 'And what's the specialist rope rescue team?'

None of this sounded good. All she could think about was the children involved in the crash. What did this mean for them?

Stan's face was pale. 'It means that the banking is too dangerous for our crews to work on, that, plus the added complication of being in water means we need the specialist crew.'

'Will it delay me getting to the children?'

Stan averted his eyes, obviously not wanting to give her the answer. He hadn't answered the other part of her question. He hadn't mentioned Callum. And the driver's comment had made her ears prick up. *Let's hope he got out of bed on the right side.*

The last thing she needed right now was a prima donna firefighter getting in her way when she had kids to attend to. 'Is Callum a bit on the crabbit side, then?' she asked as they pulled over to the side of the road. A bad-tempered man she could deal with. As long as he didn't interfere with her job.

'Only on a good day,' muttered Stan as he jumped from the rescue vehicle.

Jessica opened the door carefully, to avoid the passing traffic on the busy road. The police had cordoned part of it off as best they could. But the constant flow of traffic was unnerving.

The cold air hit her straight away. Biting cold, sneaking under the folds of her jumpsuit, made her wish she was wearing a hat, scarf and fleece and not just the thin gloves she'd been handed.

She flinched at the sight of the crash barrier, twisted beyond all recognition and lying like a useless piece of junk at the side of the road.

There were raised voices to her left. She turned just in time to see a broad-shouldered man snap on his harness and disappear down the side of the banking, with the vain words 'Risk assessment' being shouted after him by his colleagues.

A sense of unease came over her body. A vague awareness trickling through her. Callum—that's what they'd said. It couldn't possibly be Callum Kennedy, could it? She hadn't seen him since school and had no idea where he'd ended up. But there was something vaguely familiar about the body that had just disappeared over the edge.

Her footsteps shortened as she reached the edge of the steep bank. Someone touched her shoulder, looking at the sign on her back. 'Oh, good, the doctor. Let's get you harnessed up.'

She lifted her legs as she was clipped and harnessed and talked through the motions of the descent. Her bag was sent down ahead. A burly firefighter appeared next to her. 'You'll go down with me. Have you done this before?'

She peered over the edge again. Thirty feet of steep descent. How many times had the minibus rolled on the way down?

She could see it now, lying on its side in the Clyde, the icy cold water surrounding it. There was a flurry of firefighters around it. Some on top, trying to get through the windows, some on the banking, surrounded by other pieces of equipment.

'Get me down there.' Her eyes met the firefighter's and the whispered words grew more determined. 'Get me down to those children.'

He nodded and spoke into the radio clipped to his shoulder. 'The doc and I are on our way.'

She took a deep breath and turned with her back towards the water, edging down the side of the bank in time with the firefighter. It was slippery work. A thin layer of frost had formed over the mud at the side of the bank, her simple shoes giving her literally no grip. The firefighter's firm hand in the small of her back kept her from slipping completely. Even through her gloves the biting cold was already making her fingers numb.

She looked over her shoulder. 'How much further?'

'Keep your eyes straight ahead, please.'

Her anxiety was building. She wanted to get down. She wanted to help those kids. But she needed to get down there in one piece.

'Who is Callum? Is it Callum Kennedy?'

The firefighter's eyes gave a spark of amusement. 'Know him, do you?'

She wrinkled her nose. 'I'm not entirely sure. I think so. I went to school with a Callum Kennedy, but I didn't get a good look at him before he went over the edge.' She shrugged her shoulders, 'I'm not even sure he would recognise me now.'

The firefighter gave her a little smile, 'Oh, I'm sure he would.'

'What does he do exactly?'

'He's the head of the rope rescue unit. He'll be in charge down here.' They were inching closer and closer to the bottom.

'And is he any good?' She bit her lip. It might seem a little cheeky, but Stan had already mentioned he could be crabbit. She needed to know that he wouldn't get in her way. That he wouldn't stop her doing her job with these kids.

'Put it this way—if me or my kids were stuck anywhere that a rope rescue was needed?' He lifted his eyes skyward. 'I would be praying to the man upstairs that Callum would be on duty that night. He's the safest pair of hands we've got—particularly near kids.' He caught her around the waist. 'That's us. Let me just unhook you from this line—but we'll leave your harness on. You'll need it to get back up and they'll hook you up to another one if you're near the water.'

'Where's the doc?' came the shout.

Jess swivelled around, looking for her bag. 'I'm here. I'm coming.'

Several of the firefighters were forming a line, passing two little kids along to the edge of the bank. Jackie appeared at her side. 'Let's go.'

They reached the kids just as they were placed on warm blankets on the ground. Jess worked quickly, gently feeling over their little bodies for signs of injuries as she spoke to them in a quiet voice.

'Need some help?'

She nodded at the firefighter next to her. 'Heat them up. There are no obvious injuries. But they're in shock.' She turned back to the minibus. Now she was closer she could see every dent, every bash, every hole in the metalwork.

It made the chill seem even worse. 'Are these the first two?'

The man next to her nodded. 'Do we have a number yet? How many kids are injured?'

'Twelve. That's the figure we have for the moment. Just awaiting confirmation.'

She moved over to the side of the slippery river's edge as an adult was passed along and dealt with by the paramedics. She could see the hive of activity going on within the bus, hear the whimpering cries of the children.

'Can I get over there? Do you need me to get into the bus?' Her anxiety was building. She couldn't stand here and do nothing. It just wasn't in her nature. She needed to be at the heart of the action. It was her job to prioritise, triage and treat the sickest kids. She needed to be next to those children.

Her voice must have carried in the cold air, because a head whipped up from the bus. The man was lying across the windows, reaching down to grasp a squirming child, and his eyes connected with hers.

'Stay *exactly* where you are.'

Callum. Callum Kennedy. Absolutely no mistake.

She saw him flinch visibly as his brain made the connection of who was standing on the riverbank.

He'd recognised her? After all these years?

The cold hard air hit her lungs. She must have sucked in a bigger breath than normal. Her skin prickled.

How did she feel about seeing Callum Kennedy thirteen years on?

Unprepared.

Like a seventeen-year-old again, standing in a dark nightclub and willing herself not to cry as they broke up. It had been the right decision. The sensible decision. They had both been going to university, she in Glasgow and he—after a wait of a few years—in Aberdeen. Their relationship would never have worked out. It had been best for them both.

It just hadn't felt that way.

She pushed her feet more firmly into the ground, trying to focus her attention. Callum's gaze hadn't moved. It was still fixed on her face.

She could feel the colour start to rise in her cheeks. It was unnerving. But why the flinch? Was she really such an unwelcome sight after all this time?

Or maybe she was imagining this—maybe he'd no idea who she was at all.

Callum couldn't believe it. He was holding a child firmly by the waist, while a colleague released him from his seat belt.

But Callum's eyes were fixed on the flyaway caramel-coloured hair on the riverbank. Running up and down the thin frame that was in no way hidden by the bright green jumpsuit.

A sight he hadn't seen in thirteen years.

A lifetime ago.

His childhood sweetheart, here on the banks of the Clyde, at the scene of an accident.

He'd always wondered if he'd come across her sometime, some place.

As a firefighter he'd been in and out of most of the A and E departments in the city. But in all these years he'd never glimpsed her, never seen her name on any board.

He knew that Jessica had gone to university to do her medical training, but had no idea where she'd ended up, or which field she'd specialised in.

And now he knew. She was somewhere here in Glasgow, specialising in paediatrics. Why else would she be here?

Would she even remember him? It looked as though she had—even though he'd filled out considerably since the last time they'd met. She, on the other hand, looked as if she'd faded away to a wisp.

Although he could see her slight frame, the most visible changes were around her facial features and structure. And it wouldn't have mattered how many clothes she was bundled up in, he would have noticed at twenty paces.

It struck him as strange. The young Jessica he remembered had had an attention-grabbing figure and a personality to match. Every memory he had of her was a happy one. And for a second he felt as if they could all come flooding back.

There was a tug at his arms, followed by a sensation of relief and a lightening of the weight in his arms. He pulled upwards automatically. The little guy's seat belt had been released.

He pulled him up and held him to his chest, capturing the little body with his own, holding him close to let a little heat envelop the shivering form. The little boy wasn't even crying any more. He was just too cold.

He held the boy for a few seconds longer. He looked around four, just a year younger than his own son Drew. He couldn't help the automatic paternal shiver that stole down his spine at the thought of something like this happening to his son. It didn't even bear thinking about.

His only relief right now was that he hadn't signed a consent form for the school to go on any trips this week, meaning that his little Drew was safely tucked up inside the primary school building.

The temperature in the minibus was freezing, with water halfway up its side-on frame. They were going to have to move quicker to get these kids out in time.

'Callum! Callum! Pass him over, please.'

Oh, she'd recognised him all right. The authoritative tone made no mistake about that.

'Okay, little guy, we're going to get you heated up now.' He ruffled the little boy's hair before he passed him over to the arms stretched out towards him. He didn't have time to think about Jessica Rae now. Too much was at stake.

He thrust his head back inside the minibus. 'How are we doing?'

John, one of his co-workers, lifted his head. 'I'll have two more for you in a second. But I need some more light in here.'

Another voice shouted from the darkness, 'I think I've got one with a broken leg and another unconscious. Can we get a paramedic or a doctor in here?'

Callum lifted his head back up. The light was fading quickly, even though it was only afternoon. Winter nights closed in quickly—by four p.m. it would be pitch black. He didn't think twice. 'I need a paramedic or a doctor over here, please.'

He could see the quick confab at the side of the river. Jess was issuing instructions to the nurse with her and the paramedics and ambulance technicians at her side. Things were going smoothly out there. Two of the children and one of the adults had already been transported back up the slippery bank. The latest little guy was still being assessed.

Jess moved to the side of the bank. He could see the impatience on her face as she waited for her safety harness to be clipped to the harness point on the shore. She shook her head at the waders she was offered, grabbed at a hand that was offered and started to climb towards the minibus.

It was precarious. The Clyde was not a quiet-flowing river. It was fast and churning, the icy-cold water lapping furiously at the side of the minibus as it penetrated the interior.

The minibus was moving with the momentum of the river and Jess slipped as she climbed over the wing of the minibus, the weight from her pack making her unstable. She was just within Callum's reach and he stretched out and grabbed the tips of her fingers with a fierce, claw-like grip.

'Yeowww!' Her other hand flailed upwards then closed over his, and he steadied her swaying body as she thudded down next to him.

The red colour in her cheeks was gone, replaced with the whiteness of cold. 'Thanks,' she breathed, the warm air forming a little steamy cloud next to them.

'Fancy seeing you here,' he murmured, giving her a little smile. It had been impossible to spot from the riverbank, but here, up close, he had a prime-time view of the thing he'd always loved most about Jess—her deep brown eyes.

The smile was returned. That little acknowledgement.

That in another time, another place…

The memories were starting to invade his senses. Jessica in his arms throwing back her head and laughing, exposing the pale skin of her neck—skin that he wanted to touch with his lips.

His brain kicked back into gear. This was work. And he never got distracted at work.

'Have you done anything like this before?'

She pulled back a little. It was the tiniest movement, a flinch almost, as if she was taken aback by his change of tone.

She shook her head and her eyebrows rose. 'An overturned minibus in a fast-flowing river with lots of paediatric casualties?'

The irony wasn't lost on him. He might do this sort of thing day in, day out, but Jess was usually in the confines of a safe, warm, comfortable hospital.

She hunched up onto her knees and pointed at the harness. 'I've never even had one of these on before, let alone abseiled down a hillside.' She wiggled her hips and tried to move her tether. 'These things aren't too comfortable, are they?'

It struck him—almost blindsided him—how brave she was being. The Jessica Rae he'd known at school hadn't even liked contact sports. He closed his eyes as an unguarded memory of other activities of a physical nature swam into his mind.

Focus. Focus now.

He knelt upwards and grabbed her around her waist, trying not to think about how it felt to be touching Jessica Rae again after all these years. Trying not to remember how her firm flesh used to feel beneath his fingers. What had happened?

'I'm going to lower you down, Jess.' He peered through the side window next to them, which had been removed. 'Your feet will get a bit wet because there's some water on the floor. Are you okay with that?'

She nodded. She didn't look scared. She didn't look

panicked. But there was a tiny little flicker of something behind her eyes. She looked in control.

He shouted down into the minibus. 'John, I'm going to lower the doc down. Can you take care of her?'

She started. 'Take care of me?' It was almost as if he'd just insulted her. 'Don't you mean take care of the kids?'

But Callum wasn't paying attention. He was back in rescue mode. 'There are two kids in the back who need your attention. One unconscious, the other with a broken leg. It's too cramped in there to take your bag down. Shout up and tell me what you need.'

Their eyes met again as she shrugged off her pack. 'Ready?' She nodded and he lowered her down slowly into the waiting arms of the firefighter below, praying that things would go to plan.

'Sheesh!' Her feet hit the icy cold water and it sent the surge of cold right up through her body. No one could stand in this for long.

It took her eyes a few seconds to adjust to the gloom inside the minibus. The mottled daylight was still sending shadows through one side of the bus, but Callum's body and those of the other firefighters lying across the windows was blocking out the little light that was left.

A flashlight was thrust into her hands. 'Here you go, Doc.' She turned it on immediately. The first sight was the way the water was lapping quickly around them. She felt the vaguest wave of panic. 'Is the river rising?'

John nodded. 'Not quickly enough for us to worry about.' His eyes didn't quite meet hers.

Work quickly.

She noticed his black trousers ballooning around his

ankles and gave him a little nod. 'Did you say no to the waders too?'

He smiled. 'No room for waders in here, Doc. Space is limited.'

She nodded and she shuffled around him towards the kids. 'Are any of the kids in water?' Her feet were already numb. There was a real danger of hypothermia setting in for any kid exposed to these temperatures.

'Four.'

'Four?' She could feel a flare of panic. She was one person. How could she attend to four kids?

Callum stuck his head in the gap. 'Start with the two at the back, Jess. As soon as you've stabilised them and they're safe to move, my men will get them out. The other two don't appear injured.' He pointed to the front of the bus. 'My men are getting them out as quickly as possible.' He looked towards the back of the bus. 'The little girl is called Rosie.'

His voice was calm, authoritative. The kind of guy in an emergency who told you things would be okay and you believed him—just because of the way he said it.

She pushed her way back to a little girl with masses of curly hair, still strapped into her seat. Her leg was at a peculiar angle, and it hadn't taken a doctor to make an accurate diagnosis of a fracture. The little boy behind her, strapped into the window seat, was unconscious, but she couldn't possibly get to him until she'd moved this little girl. She took off her gloves and put her hand round the girl, feeling for a pulse at his neck and checking to see he was still breathing. Yes, his pulse was slowing and his chest was rising and falling. But in these cold temperatures hypothermia was a real risk. She had to work as quickly as possible.

The water was lapping around their little legs and would be dropping their temperatures dramatically.

She shouted up to Callum, 'I need you to pass me down the kit with analgesia—I need to give Rosie some morphine. It's in a red box, in the front pouch of the bag.' She waited a few seconds until the box appeared then shouted again, 'And an inflatable splint.'

She spoke gently to Rosie, stroking her hair and distracting her, calculating the dosage in her head. It was too difficult to untangle the little girl from her clothes and find an available patch of skin. The last thing she needed to do was cause this little girl more pain. She took a deep breath and injected it through the thick tights on her leg, waiting a few minutes for it to take effect. 'Pass me the splint,' she whispered to John.

The positioning on the bus was difficult. 'I'm sorry, honey,' she whispered, as the little girl gave a little yelp as she straightened her leg and inflated the splint around about it to hold it in place.

'Is she ready to be moved?'

'Not quite. Can you get a collar? In fact, get me two. Once I've got that on her, you can move her.'

It was only a precaution. The little girl didn't appear to have any other injuries apart from her leg. She seemed to be moving her other limbs without any problems, but Jess didn't want to take a risk.

It only took a few seconds to manoeuvre the collar into place and fasten it securely. The cold water was moving quickly. It had only been around the children's legs when she'd entered the vehicle—now it was reaching their waists. Time was absolutely of the essence here.

She was freezing. How on earth would these children

be feeling? Kids were so much more susceptible to hypo-thermia because they lost heat more quickly than adults.

Another firefighter had appeared next to John, and they held a type of stretcher between them. Space was at a pre-mium so Jess pushed herself back into the corner of the bus to allow them to load the little girl and pass her up through the window to Callum.

Time was ticking on. The sky was darkening and the level of the freezing water rising. She squeezed her way into the seat vacated by the little girl and started to do a proper assessment on the little unconscious boy, who was held in place by his seat belt.

'Anyone know his name?' she shouted to the crew.

'It's Marcus.' The deep voice in her ear made her jump.

'Where did you come from? I thought you were on the roof?'

'The water's too cold to have anyone in it for long. I told John to go ashore and dry off.'

'Tell me about it. Try being a kid.'

There was an easy familiarity in having Callum at her side. It didn't matter that she hadn't seen him for years, it almost felt as if it had been yesterday.

Callum had changed, and so had she. The skinny youth had filled out in all the right places. His broad shoulders and muscled chest were visible through his kit. The shorter hairstyle suited him—even though it revealed the odd grey hair. They were only visible this close up.

'What do you need?'

He was watching as she checked Marcus's pulse, took his temperature, looked him over for any other injuries and shone a torch in his eyes to check his pupil reactions.

She shook her head. 'This is going to have to be a scoop and run. He's showing severe signs of hypothermia. His pulse is low and I can't even get a reading with this thing.' She shook the tympanic thermometer in the air. 'So much for accurate readings.'

She placed the collar around his neck. 'I don't want to waste any time. I can't find an obvious reason for him being unconscious. His clothes are soaking—right up to his chest. We can't waste another second. Can you get me some kind of stretcher so we can get him out of here?'

Callum nodded. 'Get me a basket stretcher,' he shouted to one of his colleagues. He gestured his head to the side as the stretcher was passed down. She stared at the orange two-piece contraption, watching while he took a few seconds to slot the pins into place and assemble it. It had curved sides, handholds, adjustable patient restraints and a lifting bridle.

'This is the only way we'll get the casualties back up the steep embankment. Jump back up, Jess, we need as much room as we can to manipulate this into place.' A pair of strong arms reached down through the window towards her and she grabbed them willingly. It pained her to leave the little boy's side, but there wasn't time for egos or arguments here.

The cold air hit her again as she came back out into the open. If she'd thought standing in the icy water had been bad, it was nothing compared to the wind-chill factor. Her teeth started chattering.

'How…many more patients?' she asked the firefighter next to her.

'We've extricated all the adults. There's another two kids stuck behind the front seat, but their injuries are minor and they're not in contact with the water. We'll get to them next.'

'Has someone looked them over?'

He nodded. 'Your nurse and one of the paramedics. They had another kid who was submerged. She'll be in the ambulance ahead of you. We've just radioed in.'

The minibus gave another little lurch as the currents buffeted it. 'This thing had better not roll,' came the mumble from next to her.

Jess wobbled, trying to gain her balance. She hadn't even considered the possibility of the bus rolling. That would be a nightmare. There was a tug around her waist, and she looked to the side of the riverbank where one of the rope crew was taking up some of the slack in her line. The stretcher started to emerge through the window. At last. Maybe she'd get a better look at Marcus out here.

Callum's shoulders appeared. He was easing the stretcher up gently, guiding it into the arms of his colleagues.

The minibus lurched again. Callum disappeared back down into the depths of the minibus with a thud and a matching expletive. The firefighter next to her struggled to steady the weight in his arms, the stretcher twisting and its edge catching her side-on.

She teetered at the edge of the bus, losing her footing on the slippery side.

It seemed to happen in slow motion. She felt herself fall backwards, her arms reaching out in front of her. The firefighter who'd knocked her with the stretcher had panic written all over his face. There was a fleeting second as he struggled to decide whether to decide to grab her or maintain his hold on the stretcher.

What was it that knocked the air from her lungs? The impact of hitting the water? Or the icy water instantly closing over her head? Her reaction was instantaneous, sucking inwards in panic, instead of holding her breath.

The layers of clothes were weighing her down, as were her shoes. She tried to reach for the surface. The water hadn't been that deep, had it? She was choking. Trying to suck in air that wasn't there—only murky water. Then the overwhelming feeling of panic started to take over.

CHAPTER TWO

CALLUM HIT THE bottom of the river-filled minibus with a thud, the icy water doing nothing to slow the impact. What little part of him had remained dry was now soaked to the skin.

There was a splash outside, followed by some panicked shouts. Callum was instantly swept with a feeling of dread. The jolt had been a big one. *Please, don't let them have dropped the stretcher.*

He was on his feet in seconds, his arms grabbing at the window edge above him and pulling himself up onto the side of the bus.

The stretcher was steady, the child safe and being passed along the line. The crew around him, however, was panicking.

'Where's her line? Wasn't she wearing a line?'

Oh, no. His head flicked from side to side, searching frantically for any sign of Jess. She was the only female river-side. Everyone else was safely ashore. They could only be talking about her.

'Can you see her? Can anyone see her?'

Callum didn't hesitate. Not for a second. He saw where the outstretched fingers were pointing and jumped straight into the Clyde.

The water closed around his chest, leaving him up to his

neck with barely a toehold on the river's bed. Even after the water in the minibus, being fully submerged in the fast-flowing Clyde was a shock to the system. Every part of his body seemed to react at once. Everything went on full alert, hairs on end, trying to pull heat back into his centre.

He looked around him, shouting at the guys still on top of the bus. 'Where? Here?' He pointed to the riverbank. 'Tell them to pull in her line!'

The Clyde was murky and grey and several pieces of ice, broken from the river's edge, floated past.

He swept his arms around under the water. He couldn't see a thing. Not even a flash of the bright green jumpsuit she'd been wearing. The water wasn't too deep as he was on tiptoe. But he was a good foot taller than Jess, with a lot more bulk and muscle. Even he could feel the hidden currents pulling at his weight.

Every man working on the minibus had been wearing a line—except him. He took a few seconds to follow the lines from the riverbank to the bus, until he located the one that led directly into the river.

The firefighters on the bank were having the same problem. It took a few moments of frantic scrambling to ascertain which line belonged to Jess. They started to reel it in and Callum waded through the water towards it.

There! A flash of green as she was tugged nearer the surface.

He grabbed, lifting her whole body with one arm, raising her head and chest above the water's surface.

For the briefest second there was nothing, just the paler-than-pale face.

Then she coughed and spluttered, and was promptly sick into the river. He fastened one arm around her chest, pulling her back towards him, supporting her weight and lifting his other arm to signal to the crew to stop pulling in her line.

'I've got you, Jess. It's okay.' He whispered the words calmly in her ear. The cold wasn't bothering him now. There was no heat coming from her body, but he could feel the rise and fall of her chest under his hands. He could feel her breathe.

Relief. That was the sensation sweeping through him. Pure and utter relief.

He always felt like this after a rescue. It was as if the anxiety and stomach-clenching that had been an essential part of his momentum and drive to keep going just left him all at once. More often than that, after a rescue he would go home and sleep soundly for ten hours, all his energy expended. Building reserves for the next day so he could do it all again.

Even Drew understood. And on those nights his little body would climb into bed next to his father and cuddle in, his little back tucked against Callum's chest—just the way Jess's was now.

She coughed and spluttered again. He could hear her teeth chattering. She still hadn't spoken. Was she in shock?

There would be an investigation later. An investigation into why the paediatric consultant helping them had ended up in the middle of a fast-flowing icy river.

But right now he wanted to make sure Jess was okay. He started wading towards the riverbank, keeping Jess close to his chest. Several of his colleagues waded in towards him, sweeping Jess out of his arms and wrapping them both in blankets.

One of the paramedics started pulling out equipment to check her over. Callum pulled his jacket and shirt over his head. The cold air meant nothing to him right now—

he couldn't be any colder anyway. He gratefully accepted a red fleece thrust at him by one of his colleagues.

He pulled it over his head. There was instant heat as soft fleece came into contact with his icy skin. Bliss.

Two basket stretchers with a firefighter on either side were currently being guided up the steep, treacherous slope. The two kids with hypothermia. He could see the ambulance technicians waiting at the top of the bank, ready to load them into the waiting ambulances.

'Stop it!'

He turned, just in time to see Jess push herself to her feet and take a few wobbly steps.

'I'm fine. Now, leave me alone.' She pulled the blankets closer around her, obviously trying to keep the cold out.

He turned to one of his colleagues. 'See if someone will volunteer some dry clothing for our lady doc.'

Jess stalked towards him. Her face was still deathly pale, but her involuntary shivering seemed to have stopped. She pointed to the stretchers. 'I need to get to the kids. I need to get them to hospital.'

Callum shook his head. 'Jess, you've just been submerged in freezing water. You need to get checked over yourself. The kids will go straight to Parkhill. One of your colleagues will be able to take care of them.'

She shook her head fiercely. '*I* will take care of them. I'm the consultant on call. Neither of my junior colleagues has enough experience to deal with this. Two kids with hypothermia? It's hardly an everyday occurrence. Those kids need me right now.'

One of the firefighters appeared at his side with a T-shirt and another jacket. Callum rolled his eyes. 'You've still got a stubborn streak a mile wide, haven't you?'

He handed the clothes over to her. 'Get changed and

I'll get you back topside.' She shrugged off her jumpsuit, tying the wet top half around her middle, hesitating only for a second before she pulled her thin cotton top off underneath.

In just a few seconds he saw her pale skin and the outline of her small breasts against her damp white bra. It was almost translucent. She pulled the other T-shirt over her head in a flash. But not before he'd managed to note just how thin she was.

Jess had always been slim. But slim with curves. What had happened to her?

She zipped the jacket up to her neck. Meeting his eyes with a steely glare. Daring him to mention the fact she'd just stripped at a riverside, or to mention her obviously underweight figure.

Callum knew better.

He'd learned over the last few years to pick his battles carefully.

Now wasn't the time.

He signalled and a couple of lines appeared down the side of the steep incline. He leaned over and clipped her harness. Her whole bottom half was still wet—as was his. Spare T-shirts and jackets could be found, but spare shoes and trousers? Not a chance.

'You do realise we go back up the way we came down?'

She sighed, but he couldn't help but notice the faint tremble in her hands. An after-effect of the cold water? Or something else?

He stepped behind her and interlocked their harnesses. 'The quickest way to get you back up is to let me help you.'

He could see her brain searching for a reason to disagree.

'You want to get back up to those kids?'

She nodded. Whatever her reservations, she'd pushed them aside.

'Then let me help you. It's like abseiling in reverse. Lean back against me.'

She was hesitating, still keeping all the weight on her legs, so he pulled her backwards towards him. He felt a little shock to feel her body next to his.

It had felt different in the water, more buoyant, the water between them cushioning the sensation. But now it was just clothes. Wet clothes, which clung to every curve of their bodies.

Her body was tense, stiff, and it took a few seconds for her to relax. He wrapped his arms around her, holding onto the lines in front of them, and gave them a little tug. His lips accidentally brushed against her ear as he spoke to her. 'We let the lines take our weight. If you just lean back into me, I'll walk up back up the incline. Just try and keep your legs in pace with mine. It feels a little weird, but it'll only take a few minutes.'

He let her listen, digest his words. He could feel her breathing sync with his, the rise and fall of their chests becoming simultaneous. She put her hands forward, holding onto the same line as he was, reaching for a little security in the strange situation.

He wrapped his hands around hers. His thick gloves were in place, to take the taut strain of the line.

He felt the tug of the line and started to walk his legs up the slope, taking her weight on his body. He looked skyward. Praying for divine intervention to stop any reactions taking place.

It was the weirdest sensation. The last time their bodies had been locked together she'd been seventeen and he'd been twenty-one. A whole lifetime had passed since then.

A marriage, a divorce, a fierce custody battle—and that was just him. What had happened to her?

His eyes went automatically to her hand. He'd always imagined a girl like Jess would be happily married with a couple of kids by this age. But even through her wet gloves he could see there was no outline of a wedding band. Not even an engagement ring.

Something clenched at him. Was it curiosity? Or was it some strange thrill that Jess might be unattached?

His head was buzzing. He couldn't even make sense of his thoughts. He hadn't seen this woman in years. He hadn't even *heard* about her in years. He had no idea what life had flung at Jessica Rae. And she had no idea what life had thrown at him.

Drew. The most important person in his world.

A world he kept tightly wrapped and carefully preserved.

Drew's mother, Kirsten, had left after the divorce and costly custody battle. She was in New York—married to her first love, who she'd claimed she should never have left in the first place, as he was twice the man that Callum was. Callum had been a 'poor substitute'. Words that still stung to this day.

By that point, Callum couldn't have cared less about her frequent temper tantrums and outbursts. He had only cared about how they impacted on Drew.

Drew was the best and only good thing to have come out of that marriage.

He didn't intend to make the same mistake twice.

He'd never introduced any woman to Drew in the three years following his divorce. No matter how many hints they'd dropped.

But his immediate and natural curiosity was taking

over. He didn't have a single bad memory about Jessica Rae. Even their break-up had been civilised.

Seeing her today had been a great shock, but her warm brown eyes and loose curls took him straight back thirteen years and he couldn't resist the temptation to find out a little more when it was just the two of them. They were around halfway up now. 'So, how have you been, Jessica? It's been a long time since we were in a position like this.'

He was only half-joking. Trying to take some of the strain out of her muscles, which had tensed more and more as they'd ascended the slope. Was Jessica scared of heights?

Her voice was quiet—a little thoughtful even. 'Yes. It has been, hasn't it?' She turned her head a little so he could see the side of her face. 'I'd no idea you were a firefighter. Didn't you do engineering at uni?'

She'd remembered. Why did that seem important to him?

'Yes, three years at Aberdeen Uni.' He gave a fake shudder. 'These would be normal temperatures for up there.'

'So, how did you end up being a firefighter?'

Was she just being polite? Or was she genuinely curious? He'd probably never know.

'There was a fire in the student accommodation where I stayed. We were on the tenth floor.' He tried to block out the pictures in his mind. 'It gave me a whole new perspective on the fire service. They needed to call out a specialist team and specialist equipment to reach us.' He didn't normally share this information with people. But Jess was different. Jess knew him in ways that most other people didn't.

'That must have been scary.'

Not even close. There was so much he was leaving unsaid.

The terrifying prospect of being marooned on a roof with the floors beneath you alight.

The palpable terror of the students around you.

The look on the faces of the fire crew when they realised you were out of reach and they had to stand by and wait, helpless, until other crew and equipment arrived.

'Callum?'

'What? Oh, yes, sorry. Let's just say it made me appreciate the engineering work involved in the fire service's equipment. I joined when I finished university. It didn't take me long to find my calling at the rope rescue unit. I still do some other regular firefighting duties, but most of the time I'm with the rescue unit.' He wanted to change the subject. He didn't want her to ask any questions about the fire. 'What about you? Are you married with four kids by now?'

It was meant to be simple. A distraction technique. A simple change of subject, taking the emphasis off him and putting it back on to her.

But as soon as the words left his mouth he knew he'd said the wrong thing. The stiffness and tension in her muscles was automatic.

They were nearing the edge of the incline and he could see movement above them. The flurry of activity as the stretchers were pulled over the edge and the paramedics and technicians started dealing with the children.

'Things just didn't work out for me.'

Quiet words, almost whispered.

He was stunned into silence.

There was obviously much more to it than that but now was hardly the time or the place.

And who was he to be asking?

He hadn't seen Jessica in thirteen years. Was it any of his business what had happened to her?

The radio on his shoulder crackled into life. 'We've got the last two kids. Minor injuries—nothing significant. There's an ambulance on standby that will take them to be checked over.'

'Are all the ambulances heading to Parkhill?' She sounded anxious.

He lifted the radio to his mouth. 'Wait and I'll check. Control—are all paediatric patients being taken to Parkhill?'

There was a buzz, some further crackles, then a disjointed voice. 'Four classified as majors, eight as minors. Two majors and six minors already en route. The adults have gone to Glasgow Cross.'

'Give me your hand!' A large arm reached over the edge and grabbed Jessica's wrist, pulling them topside. Someone unclipped their harnesses and tethers, leaving them free of each other.

'Doc, you're requested in one of the ambulances.'

Jess never even turned back, just started running towards the nearest ambulance, where one of the hypothermic kids was being loaded.

Callum watched her immediately fall back into professional mode.

'Scoop and run,' she shouted. 'Get that other ambulance on the move and someone get me a line to Parkhill. I want them to be set up for our arrival.'

Callum looked around him. The major incident report was going to be a nightmare. It would probably take up the next week of his life.

He grabbed hold of the guy next to him. 'Any other problems?'

The guy shook his head. 'Just waiting to lock and load the last two kids. The clean-up here will take hours.'

Callum nodded. 'In that case, I'm going to Parkhill with the ambulances. I want to find out how all these kids do. I'll be back in a few hours.'

He jumped into the back of one of the other ambulances, where the paramedic and nurse were treating the other hypothermic kid. 'Can I hitch a ride?' He glanced at the nurse, who was balanced on one leg. 'Did you hurt yourself?'

The paramedic nodded.

'Ride up front with the technician. We're going to be busy back here.'

The nurse grimaced, looking down at her leg. 'I'm sure it's nothing. Let's just get these kids back to Parkhill.'

Callum jumped back down and closed the doors, sliding into the passenger seat at the front. Within seconds the ambulance had taken off, sirens blaring. Great, the paediatrician had ended up in the Clyde and the nurse had injured her ankle. The major incident report was getting longer by the second.

It wouldn't take long to get through the city traffic at this time. He pulled his notebook from his top pocket. It was sodden. Useless, soaked when the minibus had tipped and he'd landed in the water.

'Got anything I can write on?'

The technician nodded, his eyes never leaving the road, and gestured his head towards the glove box, where Callum found a variety of notebooks and pens.

'Perfect. Thanks.' He started scribbling furiously. It was essential he put down as much as could for the incident report, before it became muddled in his brain.

The number of staff in attendance. The number of victims. The decision to call out the medical crew. Jessica. The descent down the incline. The temperature and depth of the water. Jessica being called onto the minibus. His first impression of the casualties. The way the casualties had been prioritised. The fact that Jessica had landed in the water.

The feeling in his chest when she'd disappeared under the water.

He laid the notebook and pen down in his lap.

This was no use.

He wasn't thinking the way he usually did. Calmly. Methodically.

He just couldn't get her out of his head.

It seemed that after thirteen years of immunity Jessica had reclaimed her place—straight back under his skin.

CHAPTER THREE

THE AMBULANCE DOORS were flung open and Jess heaved a sigh of relief. Her team was ready and waiting.

The A and E department would be swamped. There were twelve kids with a variety of injuries to look after, as well as all the normal walking wounded patients and GP emergency admissions that would have turned up today.

Everyone would be on edge. The place would be going like a fair.

Her team sprang into action immediately as she jumped down from the ambulance.

'Is the resus room set up for these two kids?'

'All prepared, Dr Rae. Fluids heating as we speak. Harry Shaw, the anaesthetist, and Blake Connor, the registrar, will help you run these kids simultaneously. You're drookit, Jess. Wanna get changed?'

A set of scrub trousers were thrust into her hands and she gave a little smile. Her team had thought of everything.

Harry appeared at her side. 'I take it it was freezing out there?'

'Baltic.' The one-word answer told him everything he needed to know.

The second ambulance arrived and both kids were wheeled into the resus room and transferred to the trolleys. Jess ducked behind a curtain and shucked off her soggy jumpsuit, replacing it the with the dry scrub trousers. If only her underwear wasn't still sodden.

Her team was on autopilot, stripping the freezing-wet clothing from both kids and bundling them up in warming blankets.

She walked out from behind the curtains. Harry Shaw was standing at the head of one of the trolleys, doing his initial assessment. 'What can you tell me?'

She looked up as Callum appeared at the doorway and handed her a sheet of paper. 'Thought this might be useful,' he said as he walked away.

She stared at what he'd scribbled for her. *Temperature of the Clyde is currently minus five degrees centigrade. Moving water takes longer to freeze.*

It was just what she needed. The temperature to which these kids had been exposed was very important.

She walked over to Harry. 'This is Marcus, he's four. He was unconscious at the scene but I can't find any obvious sign of injury. Showing severe signs of hypothermia. As far as I know, his head was always above the water, but we couldn't get the tympanic thermometer to register on-site.'

Harry nodded. 'I need baseline temps on both these kids. Has to be a core temperature, so oesophageal temperatures would be best.'

More paperwork appeared in her hand from the receptionist. 'Nursery just called with some more details.'

Her eyes scanned the page and she let out a little sigh. 'This is Lily. She's four too. She was submerged at the scene—but no one can be sure how long.'

Harry was one of the most experienced paediatric anaesthetists that she knew. He'd already realised that Lily was the priority and left Connor to take over with Marcus. He was already sliding an ET tube into place for Lily. He took a few seconds to check her temperature. Both cardiac monitors were switched on and the team stood silently to watch them flicker to life.

Jessica's heart thumped in her chest. What happened in the next few minutes would determine whether these kids made it or not.

'Marcus's temp is thirty degrees. Moderate hypothermia,' shouted Connor.

She watched the monitor for a few more seconds. 'He's bradycardic but his cardiac rhythm appears stable. Any problems with his breathing?'

Connor shook his head. 'He's maintaining his airway. His breathing's just slowed along with his heart rate.'

Jessica's brain was racing. She was the paediatric consultant. This was her lead. But Harry was an extremely experienced anaesthetist. She wanted to be sure they were on the same page.

She turned to him. 'Warmed, humidified oxygen, contact rewarming with a warming unit, rewarmed IV fluids and temperature monitoring. Do you agree?'

He gave her a little smile over the top of his glasses. 'Sounds like a plan. I've paged one of my other anaesthetists to come down.' The nursing staff started to flurry around them, carrying out the instructions. Jessica felt nervous.

Hypothermia was more common in elderly patients than in children. Every year they had a few cases come through the doors of A and E, but she wasn't always on duty. And most of those kids were near-drownings—kids who'd been playing on frozen rivers or lakes and had slipped under the water.

Blake Connor, her registrar, looked up from Marcus's

arm. 'I've got the bloods.' He rattled off a whole host of tests he planned to run. 'Anything else?'

She shook her head. 'Right now, we're working on the assumption that he's unconscious due to his hypothermia. There's no sign of any head injury or further trauma. Keep a careful eye on him. I want to know as soon he regains consciousness. He'll probably be disorientated and confused. Most adults with a temperature at this stage start undressing. We might need to sedate him if he becomes agitated.' She scribbled in the notes then spoke to the nursing staff.

'We're aiming for a temperature gain of around one degree every fifteen minutes. Keep an eye on his blood pressure and watch for any atrial fibrillation. Is that clear?'

The nursing staff nodded and she looked around. 'Anyone seen Jackie? She was the one who brought Lily in. I need some more information.'

One of the paramedics touched her arm. 'She fell, coming back up the slope. We think she might have fractured her ankle. Once we'd dropped Lily here my technician took her along to Glasgow Cross.'

Jess felt a twinge of guilt. It was her fault Jackie had been on the scene. She'd wanted the expertise of the experienced nurse at the site. Now, because of her, Jackie was injured. It didn't seem fair.

'Lily's temperature is lower than Marcus's. It's twenty-eight degrees.' Harry had just finished sliding the oesophageal temperature monitor into place. He glanced at the monitor. 'She's borderline, Jess. What do you want to do?'

Jess pulled back the warming blankets to get a better look at her small body. Lily was right on the edge, hovering between severe and moderate hypothermia. It was a wonder she hadn't gone into cardiac arrest.

'How's her respiratory effort?'

Harry was sounding her chest. 'For a child who was submerged I'm not hearing any fluid in her lungs. Just a few crackles. She is breathing, but not enough to keep me happy.'

'Wait a minute, folks.' Jess held her hand up as the monitor flickered, going from a stable but slow heart rate to a run of ectopic beats. She shook her head.

Time was of the essence here. She needed to make a decision.

Lily was deathly pale. All her surface blood vessels had contracted as her little body was focusing its resources on keeping her vital organs warm.

Her lips and ears were tinged with blue, showing lack of oxygen perfusing through her body.

Her eyes fell on Lily's fingers and toes. Their colour was poor.

No. Their colour was worse than poor.

The blueness was worse.

The tinkle of the monitor indicated Lily had gone into cardiac arrest. Jessica leaned across the bed and automatically started cardiac massage with the heel of one hand.

It clarified things and made the decision easier.

'Harry, we're not going to wait. Call the team. Let's get her to Theatre and begin extracorporeal rewarming. Can you phone ahead? Let them know we are resuscitating.'

One of the nurses nodded and picked up the phone in the resus room. 'Paediatric ECMO in Theatre ASAP. Yes, it's one of the minibus victims. Four-year-old female, submerged, with a core temperature of twenty-eight degrees. She's arrested and currently being resuscitated. Dr Shaw has her intubated and they'll be bringing her along now.'

She replaced the receiver. 'Theatre one will be waiting for you.'

A wave of relief washed over Jessica. There was no drama. No struggling to find theatre time. It sounded as though the theatre staff was already prepared for the possibility of one of the hypothermic kids needing ECMO.

Extracorporeal membrane oxygenation worked with cardiopulmonary bypass to take over the function of the heart and provide extracorporeal circulation of the blood where it could be rewarmed and oxygenated. It had only been used in a few cases of hypothermia with cardiac arrest in the last few years, but had had extremely positive results with good outcomes for patients.

Lily was going to be one of those patients.

Jessica was absolutely determined.

Two porters appeared at either side of the trolley, ready for the move.

As they swept down the corridor towards the lifts she caught sight of Callum again, taking notes and talking to one of the nurses. He was still here?

She hadn't had a chance to think about him. She had been too busy concentrating her energies on keeping this little girl alive. She could feel the cold flesh under her hand as she pumped methodically, trying to push blood around Lily's body. Trying to get some oxygen circulating to her body and brain.

This was somebody's child. Somebody's pride and joy.

Their reason to get up in the morning and their reason to go home at night.

Any minute now some poor, frantic man and woman would turn up in A and E anxious to get news of their daughter.

Praying and pleading to hear the best possible news.

Trying not to think about the pictures their brains had been conjuring up ever since they'd heard about the minibus crash. Struggling to remember to breathe as they made the journey to the hospital.

A journey that probably seemed to take twice as long as it normally did.

Their 'normal' day had changed beyond all recognition. Had they kissed their daughter goodbye that morning before they'd dropped her at nursery? At the place they'd assumed she would be safe?

Had they spent a few brief seconds taking her in their arms and feeling the warmth and joy of cuddling a child before they'd left her that morning? Or had they given her the briefest kiss on the top of her head because they had been in a rush to get to work? Because they hadn't realised it could be the last time they kissed their child.

Would they spend the rest of their lives regretting signing a consent form to say their daughter could go on the nursery trip? The one that could have cost her life?

All these thoughts were crowding her brain. Any time she had to resuscitate a child she was invaded with *what-ifs*?

But the *what-ifs* were about her own life. She'd spent the last three years thinking about the *what-ifs*.

What if she'd been driving the car that night?

What if she hadn't been on call?

What if her husband hadn't stopped to buy her favourite chocolate on the way home?

The lift doors pinged and they swept the trolley out. She lifted her head. The theatre doors were open and waiting for them.

One of the perfusionists was standing by, already scrubbing at the sinks, preparing to insert the catheter lines that could save Lily's life.

This was why she did this job.

This was why after a year of darkness she hadn't walked away. She might not have been able to save her own child but she would do her damnedest to save *this* one.

Callum stared at his watch. It had been six hours since he'd last seen Jessica sweeping down the corridor, her thin scrub trousers clinging to her wet backside, her hand pumping the little girl's chest.

He'd felt physically sick at that sight.

Not because he wasn't used to dealing with casualties. Casualties of all ages and all descriptions were part and parcel of the job.

But seeing the expression on Jessica's face wasn't.

Everything about this situation was having the strangest effect on him. The sight of Jessica hadn't just been unexpected—it had been like a bolt out of the blue.

They'd been childhood sweethearts who'd broken up when life had moved on and they'd never moved in the same circles again. He hadn't even heard anything about Jessica over the last few years.

Her words on the steep embankment had intrigued him. *Things just didn't work out for me.*

It made his brain buzz. There was a whole world of possibilities in those words. But he didn't feel as if he could come right out and ask.

Particularly when the sick kids were the priority.

And his lasting memories right now were the way her body had felt next to his. The way they'd seemed to fit together so well again—just like they always had.

It was the first time in a long time that he'd felt a connection to a woman.

The first time in a long time he'd ever *wanted* to feel a connection to a woman.

Sure, he'd dated on a few rare occasions, but nothing had been serious. He'd never introduced anyone to Drew. It was almost as if he didn't want to let anyone into that part of his life.

Would he ever feel ready to change that?

The doors opened at the end of the corridor and Jessica walked through. She looked absolutely exhausted. There were black circles under her eyes and her skin was even paler than it had been earlier.

He was on his feet in an instant. 'Jess? How did it go?'

She reached out to touch his arm, her brown eyes fixed on his. 'The next few hours will be crucial. We've done everything we can. Lily's temperature is coming up gradually. Now it's just wait and see. I've just spoken to her parents.' Was that a tear in Jess's eye?

It was there—written all across her face—how much those words pained her. How much she hated it that things were out of her control. The only thing left to do was wait.

She flicked her head from side to side. 'I need to get a report on all of the other kids. I need to find out how they are all doing.'

'No.' He rested his hand on her shoulder. 'You need to take a break. Come and sit down. Have a coffee, have something to eat. You must be running on empty, you know that can't be good for you.'

He could see the struggle in her eyes. 'I just can't, Callum. There were twelve kids in that accident. I'm the consultant on call. They're my responsibility.'

Callum glanced at the notes in his hand. 'Four have

already been discharged. Another four have been admitted to the paediatric unit with mild hypothermia, a head injury, and some bumps and scrapes.'

Her eyes widened. 'How do you know all that?'

He gave her a little smile. 'It's part of the investigation after any major incident for the rope rescue crew. I always need to find out the outcomes for the victims. We need to look over everything that we did to make sure there were no mistakes.'

'And were there?'

He frowned. 'Apart from our doctor ending up in the Clyde? And your nurse fracturing her ankle?'

A little smile danced across her weary face. 'I don't think you have much control over tides and currents—no matter how much you want to. And Jackie? That's my responsibility. It was me who asked her to come on the rescue.'

He shook his head. He hadn't been able to shake the picture from his mind of Jessica falling into the icy river. It had made him feel sick to his stomach and would have to form part of his investigation.

'It's my job to make sure everyone is safe at the rescue site. It's my responsibility, not yours.'

Her shoulders relaxed a little. This was probably the first normal conversation she'd had all day. 'Do you want to fight me for it?'

'Will I win?' he quipped.

'Did you ever win?' she quipped back equally quickly.

He smiled. This was the Jess he'd once known.

He glanced at his notes. 'What about the other kids? I know about Marcus and Lily, but that still leaves another two.'

'One was Rosie, she was on the bus next to Marcus. The

other is a little girl called Kelly. Both have broken limbs and were taken to surgery by the orthopaedic surgeon.'

'I'll need to follow them up for the report.'

She paused for a second, as if trying to find words. 'It was nice to see you today, Callum, even though it wasn't the best of circumstances. I'm glad you're doing well.'

Something sparked in his brain. She was just about to say goodbye. And he didn't want her to. He didn't want this to be the last time he saw Jessica Rae for another thirteen years.

'But how are you doing, Jess?' The words were out before he had a chance to censor them. Should he really be asking her something like that?

Her eyes lowered, breaking contact with his. Had he offended her? He could see her taking a deep breath.

'If you need any assistance with the investigation, feel free to come back and talk to me.' It was a deliberate side-step. A deliberate attempt to move the conversation back to something more professional.

'I'll need a statement from you about the events.' He would. It wasn't a lie. Any event like this always needed information from all the professionals involved. Not least the one who had landed in the middle of the Clyde.

'That's fine, but can we do it some other time? I really want to check on the kids.'

What she needed to do was to rest. She looked as though a long night's sleep would do her the world of good. But he already knew that wasn't going to happen.

'Of course we can do it some other time. I need to follow up the adults at Glasgow Cross—I'll do that tomorrow. Then I'll come back here to see how the kids are doing.' He hesitated, just for a second. 'Will you be available at any point tomorrow?'

He was hopeful. He was more than hopeful. This might be work, but more than anything right now he'd like to see Jessica again. Any way he could.

She nodded. 'Leave it until later in the day. I'll be busy first thing in the morning with ward rounds and reviews.'

He gave her a little smile and he couldn't help the words that came out of his mouth. 'I'll see you then.'

There was a moment of hesitation, a flicker of something going through her eyes, and it struck straight at his heart. Was it panic? Was it fear?

Her shoulders had pulled back a little, moving away from him, and the urge to reach out and pull her back towards him raced through his mind.

Why would the simplest of words cause this reaction? Jessica had always been a fun-loving, gregarious young woman. And even though he hadn't seen her in thirteen years this seemed wrong to him. Out of character.

But did he even know Jess's character any more?

It took a few seconds, but Jess seemed to gather herself and gave him the slightest flash of her brown eyes. 'Tomorrow's fine, Callum. I'll see you then.'

She turned and walked down the corridor. He couldn't tear his eyes away from her.

Now, when she was wearing only thin green theatre scrubs, he could see that her weight loss was dramatic. He flinched, remembering having seen the outline of her ribs on the riverbank. Now he could see her legs and hips. Hips that had been pressing up against his earlier.

He'd reached the bottom of the corridor, near the nurses' station in A and E. He recognised one of the sisters— they'd gone to a few study days on some aspects of community safety.

He walked over to her. 'Hi, Miriam, how's things?'

The older woman looked up and shot him a friendly smile. 'Hi, Callum. I take it you were dealing with the kids in the minibus?'

He nodded. 'Not the best day of my life. One of your doctors was out helping us—Jessica Rae?'

Miriam looked confused for a second then waved her hand. 'Oh, you mean Jessica Faraday. I know she's reverted back to her maiden name but I can't get used to it. She's fabulous. One of the best consultants we've got. The kids were certainly in safe hands with her.'

Callum could feel himself furrowing his brow. 'Jessica Faraday? She was married?'

Miriam finished typing something on the computer. 'Yeah.' She was distracted, concentrating on the words in front of her.

'But she's not now?' Callum couldn't help but probe. Curiosity was killing him.

Miriam met his eyes. 'Sadly not.'

Things just didn't work out for me.

Jessica's words echoed in his brain. He still didn't know what they meant, and it just didn't seem right to be asking someone else. It didn't matter that Miriam was a colleague—one he'd spoken to on many occasions—he just didn't feel he could ask anything personal about Jess.

It was an invasion of her privacy. He had no right to ask anything about her. It didn't matter that his curiosity was currently burning so fiercely in his stomach it would probably cause an ulcer.

Suddenly he was conscious of what he'd just done. He'd been around hospitals long enough to know that even the simplest and vaguest questions could be entirely misinterpreted.

Miriam had gone back to her paperwork—not in the

least interested in why Callum was asking questions about Jessica. Thankfully, she had a hundred other things to worry about. The last thing he needed was rumours starting to spread in a hospital. He didn't want anyone to get the wrong impression.

What was the wrong impression?

He had no idea what he thought about all this.

All he knew for sure was that the haunted look in Jessica's eyes was going to stick in his brain for the rest of the day. And probably most of the night.

This was wrong. He shouldn't be thinking about her at all.

He had Drew to worry about. His little boy was his entire life and he didn't want anything to get in the way of that. He *wouldn't* let anything get in the way of that.

The custody battle had been fiercely fought, sapping all his energy and strength. And whilst he'd been on dates in the last year or so, no woman had really attracted his attention. No woman had ever been introduced to his son.

And that was way he intended to continue.

He should walk away.

He should run.

But somehow he knew that come tomorrow afternoon he would be right here.

Right here, waiting for Jessica.

CHAPTER FOUR

CALLUM STARED AT the clock and pulled out his cellphone again. *How is Drew?* he typed.

Drew had been clingy last night. Definitely not normal for him. He hadn't wanted to go to bed and had just said he didn't feel good.

After a day stuck in the freezing-cold Clyde, all Callum had wanted to do was hold him close. So he'd broken all his own rules and let Drew come into bed beside him.

There hadn't seemed to be anything obvious wrong with Drew. His temperature hadn't been raised. He hadn't had a rash. But he'd had a restless night and when he'd stirred his porridge around his plate that morning Callum had looked at the pale little face and had known he couldn't send him to school today.

Thank goodness for good friends. Julie and Blair were always willing to help out any way they could.

His phone buzzed.

Not eating and a little tired. But managing to watch the TV. Don't worry. Julie.

Don't worry. Fat chance.

The door next to him opened. Jess. He stood up straight away and walked over to her. 'How are you? Are you okay?' She looked a little better today. There was some colour in her cheeks, her caramel-coloured hair hung in waves around her shoulders and her pink woollen jumper gave the illusion of some curves.

There it was again. The little surge he'd felt yesterday when he'd seen her. That buzz of attraction. He hadn't imagined it. He hadn't imagined it at all.

She gestured down the corridor. 'I'm fine. Honestly. No ill effects.' She gave him a little smile. She was definitely a little more relaxed today but, then, Parkhill was her comfort zone.

'How are the kids?'

Her expression was still serious. 'We've still got two in ITU, both serious but stable. Four were allowed home yesterday, another four were kept for observation overnight but are being discharged today. The last two will be in for a few days, both have different kinds of fractures.'

He gave her a knowing smile. 'Busy day, then?'

She let out a little laugh. 'What? No way. We've only had another thirty admissions on top of the accident yesterday. It's practically been a walk in the park.'

'Thirty? Is there some kind of outbreak?'

She nodded. 'Yip.' She handed over a set of case notes to the secretary next to them. She folded her arms across her chest. 'It's called a Scottish winter.'

'What do you mean?'

She gave a little shrug. 'It's like this every year. Asthma and chest infections flare up and there's always an outbreak of norovirus somewhere. Public health had to recommend closing two nurseries yesterday.' She waved her hand. 'We've got a baby with chickenpox in ITU. Oh, and the usual slips, trips and falls. We're thinking of putting a sign on the door of ward 1C saying *Only people in fibreglass may pass these doors*.'

He couldn't help the smile dancing across his face. 'It's that bad?'

She gave a little sigh. 'It's just how things are. That, and all the parents that come to the desk and give it laldy.'

He smiled. 'Now, there's a word I haven't heard in a while.'

She rolled her eyes. 'It's the most accurate description. I said it the other day to one of the Spanish registrars and he was totally lost. Thing is, it's never the parents with the sickest kids who cause a scene, it's the ones who probably shouldn't even be in an A and E department and don't think they should be waiting.'

'We get our fair share in the fire service too. Last month it was a guy who called 999 every time his house fire alarm went off.'

'Did he have a fire?'

Callum shook his head. 'Nope. He just kept burning his toast and thought we should come out.'

'Thank goodness. I thought it was just us that got the crazies.'

He looked over at her. Although her outward appearance had improved since yesterday, he could still sense the tiredness in her body.

'Are you sure you want to do this today? We can do it some other time if it doesn't suit you.'

She shook her head. 'You're going to need the statement at some point and it's probably best I do it while it's all still fresh in my mind.'

'Have you got time for a coffee?'

She glanced at her watch. 'Actually, I've got a couple of hours.' She looked around her. 'Can we get out of here for a little while? I need to cover for someone tonight so I'll be here until tomorrow.'

He bit his tongue. From the look of her she'd already covered last night too. Did she really need to do it again? The thought of getting her out of this place was very appealing. Maybe some fresh air and a change of scene would lessen the tiredness in her eyes. There was no way he'd say no to her.

'Sure. As long as you don't mind travelling in a fire and rescue vehicle.'

Her eyes widened. 'You've got a fire engine sitting outside?' He could hear the edge of excitement in her voice. It was almost everyone's childhood dream to ride in a fire engine.

He laughed. 'No, I've got the four-by-four. But I'm on call and can be paged at any time, so I need to be ready to go.'

'Oh.' She looked a little disappointed. 'Does that mean you can't go anywhere?'

He shook his head, his heart clenching a little as he realised she'd looked a little sad at the prospect. 'Of course I can. But let's not go too far. That way, if I get paged I can drop you back here quickly. Is there somewhere local you'd prefer?'

She nodded. 'There's an Italian coffee shop that does great food and some killer carrot cake about five minutes' drive from here. Just let me grab my bag and coat.'

He stood for a few seconds until she reappeared at his side, wearing a thick purple wool coat and pink scarf. He smiled. 'I take it you came prepared today.'

'After yesterday? I've honestly never been so cold. The first thing I did last night was put on the fire, find the biggest, snuggliest pair of pyjamas I could and pull my duvet in front of the fire.'

The picture was conjured up in his head instantly. Snuggly pyjamas might not be the sexiest nightwear he would normally think of for a woman, but it still brought a smile to his face.

They walked outside into the cold air and she automatically moved a little closer to him, letting his body shield her from the biting wind. It was all he could do to stop his arm reaching out to wrap around her waist.

He felt on edge. He hadn't seen her in years. She had a whole other life he knew nothing about. Little things started to edge into the corners of his mind. Who did Jessica have to snuggle up to after a stressful day at work? Had she spent the night alone in front of the fire?

Curiosity was killing him. Particularly after the comment Miriam had made the previous day about Jessica reverting to her maiden name.

He had a burning sensation to find out why. It suddenly seemed really important—even though it shouldn't. Did Jessica feel the nervous edge that he did?

But Jess seemed relaxed around him. She shot him another smile as she climbed into the car. 'You would have been horrified. I even resorted to bedsocks last night!'

'Were they pink?' He started the car and pulled out of the car park.

'How did you guess?'

'Because some things don't change.' Pink had always been her favourite colour. The words had come out before he'd had time to think about them. Because nothing could be further from the truth. Things had changed, for both of them—probably more than they could ever have imagined.

Thirteen years was a long time.

There was silence for a few seconds, as if she was thinking the same kind of thoughts that he was.

She gestured to the side. 'This way.' She waited until

he changed lanes. 'I guess I always did like pink,' she said quietly. She touched the collar of her coat. 'I've even got a pink coat, I just didn't wear it today.'

Another little memory sparked into his brain. Jessica's wardrobe. She'd had the biggest array of clothes he'd ever seen. He shot her a smile. 'Knowing you, you've probably got a coat for every colour of the rainbow.'

She tilted her head to the side as if she was racking her brain. 'Emerald green.'

He raised his eyebrows.

'That's the colour I'm missing. I need to get an emerald-green raincoat and the rainbow will be complete.' She pointed in front of them. 'It's just over here. Pull in to the left.'

He halted just in front of the Italian-style coffee shop, walking around and opening the door for her.

The heat hit them as soon as they walked inside, along with a whole host of mouth-watering smells.

He pulled out a chair and helped her off with her coat, before sitting across from her and bringing out his array of paperwork. But his brain wasn't focusing on the paperwork.

Taking Jessica out of her own environment felt a little odd. It felt personal but this was business. A professional meeting. Nothing more, nothing less. No matter how casual it seemed.

No matter how *easy* it seemed.

Why did he have to keep reminding himself about that?

He pointed to the menu. 'What do you recommend?'

'Anything and everything. There won't be a single thing in here that you don't like.'

The waitress appeared at their side.

'Just a latte for me, please.'

'No.'

He couldn't help it. Her thin frame was too much for him. He was resisting the temptation to just order her some mushrooms, a portion of lasagne and some garlic bread. Things they used to eat together a long time ago and he knew that she liked.

He couldn't help but wonder who was looking out for Jess right now. Surely her friends had spoken to her quietly and told her she'd lost too much weight? It didn't matter that he hadn't seen her in years, he couldn't stand by and say nothing.

The waitress looked a little taken aback. Callum's eyes ran down the menu. 'You need more than just coffee. Order something else.'

He could see her take a deep breath, getting ready to argue with him. But he shook his head, the smallest of movements, then reached over and touched her hand. 'Don't.'

He kept his gaze steady. They'd been friends for such a long time. It didn't matter that he hadn't seen her in years. It didn't matter that fate had thrown them together. He had no idea what had happened in the last few years for Jess—and she might never tell him. But he could focus on what was in front of him.

The one thing he could do something about.

And she knew him. She knew him well.

She would know that he would never cause a scene, but she would also know that when he was determined, there was no way around him.

Her brown eyes were fixed on where his hand was touching hers. Was she annoyed? Did she think it inappropriate? Because he'd only done what had felt natural—and it didn't feel inappropriate to him.

He could see the long exhalation of breath, the relaxing of her shoulders, then she lifted her long dark eyelashes to meet his gaze.

The long dark eyelashes that used to tickle his cheeks.

The thought came out of nowhere, triggering a whole host of memories in his brain. Now, *they* could be inappropriate.

Jess's fingers moved under his. She looked at the waitress. 'What's the soup?'

'Minestrone or tomato and herb, both served with crusty bread.'

Jess pressed her lips together. 'I'll have the minestrone. Please.' She handed the menu over.

'I'll have the same—the soup and a latte.' Something fired in his brain and he remembered what she'd said in the car. 'And carrot cake—for both of us, please.' It wasn't what he would normally eat at this time. The paperwork was still in front of him. But right now it was the least of his concerns.

Would she tell him what had happened to her in the last few years? And, in return, would he be able to tell her about Drew?

He took the bull by the horns. 'You're thin, Jess. A lot thinner than you used to be. I'd rather have bought you a three-course meal than a plate of soup.'

'Who said I was letting you buy it?'

He smiled. There it was. The spark that had seemed missing at times. The spark that took him back thirteen years.

Every now and then it flared, reappearing out of nowhere. Then the thin veil would come back down and the Jessica that he had once known would disappear.

He leaned back in the chair. Sparring with Jess now

felt as natural as it had years ago. 'Oh, you're letting me. I can assure you of that.'

'Still a stubborn bossy boots, then, Callum?'

'I had a very good teacher,' was his automatic response. But it only took a second to know what he really should do. He stretched across the table and took both her hands in his. 'Actually, I'm still a concerned friend.'

He could sense her pull back a little. See her wariness at his actions.

'We haven't seen each other in years, Callum. We lost touch. You've no idea what's happened in my life and I've no idea what's happened in yours. If that accident hadn't happened yesterday, our paths might never have crossed again.'

'And that would have been a real shame.' He shook his head. 'I'm not glad the accident happened. I'm not glad those kids were injured. But I am glad our paths have crossed again. It's nice to see you.' His voice was low and the words said quietly. He hoped she could see the sincerity in his eyes.

She paused for a moment then said, 'It's nice to see you again too.' She gave him a little smile. 'You always were a pest when it came to food.' She had a glint in her eye, and he could see her visibly relaxing, sinking a little further into her chair and leaning her elbows on the desk so they were closer.

His reaction was entirely natural—he leaned forward too. 'Jessica Rae, I've no idea what you're talking about.'

She raised her eyebrows, her smile spreading across her face. She placed her head on her hands. 'What about the cookie incident, then?'

He stifled a laugh.

The memories came flooding back. A visit to the cinema with Jess asking him to hold her coffee and cookie that he'd bought her while she went and washed her hands. They'd been running late and the film had already started by the time they'd fumbled to their seats. It had taken Jess a few minutes to lift the napkin from her purchase and the scream she'd let out had caused the whole cinema to jump in shock.

'It was only a tiny nibble.' He shrugged his shoulders.

'It was a giant-size bite! And then you let me think that it was the boy behind the counter—you were going to let me go and complain.'

He couldn't stop laughing now, with the still indignant look on her face thirteen years later. 'Just as well the crumbs gave me away, then.'

Jess started to laugh too. Her shoulders shook as she bent forward and then threw her head back. Jess didn't have a delicate, polite laugh. It was loud and wholehearted, as if it came all the way from her toes.

There was something so nice about this. The way her skin glowed and her eyes sparkled when she laughed like that. The ease and familiarity of being with someone you felt comfortable around. Someone you shared a history with. Someone who made you feel as if you could look into their eyes and trust what they said.

Someone who wouldn't run out on you and your child.

Where had that thought come from?

The door to the café opened and a woman and her child bundled in out of the cold. The little boy's nose was glowing red underneath his woolly hat. He looked around the same age as Drew.

Callum pushed all thoughts of Drew's mother out of his head and leaned forward to pass a comment to Jess. But the expression on her face stopped him dead.

She'd gone from hearty laughter to deathly pale—almost as if she'd been caught unawares. He bit his tongue, stopping himself from asking what was wrong.

He had to give her time. He had to give her space. If Jess wanted to tell him something she would.

There was silence for a few seconds as he could see her gathering herself.

She nodded at his paperwork. 'This could take some time. Shouldn't we get started?'

The barriers were going up again. She was closing herself off from him. Going back to business as usual. 'What do you need from me?'

The waitress appeared and put down two bowls of steaming-hot minestrone and a basket of crusty bread. 'I need you to relax for a bit. I want to see you eat. Once you've finished we'll do my paperwork. I need a detailed statement from you.'

He didn't want the veil to come down. Because when it did Jess had the strangest look in her eyes, almost vacant, as if she was removing herself from the situation. It was obvious that she wasn't feeling any of the same strange sensations that he was. His brain was currently mush.

Being around Jess was flaring up too many memories in his mind. Sharing memories with Jess was both warming and setting off alarm bells in his head. He'd been awake most of the night, thinking about all the good times that they'd had together.

He hadn't even told her about Drew yet. And did he want to? He had no idea what he wanted to do about any of this. Could he be friends with Jessica or was it just a recipe for disaster? He'd just have to wait and see.

CHAPTER FIVE

IT WAS THE middle of the night. The snow had given way
to sleet and was currently battering the windows in the
old Glasgow hospital.

Whilst the ward was dark, most of the windows were
adorned with festive lights. A Santa, a snowman and a
reindeer stood out twinkling against the black night sky
outside. A tree with multicoloured lights flickered at the
end of the ward, and strings of icicles were hanging from
most of the windows outside the ward bays.

A few little bodies shifted under the starched white
hospital sheets and coloured blankets. Almost everyone
was sleeping—unusual for a children's ward—with only
a few little murmurs here and there. Alongside most of
the beds were chairs and stools with an array of uncomfortable parents trying to catch a few hours' sleep as they
watched over their children.

Jessica padded along the ward in her soft-soled shoes.
She loved Christmas in the children's ward. Although most
people in her circumstances would want to avoid this place,
it was actually the one place at this time of year that gave
her a little solace.

There were always people worse off than you.

Actually, no there weren't. No parent should outlive
their child.

Here, in the ward, she felt safe. Everyone knew what had happened. No one asked awkward questions. If she needed a few moments on her own, she got them.

If she needed to be amongst people and in company, it was here.

If she needed to feel of value, there was no doubt she was needed here. There was always a little one to cuddle. There was always a parent to talk to in the quiet hours of night—to give some kind of explanation, to give some kind of comfort.

Mostly, she just liked to watch the kids sleeping.

There was nothing more comforting than watching a child sleep.

Tonight she was watching Grace Flynn, a seven-year-old with a rare form of aggressive bowel cancer. She'd had her tumours operated on twice.

Grace was a beautiful child. She wanted to be a ballerina, or an air hostess, or a teacher. She changed her mind every day. But she was becoming frailer and frailer with every visit. The chemotherapy and radiotherapy were having ravaging effects on her body. The surgeries were taking their toll. The battle was becoming harder and harder.

So tonight she was taking a little pleasure in watching Grace sleep. Watching the rise and fall of her little chest.

Moments like this always pained her. What was worse? Your child dying suddenly, with no chance to say goodbye, or dying slowly, painfully right before your eyes?

Her brain couldn't even begin to compare those issues. All she knew was that she would do everything in her power to help Grace and her parents.

Hopefully Grace would be able to be discharged home with her family tomorrow and get to spend Christmas at home.

She would love that. She might be the model patient but she always had a smile on her face when she was discharged home.

Jessica walked down the corridor, watching the twinkling lights on the windows and appreciating the stillness of the ward.

It wasn't always quiet in here. Some nights it went like a fair. Some nights she didn't even see the inside of her on-call room. Then there were other nights like tonight.

She sat down at the nurses' station and tapped a few keys on the computer, bringing up the file of one of the kids admitted earlier. She would never have been able to sleep anyway.

Images of Callum were currently swimming around in her brain.

It was the oddest of feelings.

Because she didn't know how she felt.

For the last few years she'd been sad. She'd worked hard to put one foot in front of the other and try and come out the other side. And now she finally felt as if she'd reached a plateau.

She didn't cry non-stop any more. She didn't spend every day wishing she didn't need to get out of bed. She wasn't insanely jealous of every woman pushing a stroller in the street.

Oh, she still had moments when things crept up on her and caught her unawares. When she needed a few minutes to gather herself or to wipe the stray tear that appeared on her face.

But things had eased. It was still the first thing she thought about every morning and the last thing she thought about at night. But it didn't fill her every waking moment of the day any more. She'd allowed herself to think about other things. To care a little about other things.

And work was her biggest comfort. It helped her tick along. It gave her a sense of purpose. A little confidence that she did have a life worth living.

Then something like this happened.

A blast from the past, totally unexpected. Totally unprepared for.

Callum was evoking a whole host of memories. Most of which were good. Some of which were distinctly edged with tinges of pink—the way all teenage first-love memories were.

It was a little unsettling. Not just seeing Callum but the whole host of *what-ifs* that had her flooded her mind afterwards—some of which had permeated her dreams.

What if she'd married Callum? What would her life have been like? Would they still have been together after all this time?

She tried to push the thoughts away. It felt disloyal. Disloyal to the memory of her husband, Daniel, and her little boy, Lewis.

Daniel had been the love of her life. She'd been blissfully happy. She'd thought they'd grow old together. She'd *expected* them to grow old together.

But as much as she'd loved Daniel, the loss of Lewis was even worse. As if someone had ripped her heart right out of her chest and squeezed it until every last drop of blood was gone.

The pain had almost killed her.

Maybe that was why her brain was drifting into unchartered territories. If she'd stayed with Callum, Daniel and Lewis would never have featured in her life.

She would never have suffered such torment and hurt

at their loss. She wouldn't have found herself wondering if she wanted to go on. To live a life without them.

Maybe Callum was a safe memory.

She opened her eyes, looking around to see if anyone had noticed her hunched over the keyboard. Two of the nurses were standing at the door of one of the rooms but they hadn't noticed a thing.

Her pager sounded and she was on her feet instantly. ITU. She had three kids in there right now. The baby with chickenpox and Marcus and Lily from the accident. She started saying silent prayers in her head as she walked swiftly down the corridor. She looked around. It was the dead of night and there was no one else about so she took off. Her soft running footsteps echoed up and down the passages of the long building until she reached the doors and squirted her hands with gel before entering.

The doors swung open. The steady whoosh-whoosh of the ventilators was the first thing that she heard whenever she stepped inside. In most instances it was a soothing sound, often not reflecting the serious condition of the patients inside. She took a quick look around the unit. It was brighter than the rest of the hospital, even though some of lights were dimmed.

She recognised a figure next to Lily's bed and walked over quickly. Pauline, the sister in ITU, was great. She'd been there for ten years, had a whole wealth of experience and, more importantly, good instincts. Jessica trusted her judgement, and she also valued her friendship. She'd been a pillar of strength for Jess in the last few years.

'What's up, Pauline?'

Pauline shook her head. 'She's gone from bradycardic and hypothermic to the opposite. Tachycardic and high temp. Isn't it amazing how kids go from one extreme to the other?'

Jessica cast her eyes over the monitor. Thirty-six hours ago Lily had had a heart rate of fifty and now it was one hundred and sixty. 'Darn it. The ECMO should be keeping her heart rate and temperature steady. She must have an infection somewhere. How's her suctioning been?'

Pauline's lips pressed together. She hated it as much as Jess did when kids got sicker. 'She's been suctioned every four hours and there's been no increase in her secretions.'

Jessica rolled her shoulders back, trying to relieve the tension in her neck and shoulders. Everyone knew that ECMO could have complications—bleeding, infections, neurological damage and kidney damage.

Jessica unwound the pink stethoscope from her neck. 'I'll have a little listen to her chest. It was clear earlier and her chest X-ray was fine, but you know how things can change.'

She placed her stethoscope on Lily's little chest and listened for a few seconds then frowned. 'I can hear crackles in her lungs. Can I have her chart? I'll get her started on IV antibiotics right away.' She scribbled on the chart handed to her. 'Are you okay to make these up or do you want me to do it?'

Most of the nurses in ITU had extended roles. The IV antibiotics could be sent up from the hospital pharmacy but that would take time. Time that Lily essentially didn't have. Pauline nodded her head. 'It's fine. I'll do it. It will only take a few minutes.'

Jessica continued to make a few notes. 'I'm asking for another chest X-ray. I want to see if there's any change from this morning. And I'll be about for the next few hours. Let me know if you have any concerns.'

'Not planning on having any sleep tonight, Jess? You know that's not good for you.' There was concern in Pauline's voice. And it was sincere—she always tried to look out for Jess.

Jess just gave her a little smile and kept writing. Sometimes she just liked to keep her head down.

'I meant to ask you, how do you know Callum?'

The question took her by surprise. She felt on guard, even with a woman she'd always trusted. But Pauline's face was open and friendly. 'Callum Kennedy?' she asked.

'Yeah, the fireman—the rope rescue guy. He was on the phone earlier, enquiring after the kids. He knows we can't give him any specific details. He just wanted to check everything was okay. Apparently he was in yesterday too. The staff say he's gorgeous.'

Callum was in here yesterday? Why hadn't she known that? 'What did he say?'

Pauline's eyebrows rose. 'He said you went way back— that you were old friends.'

She was obviously piquing Pauline's interest, and it made her wish she hadn't asked. Jessica felt the colour flare into her cheeks. What on earth was wrong with her? Callum was a good-looking guy and in a gossip hive like a hospital it was obvious people would comment.

Pauline was still talking as she adjusted the controls on Lily's monitors. 'Even David knows him. Says he's played five-a-side football against him. Apparently he's single.' She gave a little laugh. 'He also says the firefighter football team are a bunch of break-your-leg animals. He says he always volunteers to be goalie when they play against them.'

David. The solitary male staff nurse in ITU who was usually the butt of everyone's jokes. Just as well he was fit for it. He always gave as good as he got. And it was good to have a male in a predominantly female environment. Some babies responded better to a male voice—even seemed to be soothed by it.

And he always told any little boy who woke up scared and ventilated in ITU that the same thing had happened to him as a kid.

Some people were just destined to work with children.

Then again, David had just given her a vital piece of information. Callum was single. It seemed ridiculous. He was a gorgeous man, with a good job, and was fun to be around. Women would be beating a path to his door. Why on earth was he single? And, more importantly, why would she care?

'Jess? What's wrong?'

'Nothing. Nothing's wrong.' She could hardly look Pauline in the eye. Pauline was too perceptive by half. Her cheeks were practically bursting. She felt like some crazy teenager again.

'Jess, honey, no one would ever dare say these words to you. But I will because I care about you. Things are looking easier for you, Jess. Your mood has lifted, you don't have quite as many dark circles under your eyes. And once you start eating again…'

'What do you mean, Pauline?'

Pauline bit her lip. 'I mean that if you and Callum have history, *good history*, that might be a good thing.' She hesitated then continued, 'It might be something to embrace instead of run away from.'

'You think I run away from things?'

Pauline reached over and touched her arm. 'I think that you're ready. I think it might be time to start living your life again. I think it might be time to lift your head above the parapet and see what's out there. Whether that's Callum or someone else.' She gave Jess's arm a little squeeze. 'The next step will be hard, Jess. It might be easier if you took it with someone you used to know.'

She looked at Pauline's hand on her arm. The same place that Callum had touched her. The touch that had made every tiny hair on her arm stand on end and little unfamiliar sparks shoot up her arm. It had felt odd.

She wasn't sure how she felt about any of this. She'd spent a long time with one man and the thought of another—even one who was familiar—was alien to her. There was still that burning edge of disloyalty. Right now she couldn't even consider that Callum could be anything but a friend. No matter how her body reacted to him. It didn't help that her confidence was at an all-time low.

She caught a glimpse of her reflection in one of the windows in ITU. She hardly recognised herself these days. Even she was aware of how thin she was.

She'd once been proud of her figure. She'd liked the glow about her skin. But all that had been lost in the last three years. She barely even looked in a mirror any more. She got her hair cut when it took too long to dry in the mornings. She only put make-up on to stop people commenting on how pale she looked. What man could ever find her attractive now?

'It's only work, Pauline, nothing else.' The sadness in her voice surprised even her. Why were thoughts like this even entering her mind?

'But maybe it could be something else?' Pauline had raised her eyebrows and there was a hopeful tone in her voice.

Everything about this made her uncomfortable.

'If it hadn't been for the accident, our paths would never

have crossed again. It's just some crazy coincidence. Callum isn't interested in me.'

'Isn't he? Well, he apparently asked after you while he was in.'

'He did?' She hated the way her heart had given a little jolt at those words.

Pauline finished checking the controls on the ECMO machine and recorded them in the log. 'Yes. He did.' She stared at Jess. 'All I'm saying is there's a world of possibilities out there. Just leave yourself open to a few.' She hung the chart at the end of the bed and moved across to the next patient.

Jessica gazed at her reflection in the glass. A world of possibilities.

How on earth would she cope with those?

CHAPTER SIX

CALLUM WAS BORED. Bored rigid.

He usually liked coming to study days. There was always something new to learn in his job and some networking to be done. But this guy had been droning on for what seemed like hours. It felt like he was saying the same sentence over and over again. It didn't matter that the clock had only moved on ninety minutes, it felt like groundhog day.

The door at the back of the auditorium opened and he heard a little murmur around him, accompanied by the sound of over a hundred firefighters straightening up all at once. He turned sideways, trying to see what had caused that effect. Had the chief officer just come into the room?

No. It wasn't the chief officer. It was a woman with caramel-coloured hair and a sway to her step. His mouth fell open. Jess?

All of a sudden he was paying attention to what the man at the front of the room was saying. 'Ladies and gentlemen, I'd like you to welcome Dr Jessica Rae. She's a paediatrician at Parkhill, the children's hospital in Glasgow.'

Callum tore his eyes away from Jessica for a moment—something none of the other men in the room were doing—to look at his programme. It had someone else's name on it for the next lecture.

'Dr Rae is filling in for Dr Shepherd, who had an unexpected family emergency today. We're very grateful that she could find the time to step in for us. Dr Rae will be talking to us about paediatric smoke inhalation and immediate treatment.'

Callum watched as Jessica walked to the front of the room. Her hair was shining and resting in curls on her shoulders. And she was dressed cleverly in layers to hide how thin she was, and in bright colours to complement her skin tone.

'Hey, Callum, isn't that the lady doc from the minibus accident?' the firefighter sitting next to him whispered.

'Yes, it is.' He still hadn't taken his eyes from her. She was wearing a bright blue dress that was draped and gathered at the front. She looked good. She had more colour about her face today and was wearing bright lipstick.

'Wow. She looks gorgeous.' He turned and squinted at Callum, in the way only a friend could. 'Didn't you say you knew her from years gone by?'

Callum shifted uncomfortably in his seat. He knew exactly what was going on in Frank's head. 'Yeah. She's an old friend.'

Frank let out the lowest of whistles. 'Wish my old friends looked like that.'

The hackles at the back of Callum's neck immediately rose. Frank was only voicing what every appreciative man in the room was thinking. But that didn't mean that he liked it. He wanted to put a cocoon around Jess and protect her. Hide her away from the leering glances.

He hadn't seen her in more than a week and, boy, was she a sight for sore eyes. The fact that thought had sprung into his mind alarmed him. Why, all of a sudden, was he annoyed by the fact that other men found her attractive? What right did he have to feel like that?

More than once this week his hand had hovered over the phone, thinking of a reason to phone Jess again. Looking for any excuse just to speak to her.

But then his rational side had kicked in and brought him back into reality.

Too bad reality was looking kind of blurry right now.

Jess stood up at the podium and looked around the room. When her eyes rested on Callum he saw her give a little start, before she gave him a nervous smile.

'Hi, folks. I recognise some of the faces in here today because unfortunately, in our lines of business, our paths frequently cross.' She pressed a button and the presentation appeared on the wall behind her. 'I'm going to give you some up-to-date information on the best things you can do for a child with smoke inhalation.' She lifted her hand and gestured around the auditorium. 'I'm sure it's something you've all had to deal with.'

Jessica was confident at work. She was in control. That much was clearly evident. She could probably have done this presentation with her eyes shut. And it was nice to see her that way.

Her voice was steady and clear. 'We don't expect any of you to do anything more than the most basic first aid. I'm sure you're all aware that the paramedics and ambulances aren't always on scene immediately, so my job today is to give you enough information to feel confident in your first responses.'

She lifted her hand, pressed a button on the remote and the screen behind her changed. Then she turned back and gave the room a dazzling smile. 'Now, let's begin.'

* * *

It was officially the quickest thirty minutes of her life. She hadn't hesitated that morning when a colleague had asked her to cover for him. As a paediatric consultant at a teaching hospital she was often asked to give lectures to medical students and people in other disciplines. This was a walk in the park for her.

If only there wasn't a great big distraction right in the middle of the room.

Callum was definitely the proverbial elephant in the room today.

She spent the whole thirty minutes trying to avoid looking at him. She was sure that if she caught a glimpse of his green eyes she wouldn't be able to concentrate at all.

It was strange. She should have felt happy that there was a friend in the room, but instead she felt almost like a student undergoing an examination. It was just as well the firefighters went easy on her and there were only a few questions at the end. That was the beauty of talking just before the coffee break—no one wanted to hang around for long.

As soon as she'd finished the room emptied quickly. Her heart started to thud. Would Callum leave without speaking to her? Maybe he had to network with some of his colleagues and wouldn't have time.

'Hey, Jess. That was a nice surprise.' She started at his voice and turned around quickly as someone jostled him from behind and pushed them even closer together. It looked as if it was a stampede towards the strong smell of coffee.

Her hand went up automatically and rested on his chest. She could feel the heat of his body through his thin black shirt. 'Hey, you too. I didn't expect to be here. Just filling in for a friend.'

'What happened?'

'Mark Shepherd's wife has cancer. She had a bad reaction to her chemo, so he wanted to stay home with her.'

'I'm sorry to hear that. How are the kids from the accident doing?'

She raised her eyebrows. 'You mean you haven't already phoned today?'

He squirmed. 'Okay, I admit it. I'm a bit of a stalker.'

She laid her hand on his arm. 'But only in a good way. We've got four still in, but they're all improving. With kids we just take things one day at a time.'

Callum nodded slowly. He held his elbow out towards her. 'Have you time for some refreshments before you leave?'

'Hmm, firefighter coffee. Is it as bad as I think it will be?'

'Scandalous! We're very serious about our coffee, and we're even more serious about our cakes. I can guarantee you a fruit scone.'

'Something does smell pretty good around here.' She put her hand through his crooked elbow. 'Why do I get the impression that you're trying to fatten me up, Callum?'

He rolled his eyes and pressed his other hand to his chest. 'Tragedy, you've caught me out.' His face broke into a wide grin. 'Let's call it *looking out for a friend*.'

Her heart gave a little flutter. 'Friends? Is that what we are again, Callum?'

'I certainly hope so.' There was something so nice about the way he'd said those words. Not a moment's hesitation. He didn't even need to think about it for a second.

Friends. She liked that word. It felt safe.

They walked across the corridor to the coffee room. The queue had died down a little and she had a little time to peruse the cakes in the glass cabinet. The firefighters certainly did take their coffee seriously. This was an outlet of a popular coffee house, with all their famous tempting products on display.

He placed his arm on the counter and slid a tray in front of her. 'What can I tempt you with?'

Now, there was a question.

The thoughts that flooded her mind almost made her blush.

'I'll have a light caramel latte with two shots and a piece of the banana and nut loaf, please.' The words were automatic. She was used to ordering in one of these coffee shops—she didn't need to think twice.

He seemed pleased. Pleased that she didn't spend forever fretting over what to eat and drink. Patience had never been Callum's strong point.

They waited a few minutes while the barista made their coffee. 'How did you manage to wangle a franchise in here?' she said. 'I didn't think it would be allowed.'

He pointed to a sign near the door. 'Neither did we, but the coffee was getting worse and worse and tempers were fraying. They asked what we wanted and we told them. The profits from this franchise don't go back into the overall company. We have a ballot every year to decide which charity to support.'

He gave a little shrug. 'It works in our favour and in theirs. We get to support the charity of our choice, and they get to put us on their website talking about their contributions to charity. It's good publicity for them.' She smiled at the poster supporting research into Alzheimer's disease. 'Why did you pick that one?'

He picked up the tray and carried it over to a vacant table. 'We get lots of accidental house fires started by older people with memory problems—putting things in the oven or on the hob and forgetting about them. Some have early signs of Alzheimer's. We often go out and do community safety visits and fit fire alarms for anyone referred to us. It seemed a natural pick.' His voice lowered and she could sense the sadness in it. 'It caused us three fatalities last year.'

They sat down and Jess sipped her coffee. It was just as good as it was in every shop in the country. 'I think it's a great idea. I wonder if the hospital would consider it? The hospital kitchens are great, but the staff canteen is run by an outside firm. It's nowhere near as good as this.'

'I can give you some details if you want.'

'That would be perfect.' She leaned back in her chair. 'You could quickly make me the most popular woman in the hospital.'

'I'm sure you're that already.' His voice was low and he was looking up at her from over the top of his steaming cup of coffee.

She couldn't help the little upturn at the corners of her lips. When had the last time been that she'd had a man flatter her? It had been so long ago she couldn't remember.

Sure, there had been the odd unwanted leering comment, the kind that made your stomach turn—and not in a good way.

But this was different. It hadn't been invited. Or expected.

It was just—well, a nice comment. The kind that sent a little rosy glow all through you. Something she hadn't felt in a very long time.

It was kind of weird how she felt about all this. That first glimpse of Callum on the riverbank had been a total shock. And the way her body had reacted—her *natural* instinct—had been even more of a shock.

Because her natural instinctive response to Callum had been very physical. It hadn't helped that they'd been thrust together—in more ways than one—and parts of her body that had seemed dead had suddenly sparked into life.

It was taking time to get her head around all this.

And, to be frank, she was struggling.

In a way she wished she could be that naïve seventeen-year-old again, thinking that her heart was breaking as she left her first love behind.

If only she'd known then what she knew now.

That wasn't the thing that broke your heart. Not even close.

But all her memories of Callum were good. They were safe. Even if they came with a heavy dose of passion and teenage angst.

She didn't feel afraid around Callum. And she liked the way he was looking at her. It made her feel as if she was finally worth looking at again.

Pauline's words echoed around her head. *A world of possibilities.*

'Callum, I need to speak to you about something.'

The words jerked Jess out of her daydream. A well-stacked blonde was directly in her line of vision, her boobs inches from Callum's nose. Were those real?

'We need to talk about the meeting tomorrow at city headquarters. I need to give you a report to review before you go.'

Strange things were happening to Jess. The hackles had just gone up at the back of her neck and she felt an intense dislike for this extremely pretty and apparently efficient blonde. What on earth was wrong with her? She was never like this.

'Hi, Lynn. I'm actually in the middle of something right now.'

'What?' She glanced over at Jessica—whom she'd completely ignored—with renewed interest. 'Well, I'll let you finish up. But I'll need to see you in five.'

She turned to sweep away. Jess felt a smile sneak across her face as she realised Callum hadn't stared once at the boobs on display.

'Actually, I'll be a bit longer than that.' He gave a wave of his hand. 'I'll come and find you later.'

Lynn shot him a look of surprise, but Callum wasn't even looking at her any more. His attention was completely on Jessica.

Jess's heart gave a little flutter. She'd just recognised the sensation she'd felt a few seconds ago on Lynn's approach. Jealousy.

It was almost as if she'd landed in the middle of the icy-cold Clyde again, with the freezing water sweeping over her skin.

There was something very strange about all this. Being around Callum was making her feel again, something she thought would never happen. She'd been switched off for so long that she wasn't recognising everything straight away.

This was dangerous territory. She would have to take baby steps.

But all of a sudden it didn't seem quite so scary.

She gave Callum a little smile. 'So, tell me more about uni.'

She had to start somewhere and it was as good a place as any.

* * *

'Daddy, I don't feel good.'

Callum was sleeping but the little voice jerked him straight out of the weird dream that was circulating around his brain. Jessica dressed in a clown suit. Where did these things come from?

Yesterday had been fun. They'd spent most of the time together reminiscing. Talking about their past seemed to relax Jess. And he liked her like that.

He also liked the fact he was spending time with someone he trusted. Someone he didn't need to feel wary around. Somebody who wouldn't let him down.

But right now his paternal radar was instantly on alert. Drew was standing in the doorway, his eyes heavy with sleep and his hand rubbing his stomach. This was the second day he hadn't felt great. The second night Callum had put his dinner untouched into the bin.

Over the last two weeks Drew's symptoms seemed to flare up and then die down again.

He lifted up the corner of his duvet. 'Come over here so I can see you.'

Drew scuttled across the room and straight under the cover next to his dad. Callum pressed his hand to his head. He didn't feel warm—no obvious temperature. 'What's wrong, big guy? Do you feel sick?'

According to Drew's primary teacher half the class were off with a sickness bug. Maybe some of them had even ended up in Jessica's hospital. Rumours were circulating that it was norovirus.

Just what he needed. He still had the accident report to complete and there had been another incident at work today that would need to be followed up.

'Not sick, Daddy. Just a rumbly tummy.'

'Are you hungry? Is your tummy rumbling because you didn't eat any dinner?' He glanced at the clock. Two a.m. 'Do you want Dad to make you some toast?' It wasn't an ideal situation but if it settled Drew and got him back to sleep quickly, he could live with it.

Drew lay back against the pillows. 'No. Not hungry.' He moved a little closer. 'Just rub my tummy, Daddy, that will make it better.'

'You're sure? Do want a little drink of water?'

Drew shook his head and closed his heavy eyes.

Callum's hand automatically moved into position, very gently rubbing Drew's tummy in little circles. What could be wrong?

He hated to overreact. He hated to be an over-anxious father. But the truth was he had very few people he could bounce things like this off.

His friends Julie and Blair were the obvious choice but he wasn't going to call them at this time of night.

He glanced at the clock again. Maybe he would take Drew back to the GP in the morning. The trouble was, he hated going to the GP with a list of vague symptoms. A list of *not much but maybe it could be.*

It made him feel paranoid. It made him feel as if he wasn't coping. And that was the last thing he wanted anyone to think.

Did single mothers feel like this too?

Drew was the most precious thing in the world to him. He couldn't live with himself if he brushed something off and it turned out to be serious.

Maybe he should have asked Jessica yesterday. She was a paediatrician, she knew everything there was to know about kids.

But he hadn't thought about it and that made him feel

a little guilty. He hadn't even told her about Drew yet. Should he have? Theirs was a professional relationship. Nothing more, nothing less. But a tiny little part of his brain was nagging away at him, thinking that maybe it could be something else.

He still hadn't got to the bottom of her words. *Things just didn't work out for me.*

She'd been really careful today to keep steering the conversation back to him—or work, whenever he'd asked anything vaguely personal. She'd mentioned her mum and dad, a few old friends they'd known years ago. But nothing about herself.

Maybe he should wait until he found out what that meant before he gave it another thought.

He cuddled up with his little boy. Drew was his top priority right now.

The first person he looked at in the morning and the last person he looked at at night.

And that's the way it would stay.

CHAPTER SEVEN

THE WARD WAS quiet and he'd no idea where Jessica was. The nurse had just pointed down in this general direction.

He walked past a few windows, seeing children lying in beds with anxious parents next to them.

His heart clenched slightly. He would hate to be in that position. Thank goodness Drew usually kept in good health. He still hadn't got to the bottom of that stomach ache. The GP had basically fobbed him off and Callum didn't blame him because when they'd finally got an appointment, Drew had been full of beans and jumping around the place.

It was always the same with kids.

The ward sister he'd met a few times was standing next to one of the doors. 'Hi, Pauline.'

She gave him a knowing smile. 'Hi, there, Callum. And who might you be looking for?'

He sighed. He'd known from the first time he'd met her that Pauline could read everyone instantly. Why even pretend it was anything else? He still hadn't seen Jess, so this might work in his favour.

He leaned against the doorjamb and folded his arms. 'Let's just say I'm looking for our favourite doc.' He lifted his eyebrows. 'All work-related, of course.'

Pauline nodded. 'Of course.' But the smile was spreading further across her face. She lowered her voice. 'I think our mutual friend will be very pleased to see you.'

He felt something flare inside him. That acknowledgement—no matter how brief—reassured him. Pauline and Jess were good friends. If Jess was talking to anyone it would be Pauline. It gave him a little hope. It also gave him the courage to ask the question that had been gnawing away at him.

He hesitated for a second. 'Pauline—about Jess.'

She raised her eyebrows, as if he was about to say something she didn't want to hear. She was protective of Jess and that was nice.

'Jess told me that things didn't work out for her. And I know she's reverted to her maiden name.' He unfolded his arms and held out his hand towards her. 'I wonder if you could tell me what happened. I get the feeling I'm treading on difficult ground.'

Pauline bit her lip and glanced over her shoulder. Her eyes met his. 'You're right, Callum, it is difficult ground but I think that it's something Jess really needs to tell you herself.' Her eyes looked down, as if she was hesitant to say any more. 'Life hasn't turned out the way she expected. Jess should be married with a family to love and I'm hoping that's what she'll get. Just give her a little time.'

She pointed to the next set of doors. 'She's down there. Go and say hello.'

Was this better or worse?

His curiosity had just scaled up about ten notches.

He wanted to give Jess time to tell him—he really did. There was just that little edge of wariness. That lingering feeling left by a previous experience.

Jess was nothing like Kirsten, Drew's mother. They

weren't even in the same ballpark. But it didn't stop his slightest sense of unease as he walked down the corridor.

He pushed the feelings to one side. He'd already made up his mind about what he wanted to do next. He wanted to see how Jess would react. And he wouldn't know unless he tried.

Finally he caught sight of Jess's caramel-coloured hair. She was sitting talking to a little girl with curly hair with her leg in a bright pink fibreglass cast. It was Rosie, from the minibus accident.

He stuck his head around the door. 'Knock, knock.'

Jess looked surprised to see him. 'Callum, what are you doing here?'

'I phoned and left you a message. Didn't you get it?'

She shook her head then turned to the woman sitting next to her. 'Carol, this is Callum Ferguson. He's one of the fire rescue crew who were at the accident. He helped get Rosie out of the bus.'

'It's him, Mummy! It's him!' Having a cast on hadn't seemed to limit Rosie's movements. She wiggled over to the edge of the bed. 'The one I told you about.'

Rosie's mum stood up and held out her hand. 'Callum, my daughter has been talking about you non-stop. She seems to think you're a superhero. She saw you abseil down the side of the riverbank.'

Callum felt a little rush of blood to his cheeks. This was the last thing he had been expecting. He shook his head and knelt down beside the bed. 'You're much braver than me, Rosie. You tumbled down the bank in the minibus. That must have been really scary. The way I got down wasn't scary at all.'

Rosie held out her hands and reached round Callum's neck, giving him a big hug.

Jessica was watching. Watching—and trying to keep the smile from her face at his appearance. Callum seemed totally at ease, not in the least fazed by the little girl's action. Thank goodness. She had him on some sort of pedestal.

But it was kind of nice. Almost as if he was used to being in contact with kids.

Callum leaned back and tapped the pink cast. 'How is your leg? I love the colour of your cast.'

Rosie smiled. 'Thank you. Dr Rae and I have the same favourite colour. That's why I picked pink.'

'Well, I think it looks great. Your leg will be all better soon.'

Jess stood up and gave Carol and Rosie a smile. 'I'll leave you two. You can give me a call if you need me.' She nodded her head towards the door. 'Callum?'

She could smell his aftershave. It wasn't familiar. It was different from the one he'd used the day they'd abseiled back up the slope. It was more spicy, with richer tones. She liked it.

They walked along the corridor. Callum waved his hand, in which he had a big brown envelope. 'I've typed up the statement from the other day. I need you to read over it and sign it.'

She felt a flutter of disappointment. Business. Purely business. That's why Callum was here. Not for any other reason. A strange lump was forming in her throat. Once she'd signed the statement she would have no reason to ever see Callum again.

Her heart had leapt when he'd appeared. She hated it when it did that. She kept telling herself over and over again that this was nothing. This meant nothing. Just some wild, crazy coincidence that their paths had crossed again. This was work-related.

He turned to face her and she tried hard not to stare at his chest, which was instantly in her view.

She raised her eyes to meet his bright green ones. It was one of the first things she'd ever noticed about Callum, his startling green eyes.

'I can read the statement now, it will only take a couple of minutes.' There was no point turning this into something it wasn't. She saw him glancing at his watch, it was nearly six o'clock in the evening. He would be finished for the day—just the way she should be. Was he worried about being late? Did he have a date? Maybe that blonde from the fire station?

She hated the way that thought made her stomach curl.

'Have you finished for the day?'

'What?'

He'd moved a little closer and was towering over her, an impatient edge to his voice.

'I mean have you finished? You can't be on call again. I want you to come somewhere with me.'

She pulled back a little. There was something a little weird about him. Was he nervous?

She looked around her. The ward had quietened down. All patients had been seen, all prescriptions and instructions written. 'Yes, yes, I'm finished.' She was feeling a bit bewildered. A few seconds ago she had been sure everything was business as usual. He needed a signature to get the job finished so he could be on his way. And that had made her sad.

Now what?

A smile broke across Callum's face. 'Then get your coat.' She was turning towards her office when she heard him mutter something under his breath. 'You've pulled.'

She let out a burst of laughter and spun back around. 'Did you just say what I think you did?'

It had been a joke between them. A daft teenage saying that both had used years before. But it came totally out of the blue and instantly took her back thirteen years.

Callum's shoulders were shaking. 'Sorry, I couldn't resist it.'

Jessica stuck her hand around the office door and pulled out her woollen coat. There was a flash of bright pink. 'Think you can cope?' she asked as she wound her purple scarf around her neck and fastened the buttons on the bright coat.

He just nodded. 'You did warn me about the bright pink coat, and knowing you I wouldn't have expected anything less. Do you have gloves?'

She stuck her hands in the coat pocket and pulled out a pair of purple leather gloves. 'Sure. Why?'

'It's a nice night out there. Just a little dusting of snow. I'd like to walk instead of drive. Are you okay with that?'

She pulled out a woolly hat and stuck it on her head. 'I'm game if you are. But you've got me curious now. Where are we going?'

He gestured towards the door. 'Let's find out.'

They walked quickly through the lightly falling snow. It was pitch dark already—darkness fell quickly in winter in Scotland. The streetlights cast a bright orange glow across the wet pavements.

'So where are you taking me?'

Callum drew in a breath. He was still getting over the fact he'd asked her. It had been totally instinctive. He'd only made the decision once he'd set foot on the ward—particularly after what Pauline had said to him. The words had come out before he'd even had a chance to think about them. A signature would have meant he'd have no excuse to see Jesssica again. And he wasn't quite ready for that.

Drew was at mini-kicker football tonight. He went every week with Julie and Blair's son. One week Callum gave them dinner and took them, the next week Julie and Blair took them. Drew wouldn't be home until after eight o'clock.

'That would be a surprise.'

'Hmm…a surprise. How do you know I still like surprises?'

He gave her a little smile. 'It's an educated guess. Some things are just part of us—like our DNA. I'm working on the premise that the fundamentals haven't changed.'

They turned a corner and started walking along one of the main roads. It was busier now, the crowds jostling along all seeming to be headed in one direction.

The strains of Christmas music could be heard above the buzz of the crowds around them. Jess stopped a few times to look at the Christmas displays in some of the shop windows. Finally, he placed his hand in the small of her back as he guided her around the corner and into George Square.

'Oh.' He heard the little bit of shock in her voice as the recognition of where they were sank in. The square was bustling, packed with people here to see the annual switching on of the Christmas lights. A huge tree stood in the middle of the square, already decorated and just waiting for the lights to be lit. The Lord Provost already stood on the stage, talking into a microphone and trying to entertain the crowds.

'You brought me here? I can't believe you remembered.' Her voice had gone quiet, almost whispered.

This had been one of their first dates, coming to see the annual switching on of the Christmas lights in George Square. He hadn't planned this. He hadn't even thought about it. But as he'd driven to the hospital tonight he'd heard the announcement on the radio about the switch-on. It had almost seemed like a sign—a message. He'd had to ask her to come along. If only to try and take a little of the sadness out of her eyes.

'There's so many families,' she said as she looked around, dodging out of the way of a little girl with long blonde hair running straight for them.

'Yeah, there always are.' Lots of people brought their families to the turning on of the lights. It was entirely normal. But he couldn't help catch the little edge of something else in her voice.

'Over here.' Callum put his hand on her back again and guided her over to one of the street-vendor stalls. The smells of cloves, mulled wine and roasted chestnuts were all around them. Callum bought two cups and handed one over to her.

'Want to take a guess at what colour the tree lights will be this year?'

Jessica leaned against one of the barriers, sipping her mulled wine and watching the people around them. It was obvious that her brain was trying to take in their surroundings. 'They were purple the first year that we came here.'

'And they were silver the year after.' He kept his voice steady.

'And red the year after that.'

It was clear that they both remembered and for some reason it was really important to him that it was imprinted on Jess's brain just as much as it was on his. Half of him had been sure she would know why he'd brought her here, while the other half had been in a mad panic in case she'd turned around with a blank expression on her face.

'They were blue last year,' he murmured, not really thinking.

Jess spun round, the mulled wine sloshing wildly in her cup. 'You were here last year?'

Yes. He'd been here with Drew. But it had turned out Drew didn't really like the turning on of the lights. It was almost as if there was a little flare of panic in Jess's eyes. Did she think he'd been here with another woman?

Maybe this was it. Maybe this was time to tell her about Drew. It seemed natural. It was a reasonable explanation for what he'd just said. But the look in her eyes, that and the wistful tone in her voice when she'd remarked on the families, made him think twice.

'I was here with some friends.'

'Oh.' She seemed satisfied with that answer and rested her forearms back on the barrier.

The crowd thickened around them, pushing them a little closer together as people jostled to get a better place at the barrier. Callum wound his arm around her waist, holding her firmly against him, to stop anyone coming between them. The countdown around them started. Ten, nine...

It was the smallest of movements. Jess rested her head on his shoulder then a few seconds later he felt her relax a little more and felt some of the weight of her body lean against him.

A grin spread across his face. It wasn't like anyone could see it but it had been automatic and was plastered there for the world to see. Three, two, one.

'Woah!' The noise went around the crowd as the lights flickered on the tree, lighting up the square in a deluge of pink and silver.

'Pink! It's pink!' Jess yelped, as the wine sloshed out of the cup and she turned to face him. Her eyes were sparkling, her excitement evident. It was the first time since he'd seen her again that she looked totally carefree. Totally back to normal.

Her face was right in front of his, her brown eyes darker than ever before and their noses almost touching. He could see the steam from her breath in the cold night air. He placed his cup on the barrier and brought his hand to her hip, matching the hold of his other hand, and pulled her a little closer. He gave her a smile.

'My plan worked. I told them that pink was your favourite colour and that you'd be here.'

She let out a laugh and placed her hands on his shoulders. She didn't seem annoyed by him holding her. She didn't seem annoyed at all. In fact, if he wasn't mistaken, she was edging even closer.

Her dark eyes were still sparkling, reflecting the twinkling lights around them, 'Oh, you did, did you? I bet that took a bit of planning, especially as you didn't even know if I'd agree to come on a walk with you.'

He pulled her even closer. 'Oh, I knew. I was absolutely sure you'd come with me.'

He could turn back the clock. He could flick a little switch right now and this could be thirteen years ago. Standing almost in this exact spot.

She tilted her head to the side. 'Well, that was a bit presumptuous, wasn't it?'

He shook his head. 'I don't think so. But this might be.'

He bent forward. People around them were still cheering about the Christmas lights, breaking into song as the music got louder in the amplifiers next to them.

But Callum wasn't noticing any of that. The only thing he was focused on was Jess's lips.

And everything was just like he remembered. Almost as perfect.

The last time round Jess had tasted of strawberry lip gloss, and this time she tasted of mulled wine. He could sense the tiniest bit of hesitation as he kissed her, so he took it slowly, gently kissing her lips, teasing at the edges until she moved her hands from his shoulders and wrapped them around his neck, kissing him right back.

And then everything *was* perfect.

CHAPTER EIGHT

CALLUM LISTENED TO the NHS helpline music with growing impatience. It was funny how all rational thought flew out of the window when your child was in pain.

Drew was clutching his stomach again. He was pale and feverish, and he couldn't even tolerate fluids. But the pain was making him gasp and sob and Callum was feeling utterly helpless.

He glanced at his watch. It would be nearly midnight by the time the NHS helpline put him through to one of the nurses—and he told Drew's story *again*—then they would have to drive out to one of the GP centres. Who knew when his son would get some pain relief?

No. He couldn't wait that long.

As a member of one of the emergency services, he hated it when people used the services irresponsibly. But this didn't feel irresponsible. This did feel like an emergency. And he could explain later why he hadn't been prepared to wait for the helpline.

Jessica was on call tonight. Should he take Drew to Parkhill?

He hadn't even told her about Drew yet, and this would be a baptism of fire. But as Drew's father he couldn't think of anyone he would trust more with his son. He'd seen Jessica at work. He'd heard her colleagues talk about her.

She was undoubtedly a great doctor, who cared about her patients.

He was supposed to be taking Jessica out for dinner in a few nights' time. He'd been hoping to tell her about Drew then, and also to explain why evening dates could prove to be difficult. After a day of work he really didn't like to ask someone to babysit his son. He wanted to spend time with him. And he was hopeful that Jess would understand that. But now that would all have to wait.

Within minutes he had Drew bundled up into his booster seat, still in his pyjamas and wrapped in a fleecy blanket.

The roads were coated with snow and deadly quiet. Anyone with a half a brain was tucked up in bed. The only other traffic on the roads at this time of night was the gritters. He made it to the hospital in record time, parked in one of the emergency bays and carried Drew inside in his arms.

'I need to see Jessica Rae right away.'

The receptionist looked up, her face unfamiliar. 'Can you give me your details, please, sir?'

'Jessica Rae—I know she's on duty tonight. I want her to check over my son.'

The receptionist plastered a weary smile on her face. 'Give me your son's details. I'll get one of the doctors to see him.'

Callum felt his patience at an all-time low. 'Page Jessica Rae for me—*now*!'

One of the triage nurses appeared at his side and gave a knowing smile to the receptionist. They were probably used to frantic parents, but it didn't excuse his behaviour. 'Come with me, sir, and I'll start the assessment procedure for your son.' She reached over and brushed Drew's fringe out of his eyes, taking in his pale colour and the sheen on his skin. 'Let's get some obs.'

Callum felt himself take some deep breaths as he followed the nurse down the corridor. She was ruthlessly efficient, taking Drew's temperature, heart rate and blood pressure, then putting some cream on the inside of one elbow to numb the area and prepare it for a blood sample to be taken. As she scribbled down Drew's history, then held a sick bowl to let him retch into it, she gave Callum a tight smile.

'I know you asked for Dr Rae, but she's in surgery right now. She will see your son, but he needs some other tests done and some blood taken in the meantime. I'm going to ask one of the other doctors on duty to see Drew right now.'

There was something in the way she said the words. The quiet urgency in them. As if she suspected something but wasn't prepared to say it out loud. She had that look about her—the nurse who'd seen everything a dozen times and could probably out-diagnose most of the junior doctors.

'What do you think's wrong?'

She gave the slightest shake of her head. 'Let's leave that to the doctors, shall we?'

He tried his best not to erupt. To tell her that he didn't want his son to wait a second longer.

She glanced at him as she headed to the curtains. 'I'll get the other doctor now. The sooner Drew is seen, the better. Then we can get him some pain relief.'

He nodded automatically. Pain relief for his son. That's what he wanted more than anything. Anything to take the pain away from Drew.

'Dr Rae, there's a kid with an acute abdomen in A and E. Father is insisting you see him.'

Jessica pulled off her gown and gloves and dumped them in the disposal unit. 'Really? What's the name?'

'Kennedy. Drew Kennedy.'

She shrugged. She was the consultant on call. She'd see any kid with an acute abdomen anyway. 'I don't recognise the name, but tell them I'll be right there.'

She gave her hands a quick wash, trying to place the name. None of her friends had a son called Drew. And the surname? Well, there was only one Kennedy that she knew.

Her stomach gave a little sinking feeling as she rounded the corner into A and E. It couldn't be, could it?

No. Not a chance.

It couldn't be a nephew as Callum didn't have any brothers or sisters.

And Callum would have mentioned something as important as having a son. Wouldn't he?

But as she walked over to the curtains she recognised the frame hunched over the little figure straight away.

She froze.

She wanted to turn on her heel and run away. She wanted to disappear out of the hospital and take a minute to catch her breath. To try and get her head around the thousand thoughts currently spinning around in her brain.

But that was the second that Callum looked up. And his relief at seeing her was plastered all over his face.

She'd seen that look a hundred times. The parent worried out of their mind about their child. Hoping against hope that their worst fears weren't about to be realised.

Professional mode. No matter how she felt, or what her questions were, she had to move into professional mode right now. There was a sick little boy to be dealt with.

She kept her voice steady and calm. 'Callum? I didn't

expect to see you.' She picked up the chart, her eyes skimming over the notes and observations. 'Is this your son?'

Calm. Rational. That's how she was hoping she sounded.

Callum had the good grace to look embarrassed. 'Yes. This is Drew.' There was a shake to his voice. He really was scared for his son—he must be. He'd deliberately brought him here and asked for her, even though he'd known she would have questions. 'He's five and he's had a sore stomach on and off for the last two weeks. We've been back and forth to the GP with no diagnosis. But tonight he's much worse.' He lowered his voice. 'Sorry. I was going to tell you about Drew at dinner on Saturday.'

Her brain was still stuck on the 'five' part. She tried not to wince as she glanced at the date of birth. Drew was almost the same age as her son Lewis would have been.

She tried not to let the tight squeeze around her heart affect her. Everything was so unfair. Callum had the little boy she should still have. A little boy he hadn't even mentioned.

She took a deep breath and looked over at the little boy on the bed. The junior doctor had done everything he should, but he hadn't made any provisional diagnosis. Which meant he was stumped.

'Hi, there, Drew. I'm Dr Jessica. Do you mind if I have a look at your tummy?'

'No. Daddy, don't let them touch my tummy again.' She could hear the distress in the little boy's voice. The fear of someone touching a part of him that was already very painful.

She looked at the chart, making sure he'd been given some analgesia. 'Hasn't the medicine helped your sore tummy? It should have made it feel a little better.'

The little boy shook his head. 'It's still sore.'

'Can you tell me where it hurts if I promise not to touch?'

He nodded. His face was pale. 'It started in the middle but now it's over here.' He pointed to his left side.

She pointed to the IV in his arm. 'I'm going to put a little more medicine in here. It will work really quickly and help your tummy.' She nodded towards the nurse. 'Can I have point two milligrams of morphine, please?'

She waited a few minutes until the nurse returned with the syringe and ampule for her to check before administration. She prescribed the dose and signed the ledger before giving Drew the analgesic. She placed her hand on his forehead and bent down to whisper in his ear, 'It will start to work really quickly, I promise.'

Some doctors didn't agree with giving analgesia to paediatric patients before a diagnosis was made. They thought it could mask abdominal symptoms and delay a diagnosis. But Jessica had read a whole host of studies with evidence that analgesics reduced pain without interfering with diagnostic accuracy. Besides, Jessica could never leave a child in pain.

Right now, Drew was showing most of the signs and symptoms of appendicitis, but the pain for appendicitis was associated with radiating to the right, not the left.

She bent down and whispered in Drew's ear. 'Okay, I know I'm a lady doctor but I need to have a little check of your testicles. Do you know what they are?'

He shook his head.

She lifted her eyebrows. 'Your balls.'

He gave a little giggle.

She nodded. 'All I'm going to do is have a little feel to make sure they are where they're supposed to be. It will only take a few seconds, and it won't hurt, okay?'

He nodded and she checked quickly. It was important with boys to rule out a twisting of the testes, but everything seemed fine.

She did another few tests, one—the McBurney's—the classic indicator of appendicitis. But nothing was conclusive.

Drew's guarding was evident. Something was definitely going on.

The nurse appeared at her side. 'Drew's blood tests are back. They're on the system.'

Jessica gave a nod. No wonder the junior doctor had been puzzled. *She* was puzzled. 'Let's get an IV up on Drew and I'm going to order an abdominal ultrasound to see if we can get a better idea of what's going on.'

She walked over to the nearest computer and pulled up Drew's blood results. His white-cell count was up, just as expected in appendicitis. She gave a little nod of approval as she saw the junior doctor had grouped and cross-matched his blood too, in case surgery was needed at a later time.

She looked over at Drew again. He was curled up in a ball, guarding his stomach like a little old man. And the strangest feeling came over her.

She unhooked her pink stethoscope from her neck. 'Drew, I'm just going to have a listen to your chest. It will only take a few seconds.'

She placed her stethoscope on his chest, waited a few seconds then took a deep breath and repositioned it.

She looked sideways at Callum. 'Has Drew ever had a chest X-ray?'

He shook his head. 'I don't think so. He's never had any problems with his chest. Why? What's wrong?'

Jess signalled to the A and E nurse. 'Can you arrange a portable chest film for me—right away?'

The nurse nodded and disappeared for a few minutes. There was always a portable X-ray machine in the emergency department.

Callum walked over to her. 'What is it?'

She placed her hand on his chest. 'Give me a minute. I need to check something.' She wrinkled her nose. 'Have you ever had a chest X-ray?'

He rolled his eyes. 'Jess, I'm a fireman. I spent years working with a regular fire crew. Every time I came out of a burning building I had a chest X-ray.'

She nodded, it made sense, 'Right. So you did. And no one ever mentioned anything?'

He shook his head. 'Are you going to tell me what's going on? I'm going crazy here.'

She reached over and touched his hand. It didn't matter how upset she was right now. She'd even pushed aside the conversation she wanted to have with him right now. 'Callum, do you trust me?' Drew was the only thing that currently mattered.

His eyes flitted from side to side. Panic. Total panic. He ran his hand through his hair. 'Yes, of course I do, Jess. Why do you think I brought Drew here and asked to see you? There's nobody I trust more.'

The horrible reality right now was that she understood. She understood that horrible feeling of parental panic. That *out-of-control* sensation. She did. More than he would ever know.

She wrapped her other hand over his. 'Then just give me five minutes. Let me have a look at a chest X-ray for Drew. I promise, I'll explain everything.'

She saw his shoulders sag a little, saw the worried trust in his eyes.

She was telling herself that she would do this for any parent. That she *had* done this for any parent. But her conflicting emotions were telling her something else entirely.

The X-ray only took a few minutes and she pushed the film up onto the light box. It took her less than five seconds to confirm her diagnosis.

'Can you stay with Drew?' she asked the nurse.

'What is it?' The stricken look had reappeared in Callum's eyes, but she shook her head, pulled the chest X-ray down from the box and gestured with her head for him to follow her.

She opened the door to a nearby office and pushed the film back up on the light box inside. She flicked the switch and turned to face Callum.

'Drew has a condition called situs inversus.'

'What? What is that?'

She took a deep breath. 'It literally means that all his organs are reversed, or mirrored from their normal positions. Everything about Drew's symptoms today screamed appendicitis. Except for the positioning of the pain. Most people have their appendix on the right side. One of the true indicators of appendicitis is pain in the right iliac fossa.' She pointed to the position on her own abdomen to show him what she meant. 'But Drew's pain is on the other side—because his appendix is on the other side.'

'What does this mean? Is it dangerous? And how can you tell from a chest X-ray?'

She placed her hand on his shoulder. 'Slow down, Callum. One thing at a time.'

She pointed to the chest X-ray. 'Drew's heart is on the right side of his chest instead of the left. I can see that clearly in the chest X-ray.' She pointed at the lungs. 'I can also see that his left lung is tri-lobed and his right lung bi-lobed. That's the reverse of most people. This all gets a little complicated. It means that Drew's condition is known as situs inversus with dextrocardia, or situs inversus totalis.'

She tried to explain things as simply as she could. 'This is a congenital condition, Callum, it's just never been picked up. It could be that either you or his mother has this condition. It seems less likely for you as it would have been picked up in a routine chest X-ray.' She gave her head a little shake. 'It could be that neither of you has it. It's a recessive gene and you could both be carriers. Around one in ten thousand people have this condition.'

'Is it dangerous?'

She bit her bottom lip. 'It can be. Particularly in cases like this, when things can be misdiagnosed. But Drew's been lucky. Some people with this condition have congenital heart defects, but as Drew's been relatively unaffected that seems unlikely. It's likely if he had a congenital heart defect he would have had other symptoms that meant the condition would have been picked up much sooner. We'll do some further tests on him later. Right now we need to take him for surgery. His appendix needs to come out. How about we take care of that now, and discuss the rest of this later?'

He was watching her with his deep green eyes. She could see that he'd been holding his breath the whole time she'd been talking. He let it out in a little hiss. 'Will you do the surgery?'

The ethics of this question were already running through her mind. She had treated the children of friends on a number of occasions. It wasn't something she particularly liked to do—but in an emergency situation like this, the child's health came first.

'I'm the physician on call tonight. So it's up to me to perform the surgery. Would you like to find someone else to do it? That's always an option if you feel uncomfortable.'

He was on his feet instantly. 'No. Absolutely not. I want you to do it. I trust you to do it.' He looked her straight in the eye. 'There's no one else I would trust more.'

Things were still bubbling away inside her. It wasn't the time or the place, but she still had to say something.

'This isn't exactly ideal, Callum. And I'm not entirely comfortable about it. The surgery isn't a problem. There will be a registrar and an anaesthetist in Theatre with me. I'll need to go over the risks with you and get you to sign a consent form.'

She hesitated and let out a sigh. 'I kissed you a few days ago, Callum, so that complicates things for me. Obviously I didn't know about Drew…' she held up her hand as he tried to interrupt '…because you chose not to tell me. So, because I haven't met your son before, and don't have a relationship with him, that makes things a little easier.'

Her hands went to her hair and she automatically started twisting it in her hands, getting ready to clip it up for Theatre. She kept her voice steady. 'I'll perform your son's surgery and look after him for the next few days. I'll take the time to explain his condition and give you all the information that you need. After that? I have no idea.'

'Jess, please just let me explain.'

'No, Callum. Don't. Don't make this any more complicated than it already is. I've got more than enough to deal with right now.' She pointed back through the open door towards the curtains, where Drew was still lying on the trolley with a nurse monitoring him. 'Make yourself useful, go and sit with your son.' She walked out of the room, muttering under her breath, 'You don't know how lucky you are.'

Callum watched her retreating back and took her advice.

The nurse gave him a smile as he appeared back at Drew's side. 'You were lucky,' she said. 'Our Dr Rae is a fabulous paediatrician. Not everyone would have picked up that diagnosis.'

He gave a little nod. That didn't even bear thinking about. If he'd taken Drew elsewhere and some other physician had missed this...

It made him feel physically sick to his stomach.

He stroked his hand across Drew's forehead. His son was a little more settled, the morphine obviously helping to a certain extent. Drew was the most precious thing in the world to him. He couldn't stand it if something happened to his son.

It was obvious he'd hurt Jessica's feelings by not telling her about Drew. And he wished he could take that back.

But it was too late now.

He'd explain to her later—once this was all over. He really didn't tell women about Drew. Drew was precious. He was a part of his life he kept protected, tucked away. And he had intended to tell Jessica about him. He'd just wanted to wait a little longer until he was sure they might have some kind of a chance at a relationship.

A relationship? Where had that come from?

He hadn't had a real 'relationship' since he'd broken up with Drew's mother. But Jessica was different. She was Jessica. His Jess. Someone he'd known a lifetime ago. And someone he hoped he could trust around his son.

Someone he could introduce to his son without wondering about other motives. Whether they might only really be interested in him, and not his son. Whether they might only be interested in dating a firefighter. Or some other crazy reason.

There wouldn't be any of that with Jess.

Jessica was a paediatrician. She must love kids. Why else do this job?

And she'd been interested in him when he'd been a pre-university student with no idea about his potential career prospects. So he didn't need to worry about that.

Drew opened his eyes and stared at him. 'Where did the nice lady go?' he murmured.

'She'll be back soon. She's going to make your tummy better.'

'Is she? Oh, good.' His eyelids flickered shut again.

He'd make it up to Jess.

He would. And he'd try to get to the bottom of the haunted look in her eyes.

He just had to get his son through this first.

Jess pressed her head against the cool white tiles in the theatre changing room. It was no use. She couldn't take the burning sensation out of her skin.

Thank goodness this place was empty. As soon as she'd slammed the door behind her the tears had started to fall.

It was so unfair. Callum had a son the same age as Lewis. Or the age Lewis would have been if he'd survived. A little boy he got to cuddle every day. To read stories to.

What kind of conversations did a five-year-old have with their parent when they were lying in bed at night, talking about their day?

A little boy he'd got to dress in his school uniform and photograph on his first day of school.

All the memories that Jess wished she had.

All the memories she'd been cheated out of.

Just when she'd thought she was getting better.

Just when she'd thought she could finally take a few steps forward.

Of course she had friends who had children the same age as Lewis would have been. She hadn't cut them out of her life. She couldn't do that.

She was a paediatrician, for goodness' sake. She couldn't spend her life avoiding children of a certain age. That would be ridiculous.

But sometimes it was difficult. And they were good enough friends to sense that. To know when to hold her close. To know when to give her a little space. It was a difficult path, a careful balance.

But this was different.

This was Callum.

An old friend, who was evoking a whole host of memories.

First Callum had appeared in her life. Then he had kissed her.

He'd raised her hopes, given her a glimmer of expectation that there might be something else out there.

And now this.

She was hurt. She was upset.

Upset that Callum hadn't told her about his son.

But the horrible coiling feeling in her stomach was something else.

She was jealous.

Jealous that Callum had a son and she didn't.

It was horrible realisation.

She'd seen the interaction between them. The stress in Callum's face when he was worried sick about his son. The slight tremor in his hand after she'd explained the surgery and the possible complications and he'd signed the consent form. The trust in his little boy's eyes, for him, and, more worryingly, for her.

She gave herself a shake. Children looked at her like that all the time.

The doctor who could make them better. The doctor who could take their pain away.

So why was it different that this was Callum's son?

An appendectomy was routine to her. Even though Drew's appendix was on the opposite side of his body. It shouldn't complicate the procedure for her. It was just a little unusual.

Maybe it was something else?

Callum was trusting her. Trusting her with his son.

And although she was worthy of that trust, it terrified her.

Because she knew what it was like to lose a child.

Other people in this world had lost a child. Other parents in this hospital had lost—or would lose—a child. She'd had the horrible job of losing paediatric patients and dealing with the bereaved parents herself.

But this felt very different.

No one in her circle of friends had lost a child.

She wouldn't wish that on anyone. Ever.

No parent should outlive their child.

No parent should spend the rest of their life looking at the calendar and marking off all the milestones that their child had missed.

She started to open packs and change, putting on a fresh set of theatre scrubs and tucking her hair up into the pink theatre cap. She had to get her head away from those thoughts. She had to get her head back into surgeon mode.

She walked through to Theatre and nodded to the anaesthetist, who was poised ready to start scrubbing at the sink.

Her registrar appeared at her side. 'I was just looking at the chest X-ray of the little boy for the appendectomy. Fascinating, I've never seen a case of situs inversus before—have you?'

She shook her head. 'No, I haven't.'

Alex started scrubbing next to her.

He was staring ahead at the blank wall as he started automatically scrubbing his hands, nails and wrists. 'I'll probably never see one again in my career. This might be interesting to write up.' He turned sideways, 'Can't there be complications in these kids? Heart defects and other problems? Some kind of syndrome?'

He was starting to annoy her now. He was clinically excellent, but a little too removed from his patients for Jessica's liking. In her book caring was an essential component of being a paediatrician.

'Yes, there can be a syndrome—Kartagener syndrome. People with situs inversus may have an underlying condition called primary ciliary dyskinesia. If they have both they are said to have Kartagener syndrome.' She started scrubbing her nails with a little more ferocity. Just what she needed—a registrar who permanently thought the glass was half-empty.

She preferred the other approach—the glass half-full approach. Especially when it came to children.

'You know, Alex, I've got a really sick little boy out there. His dad only brought him to our A and E department because he's a friend of mine, and the GP has been fobbing off his son's symptoms for days.' She shook her hands to get rid of some of the water then started to dry them on a sterile towel.

'I'd like you to think about that before we start. I'd like you to stop thinking about this little boy as a case for a medical journal. Think about him as a little boy who loves playing football, watching cartoons and eating chocolate cereal for breakfast. Think about him as the light of someone's life. Because the patient comes before the disease in every set of circumstances.'

She pointed to the door.

'Out there we have a father who is worried sick about his little boy. And even though I've been clear with him and given him the rundown of the surgery and the complications, he's sitting out there right now, wondering if his little kid will have peritonitis, develop septicaemia or be the one in a million who will have a reaction to anaesthetic.'

The theatre nurse came over and held out her gown for her. She thrust her arms into the sleeves and snapped her gloves in place. 'So let's make sure that I don't have to go out there and give him any bad news.'

She glared at him and stalked over to the theatre table.

You could have heard a pin drop.

She knew she'd been harsh.

She never acted like that at work.

And the staff in here all knew her personal set of circumstances. They understood exactly where she was coming from.

Harry Shaw, the elderly anaesthetist—who stood in as Father Christmas every year with his grey hair and beard—gave her a smile.

His voice was low. 'You can do this, Jess.' He gave a little nod of his head. 'It'll be a walk in the park.'

She watched as the trolley was wheeled in. She could only pray it would be.

CHAPTER NINE

'Wow—just wow.'

'What are you talking about, Pauline?'

The sister from ITU gave her a smile and pointed behind her at the delivery guy, who could barely be seen beneath the beautiful spray of pink, purple and orange gerberas. Jess was on her feet in an instant, reaching up and touching one of the petals. 'Aren't they gorgeous?'

Pauline was quicker, pulling the card from the top of the bouquet. She spun it around. 'Hmm… "For Dr Jessica Rae."' She held the card next to her chest as Jess reached over to snatch it. 'I wonder who these could be from?' She took a few steps away. 'I'm guessing Mr Tall, Dark and Very, Very Handsome. Otherwise known as Callum Kennedy.'

Jess felt her cheeks flush. 'Stop it!' She grabbed the card, putting it into her pocket without reading it.

Pauline tutted. 'I'm disappointed. He's a member of the emergency services, he should know better.'

'Know better about what?'

Pauline waved her hand. 'That we don't allow flowers in ITU.'

Jessica accepted the huge bunch of flowers and gave Pauline a smile. 'But these flowers aren't for ITU, these flowers are for me.' She pushed open the door to her of-

fice and placed them on her desk. 'Wow. Where on earth
did he get these at this time of year?'

Pauline stood in the doorway and folded her arms over
her chest. 'Must have paid a pretty penny for them.' She
turned on her heel and walked away. 'It must be love.'

Jessica's stomach plunged. 'No, Pauline.' She pointed
at the flowers. 'These are just a thank-you for looking
after Drew.'

'Honey, a thank-you is a bunch of flowers from a supermarket. An enormous bouquet, delivered by a courier,
that's a whole lot more.'

Jess sank down into the nearest chair. 'Oh.'

'Oh? That's all you can say? Just "Oh"?' She sat next
to Jess.

'What did the card say?'

Jess bit her lip. Did she really want to get into this conversation? She dug into her pocket again and pulled the
card out. Pauline was right, this wasn't just a thank-you.
And she had a sneaking suspicion what it might be.

She read the message.

This was gigantic apology *and* a thank-you.

'What is it?' Pauline leaned forward and touched her
hand.

'It's an apology.'

'An apology? What's Callum got to apologise for?' Her
eyes narrowed, she was automatically moving into protective mode.

'It's…it's awkward.'

'What's awkward about it?'

Jess let out a sigh. 'He didn't tell me about Drew. The
first time I found out was when he brought him in with
appendicitis.'

Pauline's mouth fell open. 'How long have you known this guy?'

'Since I was a teenager. But I hadn't seen him in thirteen years. And I hadn't kept up with what was going on in his life.' Her voice dropped. 'Just like he hasn't kept up with what's happened in mine.'

'You haven't told him?' Pauline's voice was incredulous.

'It hasn't come up.'

'Just like his son didn't come up?'

Jess put her head in her hands and leaned on the desk. 'This is a mess.'

'Yes. It is.' Pauline never pulled her punches. It was one of the things that Jessica liked best about her.

She placed her hand at the side of her face. 'So, this guy—who you used to know thirteen years ago—and you only met again a few days ago, and brought his son to A and E, even though he hadn't told you about him?'

Jessica nodded.

'He brought his sick son to see *you*.' She emphasised the word strongly. 'Even though he knew that might make you mad. Even though he knew you might have a thousand questions. It was more important that he thought about the health of his child and—after seeing you in action— brought him to see a doctor he trusted with the health of his son. Doesn't that tell you what you need to know?'

Jessica flopped her head back into her hands. Someone else saying the words out loud made it all seem so much more straightforward. So much simpler.

She felt Pauline's hand on her back. 'Jess, what is it that you want?'

'What do you mean?'

'I mean, what are you ready for? I thought it was time for you—time to take some steps and move on. Callum seemed like a good idea. But maybe he's got as much baggage as you do.'

'And if he does?'

Pauline rolled her eyes. 'You need to think about this, Jessica. What do you want?' She pointed to the flowers. 'Are you ready to accept Callum's apology and whatever else that might mean?'

'I don't know. I mean I'm not sure. I was hurt that he didn't tell me about his son.'

'And what about Drew?'

'What do you mean?'

Pauline moved her hand to her shoulder. 'Look at me, Jess. I'm going to ask a hard question. How do you feel about having a relationship with someone who has a son?'

Jess's head landed back on the desk. 'I don't know. I mean, I *really* don't know. Drew's lovely. He's a great little boy. I've spent a little time with him on the surgical ward. He's made a good recovery and he's ready for discharge.'

'Is he ready for you?'

'What do you mean?'

'Do you and Callum actually talk to each other? Where's Drew's mother? She hasn't been to visit. She isn't named on the consent form.' Pauline dropped her voice and said almost hesitantly, 'Is she dead?'

'No. I don't think so. When I asked Callum to sign the consent he said something about Drew's mother being in America and him having full custody. I'm not really sure what happened there. I know she's been on the phone to the ward staff a few times every day.'

'Ah, so there's no other woman to get in the way?'

'Pauline!'

She smiled at Jessica. 'So what? I'm being a little mercenary. I have a friend to think about.'

Jessica's eyes drifted over to the flowers. They were beautiful and the irony of the blooms wasn't lost on her. Gerberas were her favourite flowers—had been for years. She was surprised that Callum had even remembered that, but there was something nice about the fact that he had.

She stood up quickly. 'I need to go for a few minutes.' She looked about the unit. 'Is everything okay in here? Do you need me to see anyone before I go?'

Pauline shook her head. 'Everything's fine and, don't worry, I'll look after your flowers for you.'

Jessica rolled her eyes and hurried down the corridor. She glanced at her watch. Although the hospital allowed parents to stay with their children at all times, most parents went away for an hour or so each day to freshen up and change their clothes.

The surgical ward had been a no-go area for the last few days. Callum was there constantly with his son. Just as she would have expected.

She'd had to review Drew a few times every day. His recovery was going well and it was likely she would discharge him today.

But every time she'd been anywhere in the vicinity Callum had tried to speak to her. She'd fobbed him off as best she could. The flowers were the biggest message yet that he was determined to apologise and pursue this.

She just wasn't sure how she felt.

Her stomach churned as she walked down the ward. It was ridiculous. She spent all day, every day in the presence of kids. Why on earth would this little boy be any different?

Because he was Callum's.

Because this could be something entirely different.

If only she could be ready for it.

Drew had a little DVD player on his lap and was watching the latest Disney movie. Although he had his clothes on, the curtains were pulled around his bed and lights in the room dimmed. Most children who'd undergone an anaesthetic took a few days to recover fully. A nap time in the afternoon was common—and when most of the parents took their chance to go home, shower and change.

'Hi, Drew.' Jessica took the opportunity to sit down next to his bed. 'What are you watching?'

He turned the screen around to show her. She nodded in approval.

'So, how are you feeling?'

'I'm good. When can I go back to mini-kickers?'

She wrinkled her nose. 'Is that some kind of football?'

He nodded. 'I go every week with my friend Joe. I love mini-kickers. It's my favourite.'

'Well, we can't have you missing your favourite for long. Lie back and let me have a little look at your tummy.'

His wound was healing well. The edges were sealed and there was no sign of infection.

'This is looking great, Drew. The stitches that I used will disappear on their own. But you also have some stitches inside your tummy and if you do too much, too quickly, then it can hurt.'

'Tomorrow?' He was serious. His little face was watching her closely.

So this was how a five-year-old boy thought. Couldn't see past the football. There was something so endearing about that.

She laughed. 'No. Not tomorrow. Maybe two weeks— if you're feeling okay. Do you like school? Because if you do, it will be all right to go back to school next week.'

He wrinkled his nose. 'School's okay. I like school dinner. Mrs Brown makes the best custard.' He leant forward and whispered in her ear. 'The custard here isn't nearly as good.'

'Really? I always thought the custard here was quite good.'

He shook his head and gave her a look of disgust. 'Oh, no. Mrs Brown's custard is *much* better.'

He was a lovely little boy, with Callum's searing green eyes and a real determined edge about him. They were so alike she could have picked him out from a room filled with a hundred kids.

'What's your favourite subject at school?'

It was something that preyed on her mind from time to time. She'd often wondered what her own son would have enjoyed most at school.

'Dinosaurs or volcanoes.' Drew was absolutely definite about what he liked. He tilted his head to one side. 'And I quite like the sticky tray.'

'The sticky tray? What's that?'

'For making things. I was making a Christmas card for my dad a few days ago at school. I've picked blue card and I was sticking a snowman on the front.'

'Ah.' Jess gave a smile. 'What were you using for the snowman? Was it some cotton wool—like the kind we have in here?'

'Yes. It got kind of messy. The glue stuck to my hands and then the cotton wool got all puffy.' His face was all screwed up, as if he was remembering the mess he'd made.

Jessica leaned across the bed. 'It doesn't matter if you made a mess. I'm sure your dad will love it.'

'But I'm not finished yet. I still need to put some glitter on. I want to put some stars in the sky.'

'And that will be gorgeous, Drew. Then it's my job to get you back to school so you can finish it.'

Drew shook his head. 'That one got a bit messy. Can't you help me make another one?'

Jess hesitated. Everything in her head was screaming no.

She was a hospital consultant. She had a hundred other things to be doing right now.

But for the strangest reason none of them seemed particularly important. Here was an opportunity to do something nice. To do the first real Christmassy thing she'd done in…goodness knew how long.

She hadn't even put her Christmas decorations up for the last three years. It had hardly seemed worthwhile when she wasn't really in the mood. They were lying stuffed in a box in her loft somewhere. Maybe she should think about pulling them out.

She smiled at Drew. Yes, she could go and ask one of the play advisors to come and help Drew make a card.

But he had a really hopeful look in those green eyes.

How could she possibly say no?

She walked over to one of the play cabinets and pulled out a drawer. The hospital's own kind of sticky tray. She lifted up the vast array of coloured card and fanned it out like a rainbow in her hand. 'What colour card would you like?'

Callum strode down the corridor. He hadn't meant to be so long. But three nights of sleeping in a hospital chair did strange things to your body.

He'd stepped out of the shower and had only meant to sit down for a few seconds at home. The next thing he knew he had a crick in his neck and was hopping about the place, trying to get dressed in the space of five seconds.

If he was lucky, today would be the day he got to take his son home. And as much as he liked going to the hospital and getting to see Jessica every day, he'd much rather have his son safe at home.

He'd promised Drew's mother that they could Skype tonight. She usually did it every week with Drew and had been annoyed that she hadn't been able to see him while he'd been unwell.

It was just as well children were so resilient. Drew had seemed to get over his mother's abandonment within a matter of weeks. Probably because he'd been surrounded by people who loved him. But Callum could never forget the impact it had had on his son. What kind of a woman did that?

He turned the corner, ready to head into Drew's room, and stopped dead.

It was a sight he'd never expected to see.

Drew looked nothing like the child he'd been a few days ago, pale-faced and in pain. Today he had colour in his cheeks and sparkle in his eyes.

Drew and Jessica. Paint was everywhere. Cotton wool was everywhere. Glitter was everywhere, including smudged all along Jessica's cheekbones. But most importantly Drew was smiling, Drew was laughing. His attention was totally focused on Jessica. And the way he was looking at her...

It tugged right at Callum's heartstrings. Kirsten, his ex-wife, had never been the most maternal woman in the world. And since she'd left Drew had never really had a female presence in his life, that female contact. Sure, there were his friends Julie and Blair, and Julie was fabulous with Drew. But he didn't see her every day—didn't have that kind of relationship with her.

This was the first time he'd realised what his son had been missing out on.

He felt a sharp pain in his stomach. He'd always felt as if introducing Drew to any of his girlfriends would have been confusing for a little boy. Taking things a step too far. He wanted to protect Drew from all of that. And to be truthful he'd never been that serious about any of them. He couldn't stand the thought of different women yo-yoing in and out of his son's life.

Then there was that lingering dread of introducing Drew to another woman, only for her to change her mind and speed off into the sunset, leaving him to pick up the pieces.

But maybe he had been wrong? Maybe he'd been cheating his son out of so much more.

Jess seemed so at ease with his son. But, then, she should, she was a paediatrician, she loved kids. It was the field she'd chosen to work in.

It made him even more curious. Why didn't Jess have kids of her own? It was obvious she would be a natural.

It almost seemed a shame to interrupt this happy scene, but he had to. He wanted to know if he could take his son home. He cleared his throat loudly. 'What's going on in here?'

Drew's eyes widened in shock. 'Hide them, Dr Rae! Hide them!' He cupped his hands over whatever it was he'd been making.

Jess jumped to her feet and stood in front of the table they were sitting at, opening up her coat to block his view. She gave Callum a wink then turned her head over her shoulder towards Drew. 'It's okay. He can't see a thing. Put them in the envelopes now.'

There was the loud sound of shuffling behind Jessica's back, along with little-boy squeals of excitement.

But Callum was kind of stuck in the view right in front of his eyes. Jess was wearing a red woollen dress, which clung to her every curve, leaving nothing to his imagination. He was kind of glad that her white coat normally covered this view. He didn't want everyone else seeing what he could.

Jess sparkled. Literally. Blue and silver glitter along her cheekbones.

He lifted his thumb up and touched her cheek. 'You got a little something on here.' He brushed along her cheekbone then his fingers rested under her chin. He half expected her to flinch and move away, but she didn't. She stood still, fixing him with her deep brown eyes.

A man could get lost in eyes like that.

If he wanted to.

He stared down at his thumb. 'Is this a bit of a give-away?'

She shook her head and glanced over her shoulder again. 'How are you doing, Drew? Nearly done?'

Drew held up two giant white envelopes, looking ever so pleased with himself. 'Done!'

He stood up, but stayed behind Jessica, putting his hands on her hips and sticking his head around. 'Wait till you see what I've made you, Daddy.'

Callum knelt down. 'I can't wait. I'm hoping we can go home some time today. What do you think, Dr Rae?'

Jess brushed her hair back from her face, leaving traces of glitter everywhere, including shimmering in the air between them. 'Oh, wow! I guess we went all out with the glitter, then.'

'I guess you did.' She was still smiling at him. Not avoiding him. And not avoiding Drew. Did this mean she'd finally forgiven him? She might give them a chance at... something?

'What do you think, Doc? Is Drew ready for discharge?'

He could almost see the silent switch—the move back into doctor mode. 'Yes, I think he is. His wound is healing well. We've done a few other tests—an ECG and an ultrasound of his heart. There's been no sign of any problems.' Her face became serious and the smile disappeared for a few seconds.

'Right now I'm assuming that Drew's situs inversus in straightforward. But I understand you might want to talk to someone about it. So, even though I don't think Drew will need any kind of follow-up, I've asked for one of the other consultants who specialises in genetic conditions to give you an appointment so you can discuss any concerns that you have.'

Callum pulled back a little. 'But why? Can't I just talk to you?' The words she was saying made sense, but that didn't mean that he liked them.

She shook her head. 'I don't think that's a good idea. I performed Drew's emergency surgery, but I probably have a conflict of interest here.'

He raised his eyebrows. 'A conflict of interest, what does that mean?'

'You know what that means, Callum.'

'But you must have treated a friend's kid before?'

She nodded slowly and stepped a little closer, lowering her voice and glancing in the direction of Drew. He'd become bored by their chatting and was now doing a jigsaw at one of the nearby tables.

'Yes, I have treated children of friends before—but usually only in an emergency. I wouldn't willingly be the paediatrician for any of my friends' kids. It crosses too many boundaries—complicates things and leads to confusion all round.' She tilted her head to the side and gave him a little smile. 'I'm sure you understand.'

'Actually, I don't.' He folded his arms across his chest. 'What do you mean?'

'Friends. Is that what we are?'

'Of course.'

He didn't like it. He didn't like it at all. It didn't matter that the concept of only being friends with Jess had circulated in his mind for days.

In the cold hard light of day he didn't like that.

He wanted more.

He wanted to be more than friends.

The kiss had started something.

No. That was rubbish. Something had started more than thirteen years ago.

There was unfinished business between them.

'What if I don't want us to be friends?'

Her head shot up. 'What?' There was that fleeting look across her face again. She was hurt. But she wasn't getting his implication. She was thinking he didn't *even* want to be friends. Not that he wanted something more. It was time to put that right.

He stepped closer and placed his hand on her hip. 'What if I wanted us to be more than that?'

Her pupils widened and her tongue shot out and licked her lips. Her eyes darted to the side, obviously to see if anyone was watching. He pressed his fingers a little more firmly into her hip, pulling her closer to him.

Drew hadn't even noticed what they were doing, he was still engrossed in his jigsaw.

'I'm not entirely sure what you mean,' she murmured.

'Truth be told—neither am I.'

His other hand settled on her other hip, feeling the wool under his fingertips, along with the outline of her hip. He still had to find out what was going on with Jessica. He was no closer to that than he'd been a few weeks ago. She played her cards close to her chest.

But Drew was happy. He'd warmed easily to Jessica. He liked her. She made him smile. And after what he'd witnessed today he was willing to take some baby steps.

'But let's find out.'

She lifted her hand and touched the side of his face, her hand trembling. She bit her lip. 'What if I'm not sure?'

'Then we take it slowly. We find out together. Are you willing to try that?'

His heart was thumping against his chest wall. An answer had never seemed so important. He wasn't even entirely sure what he was asking. This was all new territory for him. New territory for them both.

He glanced over at Drew. 'How about a date? A family date?' He'd never done that before. It wasn't just a step for him—it was a leap. But maybe now was the time to find out.

He could see something fleeting pass through her eyes. A moment's hesitation. Did she want to say no? Did she want to walk away?

There it was again. Her tongue licking her dry lips. What kind of effect was he having on her?

'Let's embrace the time of year. I promised Drew I

would take him to see Santa at Cullen's Garden Centre in Largs on Saturday. They usually have a huge play park and real live reindeer for the kids to see. Do you want to come along?'

A nervous smile came across her face. 'A play park? Is that really a good idea after an appendectomy?'

He pulled her body next to his and gave a sexy smile. 'Oh, I think we'll be fine,' he whispered in her ear. 'We'll have medical supervision.'

The smile on her face seemed genuine now. 'I guess you will.'

CHAPTER TEN

HER BEDROOM WAS a mess.

No, her bedroom looked as if a tornado had swept through it.

Every jumper and pair of jeans she possessed was scattered across her bed. Along with every raincoat, woollen coat, hat, glove and scarf. It was a beautiful eruption of colour, but Jess was still standing in her bra and pants. No further forward than she'd been an hour ago.

She picked up the phone next to her bed and pressed the automatic dial. 'Pauline? Help.'

Her friend sounded as if she'd just woken up. 'What is it, Jess?' she groaned.

'What do I wear?'

'Tell me you're joking.'

'No. Why?'

'You phoned me at this time in the morning to ask me what to wear to meet Santa?'

Pauline already knew about the date. She just didn't appreciate the agonising Jessica was doing over her wardrobe.

Jess sagged down onto the bed. 'Please, Pauline. Tell me what to wear.' She sounded pathetic and she knew it. This was the behaviour of a teenage girl, not a grown woman with a responsible job.

But Pauline's voice came through loud and clear. 'I would have thought that would be obvious, Jess. You're going to meet Santa—you wear red. Wear your Christmas jumper—the one you wore on the ward last year. Drew will love it. And your skinny jeans and your big red boots. There. That's you sorted. Anything else, or can a girl get back to sleep?'

The picture was forming in Jessica's mind. She hadn't even considered her novelty knitted jumper with the great big Christmas pudding on it. It would be perfect. She stood on tiptoe and yanked it out of the back corner of her cupboard. 'Thanks, Pauline. I'll see you tomorrow.' She hung up the phone and held the jumper in front of her for a second before quickly pulling it over her head. Pauline obviously had better vision than she did. The jumper, along with her skinny jeans and red chunky boots, was perfect. She even had a red coat she could wear too.

She glanced at the clock again. She couldn't believe she was this nervous. It seemed ridiculous. This was a simple trip—a chance to get out of Glasgow and have a nice drive along the Ayrshire coast until they reached the garden centre outside Largs.

She should be calm about this. She should be relaxed. She fastened her red coat and wrapped her scarf around her neck. The forecast today said it would be cold—really cold—so she wanted to wrap up warmly.

Her make-up was already on. Even though she hadn't managed to choose her wardrobe, when she did wear make-up it was always the same—some light foundation, some mascara and a little bit of red lipstick. It seemed to give her the little bit of colour she always lacked.

There was a toot outside and her heart leapt into her mouth. Oh, no. They were here.

Why had she agreed to this?

What if Drew decided that he hated her?

What if she just found this all too hard?

She walked down the stairs and sat on the bottom step for a few seconds, taking a few deep breaths. She could do this. She had *chosen* to do this. And she had to remember that.

No one was forcing this on her—no one.

Callum had lit up something inside her that had been dead for a long time.

And no matter how much she tried to deny it, it had felt good.

Then there was Drew. He was a gorgeous little boy. Being in his company was easy. With his big green eyes and determined manner it was easy to like him.

The fears she'd had about constantly comparing him to Lewis weren't there. Lewis was a totally different little boy.

She took a sharp breath. That thought.

She did that frequently. Still thought about Lewis in the present tense—as if he was still there. Did all mothers do that? Did all parents who had lost a child still think of their child in the present tense?

Was that good or bad? She wasn't sure.

Things were changing. She was changing. Yesterday she'd even pulled the box out of the loft with her Christmas decorations and tree. It had been hard to look at them again, the pink and purple globes brought back so many memories of previous happy Christmases in this house. So last night when she'd been shopping in the supermarket she'd bought a whole host of new decorations—silver ones. It felt different. It felt right.

The pink and purple ones held too many memories. The

silver ones were new. With space available for memories of their own.

The car tooted again and she stood up, trying to ignore the fact her legs were shaking. She stared at herself in the mirror in the hall, taking in the look of absolute fear on her face.

She picked up the fake-fur-trimmed hat on the table in the hall and stuck it on her head. 'You can do this,' she told her reflection. She closed her eyes for a second.

Harry Shaw's face drifted into her mind. The expression on his face that day in Theatre when she'd just been about to operate on Drew. *You can do this, Jess. It'll be a walk in the park.* And he'd believed it. She had been able to tell by the expression on his face.

She opened her eyes and stared at her reflection again, adjusting her hat in the mirror. She looked herself in the eye and repeated the mantra, 'You can do this, Jess. It will be a walk in the park.'

She gave herself a little smile then headed out to the car, pulling the door closed behind her.

Now, if only she believed that.

Callum's fingers were drumming nervously on the steering wheel. Drew was happy. He was watching his favourite DVD in the back seat of the car, oblivious to his father's tension.

Callum squinted at the address again. This was definitely the right number. And he was definitely in the right street. He peered at the front door again. It was lovely, white with a stained-glass panel. He was sure he could see movement behind it. What was taking Jess so long?

He looked up and down the street. This was definitely one of the nicest areas of Glasgow. The street was filled with well-kept town houses with private drives and neat gardens. Wouldn't a town house be a little big for a single woman?

He shook that thought out of his head as the door opened and Jess came out. She was dressed in red today with a dark hat pulled over her ears.

There it was again. Even though he kept trying to ignore it. He was sure if they had him on one of those twenty-four-hour cardiac monitors his heart rate would shoot up every time he saw her. Jess was definitely wreaking havoc and adding to his chances of heart disease.

She gave him a little wave as she pulled the door closed behind her and started down the steps. Instead of walking around to the passenger side, she stopped and pulled open the rear door. 'Hi, Drew, how are you doing?'

Drew looked up from his DVD. 'Hi, Dr Jess. I'm good. Can I go to mini-kickers this week instead of next?'

She laughed. 'I can see five-year-old boys obviously have a one-track mind. I tell you what—let me think about it. Let's see how you do with Santa today.'

'Okay.' He pointed to the TV in the rear of the driver's seat. 'Do you wanna watch the dinosaurs too?'

She gave a little smile as she glanced at Callum. 'No, thanks. I'd better sit up front with your dad in case he gets lonely.'

'Aw, okay, then.' His eyes fixed on the screen again as she closed the door and walked around to the passenger side.

She slid in and started to unfasten the buttons on her coat. 'I was so worried about how cold it was going to be I totally forgot about the fact we'd be in the car for an hour.' She pulled her hat off her head, leaving her curls sticking up in all directions.

She seemed happy. She seemed relaxed and Callum felt himself heave a sigh of relief. He'd been so worried about this.

Worried that she'd change her mind.

Worried that she'd phone him and back out.

And although her face seemed relaxed, he'd noticed the way her hand was gripping her bag. Take things slowly. That's what they'd agreed.

He started the engine again and they pulled out onto the motorway, heading down towards Ayrshire. It was a bright day, with just a little nip in the air. Not quite cold enough to freeze yet and little chance of ice.

The road to Largs was always busy. It wound through various towns all haunted by a million sets of traffic lights, but the scenery made up for the slow-moving traffic.

'I didn't expect it to be so busy.' Jessica had leaned back in her seat and was changing radio stations for most of the journey. 'I thought people only went to Largs in the summer for the ice cream.'

He smiled. 'When was the last time you were in Largs?'

She frowned. 'I think I was a child. We were going to Millport for the weekend and had to get the ferry from Largs.'

'Did you get your picture taken on Crocodile Rock?'

She gave a little gasp. 'Hasn't every Scottish child got their picture taken on Crocodile Rock?'

He laughed. 'I've not taken Drew there yet. Maybe that's a trip for the summer.'

'What's Crocodile Rock?' came the little voice from the back of the car.

Jessica twisted round in her seat to talk to him. 'It's a rock that looks like a crocodile. Some people painted it red, white and black years ago and when I was a young girl everyone went to Millport in the summer and got their photo taken standing on Crocodile Rock.'

'But crocodiles are green!'

Callum tried not to laugh. Only a child's logic could say something like that. 'I'll show you some pictures of it later, Drew. I've got a photo taken standing on the rock. If you like it I'll take you over in the summer to see it.'

'Does it bite?'

'No, silly, it's a rock.'

Drew settled back into his chair. 'How far until we see Santa?'

Callum glanced at the road signs. 'About another ten minutes. We'll be there soon.'

'I'm hungry.'

'So am I,' Jess piped up. 'We'll get something to eat when we stop, okay?'

It was almost a relief to hear her say that. Even better was the sound of her stomach rumbling. It was like music to his ears.

She pressed her hand over it. 'Oops, sorry!'

It didn't take long to reach the garden-centre car park and Drew's DVD was instantly forgotten when he saw all the 'Santa's Grotto' signs. 'Look, Dad!' he shouted. 'They've got a sleigh and everything!'

He was out of the car like a shot and over at the painted barrier advertising Santa at the garden centre.

Jessica felt her stomach churn. He was so excited he was practically jumping up and down. It was so nice to see. So nice to experience. Lewis had been too little to really comprehend Christmas. Although he'd liked the presents, he'd still been a little scared of the man in the big red suit.

She felt Callum's arm around her waist. 'Everything okay?' Sometimes she felt as if he could almost read her mind. As if he knew when her thoughts were drifting off and taking her out of the present time and place.

She reached over and put her hand on his chest. 'I'm fine. I guess we'd better get in there before Drew bursts his stitches.'

They walked through the garden centre, past the blue-lit trees lining the driveway and fake snowmen and animals. Inside the garden centre they had a path to Santa's Grotto and another to meet the reindeer. Callum went to the nearby desk to buy tickets. It was already getting busy in the centre, with lots of families and children arriving all the time.

The entrance was gorgeous. It was filled with a huge variety of pre-lit trees, sparkling in a variety of different colours. There were shelves and shelves of lighted ornaments, coloured parcels, little nativity scenes, sequin-covered trees and models of little Christmas villages playing music. On the surrounding walls were thousands of tree decorations, all hanging in different colour schemes to make selections easier.

All around the place children were squealing with delight at seeing something new or squabbling over their favourite tree ornament.

Jessica felt a little hand slip into hers. She looked down and Drew was staring up at her with anxious eyes. She knelt down next to him. 'What's wrong? Don't you feel well?' She couldn't help it, she was immediately moving into doctor mode.

He shook his head. 'I couldn't see my daddy,' he whispered.

Jess smiled. From down here, in amongst the jostling throng of people, it was hard to make anyone out, particularly for a little boy who had been running to and fro between the attractions. But her bright red coat would be easily visible. When she stood up she could clearly see Callum's back at the ticket booth, but she wasn't a little boy.

She slipped her hand out of her red leather glove and grabbed Drew's hand again. The heat was rising in the garden centre so she unfastened the zip on his jacket. It was even nicer holding hands, skin to skin. Drew seemed relieved to have found her. His immediate trust in her was so apparent.

Callum appeared next to them and waved the tickets. 'All the visits are timed. We can't see Santa until eleven-thirty. Want to get something to eat and then we'll go and see the reindeer?'

They nodded and followed him into the busy café. 'Have a seat, you two, and I'll get us some food.'

Jessica and Drew sat down at one of the nearby wooden tables. The whole café was decorated for Christmas with tinsel, garlands and Christmas holly wreaths hanging all round the walls. There was a cup filled with crayons on every table along with ready-made Christmas colouring sheets. Drew wasted no time and started to colour in a picture of the North Pole. 'Have you given your daddy your card?'

He shook his head. 'We posted the other one to mum in America. Dad helped me write the envelope. But I hid his under his pillow this morning.' Drew giggled. 'He won't find it until we get home.'

Jess smiled, watching Callum's back as he pushed his tray along the rack, picking up food as he went. He hadn't even asked her what she wanted to eat. She had a sneaking suspicion he was trying to feed her up. And she didn't feel insulted or annoyed. It was kind of nice that someone wanted to look after her.

The tray landed on the table a few minutes later with a glass of milk and a bacon roll for Drew, some toast with scrambled egg for her, and a full breakfast for Callum. He lifted some other plates onto the table with some home-baked scones, along with a caramel latte for Jess.

He really did have the best memory in the world. All the things in the world she liked.

'Okay, everyone?' he sat down in the seat next to Drew and admired his crayoning. 'Let's eat and then we'll have a walk around the garden centre while we wait for our turn.'

Jessica looked around the room. It was full of families, all here either to buy a Christmas tree or pay a visit to Santa's Grotto. It had been such a long time since she'd been to a place like this.

She used to love visiting garden centres—especially around Christmas. She could easily have spent all her time off visiting one after the other, buying something in every place that she visited.

Something on one of the walls caught her eye. Little silver and red hearts, bunched together with bells to be hung from a Christmas tree. They were beautiful and just the sort of thing she would have picked in years gone by.

Callum followed her line of vision. 'Do you like them?'

She nodded slowly. A lump had appeared in her throat and she was too nervous to talk. She tried to clear her throat. 'I…I've changed my colour scheme. They would be perfect.'

He reached across the table and touched her hand. It was as if he knew. As if he'd just looked inside her head and saw that for a second she was struggling. 'Then we'll stop and get them before we leave. They look beautiful.' He took a sip of his coffee. 'Will your tree be red and silver this year?'

She shrugged. 'I bought some new silver decorations yesterday. I hadn't got much further than that.'

'Didn't you see the sparkly red ribbon near the door? It was on one of the trees.' Drew gave a little sigh. 'It was lovely.' Then he said quickly, 'But it's for a girl. It would be nice on your tree.'

'What colour scheme do you guys have?'

Callum choked on his coffee. 'You're joking, right? There's no colour scheme in our house. It's like a hotch-potch with every colour of the rainbow.' He smiled at Drew. 'Our colour scheme is whatever Drew's made at nursery or school that year. Right, son?'

Drew nodded and laughed. 'I've made lots of decorations. Daddy puts them all up on the tree.' He leaned forward and whispered in Jessica's ear, 'He says it doesn't matter if they're wonky.'

She felt a little tug at her heartstrings. She could just imagine their jumbled tree with haphazard decorations all made by a little boy. She wished hers could look like that.

Her silver and red decorations would seem drab in comparison. Suddenly the step she'd decided to take didn't seem nearly far enough. Not by a long shot.

She picked up a crayon and started to help Drew with his drawing. Callum's eyes were on her. He must have questions. But when could she tell him?

When could she tell him that there was a reason she wanted to take things slowly? It seemed almost deceitful when he'd invited her on a trip with his son.

He was still watching and smiling cautiously as he split the scones and put butter and strawberry jam on them. It was official. He was trying to feed her up. And he was doing a good job—it was the most she'd eaten in months.

But she didn't have the normal feelings she had around

food. Mostly she was uninterested or dissociated herself from it. These last few weeks she'd started to notice the beautiful aromas of food again—instead of just the smell of coffee. In the garden centre today food smells were abundant. From the freshly baked scones and other cakes to the smells of bubbling soup, bacon and toasted cheese. Today was probably the first time in a long time she'd felt truly hungry.

'Is it time to go and see Santa yet?' Drew could barely contain his excitement and it was so nice to see.

Jessica stood up and held out her hand towards him. 'Why don't we go and see the reindeer? Maybe your dad will be able to take a picture of them for you. How cool would it be to show your friends at school that you met one of Santa's reindeer?'

Drew jumped up like a shot. 'Oh, yes, Daddy! Could I take it in for show and tell?'

Callum was smiling again and stood up. He looked at his watch. 'We've still got half an hour to kill. I think we can take some pictures of the reindeer.'

Drew sped down the path ahead of them, giving Callum a few seconds to reach and grab Jessica's hand. It didn't feel strange. It didn't feel unnatural.

Just as holding Drew's hand earlier hadn't felt unnatural. In fact, it had felt entirely normal.

An older couple was walking down the path towards them and stood aside to let Drew barrel past them. The older man laughed. 'What a lovely family,' he remarked.

Jessica felt herself catch her breath. Her feet were still moving, still walking down the path, but she felt every muscle in her body stiffen.

That's what they must look like.

A family.

An ordinary family.

She felt Callum squeeze her hand. He could sense it. He could sense her unease again. It must be killing him that he didn't know what was going on.

She so wanted to tell him. She so wanted to tell him right now before she burst into tears in the middle of Santa's Grotto.

Guilt was crawling all over her skin. Was this a betrayal? A betrayal of the memory of Daniel and Lewis—the people she'd thought she would spend the rest of her life with?

She could feel that horrible tight feeling spreading across her chest. Her breath was catching in her lungs.

Callum's feet stopped moving and his hand slid out from hers, turning her round to face him and sliding his arms around her waist. She couldn't lift her head to look at him. It was too hard right now as she was struggling to breathe.

This was wrong. Wasn't this usually the stage that single men ran away? When they heard someone mention something about a family?

Instead, Callum was taking it all in his stride. He pulled her a little closer and whispered in her ear, 'Just breathe, Jess. I don't know what's wrong, but this is a good day.' His voice was steady and calm. 'Wherever you are, know that I'm right here. Breathe.'

His hand rubbed gently up and down her back. A few people wandered past. Drew had raced on ahead and was out of sight. To the rest of the world it must just look as if they were taking a few seconds for a sneaky cuddle. Only Jessica knew the demons she was currently fighting in her head.

Gradually, the feeling across her chest started to ease. Her muscles started to relax. Callum released his grasp and pulled back, stroking her hair from across her face. 'Okay?'

She nodded. She didn't know what to say right now. How on earth could she explain what had just happened? What had caused that reaction in her?

He took her hand again. 'Ready to see some reindeer?'

It was as if he knew better than to ask right now. But even though his gaze was kind she could see the questions in his eyes. There was no judgement, only wonder.

She squeezed his hand. 'I would love to see the reindeer.'

They walked down the path to the outside stall where the reindeer were. Drew was already standing agog. Of course none had a red nose, but the names of Santa's reindeer had been stencilled across the top of the stalls.

It was a wide paddock, with two members of staff—albeit dressed in elf costumes—on duty at all times. Jessica didn't know what she'd been expecting, but the reindeer seemed happy. They walked to the fence, and under the guidance of the staff allowed the children to stroke their coats and touch their antlers. They seemed healthy and in good condition.

Jessica had heard horror stories in the past about animals kept in children's play parks but it certainly wasn't the case here. In fact, the staff seemed enthusiastic, answering all the children's questions about the reindeer upkeep, with a few North Pole stories flung in for good measure.

'Can I get my picture with Comet, Dad?'

Callum nodded and knelt down as Drew posed next to the reindeer. Jessica waited until he'd finished then gave him a nudge. 'Go and stand next to Drew so I can take a picture of the two of you.' He obeyed and she snapped away happily. These would be great photos for Drew's show and tell at school.

'I want a picture with Dr Jess too!' shouted Drew.

Jess flushed. 'It's just Jess, Drew. You don't need to call me Dr Jess any more.'

Callum raised his eyebrows at her, obviously wondering if she would object to having her picture taken, but she swapped places with him and put her arm around Drew, letting Comet take pride of place in the background of the picture.

It was so easy to be around them. Drew had so much energy. No one would guess how sick he'd been a week ago. And Callum was every bit the doting dad that she'd expected him to be. It was so nice to see. And so easy to be a part of.

'Is it time yet, Dad?' Drew was bouncing up and down on the spot.

Callum looked at his watch. 'It's nearly eleven-thirty. Want to go down to the grotto?'

'Yippee!'

It was only a few minutes' walk. The path was lined with frost-covered decorations and houses. Christmas trees with green lights and gold stars lined the path, with red berry lights around the door of the grotto. Drew couldn't resist peering through the windows.

The garden staff had certainly gone all out to create a kids' paradise. They had staff dressed as elves, working away in a pretend workshop, piled high with sacks of toys. A little train ran around the outside of the whole complex with another elf driving it and children and parents in the carriages. 'Do we get to go on that too, Dad?'

Callum shrugged, 'I expect so.'

Jessica stood on tiptoe and whispered in his ear, 'I think

that's part of the way out. Probably to make sure you don't stay in here too long.'

The queue moved along quickly and Callum showed Drew's ticket. An elf hurried over. 'Drew Kennedy? Come over here until we check and see if your name's in the naughty or nice book.' She held out her hand towards Drew.

His eyes widened like saucers and he turned to Callum, who smiled. 'Go on,' he urged.

'They asked me his name when I bought the tickets,' he said. 'They also asked me to choose which one he'd like best from a list of toys.'

'Wow. They've really thought of everything here, haven't they?' She looked around. 'You know, I'd love to bring some of the kids from the hospital here. You know, the ones that spend half their life stuck in a ward? Things are so well organised here, it could be perfect.'

'Why don't you ask before we leave if there's any way you can arrange it?'

She gave a little nod then nudged Callum. 'Look!'

Drew gave a little gasp as the elf pretended to find his name on the Nice list. 'Fabulous!' she shouted. 'That means we can go in and see Santa.'

'Come on, Dad. Come on, Jess,' shouted Drew as he tugged at the elf's hand.

Santa's Grotto was beautiful, filled with lots of fake snow and an icy blast of cold air. Santa was bundled up in the most padded costume and thickest beard Jessica had ever seen. And he had the patience of a saint. He took each child in turn, never hurried, never concerned about what was going on around him, and sat him or her on his knee, asking lots of questions.

Drew was totally enthralled. 'Tell me everything you

want for Christmas,' Santa said with a wink towards Callum and Jessica.

Drew immediately reeled off a list of typical things a five-year-old boy wanted—a dinosaur, a racing car, a dress-up soldier's outfit. Then he stopped and pulled Santa down towards him, glancing towards his dad and whispering in Santa's ear.

Jess had a brief feeling of panic. Drew's eyes were on her the whole time he spoke to Santa. What was he asking for?

Santa smiled over at them both then spoke so quietly to Drew that neither of them could hear what he was saying. A few seconds later he handed Drew his present.

'Can I open it now, Santa?' he asked.

Santa nodded towards them. 'You'll need to ask.'

Drew jumped down. 'Can I, Dad? Can I?'

Callum swung Drew up into his arms. 'Say thank you to Santa and we'll go on the train. If you're good, you can open your present when we get to the car.'

'Yippee!' He squirmed around in Callum's arms. 'Thank you, Santa!'

They headed over to the train and Jessica laughed as Callum tried to squeeze his large frame into the carriage beside them. 'Budge up,' he said. 'It's a tight squeeze in here. This train is obviously designed for elves.'

The train ride was perfect. It started inside in the snow-covered landscape with snowmen and trees and wound its way outside to the garden centre, which was covered in a dusting of real snow and glistening in places with ice. The garden-centre staff had decorated huts to make them look as if they were still part of Santa's village.

After a few minutes the train came to a halt outside one of the buildings at the edge of the garden centre. It was a decorated barn. Jess and Callum looked at each other. They could hear the joyful squeals of children from inside. 'What on earth is in there?'

They waited as everyone alighted from the train, the elf standing at the front.

'Is there something else in there?'

The elf puffed out his already red cheeks. 'It's the winter wonderland—a children's playground.' He nodded his head at Drew. 'Your day's not over yet, pal.'

They walked inside and were hit with the wave of heat as soon as they crossed the threshold. The noise level was incredible. Every child who had visited Santa that morning had obviously ended up in here.

Around the edges of the playground were a variety of bedraggled parents sitting at tables, trying to make themselves heard above the noise.

Drew edged a little closer to his father. Jess knelt down next to him. The noise must be intimidating to a small child.

'Is there anything you'd like to go on?' she asked. Her eyes swept around the room and she put her hands on his shoulders. 'It's probably not a good idea to go on the trampoline or bouncy castle yet when you've had stitches in your tummy. But you could go over to the craft tables or into the games room if you wanted.'

Drew's hand slid into hers. 'Come into the games room with me.'

She nodded and gave Callum a smile as they made their way to the other side of the barn. He leaned over. 'This isn't like him. Normally he'd have made a beeline straight for the bouncy castle and dived straight on.'

Jess looked down at the little figure next to her. 'He's still in recovery mode. Being in hospital is a big thing for a kid. And having an anaesthetic takes a lot more out of them than you'd expect.' She rolled her eyes. 'Anyway, a bouncy castle or trampoline is the last thing he needs to be on right now.'

Callum gritted his teeth. 'Yeah, about that…'

'What?'

'I sort of bought Drew a trampoline for Christmas. He asked for it months ago and I bought it just the week before he was ill. It's sitting in the garage, waiting to be assembled. Am I going to have to say that Santa lost it?'

'What? No.' She shook her head. 'It's another few weeks yet. By then Drew should be fine. His stitches will be healed and he should be back to normal. But please tell me you've bought one of those big safety nets.' She waggled her finger at him. 'If you dare bring him into Casualty with a head injury because he's bounced off…'

He held up his hands. 'Whoa! No chance. With you on duty and knowing the abuse I would get, I can assure you the safety net is ready.' He slipped his arm back around her shoulders as they headed into the games room.

He bent his head lower. 'Anyway, I remember the days when you weren't quite so safety-conscious.'

'What do you mean?'

He started to laugh and pretended to fumble in his pocket. 'Wait until I get the list out. First, there was the day you decided we should all jump into the harbour. Then there was the time you thought it was good idea to try out that thirty-year-old sled…'

'That was a family heirloom!'

He raised his eyebrows. '*Was* being the operative word.'

She stifled a laugh. Callum brought back so many good memories. Things that she'd forgotten about for so long.

Things that she'd locked away inside the part of her mind that had stopped her from feeling joy any more.

It was so good to finally set it free again. It was so good to have someone to share this stuff with.

It was a bit quieter in the games room, with tables set with board games and a few electronic game machines. Drew didn't hesitate. He dropped Jessica's hand and raced off to watch the football game being played at the end of the room. Then he hesitated, turned round, took off his coat and hat and dumped them in her lap.

Callum pointed to one of the benches at the side. 'What do you say to another coffee? We could be in here for a while.'

'Sure. Thanks.'

The heat was building already. Jessica unfastened her coat and pulled off her hat and gloves. Callum disappeared to the coffee stand for a few moments and she leaned back against the wall.

Wow. So this was the stage Lewis would have been at. Her eyes drifted around the quieter games room and then to the noisy throng outside.

Which room would he have wanted to be in? Would he have been in the thick of things, wreaking havoc outside? Or would he have been in here, like Drew, plotting his fantasy football side?

She let out a little laugh. How on earth did five-year-old boys know how to do that?

It was so nice to sit in here and watch all the kids at their various ages and stages. And even though she was thinking about Lewis, she was thinking about Drew too.

She watched as there was a minor clash of heads outside on the bouncy castle, and for the first time she didn't go into doctor mode and run forward to intervene. It was minor—their parents could deal with it—and she didn't want to leave Drew unsupervised. Callum had trusted her to watch over his son, even if it was only for a few minutes, and strangely she was enjoying it.

She hadn't been asked to come with them as a doctor. She'd been asked as a…what? A friend? A girlfriend? A potential lover?

All the things she would have immediately shied away from a few months ago. But with Callum it all felt so easy. One look from those green eyes and she tingled right down to her toes. One brush of his hand and her whole body craved more.

It was taking her time to get used to these feelings again.

To *admit* to feeling them.

To let herself feel them without being overwhelmed by sensations of guilt and betrayal. Slowly but surely she was starting to let those feelings go.

She thought about the photo currently in her living room. A beautiful photo of Daniel and Lewis, caught wrestling on the floor together, laughing together with unbridled pleasure. It was the image that stayed in her head.

Right there, caught in that moment of happiness forever.

They would always be part of her life—a wonderful part of her life—but the shades of grey around that picture were moving.

She was starting to move.

Starting to see a life past that.

'Jessica.' Her head shot up. Drew was waving her over. 'Come and see my score. I'm the top striker!' He was jumping up and down on the spot, clearly delighted. She ran over and gave him a hug. 'Well done, Drew, that's fantastic!'

He hugged her back with the exuberance that only a five-year-old could show. It felt good. It felt natural. It felt right.

Baby steps, her brain whispered. Just keep taking baby steps.

Callum walked around the edge of the winter wonderland with the two coffees, trying not to let his 'health and safety at work' hat annoy him. The coffee area should be cordoned off to minimise the risk of scalds to all the hyperactive children who were racing around the place.

He froze at the edge of the games room. Jessica and Drew were hugging in front of the giant TV, Drew obviously excited about something.

But that wasn't what made him freeze.

It was the expressions on both their faces.

Drew's was one of pure innocence and pleasure. The joy of sharing his delight with a mother figure. The way he'd wrapped his hands around her neck and was talking nineteen to the dozen in her ear.

And the way Jessica was looking at Drew.

Like he was the best thing she'd ever seen.

It had the strangest effect on Callum. He should be happy. He should be glad that his little boy felt so comfortable around the woman he hoped would be his girlfriend.

He should be delighted that they obviously had a mutual admiration society going. So many of his other friends had told him tales of woe about new potential partners and children not getting on—this obviously wasn't the case here.

But there was the weirdest feeling in the pit of Callum's stomach.

He knew there was something else. He knew there were parts of herself that Jessica still had to reveal to him. And it didn't matter what his memories of Jessica were. It didn't matter what effects one look of those brown eyes had on his body. It didn't matter how much he kept trying to push any little nagging doubts aside.

The fact was he wanted more. More than she was currently giving.

He wanted everything. The whole package.

Whatever that might contain.

But until he knew exactly what that was, he had a little boy to put first. He couldn't risk Drew's feelings or emotions. He could see the trust in his son's eyes. He could see the way he was already forming pictures in his mind—pictures that included Jessica.

Those pictures were starting to form in Callum's mind too, but he had to be sure. He had to be certain about Jessica before things went any further. It didn't matter how much he wanted to kiss her. It didn't matter how much he wanted to hold her in his arms. After a few short weeks he knew exactly where he wanted this relationship to go.

Drew was reaching up, touching one of Jessica's curls and tucking it behind her ear as he talked to her. Jessica caught his hand in hers and planted a kiss on his palm.

That was what he wanted for his son. So much it made his stomach ache.

Jessica looked over and caught sight of him. She frowned, obviously seeing the expression on his face, and gave him a little wave. She ruffled Drew's hair and pointed back at the big screen before moving over towards Callum and taking the coffee from his hand. 'Thanks for that. What's up?'

'Nothing. Nothing's up.'

She tilted her head to one side. 'Are you sure? You looked unhappy.'

She was staring at him with those big brown eyes. *She was worrying about him.* The irony wasn't lost on him.

And she looked happier. She looked more relaxed than he'd seen her in a while. If he could forget the episode earlier, today would have been a perfect day.

There was a little sparkle about her, a little glow. Glimmers of the old Jess shining through.

She glanced over her shoulder to where Drew was engrossed again in his game. There was something different in her eyes, something playful.

She gave him a cheeky smile then grabbed his arm and pulled him round the corner, out of the line of sight of everyone. 'I wonder if I can make you feel better,' she whispered, then she leaned forward and wrapped her arms around his neck, rising up on tiptoe and kissing him gently on the mouth.

And at that precise moment all rational thought left the building.

CHAPTER ELEVEN

HER PAGER SOUNDED again. It was the fourth time in the last hour, but she'd been stuck in Theatre, performing surgery on a very sick baby with a necrotic bowel.

She pulled her theatre mask and cap off as the tiny baby was wheeled out of Theatre and off to ITU. She'd probably spend most of the night there, but she had to answer this page first.

She couldn't believe how tired she was. It was weird. For the last three years work had been her sanctuary. A place of focus. A place where she didn't have time to think about anything else.

And things here were good. Marcus and Lily, the two children with hypothermia, had both made a steady recovery and been allowed home. All the children from the accident had now been discharged and would be looking forward to Christmas with their families.

Christmas with a family. Something she hadn't even thought about for the last few years.

But the last few weeks had been different. Spending time with Callum and Drew had brought a whole new perspective to her life.

Life didn't just revolve around the hospital any more.

She didn't just wake up in the morning and stay there for as long as possible, only going home when the nurses eventually flung her out, then falling asleep straight away for the next day.

Work wasn't the first thing she thought about when she woke up in the morning. That was usually Callum and his green eyes—or Drew and whatever event he was looking forward to at school that day.

It was amazing how differently she felt about things.

In fact, tonight she'd been almost sorry that she was on call. She'd have preferred to spend more time with Callum and Drew.

For the first time in three years she was actually looking forward to Christmas. To spending it with people she loved. To have a Christmas when the focus wasn't just on being alone but sharing the time with others.

There was still the odd moment where she felt guilty. Usually in the depths of night when the feelings crept up on her unawares. When little voices in her head asked if she really deserved a second chance at happiness.

After all, she'd had her happy-ever-after. She'd been married to the love of her life and had had a beautiful son. Why should she get that chance again?

Was it fair?

Slowly but surely Callum and Drew were edging their way into her heart. Even just thinking about them brought a smile to her face.

It made her try to push the other voices away. Push them away into some dark place where she wouldn't hear them any more.

Her pager sounded again and she picked up the phone. The sister in A and E answered straight away.

'Bad news, Jessica. It's Grace Flynn. She's been admitted again. Her bloods have come back whilst we've been paging you—they're awful.'

Jessica's heart plummeted. Grace was a long-term patient. A seven-year-old with a rare form of invasive bowel tumours. She'd operated on another tumour only a few weeks ago and things hadn't looked good.

Children with cancer always had a wide team of staff looking after them at Parkhill. Grace had a paediatric consultant, a specialist oncologist, herself with her surgical skills and a whole host of specialist nurses. Even though doctors weren't supposed to have favourite patients, she'd been treating Grace for so long that she couldn't help but let the little girl have a special place in her heart.

'Have you sent her up to the ward or is she still in A and E?'

'The registrar's seen her and sent her up to the ward while we were waiting for her blood results and ultrasound. She knew her and thought she'd be more comfortable up there.'

Of course. Javier, the Spanish registrar, was familiar with the case. He'd dealt with Grace on a number of occasions over the last year. 'Ultrasound? Is there a chance her bowel is blocked again?'

She heard the sigh at the end of the phone. 'Put it this way, after a conversation with one of the other consultants he gave her a bolus of morphine and set up a continuous opioid infusion.'

Jessica sucked in her breath. News she didn't want to hear. Not for a child.

'I'll go straight up now,' she said. 'I can review the test results when I get there.'

Jessica replaced the phone and hurried up to the ward.

It didn't matter that she knew this was inevitable for Grace. It didn't matter that the doctors, family and nurses had already had discussions about future plans for Grace's care.

Her frail little body couldn't go through another round of surgery—or chemotherapy or radiotherapy. Her body had already taken all it could.

The best they could do for now was to keep her comfortable.

She pulled up the test results and her heart plunged when she saw them. Nothing was good. The blood results and ultrasound could only mean one thing. She read the notes that her registrar had written, the record of pain relief and a few further comments by one of the other consultants involved in her care and called in tonight.

There was nothing to disagree with. She would have done exactly the same things that they had done.

Grace's mum, dad and brother were sitting at her bedside, along with one of the other paediatric consultants involved in her care.

Jessica stood in the doorway for a second, trying to collect herself. She was trying to keep her professional face in place and doing her best not to cry.

Grace's mum looked up and rushed over, enveloping her in a huge, crushing hug. 'Oh, thank you for coming up to see her. I knew you'd come.'

This was breaking Jessica's heart. She had still had a tiny little glimmer of hope in her eyes—as if at any moment one of the doctors would suggest something different—something completely out of the blue that no one had thought of. But it just wasn't possible.

If there was any surgery in the world Jess could do right now to save this little girl she wouldn't hesitate. But it just wasn't to be.

Her eyes met Grace's dad's. They were strong, resolute. Resigned to their fate but determined to give his little girl as much as dignity as possible. He gave her the tiniest nod, but didn't move from his place, holding his little girl's hand.

Jess moved into the room and sat down in a chair in the corner. The lights in the room were dimmed and Grace's little chest was barely moving up and down.

Her heart was breaking. She was finding it difficult to think straight. The tension in the room was palpable. They all knew what was about to happen.

Parkhill was a children's hospital and the sad fact of life was that children did die. But it wasn't a common occurrence. None of the staff here were used to it. None of them wanted to be.

Every child's death impacted on every member of staff that worked here.

She felt a hand on her shoulder. Pauline. 'Sorry, Jess, but I need you in ITU for the baby.'

She nodded and stood up. She still had a job to do, no matter how difficult things were right now.

She walked over to the bed and stroked Grace's hair. There was a horrible pressing feeling in her stomach. She honestly couldn't do anything more for Grace, and there was a baby in ITU who needed her now.

But she couldn't just walk out of here and say nothing. This might be the last time she saw this little girl alive.

Then it came to her, the poem that she and Grace had made up one day Grace had decided she wanted to be a horse rider. It had been a wonderful daydreaming session, when Grace had decided the name and colour of her horse, where it would be stabled and how famous it would become.

Jessica bent down and whispered in her ear, 'Riding

across the fields, the wind is in your hair, holding onto Cupid's reins, as if you don't have a care. Racing through the grass, and tearing round the bend, all on a magical mission, to reach the rainbow's end.'

She felt tears forming in her eyes. In Grace's daydream that day she'd reached the end of the rainbow and found the mythical pot of gold. If only something like that came true.

She took one final look. One glimpse of the family that was about to be changed forever.

The walls were closing in around her. Suffocating her. She gave the family one final smile and left, her feet carrying her swiftly down the corridor before she unravelled any further.

Her phone beeped. Again.

She pulled it out of her pocket. *Drew and I are picking you up at nine a.m. to make sure you actually leave.*

She smiled. She was exhausted, both physically and mentally. The baby she'd performed surgery on had needed constant review throughout the night. It had been touch and go for a while. But finally, around six a.m., the little mite had seemed to turn a corner.

She rubbed her eyes. What time was it now? She looked around for the nearest window. Was it even daylight yet? Dark winter mornings were notorious in these parts. It was frequently still dark in the morning when kids were walking to school.

There was a smudge in the background of the window. The first few edges of a rising sun. She dug in the pocket of her scrub trousers to find her watch. Just before eight a.m. A feeling of dread crept over her. She knew where she had to go next.

Almost as if someone was reading her mind, the phone

next to her started to ring. One ring tone instead of two. An internal call.

Pauline picked up the phone swiftly. 'ITU Sister Jones. Yes, yes. I see. I'm really sorry.' Her eyes skittered towards Jessica, who felt her stomach tighten. 'I'll let her know. Have they? Okay, thanks for that.' She replaced the receiver and turned to face Jess, her face grave.

Jessica felt sobs rise up in her chest. Pauline's arm quickly came round her shoulders. 'Jess, it's been a big night. You were in surgery for hours, then with Grace's admission and the time you've had to spend in here…' Her voice tailed off.

'I should go back down. Back down and see the family.'

Pauline shook her head. 'They've gone home. Grace's brother was exhausted and Grace's parents decided they had to go home. They'll come back later today to make arrangements. John Carson, the other consultant, is meeting them then.'

It made sense. They would be exhausted. It would have been the worst night of their life. And John Carson had been sitting with them last night. He knew them inside out and had been involved in Grace's care from diagnosis.

Pauline placed both her hands on Jess's shoulder. 'Go home, Jess. That's what you need to do.' She glanced at the phone that was sitting on the desk. 'Go home with Drew and Callum. It's the best thing you could do right now. It's what you need right now.'

She nodded. She didn't even need to say the words.

This had probably been the second-hardest night of her life.

She'd felt herself unravel at some points. Felt as close to breaking point as she'd ever been. The only glimmer on the horizon had been the one in her heart.

Three years was a long time to nurse a broken heart. To go home to an empty house. To feel as if there wasn't much reason to get up in the morning. To wonder if anyone would miss you if you were gone.

Thank goodness she'd met Callum again. With his come-to-bed eyes and his sexy smile. The one that could stay in her thoughts for hours.

That tiny little black cloud that had still been hanging over her head needed to be banished forever. It was time to stop avoiding the subject and let him know why she found some things so hard.

She knew in her heart that he would understand. That he would support her. And that was all she could ever want. Spending time with Callum and Drew had become the most precious thing in the world to her. Something she didn't want to live without.

She gave Pauline a hug. 'Tell John I'll be available if he needs me.' She walked down the corridor and into the changing rooms. She didn't want to wait a minute longer.

If there was one thing she'd learned it was that life was too short. Life was for living.

There were only two faces in the world she wanted to see right now. And they both had a place in her heart.

Callum glanced at the clock. Two minutes to nine. Just as well this wasn't a school day. His fingers were tapping nervously on the steering wheel.

He couldn't work out why he was on edge. He just knew he was.

It was time. It was make or break.

He wanted this relationship to work. He wanted it to move on. But for that to happen there needed to be honesty between them.

He needed to know.

He needed to know what had happened in Jessica's life.

Drew had spent most of the night talking about Jessica. The glow in his eyes had told Callum everything he needed to know. His little boy had fallen just as hard as he had.

He watched the door of the hospital, willing Jess to appear, and finally she did.

She looked shattered. She obviously hadn't slept a wink last night.

Her coat was barely pulled around her shoulders and he could see her eyes searching the car park.

He gave the horn a beep and waved to her. Her face lit up and she hurried over. He expected her to jump straight in but she didn't. Instead, she opened the rear door, gave Drew a quick hug and dropped a kiss on top of his head.

'We've been waiting for you,' Drew said solemnly.

'And you've no idea how happy I am to see you,' she answered. Callum turned, watching as she enveloped Drew in another quick hug. She looked truly happy to see him—to see them both. He didn't know whether to leap for joy or let that little cautionary voice in his mind rear its ugly head.

She closed the rear door and opened the front passenger door, climbing in and sinking into the seat next to him.

'Hard night?' He could see the furrows in her brow, etching deep lines into her normally smooth forehead.

She gave a little sigh and a shake of her head, glancing across her shoulder at Drew. 'More than you can ever know.'

The words hung in the air between them. He could tell there was so much she wanted to say—but couldn't because Drew was in the car.

His little hand stretched over and touched Jessica's shoulder. 'Jess, are we going home now? Are you going to watch my movie with me? I've got my duvet on the couch for us. We can snuggle up.'

A wide smile spread across her face. Relief. Relief at the thought of getting away from the struggles of the hospital and spending the day with them. Stress free.

He felt his stomach clench a little more. Was he wrong to do this today? To ask her about her past and to put her on the spot about their future?

Part of him wanted to leave it, to stay in this happy limbo they were in. It felt like a safe place. But deep down he didn't want a safe place. He wanted much more. He wanted to be able to shout from the rooftops that he and Jessica were together. He wanted to make plans for a future for the three of them together, as a family.

He wanted to wake up every morning with Jessica by his side.

He wanted to be there to support her through whatever had happened.

He wanted to be a family.

And the only way to do that was to get rid of the elephant in the room.

He pulled out into the Glasgow traffic and started along the street. It was after nine so the morning rush was dying down. 'Want to go somewhere for breakfast before we get home?'

She shook her head. 'A duvet day with a film sounds perfect. I don't want to delay that for a second.' Her stomach gave a growl. 'But I'm starving. Do you have any bacon at home?'

'Daddy! Give her the chocolate we bought her!' Drew's voice echoed through the car. 'We bought you your favourite, Jess.'

Callum smiled and reached across her, opening the

glove box and pulling out the orange-flavoured chocolate. It had been her favourite years ago, and he expected it still was. He put the chocolate in her lap. 'That will keep you going until we get home. We stopped to pick it up on the way here.'

Silence. Absolute silence in the car.

He knew instantly that something was wrong.

Thank goodness Jess was sitting down because the colour drained instantly from her face and she looked as if she might pass out.

She swayed—even though she was sitting in the seat.

They were heading through the busiest part of town. There was nowhere to pull over and the traffic was a little heavier here so he needed to keep his eyes on the road.

'Jess? Jess? What's wrong?'

Was she sick? Maybe it was nothing. Maybe she was feeling faint because she'd been on her feet all night and hadn't had anything to eat. That would be just like Jess. Too busy to sit down for a few minutes and think of herself.

But he had the strangest feeling he wasn't even close.

'Stop the car.' Her voice was quiet, almost a whisper.

'What?'

'Stop the car!' This time she was definite.

He could see the flare of panic in her eyes. She absolutely meant it.

His head flicked from side to side, trying to see if there was anywhere to stop in the midst of the queued traffic. 'I can't, Jess. There's nowhere to go. You'll need to wait. What's wrong? Do you feel sick?'

'I'll get out here.' She flung open the door and jumped out of the car. Her bag was still sitting in the footwell of the car.

Callum was stunned. What on earth had just happened?

'Daddy? Where's Jess gone?'

'I don't know, Drew.' He looked frantically up and down the street in the direction she was walking, trying to find somewhere to pull over.

What on earth had gone wrong?

This was supposed to be a good day. How on earth could a chocolate bar cause a reaction like that?

All the nudging doubts he'd had about putting Jess on the spot vanished. Drew looked near to tears, sitting in the back of the car hugging his toy to his chest.

Something had upset Jess but she, in turn, had upset his son.

He couldn't have that. He couldn't have that at all.

This was crazy. And he couldn't let it go on a moment longer.

He'd been wrong. He'd been wrong not to sit her down and ask her right away what was going on in her life.

He'd been blindsided by her. She brought back a whole host of good memories and feelings. He loved being around her. She was beautiful—inside and out. He could see that. Even in the times she tried to hide it away.

He wanted things to work out between them.

His heart twisted as he watched the forlorn figure scurrying down the street and a whole new sensation swept over him.

He loved her. He loved Jess.

Just like he had years before.

Only this was different. This was a grown-up kind of love.

One that realised that nobody was perfect and everyone had history. And in his heart he knew she felt the same way—about him and about Drew.

So what on earth had gone wrong? He had no idea what had just happened.

But the one thing he knew for sure was that he needed to find out.

She was going to be sick. She was going to be sick everywhere.

She couldn't think or see straight.

Her hand reached out and grasped the wall, trying to steady herself.

A woman stared at her on the way past. She looked horrified. Did she think Jess was drunk at nine in the morning? Because that's the way she felt right now.

Her hand was gripping something tightly, her knuckles blanched white, her fingers growing numb.

Her hand was shaking. No, her whole body was shaking.

She leaned over and retched, trying to ignore the people walking past and looking at her in horror.

Unravelling.

She'd felt like that earlier on—in the middle of the night when she'd known Grace was about to die. She'd felt as if she hadn't had the strength to be there, hadn't had the strength to do the job she was supposed to be doing.

And now this.

Her whole world had just tilted on its axis.

In an instant. In a flash.

She stared at her hand, willing her fingers to open.

All this over a bar of orange-flavoured chocolate.

She heard the thud of feet running along the pavement. Felt a hand on her back. 'Jess. What is it? What's wrong?'

She could hear it all. The confusion in his voice. The concern.

She should have told him. She should have told him before.

Then he would have looked at her in pity and walked away. Then she wouldn't have dropped the walls around her heart and let him and his son in. Then she would have stayed safe. Locked in her own fortress where nothing could penetrate her heart and leave her exposed to hurt again.

She should have told him before.

But that would have made it all real.

Not the fact that it had happened. Not the fact that her husband and son had died. But the fact that she was telling him—telling him, as she prepared to move on with her life.

Because up until this point she hadn't really told anyone—she hadn't needed to. All her work colleagues already knew and bad news travelled fast, following you like a billowing black cloud. She was used to people whispering behind her then averting their eyes when caught.

Maybe this was what she deserved. Why should she get a chance at a happy ever after with a new family? Maybe she didn't deserve it.

All the doubts and feelings of guilt were rearing their ugly heads. How could she forget about her husband and son? How dared she?

Callum looked utterly confused. He bent down and picked up the bar of chocolate. 'You're retching over this?'

The look on his face said it all. He was at breaking point. She'd known for the last few weeks that Callum was holding back—stopping himself from saying what he wanted to.

She looked at the bar of chocolate in his hand. It must seem so pathetic, but it didn't feel that way to her.

'You don't understand—'

'You're right. I don't.' His voice was soft and he stepped closer to her, touching the side of her cheek. 'So tell me, Jess.' He glanced over at his car parked at the side of the road, where he'd left Drew on his own.

She couldn't bear to look. Couldn't bear to look at the little boy who'd won a place in her heart. Not while she felt so guilty. Frustration was building in her chest. She wanted to say so much but just couldn't find the words. They all seemed to get jammed in her throat. 'I lost them. I lost them this way.' She pointed to the bar of chocolate in his hand.

'Lost who? What way?' He looked totally confused. 'Jess, I want to understand. Really, I do. But I can't until you tell me. It's time, Jess. It's time there were no secrets between us.'

Her legs wobbled underneath her. They couldn't take her weight any more and she felt herself crumple. 'My husband. My son.' Sobs racked her body. The words were out. They were finally out there. For everyone in the world to hear. For Callum to hear.

'What?'

She couldn't stop. Now the tears had started they wouldn't stop.

She felt his strong arms on her shoulders. 'What do you mean, you lost your husband and son?'

He was crouching now, on the ground beside her. She looked up into his green eyes. He was totally thrown by all this. Probably knocked sideways.

Her voice was trembling. 'My husband Daniel and son Lewis were killed in a road accident.'

His shock was palpable. 'What? When?'

'Three years ago.' Her shoulders were shaking now.

He shook his head, his disbelief apparent. 'Why didn't

you tell me, Jess? Why didn't you tell me something like that?'

She was panicking now. People in the street were staring at them. 'I couldn't find the words. I didn't know how to tell you. I didn't know what to say.' Her breathing felt erratic, every breath a struggle. Her voice dropped, her eyes looking towards the horizon. 'It never felt the right time.'

Callum shook his head. 'How could you not tell me something as important as this?'

'How could you not tell me about your son?' The words shot out instantly. In blind panic.

He reeled back, looking as if he'd been stung.

She saw him take a deep breath and get to his feet, reaching over, putting his hands under her arms and pulling her up with him. He looked about him. 'This isn't something to discuss in the street, Jessica.'

People were staring. People had stopped what they were doing.

She looked over at the car. Drew's little face was pressed up against the window. He looked frantic and her heart went out to him. He had no idea what was happening. Just that something was wrong.

If she felt upset and confused, how must he feel?

The chocolate bar was on the ground at her feet. Tears welled in her eyes instantly. 'I can't do this,' she whispered.

'Can't do what?'

She put her hands out. 'This. Us.' She looked over at the car. 'Drew.'

She could see sadness mounting in Callum's eyes. He didn't understand. He didn't understand this wasn't about him and Drew. This was all about her.

She shook her head. 'You don't get it. You don't understand. Daniel and Lewis—they stopped to buy me my favourite bar of chocolate the night they died. They stopped at a shop just round the corner from our house.'

Her voice was breaking, trembling as she remembered, the memories rushing up so clearly and strongly, as if it had just happened a few hours ago. 'He sent me a text.' She let out a huge gasp of air. 'Daniel sent me a text saying they'd be five minutes late because they'd stopped to buy me chocolate.' She shook her head.

'The next thing I knew the sister from A and E came to find me. I was standing outside the hospital, waiting for them, wondering what was taking so long. She'd been phoned by Ambulance Control—the crew had radioed in once they knew who they were dealing with.'

Callum hadn't moved. He was still standing over her, his face unreadable. She must seem like a crazy woman, but everything seemed so clear in her head.

'What did she tell you?' His voice sounded a little wobbly too.

She looked up at him. She'd never seen his green eyes so full of conflict. She couldn't imagine how he must feel about all this. She'd never wanted to hurt him.

She'd never wanted to hurt Drew.

She took a deep breath, every part of the experience as painful now as it had been then. 'She told me Daniel had been taken to Glasgow Cross and Lewis was coming to Parkhill.' She looked off into the distance. It seemed easier to speak when she didn't have to look at him. 'That was normal after a RTA. The kids always came to us.'

'And then?'

He reached out and touched her hand, giving it a squeeze, willing her to have the strength to carry on. She could see tenderness written all over his face. She could almost reach out and touch the hurt he felt for her.

She'd been terrified to tell him. Terrified he would misunderstand.

She'd been right.

She looked at him. The tears were gone now. This was the worst part. This was the part that almost killed her.

'It was too late for them both. They were both dead on arrival. I never got to say goodbye, Callum. To my husband or my son.'

There was something so final about those words. So final, because she was saying them out loud. Her voice continued automatically—because she needed to get it all out. She'd held it in for so long. She'd wanted to tell him, but now it felt as if someone had released the dam and it had to all rush out.

'None of the staff knew what to do when Lewis arrived. It's so different when it's one of your own. Somebody else's child is just as important but you have an emotional detachment that allows you to do the job, not to think about the hopes, dreams and fears of that little person in front of you. And to a certain extent you need that. But when it's one of your own...' She met his gaze. 'The child of a friend, colleague or loved one. It's like the world stops turning. You can't function any more, autopilot just doesn't work.'

She wanted him to understand.

She needed him to understand. Because it related to why she couldn't find the words to tell him.

And he must understand it a little. He'd been the parent with the sick child.

How could she have performed surgery on Drew if she'd known him like she did now? How could she have got through that op?

He was watching her steadily. She could see the rise and fall of his chest. His words were hoarse. It was almost as if he was seeing the whole picture in his head. Feeling her pain. 'They didn't resuscitate?'

She shook her head. 'There was no point.' She couldn't hide the forlorn tone in her voice. 'I think both of them probably died at the scene. It was strange—I always thought if something like that happened I wouldn't be able to do that. That I would resuscitate for hours and hours, no matter how hopeless. But it was totally different. I didn't want my son disturbed. I didn't want people to touch him when I already knew it was pointless. I just wanted to hold him.'

She wrapped her arms around herself at the memory of it. 'Someone phoned Pauline and she came down from ITU. I held Lewis for hours. And Pauline held me.'

There was silence between them. She didn't need him to say anything—she didn't want him to say anything.

She couldn't imagine how he must be feeling.

Well, she could, but only in part.

She remembered exactly how she'd felt when she'd first heard about Drew. It had been a total bolt out of the blue. And this was much worse than that.

Callum looked deep in thought—as if a hundred different things were spinning through his mind at once.

He couldn't stop looking at his car, where Drew was. She wished she could read his mind. Know what he was thinking. He dug his hands deep into his pockets. 'So, what's changed, Jessica? You may not have told me this before but it was still there. Still circling in your head every day.'

She felt a single tear slip down her cheek. It was so hard to put this into words. She looked at the little face staring out of the car window towards her and it made her heart ache. She so wanted to hold him. She so wanted to take him in her arms and give him comfort. Because she loved him. She loved that little boy—just as much as she loved his father.

Callum's face looked more than confused—he looked numb. As if he was trying to work out where his place in all this was. She'd done this to him. It had been her.

It was all her fault.

She was hurting people that she loved. Again.

'You don't get it.'

'No, Jess. I don't get it.' He reached over and pulled her towards him. For a second they stood in the street, their heads bowed, their foreheads touching.

If she could, she would stay this way forever. With Callum holding her as if he could take all her cares and worries away.

Because this was killing her. She hated herself right now. She hated hurting those that she loved.

'It was my fault, Callum. Don't you see? It was my fault that Daniel and Lewis died. If they hadn't gone to get me that chocolate, they wouldn't have been on the road at that time. They wouldn't have had that accident.' She reached over and grabbed his hand from his pocket. 'Just like you did today. You and Drew.' She shook her head as fiercely as she could. 'I can't have that. I can't have that on my conscience. Something happening to the people I love because of me.'

He lifted his head from hers and reached up and touched her cheek. His hand was freezing. They'd been standing out in the cold for far too long. Trying to dissect their lives in the middle of the street.

She knew this was ridiculous. Everything about it was so wrong.

She'd been hurt before. She was desperate.

How could this compare to losing her husband and son? It couldn't. And yet it was hurting every bit as much.

She'd started down that road. The one that was going to lead her to a new life. She'd started to feel again.

She'd started to trust.

She'd started to love.

And there would never be anyone as perfect for her as Callum and Drew. She could never feel as much as she did now.

And it was disintegrating all around her. Slipping through her fingers like grains of sand.

Callum shifted on his feet. He looked over towards the car again and something must have clicked in his head.

'What age was Lewis, Jessica?' His voice was sharp, abrupt.

'He was two. He was just two.' She was confused. It was a natural question. But it didn't seem quite right.

His eyes darted to the car. 'So he'd have been the same age as Drew is now?' There was something in the way he said it. As if he was having a different conversation from her.

Her heart squeezed. The whole host of thoughts that she'd had at first about Drew came flooding into her mind. The comparisons with her own son, which had all faded as the weeks had progressed and she'd got to know this other little boy.

'Yes. Yes, he would.' Why was her voice shaking? Why did she feel as if she'd just sealed their fate?

'Oh, Jess.'

It was the little gasp in his voice. The way the words came out. As if his world had just crumbled in on itself.

He shook his head, very slowly. Were those tears in his eyes?

His voice was trembling. 'This was never about us, was it, Jess? This was never about me and Drew. This was about you—looking for a replacement family.'

'What? No.' She shook her head. 'Not at all.'

But Callum had switched off. It was almost as if he'd detached himself. 'You don't love me and Drew, Jess. You love the *idea* of us.' He was shaking his head again. 'I should have known.'

She couldn't believe this. She couldn't believe his brain was thinking this way. But she was so undone she couldn't think straight.

'I need you to love me, Jess. *Me.* And I need you to love Drew. For who *he* is. Not just the thought of a replacement for your own little boy. My little boy's already had a mother who walked away from him. I can't expose him to that again. I need you to love Drew with your whole heart. Love every inch of him—and every inch of me.' He was shaking his head again. 'You've broken my heart, Jess—truly you have.'

'But I do love you, Callum. I do. And I love Drew too.' Even as she said the words they sounded desperate. Like the last-ditch attempt to save something that was already slipping through her fingers.

This was over. This was finished.

It didn't matter that she'd been the one telling him she couldn't do this any more.

Part of her had still wanted him to tell her they could make it. That they could still have a chance of something.

But it wasn't to be. This was all too much for him. He hadn't signed up for this. That much was evident.

Her heart was breaking all over again.

She couldn't look at him. It was just too hard.

'We've both made a mistake here, Jess. I wanted you to

be something that you just weren't ready to be. And you wanted us to replace something that you've lost.' He bit his lip. She'd never seen him look so shattered. So resigned to their fate. 'Neither of us can do that.'

His voice was tired. 'Get in the car and I'll drop you home. It seems we both have a lot to think about.' He took a deep breath and touched her cheek one more time. 'I'm sorry about your husband and son, Jess. I really am. I'm sorry that things just haven't worked out for us.' He pointed over his shoulder. 'But right now I have to put the needs of my son first.'

He shifted slightly, blocking her view of the car. 'I want you to say something—anything—to placate Drew until we drop you off. Can you do that for me and for Drew?'

'Of course,' she whispered. 'I would never do anything to hurt Drew.'

'Too late,' he whispered as he turned towards the car and walked away.

CHAPTER TWELVE

THE DOOR OPENED and Callum jumped about a foot in the air. Drew and his little friend walked through the door, football boots in hand.

'You're back already?' He rubbed his eyes. Hadn't he just sat down?

He couldn't believe it was that time already. Julie and Blair walked into the room behind the boys and Julie folded her arms across her chest.

'Boys, go up to Drew's room for ten minutes and play. I want to talk to Drew's dad.'

Blair gave a shake of his head as he crossed the room. 'Why don't I just start running the bath and put them both in it?' He glanced at Callum on his way past. 'You're in for it, mate.'

Callum straightened up instantly. Julie and Blair were two of his closest friends. He'd never had any problems with either of them. They'd been fabulous, helping him with Drew. But even though they had a good relationship, Callum knew that Julie wasn't a woman to be messed with.

He stood up and walked towards her. 'Is something wrong?'

She waited a second, tilting her head to listen for the sound of the boys' footsteps going up the stairs and out of earshot.

'You…' She pushed her sharp finger into the middle of his chest. 'You're what's wrong. Kitchen. Now.' She turned on her heel and walked through to his kitchen.

'Ouch.' Callum rubbed the middle of his chest and started to follow her. He had a sinking feeling Blair had known exactly what he was doing when he disappeared with the boys.

Julie knew her way around the house. The coffee machine—which was only used on special occasions—was sitting on the counter and filled with water. She switched it on and turned to face him, folding her arms across her chest again.

'Right. Spill.'

Callum sat down on one of the breakfast bar stools. 'Spill what?'

She threw her hands up. 'You're the one sitting in a dark living room, staring at Christmas-tree lights. Tell me, how long were you there for? One hour? Two?'

Yeah, the Christmas-tree lights. The hotch-potch of decorations, along with the new silver and red ones that Drew and Jessica had picked out at the garden centre. Another reminder of Jessica. Along with the picture of the three of them Drew had drawn at school that was currently stuck to the fridge. Or the photo Drew had put on his bedside cabinet of him sitting on Jessica's knee at the winter wonderland.

Or the fact she was haunting his dreams. Every. Single. Night.

Julie was waiting. Waiting with her steely glare for an answer.

'I've had a hard few days at work. It's been chaos.'

'Pull the other one, Callum, it's got bells on.' She hadn't

moved. The coffee machine was starting to bubble next to her.

'I don't know what you mean.'

She shook her head and started clattering around, pulling cups from cupboards and thumping them down on his worktop. 'I'm the one who's been in the company of your little boy. Your little boy who's missing Jess. She's all he'll talk about, Callum—well, that and some promise Santa made him.'

'Drew said something?'

She nodded as she put the coffee in the machine. 'Oh, Drew said a whole lot. All about some fight and how he wanted to see Jess and you won't let him.'

Callum put his elbows on the worktop and his head in his hands. 'It's difficult, Julie. I found out something about Jessica—and it's made me rethink everything.' He shook his head. 'But Drew's hardly said a thing. He's asked a few times if she's coming round, but that's it.'

Julie pulled the chair out on the other side of the breakfast bar and sat down directly opposite him. She counted off on her fingers, 'Apparently on Monday he asked if she would be coming for dinner, on Tuesday he asked if she could go to the pictures with you both. On Wednesday he asked if she would be here after his Christmas party.' She let out a sigh. 'Whether you like it or not, Callum, this is affecting your little boy.' Her face was deadly serious. 'What did you find out?'

He hesitated. He hadn't spoken to anyone about this. It felt like a betrayal. His stomach was churning at the thought of Drew remembering every day that he'd asked after Jess. Protecting him seemed more important than ever. 'She wasn't truthful with me. She didn't tell me something really important.'

'Like you didn't tell her about Drew until you had to?'

He cringed. It felt like a low blow. And it was just what Jess had said. But from Julie's mouth it had been a lot more sarcastic. He nodded and held up his hands. 'I know, I know, but that was different.'

'Different how?'

Blair hadn't been kidding. He was in trouble.

He shook his head and waved his hands. 'Her husband and son died in a car crash three years ago. She didn't mention them at all. She just told me things hadn't worked out for her.'

Julie's hand had shot up to her mouth. He could see her take a deep breath. 'So, how did you find out if she didn't tell you?'

Trust Julie to cut straight to the chase. 'Well, she did tell me. But it was out of the blue. After she reacted badly to something and said she couldn't do this any more.'

Julie screwed up her face. 'Are you trying to talk in riddles?'

'I told you—it's complicated.'

There came the sound of shouts and splashes from upstairs. She shrugged. 'I've got time.'

Drew felt wary. The things that had been circulating through his brain for the last few days were all on the tip of his tongue. The things that had given him a pounding headache and kept him awake every night jumbled around in his head.

'It was all over a chocolate bar.'

'What?'

He couldn't keep his exasperation in check. He stood up, almost knocking his stool over, walking over to the counter and pushing some pods into the machine and propping the cups underneath.

Julie stayed silent. It must be killing her, not breaking the silence. But he knew exactly why she was doing it. She was forcing him to say all this out loud.

He placed the coffees on the breakfast bar and sat down again. 'I bought Jessica her favourite chocolate bar and I gave her it when we picked her up. After a few minutes she freaked out and jumped out of the car before I even had a chance to pull over. She said she couldn't do it. She couldn't have a relationship with me and Drew.'

Julie raised her eyebrow. 'Over a chocolate bar?'

Total disbelief was in her voice. She was waiting for the rest.

Callum sucked in a deep breath. 'Apparently her husband and son had stopped to buy her chocolate the night they had the accident. If they hadn't...' His voice tailed off.

'If they hadn't—what?'

'If they hadn't stopped she thinks they wouldn't have been killed. They wouldn't have been on that part of the road at that time of night. She thinks the accident was her fault.'

Julie sat for a few moments, biting her lip. She looked up from the coffee cup she had continued to stir. 'No. She doesn't.'

'What?' It was not what he'd expected her to say.

Julie sighed. 'Oh, Callum. This is much bigger than I ever expected. Tell me what else she said.'

He racked his brain. Did he really want to share everything Jessica had said? He'd been mulling over this for days. Going over and over things in his head. Maybe it would be useful to get another perspective.

He looked at the picture pinned to the fridge. 'It's all about Drew, Julie. This all comes down to Drew.'

'Why do you think that?'

'Her little boy—her son was the same age as Drew. If he'd lived he would be five too.' This was the hardest part. The part he hated most. 'She's looking for a replacement, Julie. She's looking for a replacement for her son—and maybe her husband.'

Julie looked shocked. She stood up sharply. 'Tell me everything. Did she say anything else to you that day? Anything at all?'

He winced. 'She told me that she loved me. She loved me and Drew and she couldn't put us in the same position her family were in. She didn't want to hurt us.'

'She told you she loved you?' Julie's voice rose.

He nodded and stared down at his coffee. He couldn't even bear to take a sip.

'She told you she loved you?' This time she was practically shouting.

'Yes. But it doesn't make a difference. She didn't mean it. It's not us that she loves. It's just the idea of us.'

Julie walked straight over to him, barely inches from his face. She looked furious. 'And what did you do then, Callum? What did you do when she told you that she loved you both?'

A horrible, cold sensation swept over his skin. Every hair on his arms stood on end. His actions had seemed perfectly reasonable at the time. He'd been so upset for her. And so upset for them too. He didn't want to be replacement for what Jess had lost. He wanted Jess to love him and Drew the way that they loved her—with their whole hearts.

'I told her to get in the car and say something to placate Drew. I told her I'd drop her off.'

'Oh, Callum.' Julie turned away. She put her arms up to her face and stood still for a few moments.

'What? I have to protect my son, Julie. Drew's the most

important thing in the world to me. I won't let anyone hurt him. Not even her.' The words came spilling out. Why did he feel as if he had to defend himself?

'Drew's been through all this before. He had a mother who treated him as if he wasn't good enough. Who walked away from him. How can I put my wee boy through something like that again?' He shook his head. 'I can't. I won't.'

Julie touched his arm. 'But Jessica isn't Kirsten, Callum. Not by a long shot. From all the stuff that you've told me about her, they couldn't compare. Surely you know that?' Her voice was wavering.

And his heart started to pound in his chest. He knew what she was saying was true. He had just needed someone else to say it out loud for him. Jess was nothing like Kirsten. He knew in his heart of hearts that Jessica would never have walked out on her son. A thought like that would never even have occurred to Jess. She was made in a totally different way.

Julie spun back round and there were tears in her eyes. She pointed to the stool. 'Sit down.'

It was *that* voice again. Do or die.

He sat down numbly. Julie should be on his side. So why did he feel as if she wasn't?

'Callum Kennedy, you've been my friend for four years. You know I love you. But sometimes you are a complete git.'

'What?'

'When you're wrong, Callum, you're *so* wrong it's scary.'

He was starting to feel sick now. Sick to his stomach. She had that horrible female intuition thing, didn't she?

'What do you mean?'

She started pacing around the kitchen, her arms flailing

around her. 'This wasn't about a bar of chocolate, Callum. This was *never* about a bar of chocolate. This was about a woman learning to let go and love again. She's scared, Callum—she's terrified. And with your reaction—frankly—who can blame her?'

'What do you mean, she's scared?'

'You and Drew—you're not a replacement family for her.' Julie looked at him in disgust. 'You could *never* replace her family, Callum.' She pressed her hand to her chest. 'They will always be with her—in here—forever. This is something totally different. Don't you see?'

He was starting to feel panicked. The last sensation in the world he ever felt. Not even in the middle of a fraught rescue. But he was feeling it now. His mouth felt bone dry. The lump in his throat was as big as a tennis ball. He shook his head. 'No. I don't see. Tell me.'

Julie reached her hands across the breakfast bar and clasped his. She looked at the drawing on the fridge. 'Callum, we both know how your son feels about Jessica. It's written all over his face. But how do *you* feel about her?' She pointed her finger to his chest again, this time a lot more gently. 'How do you feel in here?'

The million-dollar question. The thing that kept his stomach constantly churning because no matter what he did the feeling wouldn't go away. The words he didn't want to say out loud. Because then he would have to admit to a whole host of things.

Her pointed finger felt like a laser burning a hole straight through to his heart.

He looked up. 'I love her.' He could feel his voice breaking. But he didn't want it to. He took a deep breath and tried again. 'I love her, Julie.' This time the words were stronger—more determined.

It felt like a weight had been lifted off his shoulders. The acknowledgement of saying the words out loud. Admitting to himself and his friend how he felt.

Julie sagged back down into the stool opposite him. She put her elbow on the breakfast bar and put her head on her hand. 'Then what you going to do about it, dummy?'

CHAPTER THIRTEEN

THE CANDLES FLICKERED around her.

They were beautiful, spilling yellow and orange tones along the pale cream walls in her house.

The Christmas decorations had been closing in around her. A permanent reminder of another Christmas alone. Sitting in the kitchen was different. The orange and pomegranate spice of the candles was soothing. She'd been trying some deep-breathing exercises. Anything to try and take her thoughts away from the constants on her mind.

Callum and Drew.

The door rattled then the doorbell started ringing and didn't stop.

'Jess? Jess, are you in?' The door rattled again.

Her heart started to race instantly. She recognised the voice. She'd recognise it anywhere. Something must be wrong. Drew. Something must be wrong with Drew.

She ran down the hall and yanked the door open. 'What is it? Is it Drew? Has something happened?'

Callum was stuck with his hand still in mid-air—frozen to the spot. It was almost as if he hadn't expected her to answer.

She looked down at the car parked at the side of the road. Drew wasn't in it. His car seat was empty.

Callum shook his head. 'No. No, it's not Drew. He's fine.' Then he paused. 'Well, actually, he's not fine.'

'What is it?' Her stomach was clenched. Was he in hospital? Had there been an accident?

Callum stepped forward, closing the gap between them. She could smell him. His distinctive aftershave was immediately invading her senses, bringing a whole host of memories. Bringing a whole heap of regrets.

He reached up and touched her cheek. 'He misses you. *We* miss you. That's what's wrong with Drew…' He paused. 'And with me.'

It was the last thing she'd expected to hear. She couldn't breathe. All her muscles contracted.

He put his hand on her shoulder. 'Jess, please. Can we talk?'

Her brain started to race. She was confused. She'd thought he hated her. The last time she'd seen him she hadn't been able to read the look on his face. Had it been confusion? Or resignation?

She felt overwhelming relief. Drew was fine. There hadn't been an accident. She couldn't help the way her brain worked. But, then, any parent would be the same— their first thought in a moment of panic would be for their child.

Parent. The word that had popped straight into her mind.

Her reactions to Drew were those of a parent. And her thoughts about Callum? She loved him so much it hurt to even be in the same space as him.

So, if this wasn't about Drew, why was Callum here?

She tried to focus. The messages between her brain and her mouth were getting muddled. There was so much jumbling around in there.

'Jess, can I come in?'

Her feet moved backwards automatically, creating space for him to come through.

He walked into the hall and glanced in the direction of the darkened living room. He took her hand and led her inside, bending down to switch on the lights of her Christmas tree.

Christmas lights. The ones she'd been trying to avoid. The new twinkling red berries and silver stars lit up the room. They had been her fresh start. But the chance to build new memories had been destroyed. All the tiny little hopes that had started to form. All the baby steps towards some new memories—like buying the new decorations with Drew—had been wiped out.

She was trying hard to focus. Trying to make sense of it all. Part of her was angry. This was the man she'd hoped for a future with. She might not have been truthful with him, but his reaction had still hurt.

'What are you doing here, Callum?' The tone of her words revealed the exhaustion she was feeling. Every bone in her body ached. She hadn't slept for days. She couldn't eat. The truth was she just couldn't go on like this.

His hands went to her waist and she gasped. His fingers were icy cold. It was only then she realised he wasn't wearing gloves or a jacket. Why on earth was he out on a freezing night like this with no jacket? Had he been in that much of a rush?

'I came here to apologise.' His voice was deep and husky. Was he being sincere? 'I came here to apologise for how I reacted the other day when you told me about your husband and son. I'm not proud of myself, Jess. I didn't understand.'

He was apologising. She felt shocked. Then she noticed

the lines around his eyes and on his forehead. It was like a mirror image of her own face. Maybe Callum had had problems sleeping too. She shook her head. 'How could you understand? I would never wish something like that on you.'

'No. That's not what I meant.' He was babbling. 'Of course I don't know what it's like to lose a wife and child. But I didn't understand how you were feeling about us. Us—me and Drew. I got confused. I thought you were looking for a replacement. I thought you were using me and Drew as a replacement for your family.'

She pulled back. How could he think that? A million different things flew about her brain. 'But why? Why would you think that?'

Things started to drop into place. The questions. The expressions on his face. The age. This was all about Drew's age.

'Is this because Lewis and Drew would have been the same age?' For a second it felt as if someone had just dropped her back into the icy River Clyde. 'You think I would try and replace my little boy with another?'

No. It didn't even bear thinking about. How could anyone think that? She tried to keep calm. Sure, a few comparisons had swept through her brain. She'd even been a tiny bit jealous of Callum when she'd first found out about Drew. But to think she would try and do something like that?

She ran her tongue across her dry lips.

Wow. Maybe it wasn't such a leap in the dark. If the shoe had been on the other foot, might that have occurred to her? If she was the one with a child and Callum had lost his wife and child, would she wonder if he was trying to replace them?

Maybe. Just maybe. Even if it was only for a few seconds.

He pulled her closer, his chest pressing against hers. 'Jess?' He could see she was lost in her thoughts. He stared at her with his dark green eyes and she could see the sincerity on his face. 'I don't think that. I don't think that now. I was shocked. I never expected something like that had happened to you. I couldn't make sense of it in my head.'

It was easy. It was easy to feel his arms around her. It felt so good to sense him touch her skin again. But there was so much more to say. She couldn't expose her heart to this kind of hurt again. She wouldn't survive.

'Is that what you came to say?' She was trying to distance herself from all this. She could accept his apology—if that's what he wanted to offer. She could accept it, and then walk away. No matter how good it felt to be in his arms.

'No. That's not what I came to say.' He reached up and brushed her curls behind her ear. 'I came to tell you that I'm sorry. I'm sorry and I love you. Drew and I love you. I know I made a mess of this, Jess, but please don't give up on us. We want you to be part of our lives.'

'But—'

'Shh.' He put his finger against her lips then traced it over her cheekbones and eyelids. The feel of his light touch on her skin was magical. She could forget about everything else that had happened and just let this touch lull her into a false sense of security that everything would be fine.

She opened her eyes and took a deep breath.

'Don't say no. Please, don't say no, Jess. I can't be apart from you. *We* can't be apart from you.'

'But why, Callum, why now?'

'Look at me, Jess. I haven't slept in days. Neither have

you—I can tell. This…' he waved his arms in the air '…is driving me crazy. I didn't mean to walk away. I just wanted to protect Drew. I needed to know that you were there because you loved *us*, not just the idea of us.'

'But how could you ever doubt that?'

He tapped his finger on the side of his head. 'Because I wasn't thinking straight. When you told me about your husband and son, I went into defence mode—protecting my son, protecting my family.' His hand cupped the side of her face. 'But you're part of my family now, Jess. You, me and Drew. I love you. I don't want to do this without you.'

She felt herself start to shake. From one extreme to the other. Callum was looking into her eyes and telling her that he loved her. Telling her that he and Drew loved her, Jessica Rae.

She wanted to believe him. She really did.

But ten minutes ago she had been wondering just how to get through one night. And even that had seemed too much for her. Even that had been taking candles and deep breathing.

'I…I…I don't know, Callum.'

He pressed his hand to her chest. 'How do you feel? How do you feel when you see me and Drew?'

There was no doubt. No doubt for her at all. It was the one thing that was crystal clear. 'I love you. I love you both.' But even as she said the words she felt fear and she instinctively made to pull away.

Callum lowered his head so it was level with hers—so he could look straight into her eyes. 'I know you're scared. I get that now. I can deal with that. *We* can deal with that together—as a family.'

She lowered her gaze. 'But how, Callum? When I saw that bar of chocolate it brought so many memories back.

What if something happened to you and Drew? I can't go through that again.'

He gave her a smile. 'I know you're scared. But it's a big old scary world out there, Jess. You and I work in it every day. And what makes it all right is the people around us.' He took her hand and placed it on his chest. She could feel his heart beating under her palm. Thump, thump. Thump, thump.

'I can't promise you that everything will be perfect. I can't promise you that nothing will ever happen to any of us. I can't promise you that I'll never stop to buy you a bar of chocolate again. There are some things in this life we have no control over.' His other hand wound through her hair. 'What I can promise you is that I'll love you faithfully for every second that I'm here. I'll do my best to keep you and Drew safe. And if you have fears, talk to me about them. I'm here for you, Jess. I've waited thirteen years to get the woman of my dreams. I'm not about to let you escape now.'

Thirteen years. It seemed like a whole lifetime.

It had been a whole lifetime—for both of them.

'Can you give me a chance, Jessica? Can you give us a chance?'

He knew. He knew she'd been scared. He knew it had all felt too much for her and she'd needed some space.

But the love that she'd felt for Callum and his son had never faltered—not even for a second. Instead, it was growing, every single day.

'I'd like that, Callum,' she breathed. 'I'd like that very much.'

She could see the sparkle appear in his eyes. 'Then wait here.'

He turned and vanished, leaving her standing in the living room with only the red and silver twinkling tree lights.

She heard her front door open and some muffled voices then a little giggle. A little boy's giggle.

Callum appeared at the doorway with Drew standing in front of him, clutching something in a Christmas box.

'Drew!' She couldn't help herself, she rushed over and hugged him as tightly as she could. 'I've missed you. Have you been a good boy?'

Drew was bouncing on his toes. 'Watch out, Jess. You'll squash your present. I made it specially.'

She turned to Callum, shaking her head in wonder. 'But how? The car was empty. Where was he?'

It was then she noticed. Under his thick jacket and hat Drew was wearing his pyjamas and slippers. Callum wasn't the only one who'd left the house in a hurry.

Callum gave her a nod. 'I have some good friends—they helped me out, in more ways than one.'

His finger brushed her cheek again and he knelt down on one knee opposite in front of her. Drew sat on his knee and held out the box. 'This might not be the most traditional way of doing things, but it probably suits us best.' Callum smiled at his son. Drew had a huge smile plastered to his face. 'We want you to marry us, Jess, and stay with us forever. We promise to love you, for now and for always. Will you marry us, Jess?'

Drew's little hands were shaking with excitement. She reached out and took the little red box, pulling off the lid and looking inside. Her hands were trembling. A few hours ago she had been feeling helpless and miserable, expecting to spend another Christmas alone, just wishing for it all to be over.

This was the best present she could ever have hoped for.

Her eyes squeezed shut for a tiny second.

She opened them again. Yes, they were still there. She wasn't imagining this. It was really happening.

She looked inside the box. There was one of the tiny Christmas decorations that she and Drew had bought together. A tiny little red heart. Except this one had been twisted on to some tin foil to make a ring. There was a little piece of folded paper next to it.

'I made it. Jess. Do you like it?'

She looked into their smiling faces. This was hers. This was her family. For now and for always.

'I love it.' She lifted the makeshift ring out of the box and put it on her finger, watching as it gleamed in the twinkling tree lights. 'It's perfect.' She gave Drew a kiss.

He pressed the little bit of paper into her hand. 'This is the real one we've picked for you. Daddy says it's a pink diamond because pink's your favourite colour.' He looked a little sad. 'But we couldn't get it tonight.'

Jessica looked at the printout. It was beautiful. It was breathtaking. 'It's perfect.' She smiled and looked at the little red heart. 'But every Christmas I want to wear this ring, because you made it for me.'

She put her hands around Callum's neck to meet his mouth with a kiss. She couldn't have wished for anything more. A family, not just for Christmas but forever.

Drew was standing at the fireplace staring at the chimney. 'Can I write a thank-you letter for Santa?'

Callum frowned. 'But it's not Christmas yet. You've not had your presents yet.'

Drew gave him a little knowing smile. 'Oh, yes, I have. Santa and I made a deal. He's just delivered his present early.'

Jessica linked her arm around Callum's waist. 'It seems

our son has been making deals without telling us. What else do you think he asked Santa for?'

She could see the gleam in his eye. 'Let's hope it's a little brother or sister,' he whispered as he bent to kiss her.

* * * * *

SNOWBOUND WITH DR DELECTABLE

BY
SUSAN CARLISLE

First published in Great Britain 2013
by Mills & Boon, an imprint of Harlequin (UK) Limited.
Harlequin (UK) Limited, Eton House, 18-24 Paradise Road,
Richmond, Surrey TW9 1SR

© Susan Carlisle 2013

ISBN: 978 0 263 89922 1

Printed and bound in Spain
by Blackprint CPI, Barcelona

Dear Reader

My family has enjoyed a snow-skiing holiday each year for over twenty years. It is a sport that we all love and something that we enjoy doing as a family. My youngest child began skiing when he was only four, and we are now taking our third generation of skiers to the slopes.

During our last trip to the mountains I began thinking about what a wonderful setting the ski resort would be for a romance. There is nothing more breathtaking than riding a ski-lift among treetops tipped in white, while big fat snowflakes drift down and silence surrounds you. This screamed romance to me.

Hence Baylie and Kyle's story was born. They are two souls tortured by their fears. Everyone has fears—both rational and irrational—but Baylie and Kyle have let their fears define them and stop them from living life to the fullest. During their work together on the Courtesy Patrol, and through their love for each other, can they learn to live with their fears?

I'd like to thank Robin Visintin of the Courtesy Patrol at Snowshoe, West Virginia, for all her invaluable help. You and your group of volunteers make my family feel welcome every year.

I hope you enjoy reading Baylie and Kyle's snowy Christmas romance on the slopes as much as I enjoyed writing it. I love to hear from my readers. You can find me at www.SusanCarlisle.com

Merry Christmas!

Susan

Recent titles by the Susan Carlisle:

NYC ANGELS: THE WALLFLOWER'S SECRET
HOT-SHOT DOC COMES TO TOWN
THE NURSE HE SHOULDN'T NOTICE
HEART SURGEON, HERO…HUSBAND?

**Also available in eBook format
from www.millsandboon.co.uk**

DEDICATION

To my daughter, Mary Beth.
Your mother loves you.

CHAPTER ONE

DR. KYLE CAMPBELL stepped reluctantly into what at best could be called controlled chaos. The banging of skis against the floor and the clanking as they hit each other when propped against the wall was painfully familiar.

He stood in the doorway of the courtesy ski patrol building at the Snow Mountain Resort in West Virginia the weekend before Christmas. The early-morning wind buffeted his back and a blast of cold whirled by him. Why had he agreed to be here? Well, he hadn't exactly agreed. He'd been pushed into a corner and had reluctantly grunted what had been interpreted as assent. Metcalf had played on his knowledge of Kyle's past, his big heart and the reputation of the clinic in order to coerce his agreement.

As Kyle surveyed the small room full of people of all ages, wearing black ski pants and red jackets with large white crosses on their backs, he looked for the leader among them. The din of voices was high enough that he'd have to speak louder than normal to be heard.

"Hey, close the door, will ya?" someone yelled.

"Keep the noise down. You know how Baylie reacts when we're being so loud," another said.

The level of chatter dropped to a passable level.

As Kyle stepped inside, the swinging door closed behind him. A grandfather type pulled on a knit hat with the local college logo on it and grinned as he pushed past Kyle on his way out into the snowy air.

"Can you tell me where to find the head of the courtesy patrol?" Kyle asked a woman who looked to be around thirty.

"Yeah, you'd be looking for Baylie. She's over by the assignment board." She pointed across the long, narrow room.

"Thanks." Snow and wind hit him in the back as the woman opened the door again and went outside. He joined the group standing in a corner. As he approached, a feminine, almost angelic voice issued orders with drill-sergeant effectiveness.

"Roger, Mark and Sue take Snow Dream Way. We're supposed to be busy today so watch the kids closely."

Kyle liked her efficiency. When those three people moved away it allowed him a glimpse of the person to whom the voice belonged. Her straight dark brown hair brushed the tops of her shoulders as she looked back at the board. She appeared more like a kid than someone responsible for the welfare of skiers at a major resort. Maybe she was just filling in, like he was.

She called out another set of instructions and a few more people moved away, allowing him a better sight. Dressed in the same shapeless black ski bibs as many of the others, he could tell she had a trim figure. Her white turtleneck hugged her arms, covering her delicate wrists and neck. The next time she turned, her gingerbread-colored gaze met his. An inquisitive look filled them before recognition dawned.

"You must be Dr. Metcalf from the sports-med clinic in Pittsburgh. I'm Baylie Walker. We appreciate your help."

"I'm from the clinic, but I'm afraid Dr. Metcalf couldn't make it. I'm his replacement for the weekend, Kyle Campbell."

Her smile fell and she made a tut-tutting noise with her mouth. "Ooh, that's not good."

Kyle raised a brow and waited. Nothing about being at the ski resort was good as far as he was concerned. Being on the snow had once been his first love, the thing he'd lived for—but now he directed all that energy into excelling as a doctor.

Just driving here had made him break out in a sweat. The closer he'd come to the slopes as he'd driven up the mountain the harder it had been. Maybe she'd tell him that he wasn't needed. He would gladly drive the two hours back to Pittsburgh.

"There's an interview process here. You can't just show up and expect to run the slopes as part of the patrol without some instruction. I need to know you're qualified."

Her questioning of his experience irritated him. At one time he'd bet he could've outskied anyone on this mountain and most of the others. The slip of a ski, a fence and a bungling EMT had ended that.

"I didn't 'just show up'. I was told that you had been notified of the change. I understood that I would either be teaching ski school or patrolling the bunny slope. I can assure you that I'm more than qualified to do either of those," he said in an authoritative voice.

She blinked then squared her shoulders. "You may be, but I'll need to see for myself. We have rules for a reason."

This issue could be his ticket out, but the fairy-sized woman had got his hackles up. Despite not having skied for years, he didn't like the implication he might not be good enough. He'd made the choice to hang up his skis not because he couldn't ski but because he wouldn't.

"An orientation couldn't possibly be necessary in order to ski on the bunny slope." Kyle didn't even make an effort to keep the cynicism out of his voice. This situation was beginning to grate on his already strained nerves.

It had all begun when the partners in the clinic, Kyle included, had decided they should be more involved in community service. Kyle had volunteered at a community clinic in downtown Pittsburgh, but he had never had any intention of signing up as a volunteer for the Snow Mountain courtesy patrol. He had only agreed to fill in for Metcalf because he wouldn't have to ski anything more difficult than the beginner slope.

His world was good now. He was a successful doctor, he was dating, and he had a great place to live. He'd learned to deal with his loss. If it hadn't been for Metcalf getting his weekends messed up and his wife having a trip to her parents' planned for their Christmas celebration, Kyle would never have caved and agreed to take his place. Metcalf knew Kyle's skiing history, and if he'd declined it would have been hard to explain why he didn't want to work at the resort. Sharing his fear he wouldn't do. Metcalf had told the resort he had a little experience so they had agreed to give him only the easiest of slopes. With that understanding, Kyle had felt like he could make it through two days.

"Are you familiar with the mountain?" she continued as she looked back at the board.

"No."

"Great." She didn't look pleased. She turned to face him again. "I'll get someone to outfit you with a uniform.

When I'm done here I'll show you the ropes." A slight grin formed on her lips.

If he hadn't been so uptight about clicking on his skis again for the first time in ten years he might have found some humor in her pun. Beginner slopes were notorious for having rope pulls to get skiers up the mountain. Few appreciated that a rope pull was only a step better than walking up. Both methods could turn a beginner skier into a non-skier.

"Tiffani," Baylie called. A woman who looked like the quintessential snow bunny turned toward them. "Could you show…?"

"Kyle," he supplied.

"Kyle where to get a patrol jacket?"

"Sure." Tiffani gave him a smile that brought back memories. The snow groupies had used to give him the same "I'm interested" looks when he'd been on the skiing circuit. He had to admit that his ego had enjoyed them.

He returned the smile but without the same wattage of warmth, then gave his attention to Baylie again. Her lips had thinned. She'd noticed his and Tiffani's interplay. He shrugged. It didn't matter to him what she thought.

"Meet me here as soon as you're done. You have your own boots and skis?"

"In my truck." He'd dug them out of the closet. He didn't know why he hadn't gotten rid of them long ago. After this weekend they'd go to the second-time-around sports store. With a nod of understanding he turned and followed the willowy Tiffani into a back room.

Baylie regarded the new guy's wide shoulders for a second longer than she should have as he walked away. Something about his attitude said he wasn't happy about her giving him orders. She couldn't put her finger on it, but maybe it was the way he stood back from the crowd that had drawn her attention. He'd have to get over that. She ran the show as far as the courtesy patrol was concerned.

The man's looks and bearing said he was used to being the center of attention. If she hadn't been short of volunteers she might have questioned him further, but a warm body that could stand up on skis would be better than nothing on the slopes. Today she'd have to deal with the situation and keep a close eye on him. She had the idea that he wasn't going to be her most agreeable volunteer. She liked her helpers to follow directions and not question her decisions. This one was already crossing ski poles with her.

Kyle wasn't gone long before he returned in a red coat that made his dark features more pronounced. He was wearing ski boots but the buckles remained unlatched, and he carried a pair of high-end skis that few could afford. Who was this guy?

Coming out from around the counter, Baylie lifted her jacket off a peg as she moved. Slipping an arm into one sleeve, she quickly looked behind her when the jacket lightened. Kyle was holding it up for her. She finished pulling it on, zipped it and mumbled, "Thanks."

"You're welcome."

A gentleman. His deep voice made her think of a warm fire after a cold, rainy day. Soothing. She shook her head to clear that unexpected thought. She didn't need to be thinking about any man in that vein. That was one place she wasn't going to go again. Losing Ben the way she had had been too hard. She had plenty of issues to handle without adding a surly volunteer to the mix. No matter how appealing he was. She wasn't interested in being with anyone. Baylie started toward the outside door. The clomp of his boots on the cement floor matched hers as he followed.

On her way Baylie picked up a handheld radio off the dock station and gave it to him. "Here, you'll need this."

When his long fingers brushed hers, she let go, almost dropping the radio. But he grabbed it just in time. She drew in a breath of nervous relief. At the ski rack she lifted her skis from where they hung on the pegs. "So are you an intermediate or experienced skier?"

"I'm more than capable of skiing the bunny slope, if that's what you want to know."

Why the attitude? Was there some reason he wouldn't give a straight answer about his abilities? Overly self-assured men weren't her favorites. The guys in Iraq acted the same way every time they were sent on a mission. Especially Ben. It was as if he'd thought he was invincible. But he hadn't been. "A direct answer to my question would be nice."

"Then, yes, I'm experienced."

"Good. The *beginner* slope is this way." She put emphasis on "beginner". "We do not call it the bunny slope."

She didn't miss the slight upturn of his mouth.

Baylie put her skis across her shoulder and started hiking up the low, snow-covered rise.

"By the way, why is it called 'courtesy patrol' instead of 'ski patrol'?"

"Because we don't want to be perceived as the policemen of the slopes. We are here to encourage courtesy and safety. Courtesy implies a kinder, gentler way of letting people enjoy the freedom of their vacation and holidays, with a reminder to be careful."

"That makes sense. Nice idea. Unusual, but nice."

Ahead of them at the top of the grade lay the ski school.

"So there isn't a rope pull?" His voice held surprise.

Baylie smiled as she glanced at the short and slow ski lift off to their left. "No, we're more advanced than that. We don't believe in a 'glove destroyer', as we call it. Kids should learn to ride the lift. It's just as important as learning to stand on skis."

"I couldn't agree more," he mumbled as his strong strides took him farther along the slope.

When they had walked far enough Baylie stopped and placed her skis on the snow. "We'll ski down and ride up."

"Don't you mean ride up and ski down?"

"No. This is a reverse mountain. Here we stay on the top of the mountain and ski down. I know, at all the other resorts you stay at the bottom of the mountain and ride the lift up." Shoving the toe of one boot into the binding, she pressed down on her heel until the click indicated her boot was secure. Hearing no movement from the man beside her, she looked in his direction.

His skis were butted into the snow, making them stand straight up beside him. A large hand, red from being exposed to the weather and white at the knuckles, held them upright. He'd made no move to put them on. He looked off over the landscape as if in a trance.

"Is there a problem?" Baylie followed his look, seeing nothing more than the beautiful countryside covered in white. She loved this place.

"No," he said, almost too sharply. "I was just admiring the view." He placed one ski on the ground carefully followed by the other then clamped his boot buckles closed.

With a quick slip and push she had her other ski snapped into place. Done, Baylie glanced at him again. She didn't miss the small hesitation before he clicked his binding. In a smooth movement that showed his experience, his second ski went into place.

"Lead on," he said.

She pushed off.

Every nerve in Kyle's being went as taut as a tightrope. If he didn't get it together, he'd be the clown in the circus. With relief, he felt his muscles contract and release as he moved downhill. It was coming back. For him skiing again was like the old saying about it being like riding a bike.

He followed the snow pixie ahead of him with the slightest unsteady movement before he felt control returning to his body. Making a maneuver with confidence he didn't entirely feel, he slid up beside her in the lift line.

"Got your ski legs, I see. You'll need them. The beginner slope may be our easiest slope but it's also our busiest."

Had she noticed his reluctance? He couldn't—no, wouldn't—let that happen. Something about her made him believe that she didn't tolerate weakness in others, or in herself. He had no intention of letting his show. There could be no reason for questions. He looked her straight in the eyes.

"I'm aware of the type of skiers on the beginner slope. I can handle my assignment."

"It's my job to see that the resort visitors have a good time and are safe while doing it. I take it seriously, and you should too."

"Yes, ma'am," he said in a placatory tone that indicated he had no plan to yield to her position.

They slid into place to wait on their lift seat then took a chair when it came around.

Despite their difference in size, Baylie's leg brushed his, from hip to knee. A zip of awareness ran along his thigh. Even through the thickness of their ski gear he was conscious of her feminine curves pressed against him.

Her personality might be prickly, but there was nothing uncomfortable about her softness.

Baylie shifted as if trying to put space between them but the limited seating area brought her leg back against his. For that brief moment when she'd pulled away, coolness had filled the gap and was replaced by heat when her leg met his again.

She inhaled deeply and released the breath slowly. "You'll be expected to patrol this area and help anyone who needs it. Please pay special attention to the adults. The kids seem to get how to ride a lift right off but the adults can take out a group of skiers waiting in line faster than an avalanche."

Kyle couldn't help but chuckle at that turn of phrase. He'd seen it happen. They grinned at each other. For once that serious look had left her face. Where she'd been noticeably wholesome looking before, with a smile she became strikingly attractive.

Their skis touched snow again. After one unsure wobble, he skied off beside her. Success. Baylie seemed quite deft on her skis, making him all the more conscious of his lack of confidence.

"You have your radio. If you need anything, call in and someone with be here to help."

With those final words Kyle watched as she skied off down the gentle slope in the direction from which they'd come and proceeded without a pause over the side of the mountain. She seemed very confident both on the snow and in her job. At one time he had been about the latter, but not now. Taking a deep breath, he marshaled his determination to get along with the patrol leader and get through the next two days, before putting his skis up forever.

* * *

Baylie wasn't certain about the new guy.

He'd looked unsure for a moment when they'd been putting on their skis but that expression had disappeared quickly as they'd skied to the lift. If his confident attitude meant anything then he thought he could do anything well. It was one thing to be independent, another to be reckless. That she knew firsthand, and wasn't impressed by it. She'd make a point of checking on him regularly during the day. It was important for the courtesy-patrol volunteers to display self-assurance on the slopes, not superiority.

Around midday Baylie skied off the lift that stopped at the top of the mountain. She'd made her rounds a number of times and had once found the new guy helping a girl up and later stopping an experienced skier to instruct him not to ski so fast through the learner area.

This visit Baylie skied up beside him. "You seem to be catching on pretty quick."

"Most of it is just common sense," he said with a smile.

It was a nice smile that was bracketed by half-moon lines on each side of his mouth. She couldn't see if it reached his eyes because of his sunglasses but she hoped it did.

"Is the entire patrol made up of volunteers?"

"Yes. Most of them just enjoy having a free day of skiing in exchange for their help. They are snow junkies glad to be on skis."

"You are the only paid staff member?"

"I am. The management feels it makes for a friendlier resort for families to have the patrol staffed by volunteers. If the patrol consisted of all paid personnel they might think they were in authority over the skiers. The management sees us as a partner in fun. It is a subtle difference but a significant one."

He grinned. "Interesting way to think of things. I can certainly see the marketing value."

Anyway, this was more like it. She was glad to see that he seemed at ease. His smile alone was one that the resort patrons would like—especially the women.

"Enjoying yourself?" she asked.

"It hasn't been bad. I've been plenty busy."

"I told you so." She grinned at him. "Someone will be along to relieve you so you can have lunch. Do you know where to go to find some?"

"No, but I brought mine with me, anyway."

Had he made his own lunch, or did he have a significant other at home? For years her mother had packed her father's lunchbox before he'd left for the mine. It didn't matter. That information wasn't her business.

"Okay, I'll see you later." She shifted her weight and started downhill.

"You know, I don't need anyone checking up on me."

With a swift shift of her hips she pulled up on the edge of her skis, stopping. "It's my job to see how my volunteers are doing."

"Is it your job to do so every hour on the hour?"

"It's my job to do it as often as I deem necessary."

"I thought you might just like watching me."

Why, the egotistical man!

His grin said he knew exactly what she'd been thinking. She wasn't used to anyone joking with her. More than one person, especially here lately, had told her that she was far too serious.

Before she could respond, the bang from a gun being fired in the distance made her jump. She shifted precariously, ski poles searching for ground to steady herself. It had been almost a year since the blast, and she still didn't have control over her emotions when she heard a loud noise. Falling apart in front of her volunteers—and particularly this one—wasn't something she wanted to do. Kyle gave her the impression he didn't miss many details. She had to learn to handle her fear.

Before she recovered, a large hand wrapped around her upper arm and held her steady. The strength of the fingers was evident even through her bulky jacket.

"You okay?" Kyle's voice held concern.

She had the feeling that from behind his dark glasses he was watching her closely. "Yeah." She pulled her arm out of his grasp. "I'm fine." Heat filled her face, in spite of the weather. "I was just caught off guard."

"You're sure?"

Controlling the shaking of her hands, Baylie poked her ski pole firmly in the snow and pushed away. "Yes, I'm sure." But the words were caught in the wind. She reached the entrance to the intermediate slope, stopped and looked back at him. Even from a distance she could tell his brow was raised in confusion.

Hours later the radio clipped to Baylie's waist squawked, "Child down on the beginner slope." It wasn't the voice of the new guy. For some reason, his she would've recognized.

She brought the radio to her mouth. "ETA five."

Skiing fast, she made her way to the nearest lift and broke through the line. Riding up, she radioed instructions to the patrolman who had given her the report. There was a pause then the man said, "The new guy took her to the clinic."

What?

"He said he was a doctor and he'd take care of her."

He was a doctor? She'd figured since he hadn't introduced himself with the title of MD that he must be the clinic manager or a physical therapist. That didn't matter. It didn't mean he knew how to handle the kind of injuries that occurred on the mountain.

Heat filled her from head to toe. Her jaw tightened. She couldn't respond as she wanted to over the radio. She'd straighten out protocol when she was done with the patient. Working to keep her voice even, Baylie replied, "Thanks. I'll meet him there. Please patrol the beginner slope while we're at the clinic."

"Ten-four."

Baylie was going to see to it that this guy knew his place. She made the decisions on this mountain. The care of the skiers was her responsibility. It could be a liability issue if someone was further injured by one of the patrol.

She'd hardly been deposited off the lift before she was releasing her bindings and stalking into the clinic. All the way up she reminded herself that the patient came first. The last time she'd been this irate had been when she'd woken up in a hospital bed and they wouldn't tell her what had happened to the rest of the men.

Taking a calming breath, she walked through the tiny lobby of the patrol office. A deep voice and the shy giggle of a small child came from the direction of the exam room. As Baylie went through the door she found Kyle leaning over a little girl of about six years old with a cherubic face and flaxen curls. He was checking her eyes with a small penlight and at the head of the bed stood another longtime patrol member. Baylie fixed him with a piercing look. His lips went into a thin line and he shrugged before he said, "He insisted."

"I did," came the deep voice of the man examining the girl.

She spoke to the patrolman. "Please find her parents."
The man didn't dither when he left.

"Tell me what happened."

Kyle glanced at her before turning his attention back to rubbing the child's head with the tips of his fingers. Despite her anger, she had to admit he did have a gentle way about him. But he wasn't the qualified medical staff here. *She* was. He'd had no business removing the child from the slope without her permission.

"Cassie was a little late getting off the lift and it caught her in the back of the head." He continued examining the girl, looking down at her and smiling. The girl gave him a shy grin.

The man could charm a snake out of a basket. Baylie was afraid she'd have a hard time not responding to that smile if he ever turned it on her.

"The lift seat knocked her down. Mostly scared her," Kyle finished, still not looking at Baylie.

She stepped to the table. "You can go back to the slope now. I'll handle it from here," she stated in her best no-nonsense voice.

Kyle's mouth tightened and he moved away, but she sensed his presence not far behind her. He wasn't leaving. Having no intention of having an ugly discussion in front of a patient, especially a frightened child, she said no more. There would be time later to clarify the rules on this mountain.

"Hi, I'm Baylie," she said to the child, smiling reassuringly. "Cassie, can you tell me where it hurts?"

The girl put her hand to the back of her head.

"I found a goose egg in the back on the left side," Kyle said from behind her.

Moving her fingers along the girl's scalp, Baylie located a knot. "It'll be sore for a few days," Baylie told the girl. "Do you mind if I listen to your heart and check a few more things?"

"I've already done that, and she checks out fine," Kyle said, moving to the other side of the bed.

He wasn't going to leave this alone.

"Do you mind if I do it again?" she asked the girl.

The girl nodded her head in agreement.

"Good. Your mother and father should be here soon."

"Father. My mother doesn't live with us anymore." Sadness filled the girl's eyes.

"Well, how about we get you all fixed up before your father gets here?" Baylie smiled at her and pulled out her stethoscope. She began to examine the girl and was just finishing when a man's fearful voice called, "Cassie?"

With quick steps Kyle moved out into the lobby area.

"You must be Cassie's father." Kyle's rusty-timbred voice carried into where Baylie and Cassie waited. "She's fine. Just a little bump on the head. Come this way."

The men continued to talk. The man's voice lowered. Kyle had effectively calmed the father, she grudgingly admitted. Seconds later the men entered the room.

The father rushed to the girl's side. "Honey, are you all right?"

"Uh-huh. But I hit my head."

"Hi, I'm Baylie Walker, the courtesy-patrol leader on the mountain."

The man glanced at her before returning his attention to his daughter.

"Cassie's going to be just fine. You'll want to keep some ice on the bump until the swelling goes down," Baylie continued as she squeezed the girl's hand.

"That was just what Dr. Campbell was telling me."

The father had effectively dismissed Baylie. She pursed her lips and looked at Kyle. He raised a shoulder and let it fall.

"I've given Cassie a thorough exam. Other than the knock on her head she seems fine. You're welcome to take her with you but I suggest you watch her closely. You're also welcome to the disposable ice pack. If you need anything, just let me know." She stepped over to the counter, retrieved a card and handed it to the father. "You can reach me twenty-four hours a day."

"Thank you. I appreciate that," the father said, giving Cassie a hug.

"I bet a cup of hot chocolate would make that head feel better," Kyle said with a grin that did something to her insides she wasn't entirely comfortable with. His mouth could be a weapon against her if he chose to use it.

"Uh-huh." Cassie looked at her father. "Can I have a hot chocolate, Daddy?"

Her father picked her up in his arms. "Sure, honey."

Okay, Kyle officially had a great bedside manner. He might have some other grating personality issues but he'd dealt well with Cassie and her scared father. Baylie had seen none do better. Still, he had no business being so high-handed about making decisions that should have been hers.

"The best on the mountain is over at Snow Mountain Café," Baylie suggested. "You know where that is?"

"Sure do. Thank you again." The father smiled at her and offered his hand to Kyle. "Thanks, Dr. Campbell, for taking care of my little girl."

"You're welcome." Kyle ruffled Cassie's hair. "See you on the slope."

She grinned.

When the outside door to the clinic closed behind them,

Baylie turned to Kyle. "You didn't tell me you were a doctor."

"Does it matter?"

"Yes. I would've made it clear that you make no decisions regarding injuries without my approval."

"So this is a territorial thing?"

Baylie's hands went to her hips. "That has nothing to do with it."

"Then what's the problem? I saw the girl being hit and went to help. It wasn't more than I am qualified to handle by the American Medical Association."

"I'm sure it wasn't, but at this resort I make those calls. If an injured person isn't cared for in the proper way there could be problems."

"I understand. My apologies," he said in a flat tone.

Did he think she was overreacting? "The resort can be liable. Now you should understand why I was so concerned about you going through an orientation."

"Again, I agree." This time he sounded as if he meant it.

She'd give him the benefit of the doubt. "You're going to need to fill out a report as you were the one who brought Cassie in. I'll log it in the book."

Kyle moaned. "You mean even at a ski resort there's still paperwork?"

"'Fraid so." Baylie took perverse pleasure in him getting what he deserved for being so high-handed. She stepped over to a desk and turned on the computer. "Better now than later. You won't like doing it at closing time."

"If you insist."

"I do." Baylie logged onto the computer and pulled up the page he needed. She stood, letting him have the chair.

Even in heavy ski boots there was a grace, an athleticism in his movements, where others moved like bad renditions of an ostrich. It was as if he was at ease. His square jaw was already showing a midmorning shadow. Some men grew beards against the cold, but it would be a shame to cover up that strong chin or surround his expressive mouth with hair.

What had got into her? She wasn't some snow bunny out for an après-ski fling. In fact, she couldn't face another relationship. Losing Ben had been far too hard. She wasn't ready to be involved with another man—not that this one was offering. The memory of Ben was still too sharp. Hurt too much. She wouldn't give her heart again so easily.

She and Ben had been in the same company. He had been the captain, she the medic. They had known they could be in big trouble for fraternizing, but neither had seemed to let that matter. The patrol had been routine as they had been in a friendly section of Iraq. But the words "routine" and "friendly" had different meanings for her now. It had happened so fast. An IED had hit them. She had been thrown out of the vehicle, the hot burn from shrapnel in her side, and Ben had been dying beside her. She bit her lip to keep a moan of agony from escaping.

"Done," Kyle said, rolling back in the chair after clicking a key with a flourish. "I hate paperwork." The wheel of his chair hit the leg of the empty steel surgery stand and it went down with a bang and clash.

Baylie jumped, screamed and went into the brace position. Her heart shifted into overdrive and sweat beaded along her upper lip.

Kyle chuckled in embarrassment and quickly stood. He moved toward the fallen stand but jerked to a stop when he saw her. "Baylie, what's wrong?" His eyes scanned the area. "Are you hurt?"

She straightened but didn't meet his eyes. Brushing past him, she righted the table.

The loud shushing of static on both their radios brought an ocean of relief when it asked, "Baylie, is someone assigned to watch the slope while I get a bite to eat?"

Mustering control over her voice she'd never imagined she possessed, Baylie pushed the button and replied, "I'm on my way." She clipped the radio on her hip. Still avoiding Kyle's gaze, she said, "We'd better get back to work."

She glanced at him and found him still studying her. Baylie hauled on her jacket as quickly as possible. If she hurried maybe he wouldn't ask any more questions. Tugging on her knit cap, she pushed open the door to the outside. Kyle was right behind her.

As if he knew not to question what had just happened, he asked instead, "So what kind of medical training do you have to have to run the courtesy patrol?"

"I'm an emergency medical technician."

"Really? That's all?"

Was that a snarl of contempt in his voice?

"Yes, really."

"I would've expected the leadership position to require at least a doctor's degree at a resort this large."

Maybe it should, but management had hired her, and she had received positive feedback for her efforts so far. Her hand stopped in midair as she reached for her skis. Through narrowed eyes she pierced him with a look that she hoped screamed that he'd gone to the bottom of the garbage can in her estimation. "I also have advanced training in mountain rescue. I assure you, I'm more than qualified."

Still that too familiar sick feeling lingered. She'd known what to do when Ben had been hurt, she just hadn't been able to reach him. No matter how good her training, it hadn't been enough. She'd let him down—but she intended to honor his memory.

"I'll make my own judgment."

Baylie took a step forward, her eyes darkening. "Are you always this rude and self-righteous when you meet people or have you just picked me out as someone special?" She inhaled sharply and let it out in a huff. "You know, I don't care. I don't have to prove myself to a pompous MD. I don't have time for this conversation." She snatched her skis from the rack. "John's waiting for you so he can have lunch," she said, and stalked off.

Of all the arrogant, opinionated men she'd ever met *Dr. Kyle Campbell* was the worst. And that was saying something. She'd worked with doctors in the army, had been out on patrol with adrenaline junkies in Iraq and she wasn't impressed. She'd had all she could take of "I'm the man" and "I'm the best" in the military. But this doctor beat them all. Even the cold air didn't dampen the fire of ire burning through her. When this guy's two days were up she was going to send him on his way and say good riddance.

She slipped off the lip of a double-diamond trail and made quick, sharp S-turns down the slope. The wind burned her face as she rapidly crossed the trail. Her skis hit an icy spot and she had to concentrate to correct herself. The man had annoyed her enough that she was skiing recklessly. Digging in the edge of her ski, she pulled to a jarring stop on the side of the slope.

Panting miniature clouds of steam, with her heart racing, she looked out over the white run and up to the snow-kissed trees against the sapphire sky. The sun had pushed the gray clouds away. She lifted her face to the warmth and inhaled the crisp air. The mountains of West Virginia never failed to soothe her spirit. That was why she'd returned. To hide, and to survive.

CHAPTER TWO

A BITTER TASTE had filled Kyle's mouth when Baylie had stated proudly she was an EMT. Just when he had been starting to find the woman interesting. Emergency medical techs had their place. In his line of work, Kyle had to work with them. But in his personal experience an EMT with a know-it-all attitude could be dangerous. Like that guy who'd treated *him* when he'd fallen.

Baylie seemed to be on the same plane. She had to be in control. She had to make the call herself, even when others were equally qualified.

A stab of pain went through him at the memory of his accident. It had been perfect skiing conditions. Great snowfall the night before, clear sky and bright sun. Just a few wispy clouds in the sky. His parents and sister had been in the crowd, which hadn't happened often. Traveling all over the world meant he'd only seen them a few times a year. Being middle-class, blue-collar workers, his parents hadn't been able to afford to follow the ski circuit.

The event had taken place in the US, making it easier for them to attend. He'd made arrangements with his sponsors to pay for their lodging. They'd driven an entire day just to get there. He'd been the one the bets had been on to take it all, and he'd wanted them to be there to see it. He hadn't made a habit of believing his own press, but this time even he'd thought he had a chance.

He'd been almost through the run when he'd moved a fraction of an inch too far with one ski, and then he'd been in the fence. Where the crowd had been screaming, there had suddenly been nothing but quiet. His knee had taken the blunt of the stop. The EMT hadn't properly secured his foot on the stretcher, even after one of the other techs had suggested he do so. His foot had fallen off the stretcher, and that had been the end of his glory days as a skier.

Those were times best forgotten. It was water under the bridge. His knee was his only worry now.

Kyle's afternoon passed without incident on the beginner slope. He had to remind a couple of advanced skiers to slow down. He even had to threaten to take one loudmouth snowboarder's lift ticket before Kyle got the point across that he meant business.

Most of the time he spent watching children who'd finished morning ski-school practice their newfound skills. Each made their way carefully down the slope with their knees forming a wedge to slow down. They came by him chanting, "Make a pizza." If they wanted to go faster they'd make their skis go parallel to each other like "French fries".

The newbies would make it to the lift area and get on the lift to make the circuit again with broad grins on their faces. He envied them. Those had been exciting days when he'd been learning to ski. He'd been told more than once that he was a natural.

Kyle noticed Baylie a number of times as she stood talking to one of the other patrol members. She must have seen him looking at her during one visit because she skied over.

"Everything going okay?" Her words were terse. Apparently she hadn't recovered from their earlier discussion.

"Things have been calm," he answered matter-of-factly.

"Good. Slopes close at four-thirty. Please make sure everyone is off the lift and headed in." She said it evenly but her tone implied she was the boss.

"Sure." Not liking the tension between them, he offered an olive branch. "Hey, I didn't intend to offend you earlier."

"Is that an apology?"

She certainly had no plans to meet him halfway.

A voice over the radio said, "Baylie, you're needed at the clinic."

Thankfully he didn't have to answer her question. He still thought a doctor should be making the larger calls at the resort. In his case, if a sports-med doc had been made available, his skiing career might not have been ruined.

Putting the radio to her mouth, Baylie responded, "Ten-four." To Kyle she said, "You can keep your jacket overnight. Be at the patrol office at eight a.m. Slope opens at nine."

Kyle watched as she moved down the slope toward the courtesy-patrol building. There was grace in the subtle shift and sway of her hips as she skimmed across the snow.

He was usually attracted to the tall, willowy blonde types with the "help me" looks, but for some reason Baylie's compact, agile body appealed to him. The ski pants did nothing to conceal her supple curves. In many ways she was a contradiction. Outside all mountain girl, fresh and natural, while on the inside hard as nails and unyielding. The paradox made him want to know more about her.

What he didn't completely comprehend was her over-the-top reaction to the table crashing.

All Baylie planned to do was grab a pizza and head to her place to prop her feet up. The pizza parlor/bar was full of the young après-ski crowd looking for a night of fun. She stepped inside and unzipped her jacket. Despite the blast of heat that hit her, she left her jacket on. She'd only be a few minutes. Pushing her way through the throng toward the bar, she spoke to a number of people she knew. This was also the after-hours hangout for most of the courtesy patrol.

Moving around a group, her gaze met Kyle Campbell's across the room. He sat on a deep cushioned couch next to the roaring fire in the stone fireplace, which had a huge Christmas wreath hanging above it. The place had a festive holiday feel. Beside Kyle sat Tiffani, with a look of hero worship on her face as if she was fascinated by his every word.

When they had been having their heated discussion earlier his blue eyes had turned stormy, as if he was remembering something extremely unpleasant. There seemed to be nothing rational about his negative reaction to her and her qualifications. She didn't understand his attitude but it didn't matter. What he thought didn't matter.

She still held his gaze. Then with a jerk of her head she broke the connection and continued making her way to the bar. She ordered a pizza and stood against the wall out of the way to wait until it was ready. Regardless of the number of times she reminded herself that what was between Tiffani and Kyle was of no interest to her, she couldn't resist glancing in their direction. Just as she did so, Tiffani threw her head back and laughed as if Kyle had said the funniest thing she'd ever heard. Baylie curled her lip. Well, she had a pretty good idea where their evening would end.

Was that disgust or jealousy? Disgust. Definitely disgust. She wasn't interested in any man on any level and certainly not in some ego-inflated doctor.

Turning back to the bar, she saw her pizza was ready.

She paid and grabbed the box. Again, she did the bend and weave that was required to make it back to the front door. As soon as she pushed through the doors the freezing air cut through the three layers of clothing covering her chest. She placed the pizza box on the closest park-style bench and zipped up her jacket. Behind her, the doors of the bar opened. She glanced back to see Kyle coming out.

Dressed in a dark blue heavy-knit sweater with a black all-weather coat pulled over it, well-worn jeans and snow boots, Kyle looked like he belonged in this setting. He bore the air of someone who frequented the slopes, instead of those weekend warriors who bought all new clothes and showed up to impress.

"Hi." His breath was a white mist in the air.

"Hey," she said as she picked up her pizza box.

"I hope your place isn't far because that pizza's going to be frozen if it's out here long."

"Then I guess I'd better go." Baylie walked away.

She moved along the wide brick-filled pedestrian area lined with trendy shops and, above them, condos full of vacationers. Small white lights hung from the eaves and wreaths adorned the doors. This was a miniature Christmas village brought to life. Even the light poles were dressed with wreaths and red bows. She inhaled the crisp air, enjoying the sharp sting in her lungs.

She heard heavy footsteps behind her. Baylie glanced over her shoulder. Kyle was walking a few paces to the side and a few yards behind, his hands shoved into his pockets and his shoulders hunched against the wind. He'd already dumped on her occupation, and was he now stalking her?

She stopped and faced him. "What're you doing?"

The muted yellow of the streetlamp played across his startled features. His chin lifted in question. "I'm walking over to the dorm. Why? Where did you think I was going?" He stepped closer but not into her personal space. "Stalking you?"

"I, uh, no."

He looked at her squarely. "Yes, you did," he said in a teasing tone.

"Maybe I did think you were following me."

"I was, but just not with the intentions your mind was hatching."

Baylie was grateful that the light wasn't any better. Hopefully her guilt didn't show.

His grin grew. "Since we're going in the same direction, let me join you. That way you can keep an eye on me."

How could she say no to that attractive lift of his lips? "I guess that would be safer." She started walking again, and he fell in step beside her.

"So, do you live in the dorm too? Ooh, that did sound like I'm stalking you."

She laughed. Something she didn't do much of these days. "No, I have a small place next door. Since I'm here full-time I get an upgrade, such as it is."

"I just threw my duffel bag on a bunk and headed out for a burger. Place reminds me of college—dirty socks, snoring and beer cans everywhere."

She couldn't help but chuckle again. "Yeah, I know what you mean. An army barracks isn't much more appealing."

"You've been in the military?" Amazement orbited his words.

"Yeah. That's where I got my training."

He didn't comment, and she was relieved. She didn't want a repetition of their earlier conversation. They seemed to have reached a temporary stalemate.

They crossed the main paved road that divided the top

of the mountain and maneuvered around a pile of snow left by the road crew. The pavement was the line that separated the Alpine village, where all the visitors stayed, from the side of the mountain where the employees lived in considerably less luxury.

No longer in the light of the numerous security lamps, the footing became more difficult along the gravel road. Baylie slowed her pace. It had started to snow.

"What's there to do up here after the slopes close?"

His deep smooth voice and being alone together in the darkness had a far too intimate a feel. She didn't do romance. Not now, not ever again. She couldn't carry any more guilt if she failed another man. "The usual, I guess. Dinner, bars. Some people swim in the indoor pool."

"You aren't into the après-ski scene?"

"I'm sure you know the saying that those who ski all day go to bed."

"They do, do they?"

His words came out slow and rough, putting a double meaning to them that made her think of a big bed, roaring fire and no clothes. What was happening to her? She was letting this stranger get to her. Crazy stuff. They didn't even like each other. Again she was glad for the darkness. She needed to get to her place right away. "You know what I mean."

He chuckled. "Yeah. If you ski all day it's hard to stay up and party all night. You're too worn out."

"You and Tiffani looked like you were having a good time." If Baylie could have taken the words back she would have. It was none of her business with whom he spent his time. Nothing about him was her concern except what he did on the slopes between nine and four-thirty.

"So you did see us." Kyle's tone implied the statement

had a significant meaning, and he was mulling over what that was.

It was time for her to put a door between them. She'd already said too much. "Well, here's your stop." The large, functional three-floor building loomed in front of them. "I'm on down. Good night."

"Night, Baylie."

The way he said her name made her think of chocolate melting in her mouth.

The next morning Kyle pushed through the door of the patrol building. He wasn't any more enthusiastic about the prospect of being on the slopes again this morning than he'd been the day before. What Kyle did find interesting was that he looked forward to seeing Baylie. The small, gutsy live wire was interesting. Gave as good as she got. She piqued his curiosity.

For a few minutes the night before they had spoken to each other as if they could be friends. He liked her intelligence and practical manner. If he was staying longer, which he definitely wasn't, and she wasn't such a control freak, which she certainly was, and if he wanted to ski again, which he didn't... Heck, who was he kidding? They really had nothing in common.

Kyle stepped farther into the room. Baylie stood behind the counter, handing out assignments with a smile and an occasional laugh.

"Morning, Baylie." He smiled at her.

Her face sobered. "You're on the beginner slope again today. Would you mind teaching a group in ski school?"

Had he misread their amity the night before? Why was she treating him less warmly than the others? "What does it entail?"

"You'll have about six students. All you have to do is show them the basics, let them take a couple of runs down the slope and then bring them in for hot chocolate."

He didn't say anything right away.

"I'm terribly short on help today." Her voice held a hint of desperation.

"I can handle that." He gave her his best syrupy smile. The day before he wouldn't have been anywhere near as confident.

Baylie blinked twice as if she was unsure what she'd heard or seen. At least she hadn't asked him to patrol the main slopes. She'd surely have demanded an explanation if he had refused. That, he wouldn't give. He certainly wouldn't admit to being afraid.

Suddenly Baylie looked over his shoulder, squealed and circled the counter. Crossing the room in quick steps, she threw herself into the arms of a tall, lanky guy. He picked her up and swung her round. When he stopped, she slid back to her feet. Others came up and slapped the man on the back calling, "Congratulations." Seconds later, Kyle could no longer see Baylie for the throng of people with voices raised in excitement.

Who is this guy?

One of the volunteers who had been in the back room passed Kyle and he asked, "What's going on?"

"Oh, that's Derek Lingerfelt. Local hero. Just back from winning the national downhill race out in Colorado. People around here hope he'll go further. Maybe even the World Games."

That old familiar feeling of disappointment jabbed him. "So what's he doing back here?"

"Aw, Derek can't stay off the slopes so when he's home

to visit his parents, he helps us out. Even runs a class for some of the visitors. Good PR, he says."

Kyle's sponsors had encouraged him to do as much PR as possible. People had wanted to join him on the slopes— mostly women. Looking back on it, he'd really enjoyed having his ego stroked. But now he found similar satisfaction in seeing a patient improve and go back to playing a game they loved.

Derek still had his arm draped over Baylie's shoulders. There was a broad grin on her face as she craned her neck to look up at Derek. Kyle shook his head. Wouldn't it be nice to have her smile up at him with the same fondness? That was certainly an irrational idea. Baylie didn't mean anything to him. She could smile in awe at anyone she wished.

The whole scene rubbed Kyle up the wrong way. Turning his back on all the admiration, he snatched up his jacket. It was time to leave.

"We need to get to work, folks," Baylie called, breaking up the crowd of well-wishers.

When Kyle brushed by her on the way outside she gave him a quizzical look. Was his displeasure with the scene that obvious?

Less than an hour later he was so caught up in giving little kids skiing lessons that he pushed thoughts of Baylie away. As he worked with the children, showing them how to stop, start and approach the lift, he remembered the passion he'd had when he'd learned something new, he'd pushed further. What he wouldn't give to have that feeling again. First he'd done it with downhill skiing, and when that had no longer been possible, he'd turned the same determination toward medicine. He loved medicine, and had risen to the top of his field.

"Laura, you follow Mikey," he told the girl in the pink and purple suit. "Move back and forth like a snake."

The girl pushed off with a look of determination on her face. When she stopped where the class had been instructed to, she beamed up at him.

Kyle returned her smile, giving her a thumbs-up.

"You're good at this," Baylie said from where she stood just off to his left.

He couldn't help but be pleased with her praise. It was something he'd never expected to receive, and it gave him a lighthearted feeling, as if he'd accomplished something outstanding.

"We could use you every weekend." For once she didn't have that I-have-to-get-along-with-you-because-I-need-you look. She seemed truly impressed.

"Thanks. Are you checking up on me again?" He turned back to his group. "Okay, Jimmy, your turn," Kyle said to the last boy in his group as he started off.

"Just a little. So don't get a big head. It's part of my job," Baylie replied, before she skied over toward another group of pupils with their teacher.

That figured. She gave him a compliment then cut the legs out from under it. He'd sent the last skier in his group downhill and was preparing to follow when a child of about eight came flying by from out of nowhere, barely missing him. The boy's arms windmilled as he screamed, "Help!"

Without thought, Kyle pushed off, going after the boy. As the child grew closer to the advanced slope, Kyle leaned forward, moving faster. His adrenaline was already pumping when he saw the boy wobble one way then the other. If Kyle didn't catch him soon, the boy could be seriously hurt. Kyle pushed hard, picking up even more speed. As he closed in on the child, Kyle stuck his arm out and wrapped it around the boy's waist, jerking him to his chest. Cutting hard into the snow, Kyle slowed just before the slope turned steep. He took a deep breath of relief. He'd plucked the boy up just in time.

"Hey, buddy, you all right?" Kyle asked the boy suspended under his arm. The child's skis waved back and forth, hitting Kyle's shin. "Hang on a sec and I'll put you down." Kyle moved toward the side of the slope so that they'd be out of the way of the other skiers. He'd let the boy down but was still holding his arm to steady him when Baylie approached.

"You guys okay?" Her voice sounded calm but her eyes said something different.

She'd been as afraid as he that the boy was going to be hurt. Kyle looked at the child and gave him a reassuring smile then looked back at Baylie. "Yeah, I think we're fine." Kyle kicked off his skis and kneeled down to eye level with the child. "So how're you doing?"

The boy's eyes were wide and his face lacked color. He nodded he was okay.

"Good. Why don't we go get on the lift and see if we can come down the slope a little slower the next time?"

"I don't—" the boy started in a fearful voice.

"Hey," he said to the boy. "Why don't we ask Baylie..." he pointed toward her "...to watch us and see how we do?"

Kyle wasn't sure that the boy was going to answer but he finally said, "Okay."

"I don't think—" Baylie started.

Kyle looked over the boy's head to meet her gaze and shook his head.

For once Baylie accepted without argument. He took the boy's hand and towed him to a spot where it was flat enough that he could stand without being afraid he would slide down the slope. Baylie followed.

"Will you stay with…?" Kyle looked at the boy. "What's your name?"

"Levi."

Kyle turned back to Baylie. "With Levi while I get my skis?"

"Sure." She put a hand on the boy's shoulder as if she was afraid he might get away.

Kyle walked back to his skis. His knee would be screaming in pain by morning. He retrieved his skis and climbed back to Baylie and Levi. Laying his equipment on the snow, he slipped his feet back into the bindings. "I'm ready. How about you?" he asked the boy in an encouraging tone.

Levi regarded at him for a moment before saying with little eagerness, "Yes."

"Good, let's go impress the girls." He winked at Baylie. Her eyes went wide for a second before one corner of her mouth lifted slightly.

For once she looked less than in control. *Good.*

Kyle took Levi's hand and they headed toward the lift. At the top of the slope the boy balked. His small hand squeezed Kyle's through both their gloves.

He looked down at the child. "You can do this, Levi. I'm going to be with you all the way. I won't let you get hurt. Trust me?"

Kyle barely made out Levi's nod.

"Okay, here we go." Slowly Kyle led him down the beginner slope, making a crisscrossing pattern in the wide-open area. Baylie had moved away from the steeper slope. As they passed, she cheered and whistled. She skied down to meet them when they stopped and give Levi a high five. A huge grin spread across the boy's face.

"Can I go again?" He looked up at Kyle.

"Sure. Let's wait here until your instructor comes by

and you can join your friends. You remember how to slow down and stop?"

Levi nodded.

"Good. No more flying down the slope. You have to ski in control. You can save all the zooming for when you make the ski team."

The boy beamed.

Minutes later Levi rejoined his group.

Baylie's look met Kyle's. "There's more to you than meets the eye, Dr. Campbell. You were great with Levi. And your skiing ability is far better than you let on. Few people could have caught him like you did. You prevented what could have been a disastrous accident. I'm surprised that with your talent you're satisfied working the beginner slope."

"You made that call." He'd never let on how happy her assumption had made him. "If the boy hadn't tried to go down the hill again right away he might never have tried to ski again." In a number of ways, the same thing had happened to him.

"I appreciate what you just did. And I appreciate your volunteering this weekend."

"You're welcome. Now I'll get back to my job. It's a pleasure to know you." To his surprise, it was. Baylie caused his hackles to stand at attention, but something about that was invigorating. She was someone he wouldn't soon forget.

Baylie had just been dismissed. She didn't particularly like the feeling. She watched the irritating, self-important man ski off as if he owned the mountain instead of just being here for an overnight stay. She couldn't remember spending so much time calling one person so many negative names and still managing to be impressed by them.

Just what was under that thick skin of his? Something about him fascinated her, and that wasn't a good thing. Anyway, he was leaving today. That would be the end of him. Even if she had been looking for somebody in her life—which she definitely wasn't—the cocky doctor would be her last choice.

The afternoon went by with a few banged knees and scrapes to attend to in the clinic. Minutes after her final sweep of the slopes she noticed Kyle storing his equipment into a late-model SUV in the parking lot next to the patrol building. He seemed eager to leave. That would be the last she'd see of him.

Why did that thought bring a touch of sadness?

"Hey, Baylie, do you know someone named Campbell? There's a call for him. The guy said he really needed to talk to him," one of the longtime volunteers asked over the radio.

"Yeah, he's right out here in the parking a lot. I'll get him."

Taking a deep breath, she whistled. The shrill sound echoed in the clear air. Kyle looked toward her. She waved an arm, indicating he should come to her, then put her thumb and pinkie finger out to form an imitation phone. He nodded and closed the hatch on the vehicle before walking toward her.

When he got close enough to hear she said, "You're wanted on the phone."

Kyle gave her a perplexed look and headed inside.

"Hello."

"Campbell, that you? Metcalf here. I've been trying to get you on your cell for hours."

"Didn't have it on me. What's up?"

"Man, I'm not going to make it back to take over. Had a car accident. Totaled. Everyone is okay but Robbie's in the hospital with a broken arm."

Kyle was glad no one had been seriously injured, but he knew he wasn't going to like what was coming next. "I need you to finish out the week for me there. Price said he'd cover your call duty and with the clinic closed for Christmas we should be good. It's slow because of the holidays anyway. I really wouldn't ask except you'd said you weren't planning to go out and see your sister until mid-January. Will you stay?"

Kyle gripped the phone. He couldn't last seven more days. Heck, he wasn't sure he could do one more.

"Come on, it can't be that hard with your background. You know I'd be there if I could," his associate said in a far too cheerful voice.

Kyle sucked in a sharp breath. He couldn't see a way out of it without sounding completely heartless.

"I'm sorry about Robbie. I guess I've no other choice if we don't want the clinic to look like we don't honor our commitments. I'll handle it. Baylie might not even need me."

"Baylie? You found you a woman up there?"

"She's the head of the courtesy patrol." He worked to keep the displeasure at Metcalf's implication out of his voice. Baylie wasn't some bit of snow fluff. "Take care of your family."

"Will do. Thanks, buddy."

Kyle wanted to slam the phone down and say, "Right, buddy."

He turned to find Baylie watching him with an inquisitive expression on her face.

"There a problem?" she asked.

"My partner, who was going to be here in the morning, isn't going to make it after all."

"I was really counting on him," she said more to herself than to him.

"Yeah, I figured as much."

She continued, "My staff is pretty thin during the week but the crowd will still be heavy because of Christmas."

Baylie had no idea how uncomfortable he was with the idea of staying. One of the things that had made him so successful on the skiing circuit and later in medical school had been that he'd always risen to a challenge. This next week would be just that. A challenge to keep his fear locked away—and his hands off Baylie.

Baylie needed help even if it came in the form of this holier-than-thou doctor. He'd made it clear he was more than ready to be on his way. Still, she had to convince him to stay. Was he going to make her come out and beg him?

"Is one more going to make that much difference?" he asked in a formal doctor tone.

"I need your help." Oh, how she hated to admit that to this man in particular. "That is, unless you have family plans."

The long pause wasn't a surprise.

"No. Not until later next month."

"So you'll stay?'

"Yeah."

It was the least enthusiastic agreement she'd ever heard.

"Really? Uh, good," she said before he changed his mind.

"Will I still be handling ski school?"

"Sure."

The arrogant, irritating and highly attractive man was

going to be around for another seven days. Would having him here be more trouble than he was worth?

Kyle walked into the patrol building the next morning with more confidence than he'd felt in the past two days. He searched the area for Baylie. Despite all his efforts, his heart beat a little faster in anticipation. Something about being around her made him feel more alive. Maybe it was just their clash of words and ideals but, whatever it was, it stimulated him.

Not immediately seeing Baylie, he started toward the assignment board. He saw one of the volunteers he recognized from the weekend standing behind the counter.

"Do you know where Baylie is?" Kyle asked.

"Yeah, she had to check on one of the cooks over at the Always Snowing Grill. You're Dr. Campbell, aren't you?"

Kyle nodded.

"I'm Mike. I'm doing the slope assignments this morning. You're on the beginner slope. Thanks for being here. Baylie would be panicking. I can't believe we're so short-handed this year." He shook his head then went back to studying the board.

Kyle took that as a dismissal and headed toward the outside door. As he pushed on the door, it was jerked open from the other side. With a humph, a small red bullet in the form of Baylie ran into him. His arms automatically wrapped around her to prevent her from falling. Her small hands grabbed his waist. Even in the almost zero-degree weather he wished he didn't have a shirt on so her fingers could touch his skin.

Heaven help him, he had the hots for the woman and she barely gave him the time of the day. He'd never had any trouble attracting a woman before, especially when he'd been a skiing star. Then girls had flocked to him. As a doctor he'd done all right as well. But not with Baylie.

"Hey, I thought you might be glad to see me but I had no idea you'd run smack into my arms," he remarked dryly, but followed it with a grin.

She shoved away. Suddenly he wished he hadn't said anything.

Stepping back, she glared at him before saying, "Thanks for helping out, Kyle."

"You're welcome."

The displeasure left her face. "You have your assignment?"

Okay, she was back to the all-business Baylie. "I do." He'd like to see Baylie let go a little bit. With all that bottled-up angst, he bet she'd be great fun if she was ever uncapped.

"Then I'll see you later on the slope." She stepped past him and into the building almost as if she had no more patience with him.

He wasn't used to being treated as a necessary evil. He didn't like it. Claiming his skis, he headed for the slopes. Maybe the next few days wouldn't be as bad as he'd imagined. Maybe they'd be worse. He now had the added challenge of figuring out the small dynamo of a woman with the Superwoman mentality. If she'd let him.

Baylie had been shocked by the sizzle of heat that had zipped through her body when Kyle had held her. She hadn't felt that since Ben. And she might not ever again, especially as she hadn't allowed a man to touch her since Iraq. Her mind rejoiced to discover she wasn't completely numb to the attention of a male. For a second there, she'd felt a spark of being alive again. But along with it had come a feeling of disloyalty.

What was she getting so jittery about? Kyle Campbell might be eye candy but what did that matter? He'd made it clear this wasn't his first choice of a place to spend his Christmas. He'd be gone in a week.

Wasn't that what you said yesterday?

Shaking off that thought, she made sure all the assignments were given for the day. On Saturdays the number of people on the mountain doubled, but during the holidays the number could triple and therefore issues often turned into injuries. To say she wasn't looking forward to the next few days was an understatement.

Baylie managed to get away from the clinic that afternoon. Most of the morning she'd spent caring for minor injuries: a child whose finger had got pinched in a binding; a woman with stomach flu; and another with a twisted knee.

She headed down an advanced slope, taking a deep breath as she went. The fresh air always made her feel better. Just stretching her muscles invigorated her as she moved across the slope, checking on her staff as she went. Even though they were all volunteers they took their jobs seriously. She was grateful. Their patience would be tested during the week.

She'd purposely made the beginner slope her last stop. She'd been drawn in that direction from the start but had forced herself to stay away. Why did seeing Kyle tug at her so?

As she skied off the lift at the top of the mountain her name came over the radio.

"Yes?"

"We need someone at the intersection of Greenway and Sweet Ride slopes."

"Ten-four. I'll send someone right away." She headed toward Kyle, who was standing near the lift. When she slid to a stop beside him, he turned away from the activity of beginners trying to stand in line without running over each other to look at her.

"Hey," she greeted him. "I need you down the mountain to control traffic at an intersection." A look filled his eyes that she would have called panic if it hadn't disappeared so quickly.

"I'd prefer to stay here."

What? She needed him elsewhere. He certainly skied well enough to handle the assignment, so why was he balking?

"There's no one else available right now. I need you on the other slope," she said with a firmness she tried not to use with her patrol members.

"I thought we agreed I'd work here."

"We did, but I need more help down the mountain and you're the only person I can move." She wrinkled up her nose, perplexed. Who did he think he was, second-guessing her? Did he have a problem with taking orders from a woman? Or just taking orders from her? She didn't even like making her requests sound like orders. Kyle just seemed to bring out that side of her.

"Who's going to cover this slope if I'm not here?"

"That's my problem to worry about. What's your issue with going down the mountain?"

Kyle looked at her as if he'd just snapped back from the past. Focusing on her again, he said flatly, "No issue. Show me where I need to be."

CHAPTER THREE

KYLE FOLLOWED BAYLIE down the trail marked green for easiest. His heart thumped against his chest like a sledge-hammer. Sweat popped out on his forehead as he made deliberate moves characteristic of a newbie. When he fell behind, Baylie slowed and waited until he caught up.

Self-loathing rippled through him, leaving an acid taste in his mouth. He should have told Baylie no flat out when she'd said he had to move to another slope, but he'd been unable to take the blow to his pride when she'd demanded to know why not. He wouldn't appear weak. She struck him as someone who didn't accept weakness, especially in herself.

They came to an intersection and Baylie stopped well away from the flow of the skiers.

He slid up beside her.

She studied him for a moment. "Is something wrong?"

"No." The word came out more sharply than he'd in-tended. "What do I have to do?"

Her eyes widened for a second but she soon returned to business. "You need to see that skiers keep moving along in this area. They have a tendency to stop and congregate in this intersection. Congestion means danger. Just having you standing to the side wearing the patrol jacket will be enough to slow them down. You'll have to remind some of them to move on. If the area gets much busier you may need to step in and direct traffic."

He nodded. Later he'd worry about how he was going to get down the rest of the mountain so he could catch a lift up. Right now all he wanted was for Baylie to go on about her business and not witness his meltdown.

She gave him a searching look as if she knew something wasn't right before she said, "I'll see you later."

Kyle bobbed his head and half turned away to check out the intersection. When he looked around again he was relieved to see that she was moving down the slope. It had been difficult enough to make that trip over the steeper terrain of the mountain, but not knowing how his knee would react had only added to the anxiety. Thankfully it had held up. A skier whizzing by reminded him he was there to see that no one got hurt. Baylie would undoubtedly be by to check on him.

The sun was creating shadows across the snow when Baylie came around the trail to find Kyle speaking to a group of skiers.

"If I see that again I'll have to pull your lift ticket. Understood?" His voice was so stern that she almost nodded her agreement along with the group. The skiers left in a subdued manner.

"What's the problem?" Baylie asked as she reached him.

"Oh, just a bunch of college boys showing off."

"Well, I think they got the point."

"I hope so. Maybe I'm getting too old but I worry about some of these guys really getting hurt. I see too many stupid accident injuries in my practice."

"I think it's a fair concern. They happen every year. But remember, we are called the courtesy patrol for a reason."

"Yes, ma'am."

She narrowed her eyes at him and got a grin in return. Did the man take anything seriously? He certainly didn't seem to take her that way. "You ready to call it a day? We need to sweep the trail for any stragglers on our way down."

She waited as Kyle put on his skis.

"You took your skis off while you directed traffic?" she asked. She never really thought to do that, always thinking she needed to be ready to move at a moment's notice.

"Yeah. For the first time I know how a traffic patrolman in the Bahamas feels," he said.

"I've never been to the Bahamas, so I don't know what you mean."

"The policeman stands in the middle of the intersection and directs the cars that come buzzing by on either side. I learned today it's not a safe feeling. You've never been to the Bahamas?"

"No." Did he think that everyone had the money and time to just jet off to the islands anytime they wanted?

"I love it. I have a house there. Beautiful water and sand."

What would it be like to lie on a pristine beach next to this man half-naked? Ooh, that thought might melt the snow under her feet. "Must be nice," she said, pointing her skis down the trail.

As they skied Kyle remained behind Baylie and traveled at a slower speed. It was far too conservative for the skill she'd witnessed when he'd rescued the boy. So why was he hanging back? He struck her as aggressive, not someone who would let her stay ahead of her for long. Reaching the fork in the trail, she stopped. "You take the right and I'll take the left. Just make sure you stay behind the last person. Wait where the trails meet again, and we'll go down Cascade to the Snow Plow lift."

"You're bossy by nature, aren't you?" he asked in a teasing tone.

She jerked her head around to look at him.

He stood watching her with a slight quirk of his mouth. "I'll meet you, boss."

For the first time he took the lead.

Baylie made it to the rendezvous point without seeing any additional skiers. Kyle should have been waiting for her, since he'd taken the shorter of the two trails. Was he having a problem?

"Baylie, come in," came over the radio. "It's Kyle."

He didn't have to say who he was. The rusty tone of his voice was stuck in her head.

"There's a snowboarder who's fallen and busted his wrist. Do I have permission to walk him down? I've examined him and there's nothing more serious wrong. He's in a fair amount of pain, though."

"Are you past the dogleg in the trail?" She was never going to let another person join the courtesy patrol who hadn't gone through orientation and skied the slopes at least once. The volunteers needed to know how to identify where they were without question.

"Yes, just below it."

"Good. You start down and I'll head up."

"It isn't necessary for you to walk up. We'll be down to meet you in a few minutes."

The same burn of anger she'd felt day before yesterday when he'd been high-handed about caring for the young girl returned. Her thumb pressed down on the button of the radio with more force than necessary. Her sense of responsibility wouldn't let her not make an effort to move toward them. "I'll meet you."

"We are on our way to you," came his response.

She released her skis and began hiking. The people who skied on this mountain were hers to see about. She made the decisions here.

Thankfully the exertion cooled her anger. If Kyle had been standing near her when he'd made that last comment she might have picked up a ski and hit him. It didn't matter how he called the situation, she made the final judgment on how patients were handled. From what she'd seen so far he was a fine doctor but she still didn't know enough about him to trust that he knew enough about caring for injuries outside a hospital or office. In this arena, she was the one with the training.

A few minutes later Kyle's large frame came into view. He was supporting a thin, white-faced teenager with scraggly hair. The young man's jacket was zipped to his neck and one sleeve hung by his side, empty.

Baylie wanted to give Kyle a piece of her mind but she had a patient to see about first. Biting her lip to keep her scalding words in check, she climbed closer.

She gave the injured guy a reassuring smile. "I'm Baylie. I'm the courtesy-patrol medic. What's your name?"

"Rod."

"Well, Rod, Kyle and I are going to support you between us as we walk down to where the snowmobile will meet us. It should be here in a few minutes to give you a ride up."

The boy's pain was obvious on his face but he offered her a weak smile.

To Kyle she said, "We mustn't let him fall again."

"Obviously," Kyle retorted, but his displeasure punctuated the word. She hadn't followed his directive and it irritated him. That suited her. He'd made her mad and she wasn't over it either, no matter how much help he'd been. Thankfully Rod was in enough pain that the silent war going on around him didn't faze him.

When they reached the spot where she'd instructed the snowmobile driver to meet them, Baylie pulled off her jacket and laid it on the snow.

"What're you doing? Don't we need to be moving on down the mountain?"

Baylie didn't miss the frustration in Kyle's voice. She looked up and said with more calm than she felt, "No, the snowmobile will meet us here. It's too dangerous to continue on foot. It's also getting too late to see well. I want to secure the wrist for travel."

"Yes, but…"

She gave him a direct look and he said no more. "I have some small splints in my pack."

Baylie turned to the young man, "Rod, why don't you have a seat and I'll check your wrist?"

She didn't need to encourage him any further. Exhausted from pain and walking, he settled on her jacket with Kyle's help. Now she was concerned he might faint. Cautiously she unzipped the jacket. Beneath, the arm was held in a sling. She discovered that the material was actually a knit shirt. She looked a Kyle. His neck was bare and turning red from the cold. So the infuriating man could think on his feet—she'd give him that.

Slowly she removed Rod's hand from the sling and laid it on the young man's leg.

Opening the pack at her waist, she located her scissors. "I'm going to need to cut your sleeve."

"Man, it's my fave," Rod complained, shaking his head in disappointment. "Okay," he finally agreed.

Baylie snipped at the material, trying to do as little damage as possible. The area around his wrist was badly swollen.

"How did this happen?"

"Fell. I put my hands out behind me to stop the fall."

She nodded and looked at Kyle, who stood like a soldier above them, and looked just as happy. "Most common injury on the mountain."

"I'm not surprised, with some of the stuff I've seen today," Kyle stated.

She looked back at Rod. "I'm going to stabilize this and get you up the mountain then off to the hospital. You have anyone staying at the resort that you'd like me to notify?"

"Yeah, my friends." He gave her the phone number of one of them and she radioed it in. She pulled an ace bandage out of her pack. Kyle came down on his knees beside her. His big body moved in closer.

"I'll support his arm while you wrap." Kyle placed his hand at the elbow and midway down the arm.

She accepted Kyle's assistance and said, "Rod, let me know if this hurts." Regardless of Kyle's high-handed ways, it was nice to have his assistance. The young man winced as Baylie made the first wrap of the bandage across his arm. "I won't take long, I promise." As quickly as she could, she enveloped the wrist. Working in tandem, she and Kyle gently secured Rod's arm in the sling again.

Baylie closed her pack, rezipped Rod's coat around him and stood. "Rod, the snowmobile will be here in a few minutes then we'll get you on the way to the hospital. You'll be ready to try snowboarding again next year," Baylie added, with an encouraging smile.

"I don't know if I'm meant to be a snowboarder."

"Sometimes you just have to keep trying," Kyle offered.

A wan smile formed on Rod's pasty face. "I'll think about it."

In the dwindling light the unmistakable buzz of a snowmobile echoed toward them. Together she and Kyle helped Rod to his feet. Baylie picked her jacket up off the ground and shook the snow from it before pulling it on. She shuddered as the coolness of the fabric surrounded her.

Kyle's hand lightly brushed remnants of snow off her back. It was hard to remain irritated with him when he seemed concerned about her well-being. He had to be cold without his shirt. "Thanks."

He gave her a curt nod.

The roar of the snowmobile's arrival drowned out further talk other than what was necessary.

"They're waiting for him at the lift. I don't want to take the chance of him falling off the snowmobile, so I want him to take the lift," she told Ken, the man driving the machine. "I'll get my skis and be at the clinic in a few minutes."

Ken nodded. "I'll see you at the top."

She turned and faced Kyle before the snowmobile moved out of sight. "Don't you ever contradict me again about patient care while on this mountain. Do you understand, Dr. Campbell?"

"Even when I'm right?"

She stared at him a few seconds before she said, "I'm doing my job on this mountain my way. I don't have to trust your judgment."

"My, I did get your dander up." He stepped a pace closer. "I was only thinking of you when I said to stay put. It's hard to walk uphill in the snow, particularly when it isn't necessary."

She glared at him. "It wasn't your call to make."

He returned her look.

This stalemate wasn't getting them anywhere. She was all done in but she wouldn't admit it to him. "Don't do it again, Doctor." She headed back up the trail. "Coming? You'd better get your skis before it gets too dark."

Kyle put his skis on and waited as Baylie did the same. It irked him that she refused to trust him as a doctor, but even more that she didn't seem to trust him as a person. Maybe there were legal issues but she was controlling to the point of being harmful to herself. She had to be exhausted but he couldn't fault her medical thoroughness. She did seem to be a skilled EMT. Granted, it had been years since his accident, but she was worlds better than the guy who'd been in charge after his fall.

"We'd better get going. We're losing daylight," she said as she pushed away.

Kyle followed at a slower pace, still unsettled because the evening shadows made the slope more difficult to judge. He compensated for his uncertainty by making the excuse that he could at least enjoy the view of Baylie's hips shifting from side to side if he lagged behind. She did have a fine backside. The trip down flew by with ease as his focus remained on her.

A lone lift operator stood next to the control building as Baylie approached. He put the radio to his mouth, letting the man at the top of the lift know that they were coming up.

"Hey, Russ."

"Hey, Baylie. Everything all right?"

"Yeah. Another snowboarder with a busted wrist. I just wish they'd get wrist guards when they buy a board, but I guess that would negate some kind of thrill that they get from thinking they are invincible."

Russ lifted his chin in acknowledgment of Kyle as he stopped beside her. Kyle returned a nod.

"Yeah, the young think they'll never get hurt," Russ commented.

Baylie couldn't agree more. She'd seen firsthand that the human body broke. She relived it nightly in her nightmares.

"Russ, we're ready to head up. I have to see that our patient gets to the hospital." She slid into position to catch the lift. Kyle moved in beside her.

Russ radioed the man at the controls and the lift started moving. Soon she and Kyle were hanging forty feet above the ground. The sun was little more than a whisper in the western sky. Flakes of snow drifted slowly down around them and the tips of the tree branches lining the slopes were heavy with snow. Under other circumstances it might have been a romantic ride.

Despite the roomier lift seat, having Kyle's large body so close did funny things to her insides. Feelings she tried to ignore. He didn't think much of her, and she didn't like his attitude. Kyle was here only because she had to have help, and that was it. They would coexist and then go their separate ways.

She shivered when she leaned back and her wet jacket pressed against the lift seat.

"You okay?"

Baylie had no idea Kyle was observing her so closely. "Just a little cold."

"Yeah. I bet. Your coat is wet. Hold my poles a sec."

She took them and watched as he stuffed his gloves into

the pockets of his coat and started taking it off. "What're you doing?"

"Giving you my coat."

"We're on a lift. You're going to drop something!"

"No, I'm not." He grabbed the collar of his jacket and pulled it over his head then stuffed the coat between their hips.

"Now you'll be cold," Baylie said.

"This is a good thermal shirt. I'll be all right. You're much smaller and need the heat more. Stop complaining and hand me the poles."

"Who's being bossy now?" After the adrenaline rush of helping a patient and then doing so much walking Baylie was miserable. Having a dry jacket did have its appeal.

"Stop stalling and get that wet jacket off. You won't be able to see to the patient if you have hypothermia."

She was cold and it would feel good to have something dry on. Handing him the poles, she began removing her jacket. When she got twisted up, Kyle took a cuff and pulled the coat until it was off. He tucked it under his arm.

"Now put mine on."

She shivered again, her teeth chattering. Grabbing Kyle's jacket, which had stayed warm between them, she slipped her arms into it. After some careful maneuvering she had it in place.

"Zip it all the way up," Kyle said in a voice that would accept no argument.

Baylie did as instructed. The jacket was huge but she snuggled it close. It still held some of Kyle's body warmth and the slight citrus smell of his suntan lotion. "Thanks," she murmured.

"You're welcome."

A few minutes later Baylie asked, "You've done this jacket exchange thing before, haven't you?"

"Yeah, a few times."

"You have some serious slope skills," Baylie offered.

That particular topic Kyle had no interest in discussing. "Thank you."

"I mean, you seriously know how to ski. You've got a natural ability."

His chest tightened. "I appreciate the compliment."

"So where'd you learn to ski?"

"Mostly Colorado." But he'd gone down mountains all over the world.

"Your family all skiers?"

He flinched at the memory of his family skiing on the weekends when he'd been growing up. His mother and father had believed that a family that played together stayed together. That had remained true until a few years ago when a drunk driver had taken his parents' lives. Now it was just his sister and himself.

What was Baylie fishing for? She hadn't shown this much interest in him since they'd met. She must be cold and out of sorts.

"Why all the questions?" He shifted, turning toward her. The seat swung, rocking her toward him then back. She smelled of alpine air and a sweet scent that was hers alone.

"I was just wondering. You ski well but you didn't seem happy about being assigned to a trail. I wondered why."

"Would you believe I don't like being told what to do?" he said in his best deadpan voice. So his apprehension had shown.

"Yes, I'd believe that. But I think there is more to it."

"I just hadn't been on skis in a number of years."

"Why?"

"What is this? Twenty questions?"

She narrowed her eyes at him and waited.

"The usual. Life, med school, starting a practice."

Baylie's look said she didn't think that was the entire story. "Feeling more confident now?"

"Yeah." He'd been on the hot seat long enough. It was time to move on to another subject. Since Baylie had opened the door to personal questions, he'd ask a few of his own. "Now it's my turn to find out why you overreacted to the surgical table falling the other day."

She stiffened and looked up at the cable ahead of them. "I don't like loud noises."

"I think there's more to it than that."

"Well, there isn't."

Kyle was disappointed to see they had reached the top of the mountain.

Baylie secured her coat under her arm and raised the safety bar, preparing to exit. "I have to see to Rod, make sure he has someone to drive him to the hospital. I appreciate your help today. I'll leave your coat at the patrol office." She headed down the beginner slope toward the courtesy-patrol building, without giving him an opportunity to respond.

With lips pursed in thought, Kyle stood in the near-darkness, watching her go. "Miss This-is-my-mountain" was hiding a secret. Everything about Baylie dared him to get to know her better. She was a puzzle and he couldn't quite get the pieces to fit. But he would. He'd always enjoyed a good puzzle.

CHAPTER FOUR

HOURS LATER, KYLE lounged in the adorned lobby of the lodge. There was a hunting-chalet feel to it. Holiday greenery was draped on every handrail with large red bows attached. The deer head above the mantel of the fireplace even had a wreath round it. An enormous fir tree filled one corner, decked with ornaments, and a hint of pine filled the air.

It had been too quiet in his room and the bar scene held no appeal. It was nice to find a peaceful spot and still have the occasional interruption of people passing by.

"Why, Dr. Campbell, I would've expected to see you at the Snow Top Bar instead of here with your feet by the fire."

He looked up. "What're you doing here, Baylie?"

"I was going to ask you the same thing. The employees and volunteers aren't allowed to loaf in this area. It's for guests only."

Baylie wore a sweater whose material hugged her feminine figure and showed off her small but high breasts flawlessly. Her slim hips were covered by jeans and her feet were encased in fur-lined boots of the popular style. She carried a down-filled jacket in one hand. All in all a very appealing woman.

The aqua color of her top perfectly complemented her dark tresses swinging freely around her face. He'd only seen her hair sticking out from under a cap or messy from having had it covered. It looked soft, silky and thick. He had a sudden urge to touch it. If he hadn't known better he could have mistaken her for one of the college students on the mountain with their family. She screamed sex appeal, and his body was responding to the call.

"So part of your job is to police this area too?"

Her hands went to her hips. "No, I was called to see a child who had a stomachache. I'm on my way out."

"Since you're here, how about joining me for a cup of hot chocolate? Someone said they make a good one in the Lodge Café. I'll even share my foot space by the fire." He grinned.

"I don't think so."

"I hate drinking alone. Maybe we could find something that we like about each other." He shrugged his shoulder. "If not, find something else we both dislike. Come on, Baylie, live a little."

Pain flashed into her dark eyes before she said, "Thanks, but still not interested."

A log rolled off in the fire with a thump and a shower of sparks. Baylie looked around frantically before her eyes met his. Why was she so skittish?

Kyle stood. "It didn't fall out. It's fine." He picked up a poker and pushed the log farther into the fire.

"See you tomorrow. Eight-thirty sharp," Baylie snapped. She was already headed across the lobby toward the entrance by the time he finished securing the log.

"Hey, wait up." What was her hurry? It wasn't that late in the evening.

"I'm tired."

He caught up with her. "There it was again. Why the over-the-top reaction?"

"I don't feel like discussing it with you." Her feet kept moving.

Frustration gnawed at him. "I'm just trying to help."

She glared at him and pulled the huge wooden door open.

"What makes you think you can help?"

He had no doubt that the question was a rhetorical one.

As she stepped out into the crisp night air, she zipped up her jacket. Without slowing her pace, she headed down the walk in the direction of her place. Not taking time to retrieve his jacket, Kyle shoved his hands in his pockets and hunched his shoulders against the cold. Behind, he walked faster to catch up with her.

She glanced back at him a couple of times but didn't invite him to join her. Had he struck a nerve? When she passed the bunkhouse, she slowed and turned. "Didn't you miss your stop?"

"Nah, I have a room over at the lodge. So I am entitled to hang out there. I can even bring a friend. Would you like to be my friend?" he asked with a grin.

She made a small sound of disgust and stepped his direction. "You have a room at the lodge?"

"Yeah, I decided I'd outgrown dorm life. So I took a unit for the week. Very comfortable. The only snoring that will disturb me is my own." A burst of wind cut through his sweater and jeans. He stamped his feet. Surely she would invite him in to warm up.

"Then why're you over here, slumming?"

"I was making sure you got home okay." He stepped closer. "You seemed upset and there's a bunch of drunken college guys out tonight so I thought you needed watching over."

Kyle's heart skipped a beat as Baylie stomped toward him. She was beautiful in her anger. Her hair blew away from her moonlit face, her black eyes were wide and her lips pursed. What would it be like to kiss that exquisitely formed mouth? She came within his arm's length. "I can take care of myself, thank you," she spat. "You can go on back to your high-dollar lodging now."

"What? It bothers you that I'm showing concern for another human? The Hippocratic oath says I have to. Or is it that I dare show concern for the self-sufficient, I-can-do-everything-by-myself Baylie?"

She harrumphed and turned toward her place.

In midmotion he grabbed her shoulders and held her in place. "What gives, Baylie?"

She wiggled out of his hands. "I don't know what you mean."

"I think you do. Are you running from me or something else?"

"I'm not running from anything. And don't let your ego convince you that I'd ever run from you. What you don't understand is that not every woman is going to fall for a handsome doctor."

"So you think I'm handsome?" he said in a teasing tone.

She groaned but the corners of her mouth lifted. "That would be the one word in this conversation you'd pick up on."

"Oh, I heard the rest, but I just don't believe it. In fact..." he stepped closer "...I think you're running because you like me better than you let on."

"What makes you believe that?" She lifted her chin and looked straight into his eyes before lowering her head.

"The way you seem to get all feisty and confrontational when I try to have a conversation with you or when I ask you to spend any time with me. It's as if you're deliberately trying not to like me."

"That's not true. I don't even give you that much thought. I'm just not interested."

"Yes, you do. And, yes, you are. Like now." Kyle moved into her personal space. She didn't move back. He liked that. She had spunk. If he kissed her, would her resistance crumble?

"I don't play snow-bunny games. You're here to help out. That's all there is to it."

"You sure do have a big list of don'ts so I'll add another one." His hands found her waist. He pulled her to him then his lips captured hers. It wasn't a forceful kiss. Instead he questioned, searched.

Her lips were plump and cool. As he pressed his mouth closer, hers warmed. He wanted more. Just when she leaned in to return his kiss, she suddenly pulled away.

"Look, I'm not yours or anyone else's after the slopes close. If you want a woman I'm sure Tiffani is available." She turned and climbed the steps to her door.

"I don't want Tiffani. I want you," he called, before she shut the door, leaving him out in the cold.

The next morning Kyle only saw Baylie briefly. She'd avoided him, as he'd expected. He'd enjoyed their kiss and despite her bluster he believed she had too. He wasn't used to expending so much effort to get a woman to spend time with her. She was pushing him away and that added to her mystique. What was behind all that huff and puff?

Kyle hadn't balked at being assigned to the same spot on the mountain he'd had the evening before. If he'd thought the crowds of crazy skiers had been over the top yester-day, today was much worse. The day wasn't passing fast enough. Midafternoon, a call came over the radio. "Bay-lie, we need you on Steep and Deep."

"What's the problem?" came Baylie's voice.

"Looks like a severe leg break."

"Location?"

The guy's voice came back with details of where the victim lay.

"Ten-four. Be there in ten."

Kyle had gone to medical school to care for this type of injury. Without any thought, he shoved off and skied toward the slope where the accident had occurred. He'd studied the trail map the night before. It wasn't far away. He listened to Baylie busily giving directions over the radio as he went.

Making tight turns, he kept his shoulders facing down-hill and moved harder and faster than he had in the past ten years. His heart beat wildly in his chest. He had to make sure that the same thing didn't happen to this skier that had happened to him. There was a twinge in his knee, reminding him that it had been repaired. That he could deal with. Otherwise it seemed he'd slipped back into the groove he'd known so long ago.

Kyle had been impressed with Baylie's decision-making and skills so far but leg injuries were his specialty. In this area he wouldn't back down. He'd give her no choice but to accept his suggestions.

He found the correct slope, one easier than the one he'd just skied. He gained speed. Minutes later he slid up near the group of people surrounding the injured person with a flourish and a fan of snow flying out beside him. For an instant he relished having done it.

As he removed his skis, Kyle glanced around the area. There was a small trickling creek that ran over gray rock where trees had fallen at different angles across the water. Kyle laid his skis off to the side and pushed through the crowd.

A middle-aged man lay half on the snow and half on the wet, rocky ground. He must have lost control and skied off the slope. The one sure thing about skis was that they would stop in an instant when not on snow. The man's right foot lay at an angle that made it clear to Kyle the man had a compound fracture.

He looked around. Baylie had yet to arrive. This man's injury was severe enough that Kyle wouldn't wait for her instructions, not even to make her happy. Whether or not the man ever walked correctly again could be affected by what happened in the next few minutes.

Next to the injured man and on his knees was the skiing hero Baylie had hugged the day before. Kyle wished she'd smile just once at him like she had when she'd seen this kid. Then again, maybe his heart couldn't stand it if she did. "You the one who called this in?"

"Yeah. What're you doing here?" the kid demanded.

"I'm a doctor." Kyle turned to the injured man. "I'm Dr. Kyle Campbell. More help is on the way. Right now I'm going to see if I can make you more comfortable." Carefully, he started running his hands along the length of the man's leg. "What's your name?"

"Tom Moore," he whispered, and pain circled each word.

"Tom, I see you had a yard sale here." The injured man gave him a wincing smile.

Kyle had experienced a number of "yard sales" in his skiing career when he had fallen hard enough to knock off all his equipment and send it flying in four different directions.

"Yeah, I guess I did. The kids are going to enjoy this."

Kyle patted his shoulder. "Yeah, the ribbing at the Christmas dinner table will be tough for years to come." To the kid he said, "It's Derek, isn't it?"

The kid nodded yes.

"Tom, this is Derek. Right now, we're going to try to keep you as warm as possible. I need you to help me, Derek." Kyle started removing his jacket. "Tom, how did this happen?" Kyle half listened. He'd asked Tom the question just to keep him alert.

"We need to get a jacket under him and one over him," Kyle told Derek. "We've got to keep his core warm. Prevent shock. I'll lift his shoulders while you slide my jacket under. Try to get it as far down as his waist."

Baylie arrived as they finished. Her eyes narrowed and her mouth turned down. As he'd expected, she didn't look pleased to see him. So what else was new?

"He has a compound fracture to his femur," Kyle informed her. "Derek, take your jacket off and cover his chest." The young man did as Kyle instructed.

Baylie pursed her lips tightly but said nothing. She was a professional and her concern for the patient had to come first. She'd save her dressing down until the patient was out of hearing range. She brought her radio to her mouth. "ETA on the stretcher?"

"Ten."

She moved toward the man and placed her emergency bag beside her. "Hi, I'm Baylie Walker. I'm part of the courtesy patrol. We're going to get you up the mountain and to the hospital as soon as possible."

"It hurts," the man moaned.

She touched his arm. "I know. We'll help with that too."

Baylie might be a tough leader but she knew how to calm a patient and make them feel as if they were getting the best of care. He had to admire that about her.

Two additional patrol members joined them.

"Please see that the crowd keeps moving," Baylie instructed them. "We'll have our hands full, without rubberneckers getting hurt."

"While you organize things, I'll start seeing to the leg," Kyle said. "Hand me the scissors."

Baylie glared at him, her eyes snapping. She wasn't just annoyed; she was livid. Opening her mouth as if to say something, she glanced at the patient then jerked the scissors out of the pocket on the side of her bag and handed them to him. She opened the bag and pulled out a stethoscope with more force than necessary.

He didn't have time to calm her ruffled feathers. The man's leg depended on him getting to work. "Tom, you're going to need to stay as motionless as possible while I see to your leg. Derek, help hold him still."

"Okay," Derek said, placing a hand on each of the man's shoulders.

Kyle moved carefully across the rocky ground to where Tom's leg lay at an odd angle. One awkward step in the cumbersome ski boots and Kyle would do damage to his own leg. Kneeling, he began cutting away the man's ski bib leg. Working from the bottom along the outside of the calf, thigh and up to the hip, he split the pants open.

Baylie picked up Tom's wrist to start taking vitals. She called them out. At least he wasn't in cardiac distress. Finished with the bib leg, Kyle cut through the thermal underwear, taking special care around the swollen area. As he continued the material opened and the femur was exposed.

Baylie whispered, "Eee."

The ends of the bone were jagged and pointed. Her gaze met his for a second. Was that a flicker of unease in her eyes? It quickly disappeared, replaced by determination.

It was a bad break. Kyle's stomach rolled and a bitter taste filled his mouth. This wasn't going to be an easy surgery fix or a stress-free recovery. He knew that from experience. Shaking off the melancholy outlook, he regained his focus. "Baylie, I need clean bandages over that open wound. Preventing infection is paramount."

She pulled her bag closer and dug until she found four-by-four gauze packages. She would be hurling fire and brimstone over his head when they were done here.

"Stop any bleeding you can but don't apply too much pressure." Thankfully, the cold weather slowed the flow of blood.

"I understand." Baylie looked at him. "How you doing, Tom?" Her tone was one of concern and caring. She covered the entire area with a large clean cloth and secured it carefully.

"I'm going to check for further damage, Tom. I'll try not to hurt you any more than necessary." Kyle moved his hands along the man's leg, gently probing.

The man groaned and closed his eyes.

"As soon as the stretcher gets here, I'll start an IV," Baylie said.

"Good. We also need to get this leg splinted and the boot off ASAP. We're racing against the swelling with every minute that passes."

"Dr. Campbell, can I speak to you a minute?" Baylie asked him in a tone that implied she wouldn't accept no as an answer.

Still, he had to try. "Can it wait?"

When she said nothing, Kyle glanced at her. She pierced him with a look. She stood and stepped far enough away that neither the patient nor Derek could hear. Kyle joined her, standing so that his back was to the injured man.

She moved close and said in a steely voice, "You don't make the decisions here. I do. They'll handle the boot removal at the hospital. We can't take a chance on damaging his leg further."

"The boot has to come off. I know what I'm doing. I'm a sports-med doctor. I've treated injuries this bad numerous times. If we don't remove the boot it could very well mean the man never walks again."

Her mouth drew into a thin line. She clearly didn't want to agree with him.

"Baylie, don't let the rules cloud your common sense. These boots…" he kicked at the snow and ice on the slope "…are heavy. If his foot swells much more we won't be able to take it off. Even cutting off these things at the hospital can be difficult. You know it's the right move."

Her look clashed with his. "You're going to do it whether I agree to it or not."

His gaze didn't leave hers. "I am. It's the best thing for the patient."

"You know I could stop you."

"You could, but you won't." His gaze never wavered.

"You're that sure of me?"

"I know that above all you want the best for your patients. I think you know that I do too." By medical hierarchy and education, he was the senior medical person here but ultimately she had to agree.

"If you're wrong…" Baylie said softly.

"I'm not wrong. Trust me."

She looked at him long and hard before saying, "I'm

handling the splinting and transfer. Understood? You can see about the boot removal."

With a roar the snowmobile pulling the sled stretcher came up the slope. Before it completely stopped, Baylie was on her way toward it.

What had Kyle done to make her think she could trust him? He'd been great with the kids in ski school, had been concerned about her on more than one occasion; he had dealt with a distraught parent with skill and reassured a snowboarder when he'd thought his days on the slopes were over. Maybe there was reason to trust him, to value his judgment.

"Ron, we need the thermal blankets and the large emergency pack," she told the driver.

The man jumped off the machine and lifted the seat. Pulling out blankets, he handed them to her. With her arms full, she returned to the patient. "Derek, tuck these around and under him, leaving the leg exposed."

By the time the blankets were in place, Ron had brought the larger supply bag.

"Switch places with me," she said to Kyle. He leaned back and she maneuvered past him in the tight place between the trees and rocks surrounding them. As her body brushed his she was reminded of how much larger he was than her. What would it be like to always feel the shelter of his body?

"As I move the foot around, you support the leg." She gave Kyle a level look.

"I'll follow your lead," he responded.

Yeah, until I do something he doesn't agree with. "Good. Ready?"

"Yes."

"I only want to straighten the leg as much as necessary

in order to splint it well." She cupped the heel of the man's injured leg and shifted it into a more normal position while Kyle gently held the leg above the break. "All right, let's get splints on this. Ron, get the long splints off the stretcher."

The man headed back toward the snowmobile, returning with long narrow boards. He placed them on the ground near Baylie.

"Ron, go around and get opposite Kyle so you can help hold these splints in place."

The man did as instructed.

She placed one splint between the man's legs and one along the outside of the man's leg that extended up to his hip. After some careful shifting, they finally had the splints in place.

"Tom, how're you doing?"

The man's face was contorted in pain but he nodded.

"Okay, let's secure these in place. Watch the break area. We need to get him off this slope before hypothermia becomes an issue." She pulled rolls of wide tape out of the bag. Ten minutes later she said, "Get that stretcher over here. Derek, Ron, guys," Baylie shouted to a couple of patrolmen who had just skied up, "we're going to need help lifting this."

The two new volunteers brought a backboard from the sled and placed it alongside the man.

"Kyle, you support the upper part of the leg and I'll take the lower."

"Understood," Kyle responded in a no-nonsense voice.

"Okay, guys, we're going to need you to lift evenly and steadily. Watch your footing. We can't afford any additional accidents. Remember, lift from the knees."

The men all nodded.

Baylie stood and then went down into a squat. Kyle did also. Had he winced when going down on one knee?

"Problem?" Baylie asked him.

"None. Let's get this done."

"On three we lift." She waited until they all confirmed her directions. Baylie turned to the patient. "Tom, we're going to lift you onto the backboard then get that boot off before you go for a little ride."

The man nodded and closed his eyes.

"You ready?" She looked at Kyle.

He slid both arms under the man's leg. "Ready."

"One, two, three, lift."

Kyle helped lower their patient gently to the backboard. With efficient, swift, knowledgeable movements the man was strapped to the board. Kyle moved around Baylie until he was beside her at the man's boot. She gave him no argument but by her tight-lipped look she still wasn't sure about his plan. Unlatching the three buckles and the power strap, he spread the hard plastic lips at the top of the boot as wide as possible and pulled the tongue forward as far as it would go.

"Baylie, hold the leg just above the boot as steady as you can while I get this off. Derek, help Baylie." They both moved to do as he'd asked. Kyle placed a hand on the heel of the boot and tugged gently, slowly inching it off. The foot was already swollen, making it difficult to maneuver the boot. Carefully, Kyle tugged, moving it past the most difficult turn. He had to apply more force than he wished, but it was moving. Tom cried out as Kyle made the last effort.

"I'm glad that's done. The weight of the boot would likely have caused more damage while he's being transported," Kyle said as he stood. His knee throbbed. He looked at the patient, who'd passed out. While Baylie finished wrapping and adjusting the blankets to keep the limb warm, Kyle took the man's vitals.

"You did a good job with the boot," Baylie commented quietly.

He wanted to thump his chest with his fists. "Thanks. You do know by definition that was a compliment," he mumbled, for her ears only.

"Let's get him on the sled," Baylie called, ignoring him. "Okay, on my word."

Each of the four men took a handhold on the board. "Lift."

As they carried the injured man toward the snowmobile, Derek's foot slipped.

"Watch it!" Baylie called.

The patient listed in Kyle's direction. He strained to keep the board level, having to apply pressure to his bad knee until Derek found his footing again.

With Derek back in place they made it to the sled without further incident. When the patient was positioned on the sled and they were ready to go, Baylie said, "Take it easy, Ron. I'll meet you at the lift. I'll radio and let them know to expect us."

Ron nodded and the snowmobile rumbled to life.

Kyle picked up his jacket and shook it out before heading toward his skis. He was going up with her. Baylie wouldn't like it, but he was going anyway. He waited as she put on her skis.

His knee had progressed from ache to hurt. As Baylie shoved off, he followed. She went down the mountain proficiently. Small and compact, Baylie made turns he was tentative about performing. It was a pleasure to watch her go.

By the time he reached the lift, she already had her skis off and was carrying them through the crowd. The lift was no longer in motion and the snowmobile was pulled up close. He followed Baylie's lead and headed toward the snowmobile.

She, Ron and a couple of the lift operators were removing the patient from the sled. Kyle handed his skis to a man standing in line and hurried to help.

"Baylie, let me get that."

Her eyes cut to him, making it clear that she didn't appreciate him implying she couldn't do her job. Without another word he stepped up and took a handle. She was dainty but she made a Herculean effort to do her part. A few minutes later the patient was securely and safely strapped to the lift. To the average observer, it looked as if the patient was suspended in the air above the seat when he was actually locked into place.

"Thanks, guys. Good work. I'll ride up in the seat ahead so I can be there to get him to the clinic. The ambulance is already on the way."

Kyle thanked the man for holding his skis and joined Baylie in the lift seat. Seconds later, the lift started running.

"I didn't invite you to ride up with me," she stated. Her anger hadn't cooled.

"Isn't that a little juvenile after we just worked so well together?" They had made a good team.

"I'm not going to get into an argument with you right now. I still have a patient to see about. We'll talk later." She turned around to look back at their patient. When she did so her butt shifted, coming into contact with his thigh. She quickly straightened in the seat, causing the chair to swing.

He grabbed her arm. "Hey, be careful. I don't want to have to haul you up if you slip under."

"That's not going to happen. I'm not a kid."

"No, you're not," he said in a soft but emphatic voice. He knew too well that she was all woman. His body's re-action anytime she was around made it more than clear.

Baylie's head whipped around to look at him. His gaze held hers for a long moment until she broke the connec-tion. She sat stiffly beside him. The only noise was the occasional click-clack of the lift chair going over the roll-ers at the support towers. The tension between them was as thick as the snow on the slope beneath them.

When their chair reached the top of the mountain Bay-lie said, "As I organize removing the patient, would you please check his vitals one more time?"

"I'll be glad to." What had it taken her to ask him for help? "You know, you were good out there."

"Don't act so surprised. I'm well trained."

"You don't care what I think one way or another, do you?"

She glanced at him before she stepped off the lift chair. "No, I don't."

That hurt. He wasn't sure why, but it did. He wanted her to value his opinion.

Kyle followed, putting his skis down next to hers and going to stand beside her. The lift began to move, creeping closer, bringing the injured man to them. At the top of the dismount station the chair stopped. Two courtesy patrol-men joined them, and together they worked to remove the man from the lift. As they made the exchange from chair to sled again, Kyle kept a close eye on their patient. Once he was securely in place, Baylie asked the lift attendant to watch her skis and climbed on behind Ron without giving Kyle a backward glance.

The snowmobile sped off in the direction of the courtesy-patrol building. Kyle had two choices. Walk or ski. If he skied he'd have to go down and catch another lift up to get to the patrol building. The twinge in his knee said that walking wouldn't be much fun but that was what he would do.

Gathering his equipment as well as Baylie's, he started the trek through the trees in the direction of the clinic. She probably wouldn't appreciate it that he'd brought her skis but, then, she didn't appreciate much about him.

Kyle reached the courtesy-patrol building just as the ambulance was backing to the door. He stashed the skis out of the way against the wall of the building. As he started to enter to see if he could help, the ambulance attendants pushed out through the doors with the injured man.

Baylie followed close behind them as she oversaw the loading. She was a dynamo. Minutes later, with a wail of the siren, the ambulance pulled away to begin the hour-long drive to the nearest hospital.

Kyle trailed Baylie back into the building and through to the clinic area. She had to be worn out. He certainly was. The adrenaline rush and the physical labor of an emergency took a toll on the body.

"Do I need to write up part of the report?"

She turned with a look that said she was going to spit fire. "Yeah, you need to write it up. You *took* the lead! Don't you ever put me in that position—"

"Hey, Baylie." Derek lumbered into the room. "I'm sorry. I didn't mean to interrupt," he said when he saw Kyle.

"No problem. Dr. Campbell was just leaving."

"What about the paperwork?" Kyle asked, raising a brow.

"I'll handle it."

"Kyle Campbell." Derek rolled the name around in his mouth as if it were a pebble. "Your name sure does sound familiar." A smile suddenly brightened his face. "I know! You used to be on the skiing circuit. I watched you on TV when I was a kid. You were great. I was even watching the day you busted yourself up against that fence. Talk about the agony of defeat."

Kyle glanced at Baylie. He wasn't shocked to find a bewildered expression on her face. He could almost hear the wheels turning in her head as she formed questions. Turning back to Derek, Kyle said, "Yeah, that was me, but a long time ago."

"Man, you were great. I hated it when you got hurt. You were world class." He turned with the enthusiasm of youth and said, "Baylie, you should've seen this guy on skis. He was the hottest man on the slopes."

"Really?" She drew the word out as if unsure whether or not to be impressed.

"Yeah," Derek said with a passion that was truly starting to grate on Kyle's nerves. "Hey, man, could we maybe ski together sometime? I'd love to get some pointers from the great KC."

"KC?" Baylie asked, her eyes focused on Kyle with interest.

He'd not been called that for years. The crowds used to chant it before he left the starting block. But he hadn't allowed anyone to call him by his initials since the accident. At least Baylie was showing some curiosity about him, even if it wasn't for the reasons he'd prefer. He shrugged with a feeling of chagrin.

"I go by Kyle now. I'm sure I'll see you around during the week."

"Sure, man, that sounds great," Derek agreed with more eagerness than Kyle would have liked.

Turning to Baylie, he said, "I'll see you in the morning."

CHAPTER FIVE

BAYLIE HAD TO make it clear to Kyle that what had happened on the slopes today could not happen again. That discussion wasn't going to wait until tomorrow. Moreover, she didn't like being made a fool of. Kyle Campbell had done it twice, first by not telling her he was a doctor and again when he hadn't said that he had skied professionally. She could have used those skills on something more than the beginner slope from day one. Why the big secret?

She knocked on the door to Kyle's room at the lodge. Shifting her weight from one foot to the other, she knocked a second time. Was he out with Tiffani somewhere? She didn't want to know.

"Give me a sec," came a voice on the other side of the door before it was opened.

If Baylie hadn't been so put out with his actions earlier, she might have laughed at the look on his face. Astonishment slipped to amazement. His chin angled to one side in interest.

"Why, Baylie, what a nice surprise," he all but cooed.

She didn't miss the sarcasm surrounding the word "nice" while her gaze remained glued to his bare chest. If she'd noticed that his shoulders were wide before, she was even more impressed with their expanse when he didn't have a shirt on.

Swallowing a sound of admiration, her look drifted further south. A pair of baggy gym shorts covered him from hips to knees. His feet were bare. Kyle looked more like he belonged at the beach than at a ski resort. She resisted the temptation to lick her lips. Her eyes slid upward to his face.

His expression had turned to one of concern. "Am I needed?"

She gulped. "No, you're not needed," she said emphatically. More to herself than to him. She didn't want to need anyone ever again.

One thing she'd learned about Kyle was that he was always willing to help. Despite her misgivings, he was starting to grow on her. His concern for people came first, and she could appreciate that.

"Well, thanks for bursting my ego bubble. I had hoped you would need me."

How like him to turn a simple statement into an innuendo. Baylie bet he did that just to get under her skin. She hated to admit it but it did. Or had he seen her reaction to his dress—or more precisely his undress? The thought made her stomach flutter.

"So why am I being honored by a visit from the head of the courtesy patrol?"

"We didn't finish our discussion before Derek interrupted."

"I was done."

"Well, I wasn't."

"Well, you might as well come in and let me sit down while you finish lambasting me," Kyle said as he opened the door wider then walked back into the room. He dropped more than sat in the extra-large, multicolored square chair.

Was he limping?

Baylie entered and closed the door behind her. She'd been in a number of the lodge rooms but none had been this well-appointed or spacious. It figured that Kyle would be staying in the best.

Decorated in oranges, greens and browns, it had a rustic feel. In the main room there was a fireplace over which a flatscreen TV hung. It didn't surprise her to see that the TV was turned to a sports channel. Two sofas faced each other and there were two armchairs, in one of which Kyle was sitting with his right leg stretched across an ottoman. A full kitchen filled one back corner and a family-style table the other. There was a small hallway that led to what she guessed were bedrooms. This place couldn't have been more different than hers.

Obviously he was used to comfort. Had probably grown up that way. Skiing was an expensive sport that attracted families with money. Something her family knew little about.

Baylie maneuvered between the two chairs and stood in front of him. She had to force herself not to gawk at his shirtless chest. Worse, she itched to run her hands over the span of muscle and dusting of hair. Was his torso as well defined as it appeared? Where were these feelings coming from? She didn't want to have them. She had to control them.

Baylie took a deep breath and looked at Kyle's face. Was that a pinched look of pain around his mouth?

She must have taken too long studying him because he said with a huff, "Well, get on with it."

Okay, she would. She put her hands on her hips. "I thought I'd made it clear days ago that I make the calls around here. If I wasn't so desperate for help, you'd be gone."

Kyle's look didn't waver. "I won't apologize for the decisions I made today. I think what is eating you is that I have your number."

"My number?"

"Yeah. I won't let you walk all over me."

"What?" She couldn't believe he was talking to her like that.

"I'm not intimidated by your fuss and bluster."

"You're nuts."

"No, I'm not. We did good work out there. We both did what we do well. We saved a man's leg. That's what matters," he said in an even tone.

Baylie glanced down then up again. "I know. The wagon driver said they were glad to see that the ski boot had been removed. They have a devil of a time removing them at the ER. So maybe you were right."

He smiled. "That wasn't so hard, now, was it?"

"Are you trying to make me mad again?" Her eyes wandered to his chest. She blinked and jerked them back to his face.

He had a knowing grin on his face. "I wouldn't really mind doing so. I think you're rather pretty when you're hissing like a she-cat."

This handsome man thought she was pretty? Pleasure filled her, like when she had her face up to the sun on a cold winter day.

"So now that we have that settled…" Kyle looked at her expectantly.

"I have some other issues to discuss with you."

Kyle moaned. "Then why don't you take your coat off and sit down?"

Baylie pulled her coat off, sat at the end of the sofa nearest him and placed her coat beside her. She put her hands on her knees and looked at him.

"Let's hear it." He wore a placating grin on his face.

She'd entered the dragon's lair and she couldn't back down now. There had to be some way to regain control over her runaway emotions. She jumped up. "Do you think you could put a shirt on?"

His vivid blue eyes watched her intently. "Why?"

"Uh, I just think…"

He gave her a wolfish grin. "Think what, Baylie?"

"I'm not used to having serious discussions with half-naked men."

"I hadn't planned to have a serious discussion when I got dressed."

She walked to the fireplace, keeping her back to him. "Please put on a shirt."

Kyle chuckled. "Well, if it bothers you that much…"

Holding her breath, she listened as the chair squeaked and his feet made a pat-pat sound that became softer as he must have gone into a bedroom. Her breathing returned to normal for the first time since Kyle had opened the door.

A minute later he reentered the room. "Better?"

He wore a T-shirt with a state football logo on it. Even with the shirt on she still wanted to touch him.

Taking the chair again, he brought his leg up on the footstool. "You want to try sitting down now that you're not distracted?"

"I wasn't dist—"

He gave a low sexy chuckle.

The man was far too confident in his ability to rattle her. She went to a sofa and sank onto the edge of a cushion. "Look, I want to know why you weren't up front about who you are. I need to know my volunteers can be trusted."

"I told you who I was. Kyle Campbell. I didn't realize that I had to have a background check in order to direct ski traffic."

She gave him a snide smile. "I could have been using your skills and experience to better advantage. You said nothing about being a skiing star."

"To what advantage?" He made the words sound X-rated.

She pursed her lips. "You know perfectly well what I mean."

He shrugged. "I didn't think it mattered."

"I don't get it. More than once you acted as if you weren't happy to be here."

"What's not to get? I'm a doctor who hasn't been on skis for some time, nothing more."

Baylie studied him for a second to see if there was something to what he'd said that she'd missed. "World Games. Impressive."

"Thank you. I appreciate the compliment. High praise, coming from you."

"Why's that?"

"You've always acted as if my being here is only a necessary evil. A warm body to help you out on the slopes."

He had a hot body. But she'd cut her tongue out before she told him that. "I have not."

"Seen me as evil?"

"At this moment I might."

He chuckled again. Somehow that rough, sandpapery sound made her wish to hear it over and over. Kyle had a nice laugh, one that made her want to join him in mischief.

He grinned. "If we're done arguing, I'm hungry."

"We weren't arguing. We're discussing you keeping secrets."

"With you, discussing is an argument. An entertaining one but an argument nonetheless. And I wasn't keeping secrets," he stated.

"Now I think you're making fun of me."

"Maybe a little," he said with a smile. The lift of his lips was replaced by a grimace as he shifted in the chair.

"Are you hurt?" she asked, jumping up and hurrying to him.

"No, I'm fine. Just did a little more than I'm used to today."

He readjusted his leg. She had been so caught up in trying to figure him out she hadn't noticed his swollen knee. That *had* been a limp she'd seen. "Kyle, your knee! Why didn't you say something? Have you put ice on it?"

Baylie stalked toward the kitchen to find something to use as an ice pack. She jerked to a stop and swung around when Kyle's deep-throated laughter filled the room.

"This is an interesting turn of events, you showing me attention."

She rolled her eyes. "I'm sorry if I've damaged your self-esteem. Why didn't you say something over at the patrol building? I could have looked at it. At least given you an ice pack."

"And messed up your tirade about my behavior?" He gave her a big grin. One that made her want to stop what she was doing and enjoy it.

Baylie returned his smile. His mirth was infectious. "I'm done word sparring with you. I'm getting some ice for that knee."

She found a dishcloth in the stocked kitchen. Getting a handful of ice out of the freezer section of the refrigerator, she wrapped the cubes in the cloth. If he didn't have any anti-inflammatory medicine, she'd go to the patrol building and get some. She returned to where he still sat.

"Here, put this on your knee." Baylie handed the ice pack to him. "Twenty minutes on and twenty off."

"Yes, ma'am." He took the cloth and placed it on his knee, holding it in place. She moved away.

"Am I really that bossy?" Baylie asked.

"Sometimes."

"I guess you can leave the army but it doesn't leave you." She knew that far too well. Every large noise, every nightmare, and Ben remained with her.

"Why'd you join the army? You don't seem like the army type to me."

"My father is a coal miner and there wasn't money to send me to school. I dreamed of seeing the world. The army gave me both of those."

Kyle watched her too intently, as if expecting her to say more. Was he thinking about how different their lifestyles and upbringings had been? Whatever her material circumstances, she'd felt rich. Her parents loved her and she knew it.

"Hey, do you have any ibuprofen? You need to get that swelling down or you won't be able to ski tomorrow."

"Aw, there's the true Baylie. Worried about having enough help."

She slapped his arm playfully. "That's not the only reason I'm concerned. I'm compassionate toward all wounded animals." Was she really smiling and flirting with Kyle? It did feel good to let go a bit. "How about that med?"

"Didn't bring any with me. I've not had any trouble with the knee in years."

"How did you injure it?"

"I'll tell you all about it if you agree to have dinner with me."

"I don't know."

"You don't want me to have to hobble out to get something to eat with this knee, do you?"

"Playing on my guilt now, Doctor?"

"If it works." He grinned.

"All right. I guess I could pick us up something on my way back from the patrol building after I get you some ibuprofen."

"Well, don't sound so happy about the prospect of expending so much effort for me. I am starving and you are the one providing the medical care."

"Are you sure you didn't go to the wrong school? Shouldn't you be a lawyer? You do have a way of twisting words around to your best interest."

"You should hear what I can whisper in a woman's ear."

What would it be like to have that sinuous mouth speaking softly in her ear? She shivered—and covered it with a laugh. One of those deep-in-the-belly, cleansing laughs that made a person glad to be alive. "You are incorrigible. At least I know you aren't capable of chasing me around the room with that bummed-up knee."

The smile left his face, his look turning somber and unwavering. "Not right now, but I have every intention of doing so real soon."

Melting warmth flowed through her. "Is that a warning?"

"No, Baylie, that's a promise."

She swallowed hard. Was she ready for a relationship? Could she get past the guilt in order to have one? Something about Kyle made her think he was an all-or-nothing kind of guy. She was too screwed up to be anything he'd ever really want. Best not to start anything she couldn't finish. "Uh, I'm going to get that ibuprofen and some supper. Keep the ice on that knee." Baylie snatched up her coat.

"Running away won't change the facts," Kyle said softly as she closed the door behind her.

Kyle hadn't been kidding about his desire for Baylie, but he worried that she might not return. He'd laid his cards on the table, and he could have scared her off.

His heart thumped firmly against his chest when a little tap came at the door forty-five minutes later. Was it Baylie? He hadn't let himself contemplate how badly he hoped she'd come back. With more energy than he'd believed himself capable of, and a bobble in his walk he couldn't deny, he made it to the door.

"Who is it?"

"Baylie."

He smiled. She had guts and hadn't been put off by his straightforward remarks. Or was she just being the caring person she was? He opened the door.

Her heavy coat was in place again and in her hands were two sacks. Without a sideways look she headed for the table. She glanced back at him as she shrugged out of her coat. "I'm going to stick these in the microwave for a second. Can you get to the table by yourself, or do you need help?"

He would've liked to insist that she come and wrap her arms around him so he could lean on her but he didn't want to run her off. "I can make it. I'm not a complete cripple."

"You will be if you don't take care of that knee." She

pulled food containers out of one brown sack and went into the kitchen.

Kyle enjoyed the view of her behind encased in dark denim as she walked away. He never thought of himself as a butt man but he sure seemed to have a fascination with Baylie's. Lassoing his libido, he took a seat at the table.

While the microwave hummed, Baylie approached, handing him two small brown pills. "Here you go."

Kyle's fingertips trailed over her palm as he took the medicine. Her hand shook slightly as he touched her. His male pride soared. There was something between them, and not just on his part. His gaze traveled up to her full breasts, covered in a wooly pink sweater that outlined them flawlessly. He watched as they rose and fell with her breathing before his look met hers. Her attention remained fixed on his face. There were high spots of red on her cheeks that had nothing to do with being out in the weather all day. She sucked in a short breath and he lost his. She was dazzling.

Slow down, buddy. Don't panic her.

Grinning, he said, "Thanks for taking such good care of me, Baylie."

"It's my job." She pulled a takeout cup out of the other sack and handed it to him. Digging in the bag again, she removed another and set it on the table.

"I'd like to think it's more than that," he said quietly.

Her beautiful brown gaze drifted up to meet his.

The buzzer of the microwave announced their supper was warm. The moment popped like a soap bubble, but it had been there. There had been a twinkle of interest in Baylie's eyes.

She returned to the kitchen and brought the first container to him while the other heated.

"I like this kind of service."

"Don't get too used to it. I picked up an ace bandage while I was at the patrol building so you can wrap that knee tomorrow. Also some more ibuprofen for later tonight."

"So what you're telling me is that I can't count on this kind of attention regularly?"

"Yeah, that's exactly what I'm saying."

"Am I going to have to hurt myself more seriously to get extra attention?"

She stood, looking pointedly at him. "Don't even think about it. That wouldn't be a good way to get my attention."

He reached out and took her hand, slowly letting it trail through his. "So what's a good way?"

"By eating your food before it gets cold."

Once again the practical Baylie was back. He missed the playful one. Didn't she ever just let go? Do something crazy and unexpected?

The microwave buzzed again. She went after her meal and brought it to the table. It didn't pass his notice that she chose to sit on the other side of the table from him, out of touching distance.

"I was tired of pizza and burgers so I got the grilled chicken meal." Baylie poked at her meat.

Kyle dug his fork into the potatoes, putting them in his mouth. "Mmm. Good. Hits the spot. Thanks for taking pity and having dinner with me. I'd probably have called room service. It's much nicer having company at a meal."

"I doubt you have any trouble getting someone to eat with you."

"Fishing for how much I go out, Baylie?"

"I am not. You sure have an inflated view of yourself, Doctor. I was just making conversation."

"Pretty personal conversation."

"You're right. It's none of my business. But even though it is personal, you promised to tell me what happened with that knee."

"No big story really."

Baylie knew better. She'd seen him pause on the slope. He'd questioned his assignments. The fact that she'd had to ask told her it was a huge deal to him. "So what happened?"

"I was in the finals of the National Downhill competition. Instead of clearing the last gate, I hit the fence and tore up my knee. An egotistical EMT mishandled my leg and I never recovered full movement in it."

"Now I get it. Your reaction to me being an EMT. I'm sorry about your leg."

He looked directly at her. "It wasn't your fault. I was a jerk the first day we met. I'm sorry."

"What exactly went wrong? What did he do? Not do?" She was making notes not to let the same thing happen with one of her patients.

Kyle hesitated, and then took a deep breath as if this wasn't something he made a habit of talking about regularly. "I still had my boots on. My injured foot slipped off the stretcher. Not far, but far enough. The movement tore my knee further. The doctors told me that I'd never compete professionally again."

His last words sounded hollow. Kyle obviously still missed competing. Her heart hurt for him. "I'm sorry." And she meant it. "That's why you insisted on removing the man's boot today."

Kyle nodded and stabbed his green beans with his fork. "That was a long time ago. I've moved on."

She wasn't so sure about that. It might be gone but it hadn't been easily forgotten.

"That was until today."

"I have to admit it did bring back some tough memories." He pulled drink from the takeout cup through a straw then said, "I've answered your questions, so now it's your turn to answer mine. What brings you to Snow Mountain Resort?"

"I grew up not far from here. My brothers worked here so I followed along. I've been coming here on and off for years. When I was discharged from the army I needed a job and this one was open."

"So you're a local?"

"I am." He hadn't made the question sound like he was looking down on her, but she was still conscious of the difference in how they lived.

"So what're you going to do when the season is over?"

"I'm not sure. There's mountain biking in the summer, so I may just stay here."

"You're happy so far away from everything? You don't need a shopping fix once a week?" he asked, watching her more closely than made her comfortable.

Baylie's stomach cramped at the thought of being in a crowd or the loud noises of a city. She put her fork down. "No, I don't need a big city or anything that goes with it."

"That sounded pretty harsh. I enjoy living in Pittsburgh. I thought it would be tough to leave the Rocky Mountains behind but I love the rivers, the people and the sports. There's always plenty to do."

"Well, I'm more of a peace-and-quiet girl." She pushed away from the table and carried her food container to the trash.

Kyle stood and picked up his container. Baylie took it from him. "Go sit down and put that ice back on that knee."

"There you go telling me what to do again. I am a sport

medicine doctor. I do have some knowledge in this department."

"Yeah, but doctors are notorious for making the worst patients. And men are known for thinking they don't have to do as the medic orders."

Kyle wasn't going to argue those points. She was right. At least his knee had improved some with the application of ice and the meds. Disregarding her directions, he carried their drink containers to the trash. When Baylie moved past him toward the table he caught her wrist in a loose grasp. It was so delicate and fine boned he was afraid he might break it if he'd grabbed her any tighter. She looked at him. "Why don't you stay and watch TV with me for a while?"

He ran his thumb across her pulse to find it thumping rapidly.

"I don't think that would be a good idea."

"Why? Because you might find out that you like me? Or because you're afraid you might like this?"

His lips brushed hers. She didn't resist. He placed his hand on her back and brought her against him. Her curves met his, accommodating and warm. He made small begging nips at her lips until her arms slowly circled his waist. He took her mouth completely. Baylie rewarded him by kissing him in return. That was all the invitation he needed to find the treasure he was after. He pulled her closer, molding her more completely to him. Lifting his mouth a fraction, he changed the angle of his lips to further take hers. Stunned by the passion that consumed him, he shuddered.

As abruptly as a car running into a brick wall, Baylie pulled away.

"Don't do that again." She stepped out of his arms.

Kyle searched her face. "You don't mean that. You were kissing me too."

"That doesn't matter. Please don't do it again," she said in a low, dark voice.

"Why not? You liked it. I sure as hell did."

She opened her mouth.

"Don't bother to deny it. Your body will just give you away." He moved, putting distance between them. Despite her rejection, he still wanted her. "Your mind might say no but your lips on mine scream yes."

"I think you're mistaken."

"Of that I'm not. Give me a little credit for knowing when a woman enjoys my kisses."

"I do not."

He chuckled dryly. "I know you do. If you looked in a mirror right now you'd see it too."

She lifted a prettily arched brow. "That's you wishing."

"Yeah, it is." His words came out low and suggestive.

"I'm not anyone's plaything for a week. We don't even like each other. I don't like the city, and you do. You're fancy places to stay and expensive skis, and I'm not. We don't agree on anything. Those alone are enough to keep us apart."

He had no idea what she was talking about. "There you go again with the don'ts. I know we both enjoyed that kiss."

"Don't speak for me."

"You can throw all that other stuff out in front of us but you're lying to yourself if you think there isn't something going on. I'm surprised. I took you for a straight shooter. A person who knows her mind."

Baylie compressed her lips and looked at him for a long moment before she offered him a disposable ice pack that she must've brought from the clinic. When he put his hand out palm up, she slapped the bag into it. "I'd better go." She grabbed her jacket and headed for the door.

He hadn't gotten through to her. "Think about what I said," Kyle called before the door clicked closed between them.

Two days later Baylie was preparing to close the patrol office for the day when she heard Kyle hollering with a note of alarm in his voice.

"Baylie-e-e!"

"In here."

They hadn't spoken to each other since that night at his place, apart from Baylie giving him instructions on where she wanted him to be stationed on the slopes. She'd missed his needling and quick grin. And his kisses. She may not have spoken to him much but she had sure thought about his lips on hers often. The man could kiss.

Before she reached the door of the exam room, Kyle rushed in, carrying a young teenage girl in his arms. Following him were two anxious-looking adults.

"What's going on?" Baylie asked as she hurried to lower the head of the examination table.

"Difficulty breathing, rash, swelling of the face." Kyle laid the girl on the table.

"Anaphylactic shock?" Baylie asked as she handed a stethoscope to Kyle.

"That's my guess."

Baylie pulled the cannula off the hanger on the wall and fit it under the girl's nose before she turned the oxygen on.

"You start the IV while I get heart rate, respirations and BP," Kyle said.

Baylie gathered the necessary supplies. While Kyle removed the girl's jacket he spoke reassuringly to her. She gasped for breath. He called over his shoulder to the couple huddling in the doorway, "Are either of you this girl's parents?"

"No." The man stepped forward. "I'm her church youth group leader."

"What's her name?" Kyle asked as he reached for the blood-pressure cuff.

"Kelly Bishop."

"Kelly, I'm Baylie and this is Kyle and we're going to help you get better. Don't struggle to breathe. It will get better soon."

The girl's wide, fearful eyes tugged at Baylie's heart. She'd seen that same type of terror in Ben's eyes before he'd died.

"Do you know if she's allergic to anything?" Kyle asked the couple.

"There was nothing on her medical release form," the man offered.

Kyle placed the stethoscope on the girl's chest, listened then pulled the ends out of his ears, wrapping the instrument around his neck. "Do you know what she was eating?" he asked the couple again.

"I think she was having something from Wok Works," the woman said softly.

Kyle looked at Baylie and they said in unison, "Peanuts."

"I'll get the epi," Baylie said. Less than a minute later she was back and inserting the medicine into the IV line. "Kelly, you should be feeling much better in a few minutes."

Already the girl was beginning to breathe more easily. Slipping the ends of the stethoscope into his ears again,

Kyle listened to the girl's heart. Finished, he said to Baylie, "Heart rate moving toward normal."

Baylie watched the automatic blood pressure machine for the reading. "Blood pressure improving."

Kyle spoke to Kelly. "You're going to be fine. You'll need to go to the hospital for a checkup, though." His lips lifted into a charming smile. "This is the end of your peanut-eating days."

The girl made an effort to smile. The man was a good doctor. Not only his skills but his way with patients. Kelly wasn't the first person whose fearful look had disappeared after Kyle had spoken to them.

Baylie checked the girl's nail beds and found them returning to a normal healthy pink color, indicating that the oxygen level in her blood was evening out. "Kelly will need to go to the hospital for a thorough checkup," Baylie told the couple. "She'll go by ambulance because of the distance, and in case there are further complications."

The man and woman nodded their understanding.

"I'll call the hospital right now. It'll take them some time to get here. We'll monitor Kelly…" she looked at Kyle and he nodded "…until the ambulance arrives. Please plan to meet her at the hospital."

"And be sure to have her medical release form with you. It will make the paperwork smoother," Kyle suggested.

"I'll take care of that right now," the man said.

"May I stay with Kelly until the ambulance comes?" the woman asked.

"Sure," Baylie said as she pulled a couple of blankets off the storage cart and began covering Kelly.

Kyle rolled a chair over near the girl and the woman sank into it. He took vital signs again while Baylie made the phone call to the hospital. The girl quietly spoke to the woman.

When Kyle finished with the vitals, Baylie seized him by the arm and pulled him toward the lobby area out of earshot of the patient and woman.

"I like this. You missed me so much that you pulled me off into a corner." Kyle grinned.

She made an appalled sound despite the fact he'd hit pretty close to the truth. "Please be serious. I want to know what happened."

"I was standing in line, getting supper, and someone called for a doctor. I went to see what the problem was. The girl had no epi pen, so I rushed her over here."

She met his gaze. "I'm glad you were there."

"Me too."

"Thanks for helping out here."

"Why, Baylie, are you being nice to me?" he asked with a charming lift to his lips.

Baylie's blood pressure picked up its pace. "Yes, and please don't make me regret it." She returned his smile for the first time in two days.

"I shall do my best."

"You go on and get some supper. I'll watch over Kelly until the ambulance arrives."

"I bet you haven't eaten yet either. I'll go get something for both of us and bring it back here."

She began to protest but he raised his hands into the stop position. "No strings attached. You have my word."

"All right. I am hungry."

"Then I'll see you in a few." She watched as he strolled out of the building. The man was certainly growing on her.

She hoped she wasn't making a mistake by agreeing to share another meal with Kyle. She only managed to keep her attraction to him in check by seeing that they had little interaction. If he didn't keep his promise then she might lose all her self-control if he tried to kiss her. What scared her most was that deep inside she wanted him. Desired more than his kisses.

Kyle returned to the patrol building with deli sandwiches in hand to find the ambulance parked outside.

"Anything I can do to help?" he asked Baylie as he put the sack of food down out of the way.

"Yes, if you'll get one more set of vitals I'd appreciate it. I need to give her the anti-nausea med. I don't send anyone down the twisty mountain road in the back of an ambulance without a dose. There's no way she won't get sick without it."

As he went about getting vitals Kelly watched his every move. Done, he placed a hand on her shoulder. "You'll be fine."

"Thank you," she said.

He smiled down at her. "You're very welcome."

Baylie joined them and checked the IV line before adding medicine through the port. "This will help you as you go to the hospital."

The girl nodded. Kyle walked away to speak to the man and woman. The girl's eyes followed Kyle. "He's nice."

"Yes, he is." Baylie said.

"And cute."

"That too."

"I can hear you," Kyle called.

The two of them giggled.

Half an hour later, Kelly was on her way to the hospital.

"If there's a microwave around here I'll heat up our sandwiches," Kyle offered.

"There's one in the staff room." She pointed in the direction of a room off the lobby that he'd never visited. "There's a table in there. I'll join you in a minute. I have to make a couple of log notes on the girl."

"Okay, I'll find it. I'm sure hungry enough."

"I'm starting to think you're always hungry," Baylie called to his retreating form. His breath left him as if he'd taken a hard tumble on packed snow. Had Baylie just shown a sense of humor? Whatever it was, he liked it. Wanted to hear more of it. What he wouldn't do to have one of her smiles directed at him.

He stopped and looked back at her. "Baylie, are you teasing me?" he asked with a brow raised.

"I think of it more as making a statement."

"I'm thinking it's teasing. I kind of like the idea of you having a sense of humor."

"Are you trying to say that I don't?"

"I believe this is the point where warming up my supper is the better part of valor," Kyle said as he picked up the sack and headed toward the door.

"Coward." Baylie clipped with a soft chuckle.

Kyle suddenly had the desire to whoop.

CHAPTER SIX

Why hadn't Kyle kissed her? Baylie was still asking herself that question the next afternoon as she skied down Make It or Break It slope. She wasn't sure that she liked the turn of events. Days before Kyle had seemed to be kissing or trying to kiss her anytime they'd been alone. Then last night he'd kept her at arm's length.

That wasn't exactly accurate. He'd held her hand through a particularly icy area on their way to her place. They'd had a short but agreeable meal and he'd waited until she'd locked up and had then walked her home. She'd be lying if she said she hadn't enjoyed having her hand in his as they'd walked. Kyle reminded her of one of those ancient oaks on the coast of Georgia that was strong enough to have survived horrible storms. He exuded confidence and security, stability. With him she felt safe, cared for. It was something she desperately needed to feel.

Days ago it wouldn't have mattered what he thought of her, but somehow it mattered greatly now. What would he think when he learned the truth? She couldn't take the chance that she might see a look of disappointment in his expressive eyes. No, that secret was best kept. She didn't want to disappoint him like she had Ben. She'd had enough heartache.

Maybe she was making more out of Kyle being friendly than there was. He'd been on the snow-skiing circuit. He probably expected to have a different girl in every resort, and she was nobody's groupie.

"Baylie, we have an issue near Runway Lift," came a voice over the radio.

"What kind?" she asked.

"Guy down. Uh, what?" he said, as if speaking to someone else. "One of the patrol guys…" There was another pause. "Kyle says possible heart attack."

"I'll be right there. Call the top and have them send the snowmobile and put oxygen on it."

Baylie's throat constricted with fear as she sped down the slope, across another and into a glade that she didn't have time to enjoy. She was needed now. Thankfully Kyle was there. At least he would have started CPR if it was necessary. How quickly she'd come to rely on him.

She pulled to a stop, released her bindings and headed toward where Kyle was on his knees, performing CPR. She dropped down across from Kyle. He'd already pulled off his knit cap and sweat beaded on his brow.

"I'll handle the breathing. You stay on compressions. One, two, three, four, five." She leaned over and put her mouth over the man's.

His chest hardly rose. She wasn't strong enough or large enough to give the overweight man the air he needed. That old, ugly monster called panic attacked.

Keep it together.

"Breathe, Baylie," Kyle said from above her. She took a deep breath and put her mouth over the man's mouth again. This time his chest rose a little higher. But not enough.

She looked at Kyle. His gaze bored into hers. Worry for the patient was etched across his face.

"Baylie, move." He leaned over and gave the man a breath that made his chest rise visibly. "At least count, damn it," he threw at her.

"One. Two. Three. Four…" With a sense of relief that knew no bounds she rejoiced when the snowmobile arrived.

The man on the snowmobile placed the defibrillator beside her. "Hey, man," Kyle said to the snowmobile driver. "You do chest compressions while I see to the defibrillator. Baylie, help get the board in place."

Kyle's sharp, authoritative voice jolted her out of her fear. Relief flooded through her. Kyle had taken over the scene. She was glad to have his capable voice directing.

Two patrolmen carried the backboard over.

Between breaths Kyle said, "Get that under him."

She assisted in positioning the board then pulled her radio off her hip and said into it, "We need a helicopter at the grooming shed pad ASAP."

A couple of minutes later a voice on the radio said, "ETA twenty minutes."

"Ten-four," Baylie said in response, before telling the crowd that had gathered with more confidence than she felt, "Everyone, you need to move on out of the way."

"Clear," came from behind her. She turned to see Kyle placing the defibrillator paddles on the man's bare chest. "Baylie, check vitals."

She went down on her knees, jerked the stethoscope out of her bag and checked the man's chest. She looked at Kyle and shook her head.

His lips thinned. Turning up the voltage on the machine, he called, "Clear."

Baylie moved back and Kyle applied the paddles again.

"Baylie?" Hope filled his voice.

She placed two fingers on the man's wrist. Had she felt a pulse? Yes, there is was! "I got it but it's weak." She listened to the man's heart. There was a beat.

"Let's get some oxygen on him," Kyle ordered. Sitting back on his heels, he wiped the perspiration from his forehead with the sleeve of his jacket. "Baylie, vitals."

"Pulse still thready. Respirations shallow."

The clock ticked far too slowly for Baylie's nerves before the swish and whorl of a helicopter filled the air.

"Let's get him on the stretcher and to the helipad," Kyle directed. He stood in one agile movement and helped the other men position the stretcher. Another patrol member joined them.

"Hey, guys," Kyle called to a couple of people standing nearby. "Give us some help here."

The patient was so large that Baylie worried that he might not fit on the stretcher.

"On three, lift." Kyle counted.

Minutes later, the snowmobile driver, with Kyle seated behind him, was speeding toward the grooming shed and the helicopter.

All Baylie wanted to do was to go somewhere and hide. If Kyle hadn't been there that man would have died. She couldn't have saved him. Had the other patrol volunteers realized what was going on?

She collected Kyle's equipment and headed for the lift. Thank goodness it was time for the slopes to close. Her team would take care of seeing that the trails were clear. The incident report could wait until tomorrow.

Kyle knocked on the door of Baylie's place. Where was she? He'd returned to the patrol building to find his skis and poles hanging in the rack next to hers but no Baylie.

What was going on with her? She had shut down on the scene. Miss I-never-lose-my-cool had gone unresponsive.

Kyle knocked again. "Baylie, are you in there?" He listened for movement. "Come on, Baylie, I know you're in there." A light showed through one of the windows.

A couple of guys walking by showed some interest in what he was doing. He was starting to draw attention and, worse, he felt foolish talking to a door. "Come on, Baylie, let me in."

Baylie cracked the door open. "Go away."

"Let me in. Talk to me."

"Leave me alone. I'll see you tomorrow," she said without moving the door farther.

"Come on, Baylie. Let me help."

"There's nothing you can do."

"I can listen." He nudged the door back until he could see her face. She was pale, her eyes red and puffy. "You've been crying."

"Don't sound so amazed. I'm human." There was the Baylie he knew and understood.

He pushed gently on the door until she let it go. She turned her back to him, walked across the square room and flopped down into one corner of a well-worn sofa.

He didn't wait to be invited but stepped in and closed the door. On one side of the room was an efficiency kitchen, including a washer and dryer. One small light glowed. The place was a step above dorm living, but its real advantage was privacy.

Baylie's jacket, knit cap, shirt and boots littered the floor as if she'd entered and dumped them there. She still wore her skiing pants and her thermal top, which accented her breasts and showed every curve and dip.

Her hair looked as if she'd pulled the cap off but hadn't

bothered to smooth her hair. He couldn't remember ever seeing someone look more miserable. Reminding himself why he was there, he stepped over the pile of clothing and looked down at Baylie.

"What happened to you? Why'd you disappear?"

"Kyle, it isn't your business."

This wasn't like Baylie. She'd always been the head-on, bulldozer type. He didn't like the lost, I-don't-care attitude. "Aren't you at least interested in knowing how the patient is doing?"

She looked up at him with sad basset-hound eyes, filled with remorse. "Yes."

"He made it to the hospital but they almost lost him a couple of times during the transfer. We can call in a couple of hours to get a report."

"You call."

He was more worried now that he'd seen her than he'd been before he'd stopped by. She was too despondent. It wasn't like her. Concern started to eat at his gut. She was frightening him. He pulled his jacket off and threw it in a chair that matched the sofa's ugly plaid. Sitting on the couch, he left plenty of room between them. "Okay, I'm not leaving until you talk."

"I've been talking."

"You know what I mean. I'm your friend, Baylie. I care about you. Something happened out there and I want to know what." He started to take her hand but when she pulled back, he clasped his hands together and rested his forearms on his thighs.

"I don't want to talk about it."

He met her look. "But I think you need to. What happened on the slope today? What made you shut down?" he asked in a coercing tone.

She played with a fingernail.

"Tell me. I'll listen. No judgment. You have my word."

She glanced at him then looked at her hand again. He waited and when he feared she wouldn't speak she murmured, "I just couldn't take it."

He sat outwardly patient but inwardly he wanted to shake her into saying more. Everything about the way she was sitting and speaking told him she needed to get it out.

"I would never have been able to save him without you. I wasn't even strong enough to give him CPR." She lifted her shoulders and a soft sob came from her.

The urge to take her in his arms, to pull her to him and comfort her was almost overpowering. If he did, would she push him away?

"The man would've died if you hadn't been there," she said so low that he wasn't sure he'd heard her.

"I doubt that. You would've done what had to be done."

She looked at him with shimmering eyes. "You had to tell me what to do."

Baylie wrapped her arms across her middle. A wave of nausea surged one way then back crashing inside her. She'd thought about how she hadn't been able to help Ben. How she had let him down. How inadequate she was. What would Kyle think if she told him that she'd let a man die? Not just any man but someone she'd cared deeply about?

"What's going through that mind of yours?" Kyle leaned toward her. She could smell the soap from his shower mixed with a scent that was Kyle's alone. One she would know anywhere.

"When I was in Iraq there was an incident and men were killed. I couldn't save them."

"Honey, what happened?" He touched her hand but didn't hold it. His simple, reassuring action was enough.

"We were on our way to set up a medical clinic in one of the villages. An IED exploded and we were hit. I was blown out. I couldn't reach them to help. I tried but I just couldn't. Like I wasn't strong enough to help today." She scrubbed her hands across her face. Tears refused to fall.

Kyle wrapped an arm around her shoulders and pulled her to his chest. Baylie hadn't noticed he'd moved closer. She sat stiffly against him. "Were you hurt?" Alarm filled his voice.

She nodded. "Shrapnel in my side."

"Did you need to be hospitalized?"

"I spent a week there. I was told that four out of the six of us were gone." Ben was gone.

"I'm so sorry you had to go through that, but you can't blame yourself for them or what happened today. You did what you could. You were hurt. You're not Superwoman."

She broke out of his embrace, jumped up and glared at him. "It was my job to see to them. I let them down. Just like I let that man down today. He would have died!"

"I think you're overreacting. Just—"

"You got what you came for, so go." She wasn't overreacting. She'd seen the life go out of Ben's eyes. She carried the blame for not saving him. Baylie pointed toward the door.

"I'm not leaving you like this," Kyle said in an even voice, making no move to get off the sofa.

"Well, you can sit there all you want. I'm going to get a bath and go to bed." Baylie stalked through the bedroom and into the bathroom, slamming the door.

Why wouldn't Kyle leave her alone?

Fifteen minutes later the water had turned cool and Baylie stepped out of the tub, wrapped a towel around her and tucked it in place. All she wanted was to go to bed, pull the covers over her head and try to forget.

"Baylie, Baylie!"

Her eyelids jerked open but she was blinded briefly when the lamp flickered on. Kyle was standing above her. He was shirtless with his jeans on but the zipper unfastened.

"Huh?" Confusion fogged her brain. Why was he there? What was he talking about?

Kyle sank down on the mattress beside her. With a gentle hand he brushed her hair back from her face where a few strands had slipped from beneath the towel. A line etched his face between his brows. "Are you okay? You were screaming. Do you hurt somewhere?"

She stared at him.

Kyle's hand cupped her bare shoulder. It was big and warm. She wanted to huddle into the warmth. He shook her. "Baylie, honey, you're having a nightmare."

That wasn't news. She relived those horrible minutes over and over, night after night.

She rolled away from him and into a ball.

"Baylie, you're scaring me," he said.

"Ple-e-e-ase go away," she whined. Hadn't it been enough for him to have seen her melt down when they had been taking care of the heart patient? Now he was getting the full-blown effects of her dysfunction.

"Come on, talk to me. Let me help you," he said gently. "I'm not leaving until I know you're all right. You might as well look at me."

The mattress shifted and his hand reached across her,

pulling her hair away from her face. "You need to take this damp towel off your head. Come on, sit up."

Maybe if she did as he asked he would go away sooner. Permanently.

She leaned forward enough for him to pull the towel away.

The sound of him sucking in his breath made her roll toward him and look at his face. His eyes were fixed lower. The covers had fallen to her waist, and the towel that had been around her was now lying open. The look of admiration stamped on his face eased the self-loathing she felt. She wanted more of that approval. It pushed the ugliness in her life away.

"Baylie, pull the sheet up," Kyle said in a strangled voice.

"Why?"

His gaze lifted to meet hers. "Because I'm going to touch you if you don't," he growled deep in his throat.

"You want to touch me?" she whispered, confused.

"Baylie, don't do this. You're not yourself. I don't want you to regret anything you say or do in the morning." He ran a trembling hand across the stubble on his chin.

She pulled the sheet over herself.

Kyle let out a sound of relief.

"Why do you want to touch me?" Her gaze held his.

"This isn't one of our word games, Baylie. Now give me that towel and tell me where to find you something to wear."

Baylie did as instructed, causing the sheet to slip lower to just cover her breasts. She glanced at Kyle. He was looking at a spot somewhere over her head. "You know, for a doctor you sure have an odd reaction to the human body."

"Yours isn't just any body," he croaked.

She wiggled and pulled on the towel to get it out from under her. The sheet shifted farther down. Done. She handed it to him. "Why, Kyle?"

"For heaven's sake, Baylie. I don't want to have one of our debates about this."

Even if she was embarrassing herself, she couldn't stop prodding him. She wanted to feel good about herself, about something again. To feel alive again. Kyle's look of longing gave her self-confidence she'd lost in other areas of her life. She refused to give it up. She was going to grasp it and hold on for dear life.

He jerked to a standing position and glared down at her. "What do you want me to say? You're beautiful. Luscious. Desirable. I want you."

"Those are all nice. Thank you," she said quietly.

He turned his back to her, hands balled at his sides, and took a long-suffering-sounding breath. "Where are your pajamas?"

"Second drawer. T-shirt."

Kyle dropped the towels on the floor and took two steps to the small, functional dresser. He pulled on the drawer with more force than required and hauled out a shirt.

Sitting on the bed, he said, "Here, let me help you get this on."

She moved into a half-sitting position, putting Kyle's broad chest only inches from her mouth. What would it be like to place her lips to his skin?

He opened the neck of the shirt wide and held it over her head, waiting. She glanced at him. He was once again averting his eyes.

This was her sweet memory for the taking. She might not be given another chance. Maybe she'd dream of Kyle instead of what had happened that day... Baylie leaned forward and placed her lips against him. He flinched and his breath caught. His skin reminded her of warm silk. Like something she wanted to wrap around her. Kyle was holding his breath. Her lips skated an inch along his skin. It rippled. A swoosh of air came from above her head.

"Baylie." Her name was a soft breath that carried longing. "I don't want to take advantage of you. You were upset about today and then had a nightmare. This isn't the right time…"

She stuck out the tip of her tongue and tasted him. Salty sweet. She craved more.

Kyle threw her shirt to the floor, put his hands under her arms and hauled her up against him. His lips slammed into hers. He pulled away and nipped at her bottom lip before his tongue demanded entrance.

She opened for him. His tongue touched, tasted and teased hers.

He pulled her more tightly against him, pressing her breasts to his heated, hard torso. He felt so wonderful. To be desired was intoxicating.

Baylie ran her hands over his shoulders, kneading his muscles as she went, down to his biceps and back. She massaged his neck as his kisses went deeper. Her fingers buried themselves in his thick hair, pulling his mouth closer. A feeling of power washed over her to know that a man like Kyle wanted her desperately and wasn't afraid to show it. For once she didn't have to pretend to be confident. She was.

When he broke their kiss she groaned in frustration. She wanted more, demanded more.

He leaned his forehead against hers and said, "If we don't stop now I might not be responsible for what I do."

What did it take to make this man understand she

wanted him? "You don't have to be responsible. I'm a big girl. I can take care of myself."

"I know you can, but I don't want to hurt you."

"Make me feel good, Kyle." She cupped his face and kissed him, this time being the one to ask that his tongue meet hers.

Kyle shifted and stretched out on the bed next to her without removing his lips from hers. She intertwined her bare legs with his jeans-covered ones. His hand slowly caressed her hip and thigh. She shivered.

As his fingers journeyed higher they trailed over the puckered spot where she'd been injured. He paused. The tip of one finger grazed it again, circled it as if judging the size. He pulled his lips from hers.

"I'm sorry, honey," Kyle said as his gaze met hers. He pushed the covers away and brought his lips down to gently kiss the red, angry spot. "I wish it had been me instead of you." He hugged her tightly.

Baylie cupped his face and brought her lips to his. She loved kissing him. "That was the past. This…" she tugged at his bottom lip "…is the present." The tip of her finger ran along his chest.

"Mmm, I like the present."

Kyle pulled back, his focus going to her breasts. They tingled from the attention. He leaned down and took one straining tip into his mouth. Baylie feared she'd shatter from the pleasure. His tongue orbited her nipple until it grew harder, bolder and stood upright. Her center throbbed.

She arched her back, giving him greater access. Could she get enough of this kind of devotion? Kyle accepted the offering. Running a hand across her midsection and leaving a wake of fluttering along her skin, he cupped the other breast.

Just when Baylie thought she could stand no more, Kyle sucked gently on her nipple then released it. He blew on the begging tip. She trembled. Her center glowed with a craving she'd never known.

He shifted slightly until he could rub the end of his index finger over the damp, blunt end as he gave the other breast the same loving care the first had received.

Baylie's head rolled back and forth on the pillow as Kyle's skill sent her further up the mountain of need. His manhood pressed against her thigh. He was strong, hard and ready but still contained by his jeans.

She wiggled against him. He chuckled low in his throat. A sound of male satisfaction from a man who knew a woman desired him. Bringing his lips up to hers, he eased over her, putting her body securely beneath his. Her legs parted and Kyle filled the gap, pressing his length firmly against the part of her throbbing with longing.

Kyle's tongue mated with hers. She lifted her hips, begging. Suddenly he rolled away and stood, leaving her feeling bereft and desperate. Her fingers clawed the sheet over the mattress. He looked down at her with hooded eyes filled with craving and resolve. He shucked out of his pants, his manhood standing proud and tall.

The look on his face turned suddenly desperate. His head turning as if he was urgently looking for something, he swore sharply under his breath. Baylie giggled. His look shot to hers.

"Forget something? Under the sink in the bathroom. Leftovers from the resident before me."

With long steps he was out of the room and back with a handful of packets.

Her eyes widened. "I was going to make fun of a doctor who wasn't prepared but now…"

He looked down at her longingly. "Now that I have you I might never stop." Baylie's breath caught and her heart missed a beat. What would it be like to be loved by Kyle always?

With one quick tear of the package and a rolling motion, Kyle was once again beside her in bed.

She ran her hands up his chest and around his neck, pulling him to her. Kyle kissed the sweet spot where her neck met her shoulder before his mouth claimed hers. He moved his hips so that he rested at her entrance, the place that impatiently awaited his attention.

Kyle's lips left hers. He propped himself on his hands, bringing his head above hers where he could look down at her. "Are you sure, Baylie? No regrets tomorrow?" His intense gaze searched hers.

She raised her hips, taking the tip of him. "Mmm, I'm sure."

He flexed forward, going farther. She ran her hand over his chest. "No regrets…"

The last word trailed off into a sound of pure need as Kyle completely filled her. He moved, settling into a strong rhythm. Her world centered on him as she spiraled upward and burst like a star to float slowly, perfectly and completely into oblivion. Seconds later, Kyle groaned his fulfillment before his heavy body covered hers.

She'd never believed that life could be this good again. Kyle moved off her and she curled into him and slept.

CHAPTER SEVEN

KYLE HAD ONLY been worried about Baylie's peace of mind when he'd decided to spend the night on her ratty sofa. He had no intention of making love to her. Now that she'd explained what had happened in Iraq, he realized he'd had reason to be concerned. Still, that didn't give him the right to take advantage of her during an emotional time. He'd tried to resist her but, heaven help him, she'd asked one too many times.

The small bundle in his arms moved. She was a tiny woman with a giant's will. He was crazy about her. Heck, if he was truthful, he was half in love with her. Love! He could think of a lot of worse things and truthfully nothing better than loving Baylie.

Her hand floated across his chest and his body reacted. "Got any more of those packets?" she asked in a groggy morning voice.

"A few." He chuckled and looked down at her. "Why? You got something in mind?"

She smiled and her hip nudged his already straining member. "Nothing you don't."

"What about the time?"

She raised herself enough to look over his shoulder at the clock on the bedside table. "Let Mickey handle the morning assignments," she murmured, before she teasingly pulled on his bottom lip with her teeth.

"When was the last time you weren't the first one in and the last one out at the patrol office?"

"Never," she said as she pushed against his shoulders until they were flat on the bed. She straddled him. Her breasts softly swayed just above his mouth.

He grinned. "I don't imagine that will go unnoticed."

"I don't either, and I don't care," she said against his lips, then pressed forward to kiss him fully.

This was one area he didn't mind Baylie being in control. In fact, he liked it. Anything was better than the mass of insecurity he'd seen yesterday. This Baylie he recognized. Her passion for caring for people was only surpassed by her passion in lovemaking. He was grateful to be on the receiving end of it.

He easily lifted her, sitting her on him. He slid into her warm, wet welcome. He'd found home again. A place he never wanted to leave.

Thirty minutes later, as they hurried to dress, Kyle asked, "Would you like to have Christmas Eve dinner with me at the Rusty Lantern restaurant tonight?"

She stopped to look at him. "Like a date?"

"Yeah, that's kind of what I had in mind." He winked. "And maybe a little groping under the table."

She laughed. He loved the tickling windchime tones. More than that, he liked to see her relax for a second or two, not be so serious.

"Interested?"

"In the eating or the groping?"

"One or the other. Both preferably."

"That's a hard invitation to turn down. A two for one. Yes, I think that would be nice."

Kyle was surprised at their ease together that morning. There didn't seem to be any morning-after regret on her part. He shouldn't have been so worried. In fact, he couldn't remember ever having a finer morning in his life. Not even when he'd won the North American title in downhill racing. Waking with Baylie next to him in a warm bed with the snow falling outside was ideal.

"Then I'll pick you up here at seven."

As Baylie pushed socks around in her dresser drawer, he put both hands on her waist and turned her around to face him. She looked at him questioningly. Unable to resist, he leaned down and kissed her. His reward was her going up on tiptoe and slipping her arms around his neck as she leaned into his embrace. What would it be like to kiss her every morning?

One steamy kiss later, he broke the connection and rested his forehead against hers. "If I don't get out of here, that snarly boss of mine will have my hide."

She tilted her head back to look at him. "Snarly, is she?"

He kissed the tip of her nose. "Yeah, but she sure comes in a cute little package." He swatted her butt playfully and headed for the door with a spring in his step.

Baylie was thankful that Kyle had to go by his place to dress for the slopes and pick up his equipment. At least if they were both late, they weren't coming in together, which would make it far too obvious something was going on between them.

He couldn't have been a more generous lover and she couldn't remember being so uninhibited with another man. They might disagree about a number of things and be from two different worlds financially but they were more than compatible in the lovemaking department. Heat filled her cheeks just thinking about those hours in bed.

Already she was looking forward to having dinner with Kyle. That seemed to be all they did together, but this meal would be different. He'd asked her out on a date. It had been so long since she'd gone on one that she wasn't sure how to act.

The Rusty Lantern was the most upscale restaurant at the resort mountain and was located in the valley beside the lake. White tablecloths, waiters with bow ties… She needed something suitable to wear. Her wardrobe consisted of skiing clothes, jeans and heavy sweaters to get by in the off-hours. Knowing Kyle, he'd look dapper in a suit and tie. And it was Christmas Eve.

That evening, Baylie opened the door to an impeccably dressed Kyle in a suit coat over a sweater that matched his eyes.

He grinned as he stepped in the door. "You look wonderful, Baylie."

The mirror had told her that the salmon-colored wool dress added a spot of pink to her cheeks but that had deepened to a full-blown blush under Kyle's appraisal. She'd always been more tomboy than girly-girl, following behind her older brothers, but for once in her life she liked the idea of being completely feminine. Being a woman to this man was exhilarating.

Kyle kissed her on the cheek and whispered, "I'd love to swallow you up like candy but I think we need to have dinner first."

Baylie tingled in anticipation.

"We need to go if we're going to catch our ride." Kyle picked her coat up off the chair and he helped her with it.

Thankfully, the night wasn't bitterly cold. He took her

hand as they walked to the lodge. There they would board a van that would carry them down a private road to the restaurant. "I stopped in to see you around three this afternoon but the guy at the counter at Courtesy Patrol said you'd left early for the day. That you had an errand to run." He looked a little perplexed by the idea. "Last-minute Christmas presents to buy? Or was something wrong?"

"Now who's checking up on who? I just needed to pick up a few things before the store closed. No big deal." She'd bought a new dress and boots and had had her hair trimmed. She'd never done all those things before in the same outing.

The Rusty Lantern was lit by oil lamps hanging from stands with red bows around a deck that looked out over the lake. Mountains surrounded the entire region, giving the area a feeling of being nested in the woods. Baylie had never seen anything so romantic. She'd known about the place but had never had the opportunity to have dinner there. It only accommodated a small number of customers and was beyond her budget, especially during Christmastime.

She looked at Kyle and breathed, "It's lovely."

He smiled and squeezed her hand. "You're the one who's lovely."

A fuzzy feeling of pleasure invaded her. She beamed at him. Being with Kyle made her feel beautiful.

They were served hot toddies on the deck. Kyle put an arm around her waist and held her close. "You warm enough? We can go in if you like."

"No, I'm enjoying the view."

"And the company?" he asked, close enough that his breath warmed her cold cheek.

She moved away but only far enough so that she could see him. "Fishing for a compliment?"

"No. I just wanted to make sure you're happy."

She was. For the first time in too long she could say that and have it be truth. For once, the guilt she carried every waking minute had been pushed to the background, to be replaced by thoughts of how Kyle made her feel. She could say with conviction, "I'm happy."

A waiter invited them inside for dinner. They were shown to a spot in a back corner where they had a view of the moon coming up over the mountain. Lanterns with fresh greenery around them flickered as centerpieces on all the tables. A small tree with lights twinkling on it and bright red ornaments of every size and shape stood in one corner. The atmosphere was both rustic and elegant. Not unlike Baylie and Kyle themselves—simple country and suave city.

After they were served their dinner of pheasant and wild rice Baylie asked, "So have you always wanted to be a sports-medicine doctor?"

"No, not really. I was always a good student. My mother and father saw to that. If I wanted to ski then I had to keep my grades up. After I hurt my knee I decided I wanted to help people who had experienced sport injuries." He turned her hand over and kissed the soft spot at her wrist. He raised his eyes so he could look into hers.

"You had dreamed of winning it all, hadn't you?" she asked softly, gripping his hand more firmly.

"Yeah, I wanted it badly. To be the best in the world. I had worked so hard. My parents had sacrificed so much. One stupid mistake and it was all gone."

Baylie didn't say anything. Instead, she leaned over

and kissed him on the cheek. "I don't doubt that you'd have won it."

"Thanks. I've put it behind me. I'm just glad Metcalf messed up and I had to come here and ski again. I've recaptured my love for the sport again. And, better than that, I met you."

Baylie took a sip of her drink and grinned at him. "I'm glad you're here too. So when you could no longer ski you went to med school?"

"I had those good grades so I put them to use. Becoming a sports-med doc gave me a chance to help others who have experienced the same type of injuries as I had."

"And have you?"

He'd never really thought about it. "I have." There was a sense of satisfaction that went with that statement he'd not had before.

"Good." She smiled at him.

He returned her smile. It was good.

She took a sip of what she knew to be the most expensive wine the restaurant offered. "I've been meaning to ask you how your family feels about you working here, instead of spending Christmas with them."

"Mom and Dad died a few years ago. Drunk driver."

"I'm so sorry." She squeezed Kyle's hand.

"Thanks. I do miss them. I wished they had lived long enough for me to repay them for all they did."

"What do you mean?"

Disappointment filled him. "They worked hard. Both of them worked overtime so I could have enough money to travel to ski events. I had the grades for school, and got scholarships, but I still had to have money to live on. They helped all they could. They were special people."

"I had no idea. I thought you were from an affluent family." Baylie's amazement was evident in her voice.

"Why's that?"

"I don't know. Maybe the fact you ski so well. Being on the slopes a lot costs. Not to mention your skis, staying at the lodge, what you drive…the fact that you have a house in the Bahamas."

"Why, Baylie, I had no idea you were a snob."

"I am not."

"Are you surprised to find out we have more in common than you thought?"

"Truthfully, yes."

He chuckled. "Unlike you, I don't have any brothers but I do have a sister. Before you ask, she and her family are at the in-laws' and I will be visiting her in a couple of weeks to celebrate the holidays. I was asked to go along but I decided not to butt in this year. So that made me available to be here to persecute you."

"Well, that you have surely done," she said with a grin. "I'm glad to know you have someone."

"Are you going to spend any time with your family tomorrow?" Would she invite him along?

"No, they understand I have to work. We all got together on Thanksgiving and exchanged presents then."

"That's a shame. I was hoping I might be invited to meet them."

Baylie looked stricken. "I don't think that would be a good idea. My brothers tend to make more out of the situation than there is when I bring home male friends."

It hurt that she thought of him only as a friend. He wouldn't mind making it clear to her brothers how he felt about their sister. "Maybe another time."

"Maybe."

Baylie didn't make it sound like she ever intended that to happen.

* * *

An hour later as they stepped off the van under the portico of the lodge, one of the hostesses approached Baylie. "You have a message. Someone from the grooming shed has been trying to get in touch with you. One of the groomers has been hurt but not badly. Just a cut."

"Why didn't they...?" She'd forgotten her phone. Something she never did. She'd been so excited about seeing Kyle that she'd left it on her coffee table. Now she was letting Kyle affect her job. She needed to focus on what was important. He would be gone in a few days.

"Okay. I'll give the grooming shed a call right now," Baylie told the hostess. She turned to Kyle, who stood nearby. "Thank you for dinner. It really was wonderful."

"Better than the pizza and burgers?"

She smiled at him. "Much. I need to go. I have to check on all incidents so I must see if that cut needs to be sewn up or if a butterfly bandage will do."

"May I come with you?"

"That's not necessary. It won't be anything too exciting."

"Already trying to get rid of me?"

Had that been a hurt note in his voice? "No."

"Then may I ride along? I don't like to think of you going off into the dark by yourself. Come to my room and give me a minute to get on my ski clothes and then we'll head to your place."

"I'll just meet you at Courtesy Patrol. I've got some spare clothes there."

Fifteen minutes later Baylie put the phone down and called, "Come on," as she started for the door. "Charlie's out grooming without that hand getting attention."

Kyle followed her out the door while jamming his knit

cap on his head, zipping up his coat and pulling on his gloves. Baylie swung a leg over the seat of the snowmobile parked in front of the building. In what was his spot on the seat of the machine sat the "go bag", which contained her medical supplies. He picked it up, slipped the strap over one shoulder and under one arm before he took his place behind her.

His thighs encased Baylie's. Her small, firm behind fit warmly against him. He was going to enjoy this trip.

Baylie yelled over the roar of the snowmobile, "Hold on," before giving the machine gas.

Kyle rocked back then jolted forward, wrapped his arms more securely around Baylie's waist. Her breasts were cushioned against his crossed arms. Even with her bulky coat covering her, it still felt wonderful to have her in his arms.

Over her shoulder, he watched as Baylie maneuvered the snowmobile across the snow and into the night. They passed cabins where the yellow glow of lights spilled out onto the slope but they soon gave way to pure blackness only cut by the snowmobile lights. Without their light, Kyle wouldn't have even been able to see Baylie.

Around a turn, she shifted her weight and he followed her. They straightened, and he pulled her even more closely against him. His manhood responded. Baylie wiggled. Either she was teasing him or she had no idea of what she did to him. Either way, his body was appreciating the contact.

"I'm enjoying the ride," he said close to her ear in his best wolfish growl.

He was rewarded by a weave of the snowmobile before she corrected it. Maybe she did like the closeness as much as he did. They'd begun to develop something special over the past twenty-four hours, and he wasn't willing to slip back to the way it had been two days before. He would tread lightly, not wanting to take a chance on Baylie putting up barriers if she got scared. He loosened his grip on her waist. She didn't move away.

Yes!

Ten minutes later, a huge grooming machine loomed ahead of them. The row of spotlights above the cab moved toward them. The rumble of the large machine dwarfed that of the snowmobile. The groomer slowed, stopped. Baylie pulled up beside it and turned off the engine. Kyle couldn't remember when he had last been so disappointed to have a ride over.

"Oh, Baylie, I love it when you make these nighttime runs," the man in the groomer called in a teasing tone from the open door above them. "You going to spend the night with me in my big machine?"

Kyle's back bowed and the hairs on the back of his neck tingled. He shifted into fight mode. Who was this guy to Baylie? If anyone was going to spend the night with Baylie, it was *him*.

"There'd better be something wrong with your hand, Charlie," Baylie clipped back in a friendly voice.

Didn't she get that this guy was coming on to her?

Baylie stepped off the snowmobile. The cold air that replaced the heat her behind had provided proved as effective as an icy shower. Kyle groaned. At least he had the trip back to look forward to. But right now he had to figure out what was going on between Baylie and this guy Charlie.

"I'm coming up." She turned to Kyle. "Hand me the bag. I shouldn't be long."

"I'm coming along too."

"Still don't trust me, Doc?"

"I trust you just fine." Kyle tilted his head toward the large machine. "It's that guy I don't trust."

She gave him a funny look for a second. "Come on. But there isn't a lot of room up there."

"I don't mind squeezing in."

Even in the dim light Kyle didn't miss the lift of Baylie's lips as she started climbing the ladder to the metal platform where the man stood. "Charlie, sit in the seat so I'll have light to work by. You know you could've driven to the top of the mountain and let see about this in the clinic."

"I could've but I wouldn't have gotten you alone. I see it didn't matter anyway." He looked toward Kyle. "Who you got with you?"

"Dr. Campbell."

"I don't need a doctor," Charlie said as he moved back into the cab.

"You'd better not have gotten me out here for nothing," Baylie reprimanded him.

"Naw, I did cut it this time," Charlie admitted.

So this guy had lured Baylie with a ruse before. She needed to be careful, out this far by herself. This guy could have taken advantage of her. When they got back, he'd talk to her about being safe. She took too many chances.

Kyle climbed up behind Baylie, barely controlling his urge to punch the guy in the mouth. Baylie leaned over through the doorway to look at Charlie's hand. Kyle went down on his heels and looked in under her.

"Let me see it," Baylie demanded.

Charlie put his hand in hers. The stubby-fingered, work-roughened hand had a piece of cloth wrapped around it.

"Hand me the scissors, Kyle."

He knew right where to find them and handed them to her. Baylie made two snips and removed the bandage.

Underneath was a long but shallow gash. A minute later, after a good examination, she announced, "I think a good cleaning and bandaging will be enough. Hand me the bag."

Kyle pushed it toward her. She rummaged around and found some antiseptic wash and gauze.

"Kyle, hold these, please."

He put out his hand and she placed the items in it. He was now her assistant and he didn't mind. More than once Baylie had demonstrated she was qualified to do her job.

"So, Doc, you just helping out on the patrol?"

Was this guy fishing to find out where Kyle fit into Baylie's life? "Yeah."

That was the end of Charlie's interest in Kyle. He turned his attention back to Baylie. "How about a burger for lunch on Saturday?" Charlie suggested. "I'll get up early for you."

"Got to work." She continued to tend the cut.

"So, Bay, how about going to the Christmas fireworks with me tomorrow night?"

This guy wasn't giving up. Kyle had had about enough.

"All done. Keep it clean and come by and let me check it in a few days," Baylie said.

Kyle would make sure he was at the courtesy-patrol building when that happened.

"How about the fireworks?" Charlie asked, this time sounding more insistent.

"She's already got a date for the fireworks. Sorry, buddy," Kyle said with a friendliness he didn't feel.

"I see how it is." Charlie nodded his head in understanding.

Kyle packed the leftover supplies into the bag, zipped

it and pulled it across his chest, before starting down the ladder.

"Thanks, Baylie," Charlie called as she climbed off. "Sorry about the fireworks."

"Merry Christmas, Charlie." Baylie took her place on the snowmobile, and Kyle slipped in behind her. "I could have handled Charlie on my own, you know."

"Yeah, I know. But a man likes to feel like a woman's knight in shining armor every once in a while."

She turned to look at him, their mouths only inches apart. "Thanks, then." She turned round and the snowmobile rumbled to life.

Kyle put his arms around her, hoping Charlie noticed. Jealousy was an emotion Kyle wasn't used to or liked. Something in him had needed to make it clear to Charlie that Baylie was unavailable for fireworks or anything else.

Making a wide arc, she pointed the snowmobile uphill in the direction from which they'd come. Halfway along the trail she veered off to the right and along another trail that followed the ridge of the mountain. When they came out of the trees and into an open area she stopped and turned the snowmobile off.

"What're we doing?" Kyle asked.

"Shhh!"

Baylie broke the clasp he had around her waist and climbed off. She walked over to the lip of the slope and looked out into the night sky. Pulling off the bag and leaving it on the seat, Kyle followed, standing beside her. *What was going on?*

The moon was high and full in the black heavens, bathing the snow in a hushed light. The trees and rolling mountains in the distance were little more than jagged outlines. Bright pinpoints of light showed against the onyx backdrop. An amazing view. And around them pure silence. They could have been the only two people in the universe. Baylie didn't move and neither did he.

A few minutes passed before she whispered, "This is my favorite spot. Especially when there's a full moon." She gazed off into the distance. "You know how you think your life is going one way and then it turns out another way?"

Was she speaking of something specific or just waxing poetic? Either way he understood. "I do."

"But this…" she swept her arm wide "…is always what you expect."

Kyle didn't respond, not wanting to break the moment. For once he was seeing the totally uninhibited Baylie. The woman who was finally sharing her deepest feelings. No hiding. He felt honored that she was doing so with him.

"I always stop here when I'm on the slope at night. I love the peace and quiet." She said the words in a soft, worshipful voice, as if she spoke more to the world around her than to him. "It makes me feel secure," she murmured.

As in control and self-confident as Baylie was, why wouldn't she feel secure? He took her gloved hand and looped it through his bent arm, stepping closer to her. "It's amazing. Thanks for sharing it with me," he whispered.

A few minutes later he said softly, "Look, there's a falling star."

"Where?" For the first time since they had stopped the melancholy sound in her voice had disappeared, replaced by excitement.

"Right there." He wrapped an arm around her shoulders, pulling her closer, and his head next to hers. Pointing, he asked, "You see it?"

"Yes." Her warm breath brushed his cheek. The desire to turn her round and kiss her was so great it almost consumed him, but he didn't want to lose the fragile connection they'd built. What was going on between him and Baylie mattered. He wanted the opportunity to have her in his arms regularly.

"You're supposed to make a wish when you see a shooting star," Kyle said. "You going to?"

"That's for kids."

"Sometimes it's fun to act like a kid. I'll never tell," he teased, waiting. When she said nothing he stated, "Okay, then, I'll do the wishing."

His desire was to share more moments like this with Baylie.

They stood in silence for a few more minutes before she said, "We'd better go. I'm getting cold."

He hugged her close. "I know just how to warm you up."

"How's that?"

"Why don't I surprise you?" He led her toward the snowmobile.

"I'm not sure I like surprises."

"You'll like this one." Kyle gave her shoulders another squeeze. This time he took his place on the snowmobile first then she climbed on. He snuggled her to him.

Baylie pulled the snowmobile up close to one of the slope access doors of the lodge.

"Why are we stopping here?" Kyle asked over the sound of the engine.

She cut off the engine. "I've got to write up Charlie's incident report. I thought your knee might be bothering you, so I thought I'd drop you off here."

"I'd be lying if I said it wasn't speaking to me pretty loudly," Kyle said.

"You didn't have to go with me."

"No, I didn't, but I'm glad I did. You look beautiful in the moonlight and I wouldn't have missed seeing that for the world."

She laughed. "I think you might have a little Casanova in you. Do you need any ice packs?"

"Why, Baylie, you really do care."

She grinned. "Don't push it. I might decide not to."

"I used the last pack this morning, so I'd appreciate them." Thankfully, that was the truth because he would've hated to lie just to get her to come to his place. He wasn't ready for the evening to end. If she thought he or anyone else for that matter needed care, she'd show up regardless of the hour.

"Then I'll bring you a couple by on my way home."

He hoped she wouldn't be going home tonight. He wanted her in his bed.

CHAPTER EIGHT

A HALF AN HOUR later, Baylie knocked on Kyle's door. He pulled it open immediately, as if he'd been waiting for her to knock.

"Come on in. I wasn't so sure how long you would be so I was headed for a quick soak in the hot tub."

Kyle wore the same shorts he'd had on the last time she'd visited. Once again he didn't have on a shirt. She stared at the bare chest she'd so enjoyed running her hand over last night. She swallowed, afraid she was about to make a fool of herself. Didn't the man ever wear clothes when he was at home?

"I thought the heat would do my knee some good. Maybe it will take some of the soreness out of my muscles."

"I'll just leave these with you, then." Baylie pulled the chemical ice packs out of her pocket and offered them to him.

"Come keep me company. It's Christmas Eve. No one should be alone on Christmas Eve." Kyle cupped her fingertips. He looked at her imploringly, as if it was important to him that she stay.

She was such a sucker for those beautiful sparkling eyes of his. Going out into the cold to her lonely place didn't have nearly the appeal of staying awhile longer with this charming man.

"Come on, Baylie. I'm not going to be here much longer. I'd like to spend as much time as possible with you."

Her heart soared at his words while at the same time she felt a pang of sorrow at the thought of him leaving. Kyle would be gone too soon. She hated to admit it but she'd miss him. She'd tried hard not to like him but he'd gotten around that easily. Without question, he'd grown on her. "Okay."

Kyle shut the door and took her hand more firmly in his, leading her down the short hall and into a big bedroom with an equally large bed. What would it be like to share that huge space with Kyle? She blinked. Did he think she would just fall into bed with him after last night?

His bed put her ratty one to shame. They might share similar backgrounds but their lives were miles apart. His living style was luxurious.

She tried to tug her hand free. Not that she wouldn't enjoy making love to Kyle; she just refused to be considered a foregone conclusion.

Kyle chuckled softly. She blushed. He had to know what she'd been thinking.

"Relax, the hot tub is through here." Kyle pulled open one of the two glass-paneled doors to the outside. On the deck was a large hot tub sunk into the redwood planks of the deck. The water was already swirling.

He let go of her hand. "Pull the door closed."

By the time she'd turned around he'd slipped into the water up to his shoulders.

"Ah." The sound of satisfaction filled the air around them. "This is wonderful." Kyle leaned his head back and closed his eyes. "Baylie, come sit down."

She sat in one of the metal deck chairs located nearby. The bliss on Kyle's face and the whirl of the water with steam rising from it called to her. She'd love to have that water swirling around her. To relax into oblivion with Kyle.

Why hadn't he asked her to join him? In fact, he'd made no overture toward her all evening. There had been a gentle touch here, another there, a hug when they'd looked at the night sky and the lone kiss on the cheek when he'd picked her up. What had happened to the hot passion from the night before?

From having no interest in having anything to do with a man just a few days ago, she had gone to suddenly wanting this man with very fiber of her being. In only a few days Kyle had managed to make her think of little else but him, had pushed her guilt away. A jolt hit her. She was in love.

She hadn't wanted that. If she cared for Kyle so easily, what did that say about her feelings for Ben? Had they been real?

Pulling her coat closer around her neck, she pretended to protect herself from the cold night instead of from the appeal of the man unabashedly appreciating the hot tub. Baylie shivered.

What was she doing? What was she thinking? Feeling? It was silly just to sit in the cold, watching Kyle. Didn't she have any self-respect? She should go.

"You don't have to huddle there. You're welcome to join me."

She looked at Kyle. His eyes were hooded and a teasing smile curled his lips.

"I don't have a suit."

"Don't need one," he shot back.

"You've got one."

"I'll be glad to take mine off if that would make you feel

more comfortable. Come on, Baylie. You work so hard, you need to relax some."

Would it really be so bad to care for Kyle? Ben would want her to be happy. He'd encourage her to move on. "You know, if I hung around with you too much you might really corrupt me."

"I doubt that. You're smart and good at what you do. They'd be crazy not to keep you." He propped his arms along the edge of the tub as if in welcome.

Warmth that had nothing to do with her coat filled her. That had been high praise, coming from him. "Wear your underwear if it'll make you happy."

Why did she feel so timid about Kyle seeing her? He'd left few parts of her body untouched the night before. Somehow the thought of exposing herself to his gaze now made her feel nervous.

"Come on, Baylie, you know you want to," he said in a low, coaxing tone. "I'll stay on this side and you can have the other if that's the problem."

Okay, two could play this game. Mister relaxed, self-assured and incredibly sexy, I'm going to rattle your cage.

Without a word, she stood, walked to the bedroom door and opened it.

Kyle sat up, bringing his torso up out of the water. "Where're you going?"

She grinned at the sound of panic in his voice. "I'll be right back. I have a Christmas present for you."

"I didn't get you anything," he said in a regretful voice as she closed the door.

Baylie found the bathroom. Pulling off her clothes, she wrapped one of the large fluffy bath towels around her. It brushed against her sensitive skin, tantalizing already affected nerve endings. For once she felt confident. As if she'd been released from her suffering. Something that she'd carried for far too long. She felt alive again.

Baylie stepped out onto the deck, shivering as much from the cold as the thought of what she was about to do. Kyle's head turned. His eyes widened. The bobbing of his Adam's apple bolstered her resolve. She'd surprised him. Good. He didn't know it but he was in for another one.

Never having been known as a free spirit, what she was planning to do next was completely out of character. Kyle had encouraged her to spread her wings and she intended to. She only had a few more days to enjoy him before he was gone and she was going to grasp all she could. Life was very short. She knew that far too well.

Walking to the side of the tub across from him, she dipped a bare toe into the water. Kyle's gaze lifted from where the towel had given him a glimpse of her thigh. She smiled. This femme-fatale stuff was fun. She waited until she'd captured his gaze before dropping the towel and was rewarded by his eyes widening. Kyle sucked air into his lungs with a whooshing sound. Suddenly all the power was in her hands.

"You're right. This is nice. Thanks for inviting me in," she said in a syrupy voice as she put a foot into the water then continued and sank into the tub.

His eyes narrowed. "I should've known better than to tease you. By now I know you well enough to know that you would find a way to get the upper hand."

"I have no idea what you mean," she cooed.

He laughed. It was a full-bodied sound that came from deep inside him and rolled out. "Baylie, you do make life interesting. Being around you is like that thrill the moment you go over the finish line and know you've run a great race."

She let her arms float on top of the water. "Is that a compliment?"

He caught one of her hands. "The best of compliments."

"Have you ever thought about skiing in one of the Pro-Am events? There's one here next week."

"No."

Kyle made it sound as if it was out of the question. "Did your doctor advise you against skiing?"

"No."

He was a great skier. Why wouldn't he try? "It would give you a chance to compete again."

"I'd rather not. Those days are gone."

"What a waste. You're so good. You might be surprised. You might enjoy it."

"I know something I'd enjoy." He jerked her hand.

She fell against him. "Hey, you said you'd stay on your own side of the tub."

"I am on my side. You're the one who came over here." Kyle chuckled wickedly as his hand cupped her breast. He looked into her eyes. "I want to make love to you, Baylie. Not because you need me to push away a bad dream but because you want me."

Kyle would get out, dress and see her home if she asked. He'd never force her. But she didn't want to go.

She slid along his body, nudging his straining length as she went. Her lips found his. Desire found point zero low in her. Kissing him passionately, she broke away. "Why don't you take me inside and give me a Christmas gift that only you can give?" she whispered against his ear, before she ran the tip of her tongue along its curve.

He growled, stood in all his glory and stepped out of the tub. He reached out a hand and helped her out then scooped her into his arms. She opened the door for them to enter. Kyle kicked it closed and in two paces was at the bed. He eased her down on it and his body covered hers.

The slam, bang and rattle of metal jerked Baylie wide awake. What was that? Her heart pounded; her pulse raced. A film of sweat covered her skin. Even all these months later her reaction to noise wasn't getting any better.

"You okay, honey?" Kyle asked, tightening the arm around her waist and pulling her more firmly against him.

"Yes," she whispered. The noise had been nothing more than the early-morning garbage truck going over a speed bump on the road outside.

Kyle's soft snore said he'd drifted off to sleep again. She lifted his arm and carefully moved out from under it. Going to the bathroom, she looked in the mirror to find the terrified expression of someone who had lost what control they'd thought they had over their life.

Baylie put her face in her hands and started to cry. What was she doing? Pretending she had control over anything. Could have a normal relationship with a man. She was broken. Kyle didn't need to be involved with a crazy woman. He deserved better. If he knew how needy she was he wouldn't want her anyway.

She groaned. Had she heard him whisper "I love you" just before he'd entered her in the middle of the night?

Kyle was a good guy, who wouldn't stop trying to help. She wanted him to be happy, and she'd only make him miserable.

With a disgusted huff of air she started dressing. She needed to get out of there. Figure out how she was going to avoid hurting his feelings. She had to get through just two more days, and then he'd be going back to Pittsburgh. All she had to do until then was to keep him at a professional distance and that would be the end of that. Something deep inside her screamed. Kyle wouldn't be so easily put off.

Kyle stretched his arm across the bed and found that the spot where Baylie should've been had grown cool. Listening for a sound that might indicate she was in the bathroom, he was disappointed by the silence. His focus turned to the rooms in general. Nothing. Why would Baylie run off?

Throwing the covers back, he headed for the living area to check. Finding no one there, he had to accept that Baylie had left.

His chest tightened. This didn't bode well. He couldn't imagine her running from anything, and certainly not from him. There was a passion that existed between them that he'd never experienced before. He refused to let her pretend it wasn't there. Last night she'd made it more than clear that she was interested.

Less than an hour later Kyle entered the courtesy-patrol building. He headed straight for the counter, to find Ron issuing the assignments for the day.

"Where's Baylie?" Kyle demanded.

"Hey, man. Merry Christmas. Late two mornings in a row." He tsked. "I wouldn't be again. Baylie's a sticker for being on time. Even on Christmas morning."

Baylie actually knew why he was late, but he wasn't going to say that to this guy. "Where is she?"

"In the clinic, getting some supplies. First run of the day and someone cut their leg on a ski edge. She's headed to the downhill clinic to stitch them up. Better hurry if you want to catch her."

Kyle was already headed toward the exam room when Ron called, "Hey, you'll need this today." He pitched Kyle a red and white Santa hat. Kyle grabbed it in midair and then looked at Ron in question. He grinned. "We all wear them on Christmas Day."

Kyle shrugged his acceptance and headed toward the clinic again. Baylie had her back turned to the door as she stood on her toes to reach a roll of tape in a plastic storage bin on a shelf. The sun highlighted the chocolate fall of her hair through the lone window in the door to the outside.

As if she sensed him watching her, she came down on flat feet and slowly turned. Her face took on a determined look. She was shutting him out.

"I missed you this morning," Kyle said, for her ears only. "I'd hoped I'd spend my Christmas morning doing something else besides looking for you."

Baylie placed the tape in her emergency bag. "I'd forgotten my phone, and I needed to get here early. I didn't want to disturb you."

She was, without a doubt, running away. "I wouldn't have minded being disturbed," he said in a low, suggestive voice rich with thoughts of the night before.

"Kyle, I've got to go. There's a woman waiting on me at the bottom of the mountain." She pulled the strap of her bag over her shoulder and grabbed her skis, which stood by the door.

"I'll go with you."

Baylie looked as if she was going to refuse but then said, "Okay. I could probably use a second opinion on this one. I was told it's a pretty long laceration."

This was the first time she'd suggested that he might have some solid advice to offer without him forcing his opinion on her. It was a nice change from those rocky few days when they'd first met. She valued him professionally but he wanted more.

"Great. We're going by snowmobile?"

"No. We'll ski." She headed out the side door. He followed her into the snowy morning.

"My skis are on the rack. I'll be right back."

The idea of skiing down the terrain that Baylie picked made him feel a little apprehensive. His plans to hang up his equipment for good when he got home hadn't changed. But if he was going to get any answers out of Baylie, he was going to have to tough it out and ski down with her.

She looked cute with a Santa hat perched atop her head. She pushed off down the slope seconds before he arrived at the spot where he'd left her. He quickly stepped into his bindings, shoved the silly hat on his head and followed. Just as he'd feared, Baylie took the quickest trail, which included a diamond slope, and headed straight down. Kyle drew in a deep breath and tried to calm his rapid heart rate. He couldn't do it.

Veering off to the left, he went down a less steep slope that circled back into the one Baylie had taken when it became less steep. The confidence he'd gained over the past few days served him well, but he had to force himself out of his comfort zone to ski fast enough to catch up with her.

The red jackets of the courtesy patrol made finding Baylie easier. She was far ahead of him but still in sight. He wouldn't be much behind her when she arrived at the clinic. Maybe she wouldn't notice he'd gone a different way. Minutes later, he pulled up beside her. He looked at her to find her studying him.

"Why didn't you follow me down Dive Bomber?" Baylie asked. "I waited, thinking you were behind me. Then I saw you go off toward Cool Ride."

The muscle in his jaw jumped. He didn't need her asking him questions he didn't want to answer. Taking his skis off as an excuse not to meet her look, he took far more time than necessary.

"Not following me had nothing to do with your knee, did it?"

"Yeah, a little." He wasn't completely lying to her. His knee did ache some but more from their activity the night before than skiing.

"Why didn't you say something?" She studied him closer.

Leaning his skis against the rail of the porch, he looked at her. "This isn't something I want to discuss. I'm here now. We've got a patient waiting."

Baylie climbed the two steps to the porch and entered the small rustic building. Kyle followed. Would she let what she suspected go unquestioned? He didn't think so.

Inside the building, a woman in her early thirties sat on the heavy-duty stretcher. Her boot had been removed and a slit cut in the pants leg, revealing the injury. The woman was dressed like a skiing ad and had long flowing hair, but Kyle hardly noticed. She wasn't Baylie and the woman wouldn't be the person that he'd disillusioned when she learned his darkest secret. He wasn't looking forward to seeing the disappointment that was sure to fill her eyes.

Another patrol member was busy applying gauze and pressure to the woman's wound.

Baylie pulled off her hat and gloves, dropping them in one of the two institutional chairs in the room. It appeared to be a fully stocked clinic but with no frills.

"I'm Baylie Walker. I'm going to get you stitched up right away. This'll be the end of the skiing part of your Christmas vacation, though."

"And I was really improving," the woman whined. She looked at Kyle and batted her lashes. "And you are?" she cooed.

"Kyle Campbell. Nice to meet you." He smiled and came closer for a look at the wound. It was about four inches long. It would require a number of stitches and a good amount of time to close. "You've got a nasty cut there."

"Yeah, not my finest hour," the woman said with a weak smile.

"Well, we'll see that you're all fixed up," Kyle said reassuringly.

Baylie cleared her throat and looked at him. "Would you mind seeing to the cleaning while I get the lidocaine?"

"Sure." Was Baylie jealous? At least if her emotions were directed another way, she wouldn't be thinking about his issues. He pulled off and stuffed his gloves in the pocket of his jacket, which he took off and threw on the chair, along with Baylie's, and dropped the hat on top of it.

Baylie told the patrol member, "We'll take it from here. Thanks for your help. It's going to get busy out there soon. It's a Saturday and Christmas so keep your eyes open."

The man nodded. "Will do." He left.

Baylie went to a cabinet and took out a large bottle of saline. She handed it to Kyle. "You can find a plastic pan under there." She indicated a cabinet door under the small sink.

With both saline and pan in hand, he said to the woman, "I'm going to pour all of this over the wound. It will sting but it's important that we get any debris out. If any gets trapped it will cause an infection."

"Okay." She bit her bottom lip in an overly dramatic way. "I know you'll be as gentle as possible."

"I will certainly try," Kyle assured her.

He glanced at Baylie. She'd been watching them but turned back to the medicine she was drawing up as soon as he looked at her.

"Let me help you lie back. What's your name?" He

lifted the head of the stretcher and supported the woman's back as she moved.

"Charlotte."

With her in place, Kyle lifted her leg and placed the pan underneath the injured area of her calf. He removed the gauze. The wound had stopped bleeding actively. "Are you ready?"

The woman nodded and bit her lip again. He slowly let the saline wash over the laceration until the entire bottle was empty. Baylie handed Kyle a towel. He patted the excess fluid off the woman's leg and removed the pan from beneath it.

Baylie pulled a stool close to the stretcher. "Charlotte, you'll need to hold very still while I deaden this."

Kyle held the woman's ankle securely. Baylie gave him a slight nod and he asked the woman, "So where are you from?"

The woman started sharing her life story, hardly noticing what Baylie was doing.

Over an hour later Kyle applied the last piece of tape to the gauze-covered injury. Baylie had done an excellent job. He rather enjoyed playing nurse to her doctor. They made a good team. They seemed to read each other with little more than a gesture.

Baylie's name came over the radio and she stepped to the side, speaking into it. She turned back to him and the patient. "I'm needed elsewhere. Kyle, will you please escort Charlotte up the mountain?"

"I'll be glad to." He smiled at the woman.

Baylie gave him a look before picking up her belongings and heading for the door. He grinned. She was jealous.

Kyle said to the woman, "Please don't try to stand. I'll be right back in a moment."

He closed the door behind him. "Baylie, is everything all right?"

"I just need to check on a sprained wrist. I can handle it."

"You never told me what happened to you this morning."

"I'd rather not discuss it. Anyway, we both have patients to see about."

"So if we can't discuss anything, how about we just watch the fireworks together tonight?" Kyle suggested.

Baylie was already shaking her head before he finished his sentence. "I have to work. I've gotta go."

Hours later and long after dark Baylie sat at the desk in the clinic, filling out a supply order. It was a mundane job but one that suited her mood.

She'd stayed away from the clinic as long as she could after the slopes had closed in the hope that Kyle would have gone home before she came in. It had worked. She'd asked, to make sure. Hiding out wasn't the best way to handle the situation but she couldn't bring herself to tell him the truth. Kyle wasn't sharing everything about himself either. He was probably no more interested in seeing her than she was in seeing him.

Baylie's heart constricted. It was killing her to push him away, especially when all she wanted to do was huddle inside the haven that was his arms. The boom of the first round of fireworks exploding shook her, sending aftershocks through her body. She trembled.

Pulling the earplugs out of her fleece jacket pocket, she stuck them in her ears. As the next bang hit the air, Baylie squeezed her eyes shut and hunched her shoulders. The last ripple of sound echoed. She jumped up and turned on all the lights she could find. If she could've found a way to be off the mountain she would have, but someone had to man the courtesy patrol and that was her job. The next boom rent the air. She turned in a circle, frantically looking for an escape.

When the resort director had informed her she had to be available this evening, she'd known it would be difficult but she'd had no idea that her stomach would be so tied in knots. She'd hoped she could handle it better than this. Another bang filled the air and she ran to the attached room, where extra beds were kept for patients. Going to the furthest corner, Baylie huddled on the bed.

Boom, boom, boom. She quaked. This couldn't last forever. All she had to do was survive.

"Baylie?"

Kyle! Why did he have to show up now? Maybe if she didn't make a sound he'd think she was out.

"Baylie?" he called.

The sound of his heavy all-weather boots going into the clinic area could be heard between the fireworks.

"Baylie, where are you?"

Please, just go away. I don't want you to see me like this.

An extra-large explosion filled the air, and she yelped.

"Baylie?" Kyle came to the doorway. "Baylie!" He rushed to her and gathered her into his arms. "Honey, what's wrong?"

Another boom rent the air. She shivered. Kyle pulled her tighter against him, absorbing her tremors.

"Shhh. It will be okay." He gently rubbed her back. "It'll be over soon. I'm here. I won't let anything happen to you."

She buried her face into his chest and pulled her arms up snug against him. She wanted to be absorbed into his strength. He continued to soothe her over the next few minutes, softly talking through each blast until the finale made her shudder uncontrollably.

"Let me help you forget." He kissed the top of her head, her forehead, temple, cheek until his lips found her mouth. When his tongue touched hers she quivered for another reason. His hands caressed her back.

Baylie shifted, giving him better access to her lips. His kiss was one of reassurance, not demand. His hands remained around her but he made no sexual overtures. Kyle was taking care of her. It was nice. Very nice. Something she'd rarely experienced. She was usually the one being the caregiver.

"Easy," Kyle said against her lips, then lovingly kissed her again. This time he placed small fleeting kisses along her cheek and then along her jaw. "Think about how good this feels."

The sensation was wonderful.

Kyle nipped her earlobe. "How does that make you feel?" He moved on to the hollow behind her ear. "Or this?"

"Mmm."

"That's my girl. Do you like this?" He ran his tongue along the length of her bottom lip.

"Uh-huh." Baylie barely nodded.

He took her mouth again, tenderly offering a comforting kiss.

"Is anyone here?" came a call from the outer room. "Hello."

Baylie stiffened and jerked away.

Kyle looked at Baylie. Her eyes were wide and wild, the dark centers full of panic.

"Is anyone working here?" A man's voice was raised in question.

"I'll handle it until you get yourself together," he said in a hushed whisper next to her ear. Releasing her, he called, "Back here," and went out the door.

Baylie's lack of argument spoke volumes about how difficult the past few minutes had been for her.

A man with a boy of about eight with red-rimmed eyes and a face contorted with pain met Kyle in the middle of the lobby area.

"Hey, I'm Dr. Campbell. How can I help you?" Kyle said in his most professional voice, though his mind was back with Baylie huddled in the corner of the other room. All he wanted to do was to return to her, but he had a patient to see.

"My son burned his hand," the man said, taking the boy's elbow and lifting the hand higher. The boy sniffed loudly, trying not to cry.

Kyle smiled at him. "Come back to the exam room and let me see what I can do." The man and boy followed him. Kyle lifted the boy onto the end of the stretcher. Kyle took the boy's hand and looked at the angry red skin across the center of it. "So, how did this happen?"

The father hung his head sheepishly. "Playing with sparklers."

"I see," Kyle said in his best condemning voice. To the boy he said, "Let's get this clean and covered. Then it will feel better."

The boy nodded agreement.

"I'll get the saline," Baylie said behind him.

Kyle glanced around. Against her pallor, her dark eyes looked larger and red-rimmed, but there was a determined attitude to her stance. That look said that even if he told her he could handle things, she wouldn't accept it.

"The bandages are in the left-hand drawer. The ointment in the third on the left." At least she was focused on something other than her terror. She'd guarded her secret so furiously, put up a brave front so many times she'd be angry that she'd let herself fall apart. He had to admire her stamina. He'd bet she would fight for someone she loved just as zealously.

She brought the bottle of saline and a pan to the bed. Kyle placed the other items on the stretcher behind the boy. Together they cleaned and bandaged the child's hand. Kyle lifted the boy and placed him on his feet.

Looking at the father, Kyle said, "Keep it dry and change the bandage as needed. Apply this antibacterial ointment daily. It should be better in a few days."

"I will. Thank you." The man turned to Baylie. "Thank you too, miss."

"You're welcome. Please let me know if there are further problems." Baylie stood stiffly beside Kyle. The second she heard the outside door close she said, "I'm sorry you had to see that a while ago. You can go on. I'll clean this up."

He ignored her words and began putting away supplies. Baylie joined him in the effort. Done, he started turning off lights.

"What are you doing?"

"Closing up." Kyle flipped off another light.

"I'm not leaving yet."

Kyle looked at her. "Yes, you are. We need to talk and we aren't going to do it here."

"I don't want to talk."

Was she kidding? He looked at her in complete disbelief. "Baylie, what's going on between us isn't some fling. I care about you. All I want us to do is go to my place and talk."

"No."

"Do you want to have our conversation here? In the lodge lobby? Or some other place where we can be overheard?"

Afraid she would completely shut down, he tried a different tack. "Baylie, right now I'm asking as your friend. Nothing more. You don't have to talk. I won't touch you. I just want to know you're all right. I don't think you should be alone. My place is more private, that's all. Please."

She looked at him as if she was struggling to make up her mind. The old determined Baylie was back when she said, "Just to talk, and only for a little while. Then I'm going home."

Kyle put his hand up like a Boy Scout. "You have my word."

"Okay," she said softly, as if she wanted to go along but couldn't bring herself to agree readily.

They both pulled on their jackets, gloves and Santa hats, and headed out into the cold clear night. The wind buffeted them as they walked. Kyle didn't touch her, not even to support her, worried she'd retreat within herself and not open up when they got to his place.

Baylie balked when they arrived at his door. He opened it and went in first. He held the door wide, waiting for her to make a decision. She stepped inside just far enough that he could close the door but no more.

Kyle walked farther into the room, pulling his jacket off as he went. Tossing it on the chair, he said, "Now hear me out before you start saying no."

She jutted her jaw and looked pointedly at him as if she was extremely suspicious of anything that started with that statement.

"Why don't you go get a hot shower?"

She shook her head vigorously.

"So that you will feel better." He needed her to relax and trust him if he was ever going to get any answers out of her. "I'll get you something to put on, and there's a robe behind the door. While you're doing that, I'll fix you some hot tea. Then we can talk."

Kyle watched as the look in her eyes vacillated between yes and no. She must have been so tired in body and soul she couldn't make up her mind. He stepped toward her and gently took her hand. She didn't pull away, letting him know she'd reached the end of the fight. How could he help her?

Tugging her hand gently, he led her into the bedroom and then to the bath. Letting go of her hand, he turned on the water and began testing it. He looked back to find her watching him as if she were sleepwalking.

"Baylie…" Her eyelids flickered and she came back to reality. "I'll leave some clothes on the bed and the robe is hanging behind this door."

Kyle went into the bedroom and pulled the door closed behind him. He listened for movement. Seconds later there was a heavy thud of what could only be Baylie's boots hitting the tile floor.

CHAPTER NINE

BAYLIE STEPPED OUT of the hot shower feeling as weak as a cooked noodle. After drying off and toweling her hair, she pulled on the thick terry-cloth robe and opened the door a crack. Not seeing Kyle, she went out into the room. He had been as good as his word. A T-shirt with his clinic's name and logo on the front lay on the bed, along with a pair of navy sweatpants. He'd closed the bedroom door to the hallway. Just that simple reassurance was enough to say he was truly concerned about her.

Suddenly she wanted to tell Kyle her deepest fears. To share with him. Be comforted by him. Let some of the weight of her world rest on his shoulders.

Taking a breath to fortify herself, Baylie opened the door and took the first step out of the room. This one had almost been as difficult as the initial one she'd taken out of the hospital.

Kyle was sitting in the same chair he'd been in the first night she'd visited. He was flipping through TV channels, not settling on one for more than a second or two. The volume was turned low, as if he'd been listening for her.

"Hey."

His head turned immediately and he stood. She didn't

miss the hesitation when he straightened his right leg but he didn't grimace.

"Feeling better?"

She nodded.

"Why don't you have a seat, and I'll get that tea I promised. Pot's hot."

"Thank you. That would be nice." Kyle seemed unsure of himself. She'd never seen him anything but confident, unless she'd been watching closely. Now he acted as if she might bite. Kyle headed toward the kitchen. He'd changed his clothes and was now wearing a T-shirt with a resort logo on the front and a floral motif advertising the Bahamas on the back. He lived in two different worlds. Snow and Beach. She did too—the world of Happy Confidence in her job, and the Land of Terror inside. The latter was the one he'd demand to know about.

Returning with a mug of steaming hot tea in hand, he offered it to her. "I added a little sugar and cream."

She took it and inhaled the aroma. "Thanks."

Kyle returned to his chair and propped his leg up. She chose the furthest corner of one of the sofas, putting them well out of arm's reach of each other. "How's the knee?"

"Actually, better than I ever thought it would be."

He watched her for an extended moment, long enough that her look dropped to the mug. Could she find the answers in her tea to the questions he was surely going to ask?

"Baylie, we need to talk about what happened tonight. What you say stops with me. You have my word."

She looked at him then back at the mug. "It's not easy."

"No, I'm sure it isn't." His voice was soft and reassuring. "Why don't you just start at the beginning?"

He waited patiently, watching her intently. She placed the mug on the end table beside her.

"I told you about the IED accident. About how the men died and I couldn't help them." She laced and unlaced her hands.

Kyle nodded.

"The one closest to me, the one who called out to me, the one with disappointment in his eyes as I watched the life leave him, was my boyfriend." She said the last two words in a rush. Moisture filled her eyes but she refused to let it spill over onto her cheeks.

Kyle shifted in his chair to face her more squarely.

She looked at the opposite wall, anywhere but at Kyle. She couldn't stand to see his disgust or, worse, his pity. "I had no idea if the others had lived or died until I woke in the hospital. Even then I had to demand to know. That's when the night terrors began, and the fear of loud noises."

Sharing her trauma was like having a massive weight lifted off her shoulders. It felt good to tell someone of her suffering.

"Before you ask, yes, I did have some group therapy to deal with the accident. I was feeling pretty strong. But after I was released the problems with noises seemed to escalate. I can handle it as long as I don't get around crowds or places where I'm likely to hear loud sounds. That's why I took this job—a quiet place, taking care of injuries, I could handle. I'd hoped not to be put into a position like the one with the man having the heart attack. I've already realized that I'm not going to be able to work here any longer. I'll have to look for some type of job that I can handle."

Her gaze flicked to Kyle. He looked as if he wanted to argue but he kept his mouth closed.

"Now you know the whole ugly story," she murmured.

"I know this doesn't cover your pain, but I'm sorry."

She didn't miss the anguish in his voice. "I'm going to get dressed and go home now."

"Why don't you stay here tonight?"

No way was she having sympathy sex. She had that much self-respect left. "No." She stood and he mirrored the movement.

"That didn't come out right. You can sleep in the extra bed. I'll sleep in mine. I care about you, Baylie. I won't have a restful night unless I know you're okay. Please stay. If you won't stay here then I'll go home with you and sleep on your couch."

He knew how to get to her. She didn't want him to worry about her and the picture of his big body curled on her couch would have been laughable under any other circumstances.

"You can lock the door." His eyes pleaded, his gaze not wavering from hers.

"You don't give me much choice."

"That was the idea." A slight smile came over Kyle's lips.

"Good night," she said, heading for the bedroom across the hall from his.

Slipping between the cool sheets, Baylie folded herself into the fetal position and shivered from fear, heartache, ugly dreams to come and happy ones that would never happen.

Kyle lay in bed, his hands behind his head, looking up at the ceiling. It had sure been one memorable Christmas. Baylie was in pain, and he didn't know how to help her. Even if he did, he didn't know if she'd accept it. He cared more about her than about any woman he'd known. Her pain had become his.

A tiny squeak put him on alert. Had that been his bedroom door? There it was again. An almost indistinguishable noise. Hearing nothing more, he relaxed. Maybe it was from the pressure of the wind blowing outside.

"Kyle?" That was the sweetest, softest and most welcome whisper of his life.

He didn't dare move for fear Baylie would run away. "Yes?"

"Will you hold me?"

"Anytime, anywhere, honey." His heart broke, and all the love he felt for this woman poured out. He flipped the covers back. Unable to see her in the dark, he could picture her in his mind. Her feet padded along the carpet before she slipped in next to him.

"Have a bad dream?"

"No, but I don't want to." She laid her head on his outstretched arm.

"I can't promise that I can scare the dream away, but I'll help you through it."

Baylie settled alongside him. Kyle wrapped his arm around her waist and snuggled her close. He had her in his arms, and that was all that mattered.

Baylie woke to the sound of movement in the kitchen and the smell of coffee percolating. She lay in the middle of the king-size bed with the covers pulled up over her.

She groaned. Had she really come in and asked to get into bed with Kyle?

There had been a bad dream but it hadn't been as strong as those in the past. When she'd returned to reality, Kyle had been there with reassuring kisses and strong, supportive arms. He hadn't tried to seduce her. He'd kissed her face but not her lips. He'd done as she'd requested. Held her.

Or did he no longer desire her? After what he'd seen and heard, maybe he didn't want to have anything to do with someone so unstable. Either way, it was Sunday and he'd be leaving this evening. If she didn't miss her guess, he'd be gone just as soon as the slopes closed.

As much as she disliked that thought, she'd known it was coming. Their relationship had been doomed from the beginning. A sick feeling filled her middle. It terrified her to think about how much she'd come to rely on him.

She'd put on her clothes and leave before she made a further fool of herself. But her clothes were missing. Finding Kyle in the kitchen, she asked, "Where are my clothes?"

"Well, good morning to you too." His lips curved upward.

His smile always gave her a gooey feeling in her center. "I'm sorry. That was rude. You don't deserve that. I should be thanking you."

He put up a hand. "Whoa, Baylie. I'd settle for a 'good morning'."

"Good morning," she said apologetically.

"Now, isn't that a much nicer way to start the day? I washed your clothes. They should be dry in a few minutes. How about some coffee or tea while they finish? I'm sorry I don't have any breakfast to offer you."

"How long have you been up?"

"A couple of hours." He turned and took a mug from the cabinet. Filling it with hot water from a pot on the stove, he pushed the mug and a tea bag still in the wrapper across the bar toward her.

She looked around for a clock.

"Don't panic. You've got plenty of time. It's still early."

Now he was reading her mind. She took one of the stools at the bar. Opening the tea cover, she pulled out the bag and dipped it into the hot water. The process, the setting and sharing an early morning with Kyle all felt commonplace while nothing about it was ordinary. She wished it was, though.

After a bad dream Kyle had reassured Baylie. Her tears had broken his heart. When she'd settled again, wiggling her backside against him to get comfortable, it had been all he could do to control his baser instincts. He'd stood it as long as he could before he'd had to leave the bed. His body's demands to have her had been moving fast beyond his ability to resist.

He'd promised just to hold her and he intended to keep that promise.

"Baylie…"

Her fascination with the tea bag was broken when she looked at him.

"I have to leave today. Patients are expecting me in the morning."

"I appreciate your help this week. I know it wasn't what you had planned."

Why did she sound so formal? They could have been acquaintances instead of lovers the way she was acting. He didn't like the distance she was attempting to put between them.

"I don't want today to be the last time I see you."

"Kyle—"

"Let me finish. We've got something special. Something I'm not willing to let go of."

Baylie stood, knocking the stool over. As it crashed to

the floor, she grabbed the edge of the corner with both hands and recoiled.

He rushed around the bar. As he reached for her, she shoved his hand away.

Baylie stood and backed away from him. "Do you really want to have something to do with someone as messed up as me? I can't even stand to hear a piece of furniture fall."

She said the words with such venom and disgust he recognized the hatefulness wasn't directed toward him but toward herself.

"Baylie, you can get through this. I want to help. This is nothing we can't get through together." He stepped toward her but when she retreated he stopped. "You can get beyond this. I can help you get past it."

"I'm handling things," she bit out.

"How? By hiding out here?"

She made a sound of disgust. "I'm not."

"Yes, you are. Someday you'll be forced to go out into the big noisy world. What will you do then?"

She flinched as if he'd struck her.

"You don't understand," she moaned.

"What don't I understand? What it's like to be scared? Sure I do."

She stared at him as if demanding to know more.

The feeling of his chest being crushed built in him. "I've been scared every time I've put my skis on this week. I've had to force myself to take some of the assignments you gave me. I was scared when my parents died. When my dream of skiing professionally died. So *don't* tell me I *don't* understand."

"You think your loss of a skiing career compares to me letting someone die?" she all but shouted. "There is no way you can understand."

She was starting to make him mad. "You didn't let anyone die. You were injured. You did what you could. What I do know as fact is that you are using what happened in Iraq as a barrier to what we could have together."

Baylie stood taller. The defeated look left her face, replaced by one of determination. Some of the strong-willed Baylie was returning.

"You're wrong."

He half turned away from her. "No, I'm not."

"What about you? You've also been hiding out. You're a great skier but you don't even do it for pleasure anymore. You gave it up even though you loved it."

"The point is that I care and want to help."

"And just how do you plan to help me when you don't seem to be able to help yourself?"

He compressed his lips. She had him there. "I came here and skied. I didn't want to but I did it anyway. I took a step." And he had. A bubble of pride built with that admission. "What step are you trying to make? Do you care enough about us to make a step?"

She looked at him pointedly. "Have you even considered skiing in the Pro-Am event? Really seeing what you can do? The slopes you've skied are little more than bunny slopes for your talent."

That bubble popped. "No."

"Do you plan to ski again after you leave here?"

He couldn't meet her look. "No."

"Kyle, I think you need to get your act together before you start working on me. I'll take care of my issues, and you take care of yours. Now, where are my clothes?"

Baylie hated hurting Kyle, but she couldn't see any way around it.

"Come on. Baylie, let's talk this out. You're not think-

ing straight. You can't want to throw away what we have."
He put out a pleading hand.

Kyle looked as if she had punched him in the stomach.
Disbelief etched his face. It was killing her to see him in pain
and her heart ached for what had to be. She looked away.

All she really wanted to do was wrap her arms around
him. Feel his strength and reassurance. Tell him she loved
him with all her heart. Because she did.

"Baylie, look at me."

She did. His eyes sparkled with the confidence of what
he would say next.

"I love you."

Baylie held her breath. She wanted him to but at the
same time she didn't. She'd give him nothing but pain.

"And I think you care for me too."

"I don't."

"You're lying to me and even more to yourself. Take a
chance on us."

What if he found out he couldn't deal with her problem?
It would kill her if he left her. She shook her head. "I can't."

As if all the fight had gone out of him, his shoulders
slumped. "I think it is more like won't. I'm sorry for both of
us." His words were dry and flat. "Your clothes are in the
dryer through there." He pointed to a door off the kitchen
before he walked down the hall and into his room, shutting the door behind him.

Baylie had what she wanted, but it didn't feel any better
than when she was in the throes of a horrible nightmare.
She felt just as sick and scared. In the past few moments
she'd thrown away what little chance she'd had for real
happiness.

Kyle stepped out of the bathroom after his shower and into
the quiet of the room. Baylie had left. He hadn't doubted

that she would but a guy could hope. He had to get through to her somehow. He crammed into the duffel bag the few clothes he'd brought with him little over a week ago. Giving the room one last check for anything he'd missed, he made a point not to look at the bed. Those memories were so sweet they hurt.

Picking up his bag, he headed for the front door. Minutes later he stashed the bag in the SUV so he could be gone as soon as the slopes closed. Baylie needed time to cool off before he approached her again.

Kyle received his slope assignment and was headed out when Derek stopped him. "Hey, man, I heard this is your last day. Bummer. We never got a chance to ski together. I know I would've learned something from the great KC."

"Yeah, sorry it didn't work out." Kyle started to move away.

"Hey, how about being my partner at the Pro-Am event over New Year's weekend? I bet we'd take it all."

"I don't think so."

Derek slapped him on the back. "Well, if you change your mind, let me know. I think it would be awesome. And it's for a good cause. To send sick kids on their dream trips."

"I'll think about it." Kyle was surprised that he really meant what he'd said.

He was on his way out the door as Baylie entered. Her eyes were large, luminous and red-rimmed. Sadness filled them. His heart constricted. Tightening his fingers around the gloves he held, Kyle stopped himself from taking Baylie into his arms.

He nodded. It was the hardest thing he'd ever done to keep walking. He didn't like rejection any more than the next guy. All he wanted to do was snatch her up and kiss her senseless until she could think of nothing but him. Instead, he kept moving. He felt her eyes on him as he put on his skis and pushed away.

By midafternoon Kyle had been reassigned to the Cloud Nine lift. He stood nearby as skiers unloaded, helped them up if they fell and encouraged skiers to keep moving. More than once the lift operator had to stop the lift for Kyle to help one, sometimes two people to their feet. He was in the process of answering a question from a skier when a woman screamed, "Help! My boy is caught."

He turned in time to see a child of about seven hanging by his arm from a lift chair. It looked like part of his coat was caught on the safety bar. The lift had already made the turn downhill past the stop zone. The flexible automatic break bar hadn't been high enough for the boy's legs to activate it. The operator had stopped the lift but the boy was suspended fifteen feet above the granite boulders on the steep downhill side of the lift station.

Kyle moved as fast as he could to the edge of the drop-off. He reached out but couldn't touch the child. "Get Baylie over here," he called over his shoulder to the lift operator.

The mother was starting to scream hysterically. If he didn't get a handle on the situation the child was going to start squirming and fall. "Ma'am, you're going to have to stop screaming. We'll get your boy down."

The mother gulped on a sob.

He was making progress. "What's your son's name?"

"Jimmy. Jimmy Callahan." She started to sob again.

Kyle looked at the lift operator. "Take her over there and see if someone can settle her down. I've got to see about this child."

The man did as Kyle instructed.

"Jimmy, my name is Kyle. I'm going to get you down. Don't move."

The boy's back was to Kyle as he faced down the slope. All Kyle heard was a soft cry. "If you understand me, say yes. And don't look down."

"Yes."

"Good boy," Kyle called to him.

"Let's reverse this lift," Baylie called beside him. "Also move these people on."

Kyle didn't take his eyes off the boy.

"Is he caught on something or just hanging on?" she asked him.

"Caught, his mother said." He still hadn't looked at her. "Jimmy, Ms. Baylie's here. She's going to help me get you down."

"It will take a few minutes to get the machine into reverse," Baylie told him quietly.

"I'm worried about his shoulder. Depending on how strong a jerk he took when he fell there may be extensive damage to his rotator cuff," Kyle said.

"Then I'd appreciate your help in handling this."

His look captured hers for a second. "You'll always have it."

Her lips thinned and she nodded. "I have to see about getting the sled here." She pulled out her radio and spoke into it.

Kyle watched the boy as the minutes ticked away.

"Baylie, we're ready," the lift operator called.

"Slow and easy. No jerking," she instructed.

With a small shift the lift started moving. Kyle held his breath. He heard Baylie's inhalation of air. The boy swung back and forth before the chair seat crept toward him. Each movement seemed to take forever.

"When he gets close enough that I can touch him, let me stabilize him. I want to try to take the pressure off the arm," he said to Baylie.

"I'll see to getting him loose." She moved up close beside him. "Remember to watch your step. It won't do any good for you to go over the edge."

"Why, you do care after all," he quipped.

She suddenly went still beside him, but he didn't take a chance on looking at her. Instead, he found a secure stance, preparing to catch the boy. He couldn't mess up. It might mean further harm to the boy's arm. Less than a minute later the boy was within grabbing distance.

Kyle encircled the boy's waist with his arms, instead of using his hands. "I've got you, Jimmy. Don't move. Ms. Baylie has to get you undone."

He walked a step or two downward before Baylie yelled to the lift operator to stop. Once again the chair swung but Kyle swayed to counteract the shift.

Baylie seized the seat of the chair to stop further movement. "You got him?" she called.

"Yes, go ahead." Kyle held the boy against the upper part of his chest.

Baylie reached up and tugged at the strap that should have been securing the sleeve of the boy's coat at the wrist to prevent snow from entering.

While she worked Kyle asked, "How are you doing, Jimmy? Do you hurt anywhere?"

"My shoulder," the boy whined.

"That's understandable."

He looked over Jimmy's shoulder to see Baylie pulling out her scissors.

"Make sure to hold his arm. Don't let it fall," Kyle instructed Baylie.

"I understand," she said softly.

Kyle returned his attention to the boy. "So what did Santa bring you for Christmas?"

"Video games."

"Nice. Which one do you like the best?"

Suddenly the boy's weight got heavier.

"Bring his arm down to his side. We need to get it taped to him until X-rays can show how much damage there is," Kyle said.

Baylie helped to support Kyle in case he slipped by putting a hand on his back and walking beside him as they made their way to the waiting sled. With Baylie's help, he sat Jimmy on it. The boy's mother rushed over to them.

"You got your bag?" Kyle asked Baylie.

"Yes."

"I need the widest tape you have."

Baylie pulled a roll of tape out of the bag and handed it to him.

"Help me get this around him. I don't want to take a chance on taking his coat off." They passed the tape back and forth, securing the boy's arm to his side.

Done, Kyle pulled Baylie off to the side as two of the other patrol personnel settled the boy in the sled. "I'd like to go with the boy to the hospital. Look at the X-rays. Offer my services if they're needed."

Baylie nodded. "This doesn't warrant an ambulance callout, so the parents will have to drive him."

"They're welcome to ride with me if they'd like," Kyle offered.

"I'll speak with the mother."

Less than an hour later Jimmy was bundled into the middle seat of Kyle's SUV and the mother sat stoically in the front seat, having only marginally recovered from her hysteria. The father would be meeting them at the hospital after he'd packed up their belongings and checked out of their lodging.

Baylie stood nearby. Kyle approached her. He started to reach for her hand but stopped, knowing she wouldn't appreciate a public scene. "I'll be heading back to Pittsburgh from the hospital."

"I know. Bye, Kyle."

"That's all you have to say?"

"What more is there to say that we haven't covered already? Thanks for your help this past week."

He looked at her incredulously. His heart was being torn into bits and all she could say was thanks?

"Hell, if I'm never going to see you again then you're going to have something to remember me by." He pulled her against him and his lips claimed hers. She hesitated a moment before she leaned into him. Her hands clutched at his jacket. He demanded more. She gave it. His heart flew. Despite all her verbal efforts to drive him away, her kisses still pulled him to her.

He released her just as suddenly as he'd grabbed her and stepped away. Baylie teetered slightly and he reached out to steady her. "You're going to miss me."

She blinked and really looked at him for the first time. Her velvety brown eyes searched his face. Had she expected him to kiss her? Had she wanted him to kiss her? Either way, he was glad he had. They weren't done by a long shot.

CHAPTER TEN

IN THE PAST, Baylie had always enjoyed the friendly revelry during the Pro-Am New Year's event. She'd never participated but her brothers had, and she'd been there to cheer them on. She'd even looked forward to it but this year she wouldn't be in the crowd. Too much noise. Her job required her to be close in case there was an accident so she'd had the first-aid tent set up down the slope and over to the side.

The contest slope was in fine shape. The snow from the night before had left a nice base for the event. The sky was a crystal blue that reminded her of Kyle's eyes. She'd not seen him in a week and didn't expect to ever see him again. That thought always brought an ache to her heart.

There was a good turnout for the event. A number of local skiers had returned to show off their skills and the resort had recruited a number of pros, including Derek.

The loudspeaker blasted out the name of the next skier; the crowd roared then quieted. A large beep sounded, followed by silence.

Baylie couldn't see what was happening but the applause of the crowd told her that the skier had crossed the finish line. It went on for so long that she started to block out the noise. Even the names of the contestants being blasted over the loudspeaker began to blend into the background.

Busy making notes about a recent small injury, her head jerked up when the name of Kyle Campbell was announced. A lump formed in her throat. Was it her Kyle Campbell? She shook her head. He wasn't hers. She'd let him go.

What had the announcer said? Downhill? Partner Derek Lingerfelt?

Kyle wouldn't let himself focus on anything but the few feet in front of him. If he thought about what he was preparing to do or what could happen he might embarrass himself by backing out.

His heart beat at a rapid rate and his hands were sweating inside his gloves. He pulled his goggles into place. Shifting his skis back and forth in anticipation, he went into a squatting position and planted his poles. It was all so familiar yet so different.

All he had to do was to make it down the course and he'd consider it a successful run. He needed to prove that he could do it. Baylie had been right. He'd had no business telling her what she needed to do if he wasn't facing his fears either. If he could do it, maybe he could convince her that she could too.

He was grasping at any idea that he could find. The past week had been the longest of his life. He never would have thought that a woman could have him so twisted into knots. As afraid as he was that he might make a fool of himself on the ski slope, his fear of losing her forever was greater.

The beep sounded.

He pushed off, legs together and knees bent. His right knee let him know it was there but it remained strong. The first gate loomed ahead. He made it around it with a brush of his hip. The second was coming up fast. He cleared it. He'd found his rhythm. The one he remembered so well. He pushed hard. Seconds later he was over the finish line and the crowd was screaming.

His heart was pumping with joy. He couldn't control the huge smile that covered his face. That old feeling of testing himself, driving himself to do more, and the success of knowing he had done his best welled in him. He felt whole again.

When the crowd began to shout "KC, KC, KC," his smile broadened even more.

Baylie hurried to the center of the slope. Why hadn't Derek said anything about Kyle skiing today?

She tried to see over or around the heads of the crowd. Finally she maneuvered into a spot where no one obstructed her view of the starting line. Just as she got into position, the beep sounded for the contestant to start.

She'd missed Kyle. Had never imagined how much she would. She'd missed his smile, his witty banter that had managed to make her grin when she didn't want to, but most of all she'd missed his arms around her at night.

The nightmares were coming more often and with more vengeance. Many nights she'd had to force herself to go to bed because she knew they would find her when she fell asleep. The only time she had a truly happy moment was when she thought of Kyle's kisses. The last one still lingered on her lips.

Baylie's heart caught in her throat. Her hands trembled so badly she stuffed them in the pockets of her jacket as Kyle left the starting block. This had to be hard for him. She would know his body movements anywhere. He moved over the snow with knees bent low and shoulders parallel to the slope. He was flying. As he zigzagged down the course, Baylie couldn't help but admire his ability. He maintained control and form as far down the course as she could see. Kyle was a natural.

The crowd roared their pleasure. Kyle must have come across the finish line.

The announcer called, "That was Kyle Campbell with the time to beat!"

A lone voice shouted, "KC." Another joined him and another until the entire crowd was chanting.

How did Kyle feel about that? He had so quickly shut down Derek when he'd called Kyle by his initials.

Baylie couldn't deny the feeling of pride that filled her. He'd done so well. And to know that for a short time he'd belonged to her.

The next contestant's name was called. Would Kyle look for her? Did he know she was near?

If he did seek her out it would only prolong the pain. Nothing had changed. She couldn't be who he needed. He lived in a city, had a job he loved there, and she wouldn't ask him to give that up for her issues.

Baylie walked back across the slope toward the first-aid station. Halfway there, she heard Kyle call her name. She stopped. Her temperature rose above normal. Breathe, she reminded herself.

Keep it together. Act normal. Do not throw yourself at him.

She turned slowly. "Hi, I'm surprised to see you here."

"I'm kind of surprised to be here," he said with one of those grins she'd missed so much.

The warmth went to heat as his gaze devoured her. He

made no effort to conceal his hunger. "I've missed you," he said in a husky voice.

Baylie bit her bottom lip to stop herself from admitting she'd missed him too. So much so it had become a physical ache that never left. "I thought you weren't participating in the Pro-Am."

"I wasn't, but when Derek asked me to be his partner, I decided it was time I faced my fears and took a chance. Being scared has controlled my life for far too long." His look held hers.

Was he trying to make a point that it was time she faced hers? She recognized that. Continuing to live like she had been wasn't a life. But even with help it might take years for her to get better. If she encouraged Kyle, she could still end up hurting him all over again and she refused to do that. She loved him too much.

"You were good out there."

"It was tough to make that first gate. But it was easier the second time."

She didn't miss the double meaning to his words. "I'm glad for you. I know how important skiing was in your life. I'm happy you're able to enjoy it again."

"It isn't the most important thing to me," he said softly, moving closer.

Her eyes lifted to meet his. "Please don't do this, Kyle. Nothing has changed between us."

She needed to get help, but even if she did it might take years before she felt any better. She couldn't put Kyle through that.

"I think you're afraid to change. You might have to give up your pity party. I'd hoped you'd want me enough to see that. But that's something you'll have to decide on your own." He drew a deep breath. "I love you, Baylie. Want you in my life. I'm sorry that you don't want that too."

I do! She wanted to scream, but couldn't get the words out. She desired his happiness more. Something she couldn't give him.

Kyle moved near again. Close enough that she could feel his warm breath against her cheek. Near enough that she could reach up and kiss him if she let herself. He said softly and earnestly, "I won't ask again, Baylie. If you decide you want me enough to face your issues, you know how to find me."

He turned and left. An icy tear fell to her cheek.

Baylie stood in the doorway of the room in the community center. A few people mingled in groups around the large space. Others sat in chairs that formed a circle. She wanted to run, but she wanted Kyle more. Taking that step in the door and toward help had been the most difficult thing she'd ever done. The fight-or-flight mechanism within her kicked in. This time she wanted to run. But she wasn't going to.

An ache in the center of her chest grew like a mushroom out of control. She tried to inhale deeply to ease the pressure. She had to do this. For her. For Kyle. For them. She repeated it over and over in her mind.

The season had closed at Snow Mountain. She'd not seen or spoken to Kyle in over two months and she missed him like she had the minute he'd last turned and skied away. He'd demanded she get help. And she'd known he wouldn't change his mind. This time she'd have to go after him.

Trying not to think about Kyle after he'd left, she'd worked long hours every day. The nights were the worst.

If they hadn't been bad enough with the night terrors, they had been horrible from missing him. She'd reached her breaking point. Had known she had to make a change. Had to take Kyle's advice and seek help.

That had brought her here to this support group. She wanted it all. Kyle and a life with him. For that she had to get better. Had to work for it.

As she took another step into the room, one of the people came up to meet her. "Hi, I'm Callie. We're glad you came tonight."

Baylie couldn't say that she was, but hoped she might be by the time the meeting was over. Two hours later Baylie was indeed glad she'd come. For the first time in a long time she'd faced her uncertainties, had stopped running. Baylie was starting to feel good about herself. She was taking a step forward instead of cowering at Snow Mountain.

Six weeks later, much-appreciated warmth touched Baylie's face as she stepped off the plane in the Bahamas. She smiled and lifted her face to the sun. Just weeks ago she wouldn't have considered even going to a busy airport. The noise would have been more than she could have handled.

She'd not made a miraculous recovery. Every step had been hard fought. She'd attended the group meetings and had found a doctor she could relate to who specialized in her type of problem. Her issues weren't "fixed" but her progress had been noteworthy, the doctor said. Baylie's belief was that if she wanted it bad enough, wanted Kyle bad enough, she would accept nothing less.

What if Kyle didn't want her anymore when she found him? Baylie shook her head. She wouldn't allow those types of negative thoughts.

Straightening her shoulders, she headed out of the airport terminal to find a taxi. When she'd called Kyle's clinic she'd been disappointed to find that he wasn't available. Explaining who she was hadn't accomplished anything either. She had been told he was out of town. She hadn't even bothered to ask the receptionist if he'd gone to Colorado to visit his family, knowing the woman would never give Baylie that type of information. Instead, she'd asked to speak to Dr. Metcalf.

After she'd explained who she was, he'd exclaimed, "Baylie! You're the woman who put Kyle into such a tailspin."

Baylie hadn't been sure if that was a good thing or not but had hoped it meant Kyle might still care about her. Her heart had leaped at the thought.

"He's been a bear to work with. Never seen him so out of sorts and I've known him since med school. Please tell me you're trying to find him."

"I am."

With that, Metcalf had given her an address in the Bahamas, along with detailed instructions on how to find his bungalow. "There's no phone, so I guess you'll just have to surprise him." He'd chuckled. "Good luck, but I don't think you'll need any."

That had been yesterday.

Baylie spoke to three cabdrivers before she found one willing to take her to the other side of the island where Kyle's place was located. Somehow she wasn't shocked that he'd own such a secluded place. It was his getaway spot. As she rode, Baylie looked out the window at the deep green vegetation with the occasional glimpses of the beach and ocean. The lonely road slowly curved in places and then turned into a dirt road.

She was a long way from civilization. Her nerves got the better of her and she asked, "How much farther?"

"Not far," the driver said in the clipped islander English that she loved. He gave her a wide, white-toothed smile.

As they continued, her nerves went from jittery to riverdance-wild. What if Kyle had a woman with him? Maybe Metcalf didn't know Kyle as well as he thought. What if she'd hurt Kyle so badly that he just wouldn't take a chance on her? Before she could come up with another depressing thought, the cab pulled into a sandy lane where tropical growth created a tunnel. The taxi pulled to a stop.

"This it." He pointed off toward a small yellow clap-board building with light green shutters that covered the windows but were braced from the side of the house at the bottom. It was a picture-perfect bungalow.

Paying the driver, who then gave her a big smile, Bay-lie picked up her oversize purse and stepped out of the car. She watched as the taxi driver backed up the path and into the tunnel of foliage. Adjusting the spaghetti straps of her sundress, she started toward the bungalow. The light cotton fabric of her dress flowed around her legs in the gentle breeze coming off the water. Her flip-flops made a muted noise against the white sand.

She looked the part of a stress-free island visitor, but inside her stomach felt like a mass of tangled seaweed. Only by force of will had she come this far, and she wasn't running away now. What she wanted more than anything else in life was just ahead, and she wasn't giving up until she saw him.

A Jeep that had seen better days was parked beside the house. Kyle must be here. She'd been afraid she'd end up being like Goldilocks and find no one at home.

Soft calypso music filtered out from somewhere inside.

Taking a deep breath, Baylie raised her hand and knocked on the bright red door. She waited. Nothing. She knocked again. Waited. Had he seen her coming? Was he choosing not to open the door, hoping she would go away?

Now she was just imagining things. Being rude wasn't Kyle's style. Even if it had been, she was determined not to leave until she'd spoken to him. She'd not had the strength to do what she'd needed to when he'd approached her after skiing in the Pro-Am, but now she did. He'd offered her happiness then and she'd pushed him away. This time she was going to fight for it. Beg if necessary.

Pulling her purse higher on her shoulder, she stepped off the porch and followed a path around the side of the house. A large deck faced the ocean. Sitting in one of the four navy-blue Adirondack chairs on the deck was Kyle. His head was back as if he was asleep. Sunglasses covered his eyes against the afternoon brightness and his ankles were crossed and propped on the rail.

Baylie's heart went into overdrive. Would he be happy to see her?

"Kyle," she whispered.

Because she was watching him so intently she saw his body stiffen. It had gone from relaxed to alert. His head whipped toward her. It was a miracle he'd heard her, she'd spoken so quietly.

"Baylie?" He said her name with such reverence that her heart filled with hope.

In one agile movement his feet came to the wood deck floor and he stood. He pulled off the glasses and placed them on the rail, without taking his gaze off her.

He wore no shirt. Baylie's breath caught. He was gorgeous. His skin was a warm brown from being kissed by the sun. Well-worn cut-off jeans hung around his hips. If she hadn't known him as a serious doctor, he could have been the quintessential beach bum. Kyle had never looked more wonderful.

He didn't say anything for so long her heart dipped. Wasn't he glad to see her?

"How did you get here?"

Not the welcome she'd hoped for. "A taxi brought me."

"No, I mean to the island. You wouldn't have gone to the city or an airport."

"But I did." She didn't try to keep the pride out of her voice.

His look of astonishment made her smile.

"But I thought you'd be too scared."

"I was." Her eyes never wavered from his face. "But I was more afraid of losing you."

He stalked across the deck toward her, put a hand on the rail and leaped over to land in front of her. Without saying a word, his arms circled her waist and brought her against him in a bear hug. Her feet dangled in the air. That alone would have taken her breath away, but his positive reactions to her words had already done it. He eased his grip. Still holding her close, he brought his lips down to meet hers.

It was heaven on earth, being kissed by Kyle again. She'd relived his kisses so many times but none compared to the real thing. Baylie ran her hand along his neck and fanned her fingers through his hair.

Kyle's mouth left hers to trail kisses along her jaw. "I've missed you so much," he murmured, before he kissed the sweet spot behind her ear. "It's almost killed me, staying away."

She kissed his whisker-roughened cheek, enjoying the feel of being in his arms again. He suddenly stopped kissing her and took her hand. Tugging her around the corner of the deck, he led her up onto it.

"What're we doing?"

"I want to show you my bungalow."

"Now?" she asked incredulously.

He gave her a wolfish grin that made her body tingle low and deep. "I want to show you one particular piece of furniture."

Kyle led her into the dark, cool interior of a main room. He didn't let her linger long enough to see much of it. Instead, he showed her into a room with a large bed covered in a bright spread that must have been made locally. The bed faced a window that gave the room a view of the ocean. There was nothing elegant about the space, but she didn't need anything fine. She loved it because Kyle was there.

He sat on the bed and pulled her down beside him. She dropped her purse on the floor.

"I know we need to talk but my body has ached for you for weeks. I don't think I can be a gentleman."

Her hand wrapped around his neck and she pulled his mouth to hers. Her tongue teased his lips and his tongue met hers. She kissed him deeply and passionately before pulling away. "I don't need you to be a gentleman. I just need you."

He murmured his pleasure as his hands found the hem of her dress. Moving upward, his finger traced the band of her panties before he looped a finger around the thin material and tugged them off. His hands traveled upward again, removing her dress. She flexed her hips against his thigh as he worked.

"Soon, honey, soon." His hand cupped her breast and his mouth took her nipple. The fire in her burned brighter.

"Say it again," she whispered as she ran her fingers

through his hair, down his neck and over his shoulders, kneading them.

"What?"

"Honey. I've missed you calling me honey," she said, before placing a kiss on his shoulder.

"I plan to call you that always."

She boldly brushed his length with her hand as it strained behind the zipper of his shorts. "I've missed other things too."

Kyle groaned. Standing, he removed his clothes and found his place between her legs. He tenderly brushed her hair away from her face and looked into her eyes. "I'm guessing you love me as you went to so much trouble to find me."

She smiled up at him as she welcomed him into her body. "I'm guessing I do too."

Kyle had never enjoyed his beach bungalow more. Sharing it with Baylie made it paradise. She was asleep against him, all warm and perfect. He watched as the tide came in, enjoyed the cool breeze from the fan above and held her close.

As wonderful as it was to have Baylie in his arms again, he wanted her there all the time. Not just when she could bring herself to come out of hiding long enough to share her body with him. He wanted forever.

She stirred but settled again. He'd let her rest. Soon they would need to talk. He had to know why she'd really come to find him. Kyle slipped out of bed, pulled the cover over her and gave her a kiss on the head.

"Hey," Baylie said sometime later as the sky was turning pink on the horizon. She curled into the chair next to his on the deck. One of his T-shirts covered her tantalizing curves.

"I didn't ask if you had any luggage."

She smiled. "Nope. I got everything I thought I might need in my purse."

He raised a brow in question.

"My bikini fit perfectly."

"And to think I didn't even give you a chance to unpack." He grinned. They were good together. If he could just get her to see that.

"No, you didn't." She grinned and ran her hand across his forearm lying along the chair rest.

Kyle captured her hand and intertwined her fingers with his. "Baylie." His gaze found hers. "We need to talk."

She turned to face him, looking at him expectantly and her eyes serious.

What he had to say needed to be said, but what if she ran? Or refused to listen? Could he survive a second time?

"I'm glad you're here. I don't want you to think that I'm not, but I need more than just having you in my bed. I want you to marry me. Build a life with me. But that will mean living near or in Pittsburgh, flying down here, going to ball games." He paused. "Fireworks with the kids. I love you but I need to know you're taking care of yourself. I want you to let me help you."

He let go of her hand and reached over to wipe a tear from her cheek.

Her gaze didn't waver. "When you skied in the Pro-Am I knew how hard that had to be for you. I admired you for facing your fear. You inspired me."

He started to speak but she raised a hand to stop him.

"I love you so much that I couldn't stand the thought of not making you happy. I also couldn't see how I'd ever be able to do so. When you told me that you wouldn't be back, that it was up to me, I knew I couldn't live without you. I had to do something."

"Honey—"

"Let me finish. I've been going to a support group and even getting help from a psychologist to handle my fear of noise. It wasn't easy but I was able to drive into Pittsburgh, to the airport and come here. I love you and want everything you do. I'm ready to do whatever it takes to have you in my life, even live in the city. In fact, I've looked into a job. I don't think I'm ready to do regular EMT work on a large scale, especially in a metropolitan area, so I've applied to be an emergency-medical instructor. That way I can do what I love while I continue to heal."

"Come here." He pulled on her hand.

She stood, and he tugged her into his lap.

"I'm so proud of you." Putting a finger under her chin, he lifted it and placed his lips tenderly on hers. "I know you can handle anything you put your mind to. And most of all I'll always be here to help when the times are hard. I love you." He kissed her again.

A minute later, she pulled back. "So, are you going to be part of the courtesy patrol again next year?"

He grinned. "I believe I will. Thanks to you, I find I rather enjoy skiing again." He nibbled at her ear. "Is there a chance I can work with you?"

She grinned. Cupping his face in her hand, she said, "I think I'd like that. It's time for us both to stop living in the past and find our future together. On and off the slopes."

"So that means you're going to marry me?"

"You're a champion at loving me and I can't think of anything I want more than to be your wife."

Kyle's lips found hers as his hand slowly slid along her thigh and under the hem of the T-shirt.

"Don't—" she whispered.

His hand went no farther but his fingers continued to caress her skin. "There you go with the don'ts again," he teased.

She sat up in his lap so that he could see her clearly. "What I was going to say before you so rudely interrupted was don't ever stop loving me."

"Don't worry, honey." He grinned. "I never will." Kyle's lips on hers sealed his promise of today and all their tomorrows.

* * * * *

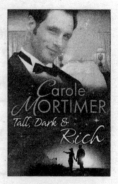